A TALE OF TWO COLORS

RED SKY STORM

VOLUME VII

A TALE OF TWO COLORS

RED SKY STORM

VOLUME VII

ANTHONY WOOD

WILL ROGERS MEDALLION WINNER

HAT CREEK

HAT CREEK

An Imprint of Roan & Weatherford Publishing Associates, LLC
Bentonville, Arkansas
www.roanweatherford.com

Library of Congress Cataloging-in-Publication Data
Names: Wood, Anthony, author.
Title: Red Sky Storm/Anthony Wood | A Tale of Two Colors #7
Description: First Edition. | Bentonville: Hat Creek, 2024.
Identifiers: LCCN: 2024939219 | ISBN: 979-8-89299-013-4 (hardcover) |
ISBN: 979-8-89299-014-1 (trade paperback) | ISBN: 979-8-89299-015-8 (eBook) |
Subjects: | BISAC: FICTION/Historical/Civil War Era |
FICTION/Crime | FICTION/Action/Adventure |
LC record available at: https://lccn.loc.gov/2024939219

Hat Creek trade paperback edition May, 2025

Cover & Interior Design by Casey W. Cowan
Cover art by Frank Tenney Johnson (1874-1939)
The Pony Express, 1924, Oil on canvas
Editing by Amy Cowan & Lisa Lindsey

For my Granny, Josie Cansata Prewitt,
whose life inspired creation of the character, Granny Thankful.

ACKNOWLEDGEMENTS

WHO WOULD I be if I didn't mention name of the one person whose friendship has enriched me from my earliest days—David Newbaker. Since our first encounter in a second grade Bible class, through thick and thin, troubled times and not, in the midst of fun and fights, we have always been the closest of friends. David's friendship has been the pattern for many of Lummy's friends throughout this series—J.A. Killingsworth, Rainy Mills, and most especially, Thomas Poole, Lummy's childhood friend and defender to the last. David, I will always cherish our wanderings on the Homochitto River, camping and fishing St. Catherine's Creek, and you being the friend "who sticks closer than a brother."

DRAMATIS PERSONAE

ANNIE "FANNY" HANDERSON: Lummy's sassy and frisky snuff-dipping friend who patched up a shoulder injury he suffered during a ferry crossing of the Mississippi River from Vicksburg, Mississippi, to Desoto, Louisiana, in search of Susannah. She was a mess. Lummy crossed paths with Annie at Desoto on his way to enlist in the Confederate Army, and when he returned to Vicksburg to enlist in the Union Army, he found her married to Beau, the owner of Handerson's Café. Annie introduced Lummy to her widowed sister, Martha. Lummy's heart was captured, and they married after the war. Lummy settled into a peaceful life with Martha and her children on the Tullos farm. Lummy visited Annie again when he and his friends traveled through Vicksburg on a mission to destroy the West-Kimbrell Gang in Winn Parish, Louisiana. Annie Fanny will always be a mess.

COLUMBUS "LUMMY" NATHAN TULLOS: Archibald and Mary Tullos's sixth child born in 1834. As the main character, Lummy leaves his home in Choctaw County, Mississippi, to begin an adventurous search to find his love, a young slave woman named Susannah, who was taken by a gambler in a card game. He finds her in Winn Parish, and they eventually marry, but nearly a year into Lummy's service with the Confederate Army in Vicksburg, he receives news of Susannah's death. He joins the Union Army to help end the war and finds new love in the process. He returns home to the Tullos farm in search of peace and quiet and finds it. His happy life is interrupted when he and his friends have to deal with two outlaw gangs decisively and with deadly force. He enjoys a number of happy years with his wife, Martha, and their family.

DAN CREEKWATER: Lummy's Choctaw friend whom he first met on the road to Winn Parish in 1859. Dan's wisdom of the Universe helped Lummy sort out his war experiences and to make his decision to join the 1st Mississippi Mounted Rifles. Lummy shared a camp with Dan in the haunts of McCurtain Creek Swamp after killing Lester, a ruffian who tried to rape and kill Lummy's family. Dan helped Lummy find his soul again. He's always around, ready to help Lummy in any way.

ELZEY BURK TULLOS: Lummy and Susannah's son who was unknown to him until he traveled to Winn Parish after Vicksburg surrendered. Because of his less than stable state of mind and the possibility of re-entering the war, Lummy decided to leave Elzey with a good family in Winn Parish until such time that he might return, which he hopes to do one day. While on the mission to end the West-Kimbrell Gang, Lummy visits eight-year-old Elzey who lives with his adopted family on the old Gilmore farm in Winn Parish.

GRANNY THANKFUL: Lummy's grandmother and faithful guide who through the thin veil comforts and protects him as he lives through difficult times and suffers with war dreams he developed from a troubled home life and horrors he endured during the war. She visits on occasion and always helps him see the grander scheme of things going on in the Universe, often using an agate stone to aid his understanding.

JASPER NEWTON TULLOS: Lummy's younger brother who served with the 1st Mississippi Light Artillery, Company C during the Siege of Vicksburg, not far from where Lummy was stationed. He and Lummy have enjoyed a number of good years living and working on the Tullos farm after the war.

JESSE COCKERSHAM: Son of Mose Cockersham with whom Lummy worked on Mr. Gilmore's farm in Winn Parish before the war. Jesse rode many miles in record time to enlist men in Winn Parish to help take down the West-Kimbrell Gang. For his effort, Lummy gives him the silver badge the people of Winn Parish gave him when he led ex-Confederate soldiers and local men to destroy Dawg Smith and his gang back in '63.

ISAIAH "ISE" HANDERSON: Susannah's brother who Lummy unknowingly met at the Battle of Franklin, Mississippi, when Lummy served with the 1st Mississippi Mounted Rifles during the war. Ise joined Lummy and friends to go to Winn Parish to destroy the West-Kimbrell Gang. On the way, they rescued a young black woman, Jenny, from evil men bent on harming her. She and Ise fall in love, and they marry after the men defeat the outlaws and return from Winn Parish.

MATT POOLE: Nephew of Lummy's childhood best friend who traveled with the band of men who destroyed the West-Kimbrell Gang. He's resourceful and a fine cook.

RAINY MILLS: Lummy first met Rainy running into his camp while being chased by coyotes on his search for Susannah in '59. They quickly became friends, and Rainy joined the others to help end Captain Tom Ford's evil reign in Choctaw County. He traveled with Lummy to help end the West-Kimbrell Gang's storm of terror in Winn Parish. Rainy stayed in Winnfield after the execution of the outlaws and married Mary Jane, wife of Lummy's dear friend, J.A. Killingsworth, who was killed in the takedown of the outlaws.

SUSANNAH: A young slave woman and Lummy's first love taken from Choctaw County, Mississippi to Winn Parish, Louisiana by James T. Gilmore, who won her in a card game. Lummy left home to find Susannah in Winn Parish and eventually marries her. He learned while stationed in Vicksburg a year later that Susannah died of measles. Lummy returned to Winn Parish after the surrender of Vicksburg to find that Susannah did not die of the measles, but rather was brutally raped and murdered by Dawg Smith and his outlaw gang. Lummy made things right by ending Smith's life. Susannah will always have a place in Lummy's heart. She visits him on occasion still.

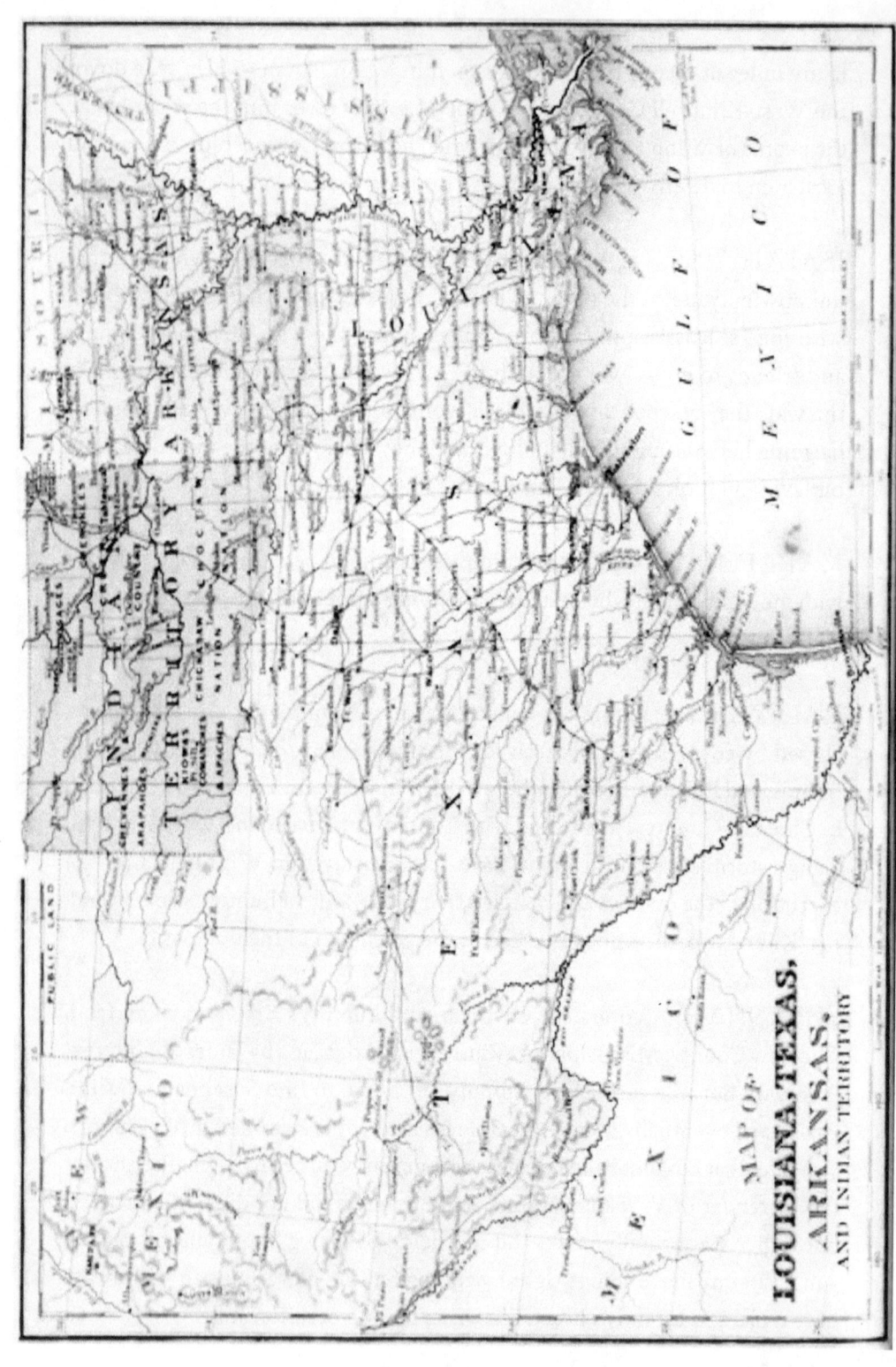

MAP OF:
LOUISIANA, TEXAS,
ARKANSAS,
AND INDIAN TERRITORY

SCAENA

CHOCTAW COUNTY, MISSISSIPPI: Founded and created in 1833 from lands ceded by the Choctaw Indians and named for them. Lummy's parents, Archibald and Mary Tullos, settled there as pioneers in 1835, and Lummy's family helped start one of the county's first Baptist churches, New Zion, in 1842. With the war over, he desperately wanted to find a peaceful life with his family on the Tullos farm only to find Captain Tom Ford and his gang terrorizing the county. Lummy, with a band of friends, ended Ford's reign of destruction. Lummy and friends traveled from the county to Winn Parish to destroy the West-Kimbrell Gang, and he returned to enjoy a number of peaceful years with his wife, Martha, and their family.

VICKSBURG, MISSISSIPPI: An important river port and railroad town that linked the east and west of the growing United States. Lummy boarded a ferry there in search of Susannah and later saw Vicksburg again from across the river as he boarded a steamer to travel south to enlist in the Confederate Army. Returning to the city after training at Camp Moore in early May 1862, he survived the Siege of Vicksburg and was paroled in July of 1863. He passed through Vicksburg on his way to Choctaw County from Winn Parish after taking down the Dawg Smith gang. He returned once again to the city to enlist in the 1st Mississippi Mounted Rifles and met Martha Brock, who became his new bride. He and his band of friends gathered at Annie Fanny Handerson's café in Vicksburg to make a plan to destroy Captain Tom Ford and his gang. Lummy traveled through Vicksburg on his way to and from Winn Parish to end the West-Kimbrell Gang's storm of terror there. Lummy has been through Vicksburg so many times, he believes if he goes to Heaven, he'll have to go through Vicksburg to get there.

WINN PARISH, LOUISIANA: Lummy traveled to Winn Parish in search of Susannah and found her with James T. Gilmore, a gambler who won slaves to set them free. Lummy joined his long lost brother and family to work on the Gilmore farm where Ben was foreman. Lummy married Susannah just before he left to enlist in the Confederate Army, and his plan was to return after the war where he and Susannah would build a life together. Returning to Winn Parish after the surrender of Vicksburg, Lummy learned the truth of Susannah's death and learned they had a son together, Elzey. Life with Susannah no longer possible, Lummy left Elzey with a good family until such time as he was fit to return for his son. A few years later, Lummy and a band of friends helped local residents destroy the West-Kimbrell Gang who had been terrorizing the parish.

A TALE OF TWO COLORS

RED SKY
STORM

VOLUME VII

PART I: LUMMY

CHAPTER 1

WHEN HOME IS HOME NO LONGER

NEAR NOON, JULY 29, 1886

Can't stay home if it ain't home no more.

"I CAN'T DO it, Jasper. I just don't have it in me anymore." I stare down at the initials T.K. on the letter and look up, tears dripping. "The war dreams come every other day. I'm old, and my hands shake. Old age plays hell on an old man." We laugh for a moment. "I can't do it, but—"

Jasper leans in. "But what?"

"I know who can."

I wad the short letter up in my hand I know was sent by Satan himself and squeeze it into a tight ball. I want to crush it to make it disappear. I throw it to the ground. "Damn that Tom Kimbrell."

I shiver like I just crawled out of Bywy Creek in the coldest part of winter. Not from fear of Kimbrell himself, but more afraid of what I'm capable of, and of what I'm willing to do with an outlaw or bully like him. I cross my arms and grip my shoulders.

Jasper whispers, "You look like a rabbit just ran over your grave."

"If you knew what I know about the Kimbrell family and what they're capable of, you'd shudder a bit, too. They are the worst of the murderin' sort, and Tom Kimbrell may be the slipperiest snake in the pit."

I look to the sky for help. Nothing.

"Damn it, Jasper, Tom Kimbrell talked his way out of a firing squad with the rest of the West-Kimbrell Gang in the Easter Sunday Massacre in Winn Parish back in '70." I notice that I'm wringing my hands. "But if I have the right man in mind to deal with him, Tom Kimbrell won't be able to talk his way out of threatening me and our family."

Jasper picks up the crumpled paper. "I'm pretty sure I know who the man is you're talkin' about. I believe he's been known to wear black."

I sit up, trying to grasp a bit of hope in my heart. "Yeah, you know him all too well."

Jasper grins. "Rainy Mills?"

"Yes, Rainy Mills."

Jasper rubs his chin. "He for damn sure is of the sort to take care of a Tom Kimbrell if there ever was one. That is, if the stories you've told me about him killing his murderous raping blood father and the judge who let that bastard get away with it are true."

I lean in. "Everything I told you about Rainy Mills is true down to that last detail."

"I believe you." Jasper stuffs the letter into his coat pocket, mumbling, "You know Mary'll want this scrap of history for the book she's writin' about the Tullos family."

I want to curse. I *need* to curse. "It's not over, dammit. Why won't people just leave it alone? Leave *me* alone?"

"Some people ain't got nothin' else to do but cause trouble for somebody else. If they didn't, they'd have no life at all."

I quote the man I hope will defend our family. "Well, it was Rainy who once told us Plato said, 'Only the dead have seen the end of war.'"

"Yeah, I remember him sayin' that sittin' around the fire up at Big Sand Rock whilst we were fightin' Captain Tom Ford." Jasper wrings his hands now. "What're you gonna do, Lummy?"

I press the owl claw Dan Creekwater gave me years ago into my wrist, but not so that it bleeds like before. "Go to Winn Parish first when I leave here, I reckon. I need to warn a few folks there that Tom Kimbrell is planning somethin' bad."

Jasper stands up. "Then I'm goin' with you, dammit!"

I rub my chin. "No, Jasper, you need to stay here and protect what family we still have. Them damned outlaws have a long and wicked arm that can stretch a long ways when they got demon doin's on their minds. No, you best stay here and watch for any trouble."

Jasper hangs his head and sits back down. "You're absolutely right, brother."

"'Sides, you gave 'em hell at Fort Pemberton, Vicksburg, and Mobile Bay. And then you gave 'em hell here when we took down Captain Tom Ford. You can defend our family. I'd feel much better if you stayed here."

Jasper snickers. "I wish Elihu was here, and ole Dan Creekwater."

I nod. "Yeah, I miss that Elihu. Nobody knows these hills better'n he did, except Dan. And there's no tellin' where that old Choctaw is."

Jasper huffs. "Probably deep in McCurtain Creek swamp somewhere tryin' to keep the skeeters away." He ponders his strategy. "I've got my guns, and I ain't alone. My boy, George Newton, is a pretty fair shot with a rifle and shotgun. His sister, Belle, is, too. Better'n her brother sometimes. She can knock a rabbit's eye out at thirty paces almost every time."

"Yeah, and the Wood brothers don't live too far, and they ain't scared."

He hands me a quart jar of their renowned moonshine made from the sweet waters of Aaron Wood's Spring.

I take a sip and laugh. "And they can fight like hell."

"Sorry this is happenin', Lummy. I just have to believe it will work itself out somehow."

"Yeah, always has, but at a great cost. A very painful cost, I might add."

Jasper stands to stretch. "I best get on home 'fore it gets dark."

I pick up my Henry leaning against a porch post and lever a round into the chamber. "And I need to pack."

I CAN'T SLEEP, so I visit the only place I find a bit of peace—the Tullos Cemetery. I spend most of the night there, finally dozing off. I don't know when. I wake to a jaybird squawking in a tree above my head. I wipe the sleep from my eyes and wander down the path from the small field of graves—likely for the last time. All are gone now except Jasper and his family, and my two daughters who visit on occasion from school in Columbus.

Sometimes I wonder. Were we ever even here? Life flies by so quickly, and too many find their graves way too early in their lives. I miss too many people whom I thought I would get to grow old with. Not to be had. My heart is sinking, and I can't stop it. As I get close to the old dogtrot cabin our family built back in 1835, a rocker creaks in slow rhythm on the porch.

It's Jasper.

"Yeah, brother, this land made us who we are, and most of us have passed on from these hills and hollers."

I shake my head. "Talkin' out loud again?"

Jasper snickers. "You ain't never gonna stop doin' that."

I shake my head and smile. "Nope, probably not." I look back up the ridge to the Tullos Cemetery. "I guess us Tullos folks will always be in the hills. Hills run thick in our blood."

"They do, since our days in Scotland before Great Grandpa Claudius came over on the boat back in the sixteen hundreds, Pa said." Jasper disappears into the old dogtrot cabin and returns with a steaming cup of coffee for me. "Here you go, brother, just the way you like it, a bit of honey and a touch of fresh cream."

I settle into Pa's old rockin' chair. "Thank you kindly." I blow on the cup's contents. "I appreciate you lettin' me stay in the old cabin all this time. I won't be much longer. I'll leave soon."

"Stay as long as you want. I appreciate how you've kept the place up. Cemetery, too."

"A body's gotta do somethin' to keep the devil away."

"War nightmares?"

"Yeah, and not just at night. They seem to be gettin' worse in the daytime, too, since my Martha left us, God rest her blessed soul. She was always a big help when I felt one comin' on." I press the owl claw into my wrist. Jasper glances over at it, and I say, "Damn thing has kept me from goin' back to the Vicksburg trenches many a time. It ain't good when that happens. Neither is this cussing that seems to have returned since Martha passed."

Jasper lifts his chin for a better look at something out in the yard. "I've been wantin' to ask, why do you leave that patch of briars in the middle of the yard over there to grow? You could just cut 'em down."

I chuckle. "Nope, ain't doin' it."

"Why the hell not? They're gettin' to be an eyesore."

"Kinda like me, I guess. An old eyesore."

"What do you mean?"

"I like to leave 'em just as they are. They remind me that some things need to stay wild and free."

Jasper squints. "Uh huh, I see."

"Some things need to be allowed to stay stubborn, like me, I reckon."

Jasper chuckles. "And a mite prickly, too."

"Yeah, and what you see on this porch is that this old stubborn prickly eyesore will be movin' on soon."

"Lummy, I didn't mean—"

"I know, but the patch makes my point. It's time for me to go. Just like them briars."

Jasper takes a long slurp of his coffee, not knowing what to say.

I look around, then smile. "This just ain't home for me no more, brother."

Jasper hangs his head. "I understand." He lifts his head with a grin. "Just so you know, my Isabell and Mary have planned a goin' away supper for you before you leave, right here at the old cabin."

"That'd be good, Jasper. Thank you."

CHAPTER *2*

REMINISCING LIGHTENS
A LOAD, FOR A MOMENT

EARLY-AFTERNOON, JULY 30, 1886

Bein' reminded of good times chases away the hurt, for a bit.

I WALK THE couple hundred yards to Jasper's house with an old jug he recognizes easily. I smile and sit on a bench next to him.

"Is that what I think it is?"

"Sure as I'm sittin' here. And as our dear departed and beloved older brother, Elihu, liked to brag, 'It ought'a be aged je-e-est about rat for drinkin'.'"

"And when we asked for a swig of his fine muscadine wine, he'd say—"

"Got no problem with it."

Jasper snickers. "Elihu was always generous in the sharing of the wine, and—"

"In the partaking of the fermented grape, as well."

Jasper leans back. "I heard a preacher say one time in church, 'The man who turned water into wine can also turn your suffering into joy.' And Elihu whispered, 'Yeah, by giving us more wine.'"

We laugh like two schoolboys whose teacher just found the frog they'd put in her desk drawer.

I wipe my eyes. "You weren't here when Elihu went off to go get us a mess of squirrels that day and the copperhead got him, were you?"

"Naw, don't recollect that I was. Why?"

"Well, you know him and his storytellin'. It might'a been the funniest one he ever told."

Jasper picks his teeth with a splinter. "Tell it." He pours us each a cup of Elihu's famous nectar.

"Of course he started off by sayin', 'I got one more story, and then I'll let you go.' That time, it turned out to be the truth. I didn't know what to expect, but he told it like this.

"A visitin' preacher had the children sit up at the front of the chapel together during a special church service one Sunday morning. He went to each child, askin', 'What's your favorite Bible story?' He came to one little girl who answered, 'When Jesus made the water into wine.' The preacher said, 'Yes, that was a great miracle, wasn't it?' She smiled and nodded. The preacher asked, 'And what does the story of Jesus making water into wine teach us?' She took a deep breath and answered, 'When you run out of wine, get on your knees and pray.'"

We laugh until tears spill down our shirts, and we spill a bit of wine from our cups. I can barely choke out, "That's the last words that ole ignert ass said before he headed into the woods and got himself snake bit."

Jasper snickers. "Yeah, but I bet he was smiling when he closed his eyes."

"And that copperhead must'a slithered off somewhere to sleep off a drunk from all the alcohol in Elihu's blood when he bit him."

Jasper grins. "Where'd Elihu hear that story?"

"He laughed and said, 'Some ole fool in a Bankston back alley I was sippin' shine with.' Anyway, that ole Elihu, what a damn good big brother." I sip a taste of his famous wine. "Yeah, I miss that boy."

Our laughter turns to silence.

I get up and stand at the top of the porch steps and look across the field where Elihu appeared so many times after one of his hunting trips. Rarely did he come home empty-handed. I take another sip of muscadine wine. "Damn that ole copperhead anyway."

"You know he wouldn't have wanted it any other way."

"Yeah, I know. That cancer on his chest was just like one that killed Pa. Guess it was better than layin' up in the bed sufferin' for who knows how long."

Jasper rocks his rocker faster. "I agree."

I shake my head. "Just another one gone too soon. And now there's only the two of us, brother."

Jasper chuckles. "Yeah, but now Eilhu's got all the time in the world and all the grapes he'll ever need to make his wine."

I grin and elbow him. "And he has the best winemaker in the house to help him out, you know, the one who turned water into wine and saved the best for last."

I pour the last of Elihu's fine muscadine wine as the sun starts to set. We touch cups and take deep draws.

Jasper hangs his head. "I wish we had one more sip with him sittin' here with us."

I look to the sky. "Me, too, brother. Me, too."

The faint sound of an old hymn wafts down from Tullos Cemetery Hill. I smile and whisper, "There he is."

I walk back to the old family cabin with an empty muscadine wine jug. And an empty heart, as well. The night will be long. Too long.

CHAPTER 3

GATHERING AT THE OLD DOG TROT

THE OLD TULLOS CABIN, JULY 31, 1886

Shall We Gather at the River is a good song,
but gathering at the supper table is much better.

M Y DAUGHTERS, DELAWARE and Rosetta, and my niece, Mary, ride up in a carriage driven by Matt Poole. My two girls jump from the buggy, rush up the steps of our old dogtrot cabin, and wrap their arms around me. I melt like butter on a summer day.

Delaware pulls back, kisses me on the cheek, and asks, "Well, how the heck are you, Pop?"

"Not as good as you with that fine command of the English language they been teachin' you in that school over in Columbus. I'm proud of you, dear."

She giggles and pulls on my beard like she did when she was just a girl.

Rosetta, six years her younger, lets go and puts her hands on her hips, like Martha used to do, and reports, "And that's not all she's been learning, Pop. Why, she's been going into town and seeing some old boy, and they got caught kissing, and—"

Delaware scowls at her sister.

I hold up my hands. "I'm sure your sister will tell me all about her adventures and escapades later tonight. Y'all get inside, wash up, and then come sit with me for a while."

They both feign sarcasm, say, "Okay, Pop," at the same time, and run inside giggling.

I hear Martha in their voices every time a word comes out of their mouths. Damn, I miss my Martha. I get a bit of pleasure from still making them obey, even though it was Martha who did most of it when they were little. I best quit this cussing I've started up again since she left us, or she'll come in a dream and tan my hide.

I step off the porch to give Mary my hand to help a lady from her carriage. "Why, Mary, it is so good to see you, my sweet dear."

"You, too, Uncle Lummy. It's been way too long."

"Yes, it has."

She nods to Jasper. "And you, too, Uncle Jasper. How's Isabell?"

He gets up to kiss her cheek. "Doin' fine, as you might expect. Keepin' me in line, that's for sure."

I snicker. "It ain't doin' no good, though. Come on up and sit a while. You're surely much easier on the eyes than this old fool."

We laugh as she hikes up her skirt, careful not to trip making her way up the steps.

I give her my spot, and she fluffs out her skirt as she sits like the lady she is.

I lean over close to her. "How's your school teachin' goin' these days?"

She puts her arm around me and says, "Well, it's like this, old timer." She giggles. "If'n it wadn't fer them dang old wild ass students, school teachin' might wud be a tol'rble way of makin' a livin'. I ain't got nary uh—"

Jasper and I belly laugh till we nearly fall out of our seats.

He says, "Now that's as fine Missip talkin' if'n I ever did heerd it, brother."

We settle down, and I stroke Mary's long, beautiful hair. "Reminds me of Ma's. I miss her."

"She was a good momma to me all those years after my mother died." She looks up the hill to the cemetery. "They are all missed, Uncle Lummy."

Jasper wipes a tear. "Ain't it so?"

It hits me. "Oh, that reminds me. I have a box of stuff for you, Mary."

"Really? The stuff?"

I nod. "You are the keeper of the family history. It's time I hand over what I have to you."

"I don't know what to say, Uncle Lummy, except thank you. I will take care of it and make sure it gets passed along into good hands."

"I know you will, dear. How's the book coming?"

"Oh, I get to work on it now and again when I can, but being single and having dedicated my life to being a school marm, it's hard to find time."

"You mean that young private who was eyein' you when he brought me that damned letter about goin' to fight John West never called on you?"

Mary squirms a bit. "Let's just say that's a story for another time." Then, she grins. "I have my eye on a schoolmaster who lives not far from here, but I'm not telling.... I will get the book done, Uncle Lummy."

"I know you will."

"What pieces of history do you have, Uncle Lummy?"

I pick up the old box Pa had made me to store my treasures in when I was a kid—arrowheads, agates, and other things a boy would treasure. I've always kept it in a special place in our barn. Since I left home back in '59, I've collected quite a few mementos worthy of the box—the cedar cross Poole carved for me, the spent bullet that slammed into my chest, and the chess set Granville made me during the Siege of Vicksburg, stuff like that. But there's one thing I'll give her today more important than all of my trinkets and souvenirs.

"Here, Mary, I want to pass all of this along to you." I pull an oiled leather pouch from my pocket.

"What are those? Letters? What's in them?"

I hand her the carefully wrapped bundle. "All the stories of our people from way back that Grandpa Temple wrote down and sent to Pa. Ma told me Pa never had much interest in them, so she saved them for me. I've kept them all these years. As you know, Temple wasn't my grandpa, but Grandpa Willoughby's brother. He was my great uncle. I never knew Grandpa Willoughby, and Ma said it was just as well because I was too much like Uncle Silas, who fought in the Battle of New Orleans with Gen'l Jackson. Uncle Silas and Grandpa Willoughby didn't see eye to eye on the idea of slavery and almost came to blows over it. That's how Pa got possession of sweet Missus Lucy, who was a slave. Pa and Ma brought her with us when we moved here, me bein' born on the way in Holmes County. Pa said she was free. She lived the rest of her life here on the farm with us, God rest her sweet soul. So, anyway, I always called Great Uncle Temple Tullos 'Grandpa', because he was the only grandfather I ever knew. He, Granny Thankful, and Uncle Silas

visited us once when I was around ten years old. Uncle Silas told me all about
his runnin's around with Sam Dale and then gettin' to the battlefield at New
Orleans just before the British attacked. It's all in there, the stories Grandpa
sent, and some I wrote down, too."

"Oh, Uncle Lummy, this is such a treasure. Thank you."

"I labeled everything in the box, but if you have questions, better ask
tonight."

"You leave tomorrow?"

"Early."

Mary sifts through the papers and trinkets, obviously looking for something specific. "Didn't you have an alligator tooth? Where did it go?"

I pause and look at Jasper. He smiles and ducks his head.

Mary shies back a little, and her face turns red. "Did I ask the wrong
question?"

We just sit and let her sort it out. It takes half a minute.

Her facial expression lightens, but it's clear she's a bit embarrassed. "Oh,
your son by Susannah, Elzey, has it, right?"

I nod. "I just don't talk about it much, but that story up till I left him after we
took down the West-Kimbrell Gang is all written down for you. It's in there."

Mary lifts out my small folded stack of writings. "Thank you, Uncle Lummy. I'll make you proud when I get a book published about the history of
the Tullos family." She gathers the box and letters and carries them to the
end of the porch where there's more light and she can spread out her new
treasures. She catalogs each piece in a little book as she retrieves it from the
box with great joy.

She stops. "Uncle Lummy, I know what most of all this is because you told
me the stories behind each piece. I like the little flags. I know that has been
very important to you, and...."

She continues talking but I get lost in thoughts of a thousand memories

"Pop! Don't you hear me? You all right?" Delaware and Rosetta are standing in the dogtrot at attention like I did when I was in the Rifles. They must
have to do that as part of their etiquette training at school. They are spitting
images of their mother, Martha, and just as pretty.

I whisper, "Yeah." I wipe a tear. "Lord, I miss my Martha."

They speak again but together softly, "We know, Pop."

Rosetta sits in my lap and wraps her arms around me. "She misses you, too, old timer."

"Old timer? Why, I can still take a switch to your backside and—"

Delaware laughs. "No you won't, Pop. You never did, and you're not going to start now."

Rosetta giggles. "We've never known you to hurt a fly, Pop. Except for just a few stories we heard that I'm sure you'd like to forget."

"You got that right. But, Mary the scholar made me give her all the details that I know about every subject I ever thought about, and—"

Mary, who sounds just like Ma when she was younger, cackles, "I heard that, old man, and I will take a willow switch to your backside if you don't watch out." She lays her head down on the table, laughing. "I cannot believe I just said that."

I mumble, "I can't help but be the happiest man on earth right now."

Jasper leans over. "So, remind me again why you're leavin'?"

I shoot him a look that says, *Don't bring that up.* "You know why, and I don't want to spend my last few moments with my girls and y'all talkin' about things I have no answers for."

Jasper throws up his hands. "You're right. Sorry."

I turn back to my girl. "You two have been the daughters every father wishes he had. I'm proud of you. I mean every word."

Delaware walks behind me and wraps her arms around me as Rosetta squeezes tighter. I'm in heaven. I could go on through the thin veil now, if the Good Lord would have me.

A voice from the cemetery speaks through a breeze. *"Creator is not quite ready for you yet, Lummy."*

DELAWARE KISSES THE back of my neck and asks, "Where are you going from here, Pop?"

"Not sure just yet. I'll send you a wire when I get there."

Delaware cries.

Rosetta stiffens her emotional resolve and announces, "Well, Pop, when you get done wandering the earth like the children of Israel in the wilderness, you come live with me. I'm sure I'll have a home and husband someday, and I'll want you living in my home."

Isabell calls from inside, "Delaware, Rosetta, would y'all come help set the table please?"

They answer together, rolling their eyes, "Yes, ma'am, be right there."

I nod for them to go. "We'll talk more in a bit, girls. Thanks for helping your aunt."

Delaware kisses me again, and Rosetta hugs me tight. They trot inside to help with the meal.

I pull another piece of history from my coat pocket and hold it up. "Here, Mary, I want to return a gift."

Mary grins. "The little Bible I sent you when you went off to the war?"

I thumb through the pages. "It is, and you'll find quite a few thoughts in here when I was goin' through the siege. I read it a lot in those days."

Jasper backhands across my chest. "Didn't do a damn bit of good, not from where I sit." He laughs at his own joke so hard he nearly falls off the bench he's sitting on.

I thump his head and snicker. "And you won't be able to sit down again until I get my boot out of you're a—"

Isabell comes to the door, wagging her finger but holding back a laugh. "Lummy Tullos! I thought Martha broke you of all that cussin'! God rest her soul." She pops a wooden spoon in her hand and tries hard not to laugh. "You and that wild and untamable brother of yours get in here, and let's say grace over supper. Lord knows you boys need to hear it."

I grin and stick my tongue out at her. "Isabell, dear, I swear I just heard my ma talkin'."

Mary laughs. Isabell just shakes her head, but with a grin.

Jasper hops up like he's been stung by a bee. "Ain't gotta tell me twice. I know when to keep my mouth shut so I get fed."

I hand the little Bible to Mary and a folded piece of paper falls out. I wince. I forgot that was in there.

"What's this, Uncle Lummy?"

"Would it be okay if you read that later? I don't need to dwell on that right now."

"Yes, sir, that's fine."

I shudder like in wintertime. It's the letter Mr. Gilmore sent me with the news of Susannah's death when I was in Vicksburg. A small glowing light up on Tullos Cemetery Hill catches my eye.

It's Susannah. Waving. I wave back, smiling, and then go inside with the others for what will be my last supper here.

CHAPTER 4

I DON'T WANT TO LEAVE, BUT I HAVE TO GO

AFTER SUPPER, JULY 31, 1886

After the last supper, there always needs to be some last words.

SUPPER'S OVER, AND the younger children have all taken to chasing lightning bugs. It's just me, Delaware and Rosetta, and Jasper and Isabell. Except for the kids romping and yelling, it's quiet.

Mary brings a straight back chair out on the porch. "I'm not missing this." She gets situated and pulls out her little notebook. She looks up from writing down the day's date and asks, "Dell, Rosey, how's school been treating you two girls?"

Delaware sits up straight like she's in class. "I love it. I never knew there was so much to learn."

Rosetta giggles. "She's learning all sorts of things in Columbus, why—"

Delaware kicks her shin, and Rosetta lets out a yell.

"That hurt!"

"It's going to hurt worse if you don't hush up, Rosey." She stares her sister down.

Jasper laughs. "That one surely is your child, Columbus Nathan Tullos."

Dell gives a mischievous grin. "Now, what was I saying before I was so rudely interrupted?"

Rosey giggles, and Dell gives her stern look, then bursts out laughing. They hug.

Mary shakes her head. "There's nothing else like the love between sisters. What's it like being in the first class of a newly chartered school, Dell?"

"Nothing short of amazing. They're calling it an experiment in education, but I tell you, I plan to graduate with a degree at the end of my four years."

Mary sniffs. "Well, the name change from The Mississippi Industrial Institute and College for the Education of White Girls to Mississippi University for Women was certainly a step in the right direction."

I have to chime in, "Shorter the name, the better."

Mary fluffs her skirt. "Yes, and it has the distinction of being the first state taxpayer funded public college for women in these United States. It's also the oldest public university in our state. Both the University and Franklin Academy, where Rosetta attends, offer education affordable for all women."

I clap my hands together. "What she means is that it's free. That makes it ve-e-ery affordable for this poor old farm hand."

Everyone snickers.

Mary laughs. "Yes, one legislator who voted for its charter said it was a Godsend for the poor girls of Mississippi."

I stomp my foot twice. "Here, here, and that'd be us. Poor as a church mouse lookin' for communion bread crumbs in wintertime."

Mary smiles at Dell and Rosey. "I believe the institution will flourish and prepare women from all over in professional training to enrich the workforce."

My heart swells to burst. "It will if they keep gettin' the quality of students like Dell, and soon Rosey."

We all sit still, enjoying the sounds of the evening. A lone owl hoots. I think of Dan.

Jasper, in the sweetest tone, asks Isabell, "I believe Lummy could use a bit of Wood brothers' moonshine, if you don't mind?"

She gives him the look that says she knows he needs a minute alone with me.

The girls get the hint. They get up to go play with the children.

Mary starts to leave, but I gently take her arm. "You stay, dear. You may want to hear this."

Jasper rubs his chin. "Just thought I'd mention that there'll be an old soldier's reunion near Winnfield come the tenth of next month."

"Oh yeah? How'd you find that out?"

"You know I keep up with the old fellows we fought with in the war who still live around here. They get mailed a list of upcoming events the boys might be interested in attending. The note on the Winnfield reunion said there'll be members of the Twenty-seventh Louisiana Volunteer Infantry there. Thought it might be good if you were to stop by there on your way to wherever you're headed."

"It's an idea, I reckon. I wouldn't mind seein' a few of them old boys, especially since John West won't be there."

"Maybe it could help with your war dreams? Talkin' with other men who might be havin' the same problem, that is."

"Yeah, maybe. I'll give it some thought."

Mary quietly asks, "Uncle Lummy, would you take down notes about what you're doing from time to time, please?"

"Yeah, I guess I could do that."

She hands me three small books like the ones Gunnard carried during the siege of Vicksburg and Sheriff Barnett wrote in when we took down Dawg Smith. Each one is as thin as the width of my pointing finger and can fit easily into a coat pocket. I thumb through the pages.

"There's nothin' in here but my name and some kind words that you wrote in the front, Mary. What am I—?"

"It's called a journal, Uncle Lummy. The blank pages are for you to write your experiences in. When you finish filling one book with your notes and thoughts, just send it to Uncle Jasper, and he'll get it to me. Then, start a new one. Three should keep you for a while, but you can find them in most any book store or mercantile."

"I can do that, or should I say like Elihu? 'Ain't got no problem with it.'"

Jasper pulls back his graying hair, smiling. "It'll be a good thing to do, Lummy. We'll get to read your story like a long letter and know where you are from time to time. And besides, I don't think the Lord's done with you yet. He's always had interesting things for you to do."

"Yeah, and maybe the writin' will help keep my head in the present when the war dreams come callin'." I drop my head, thinking how weary I am of all of that. I whisper, "But Lord, like your son said, 'Not my will, but yours be done.'"

Jasper squeezes my arm. "Now there's the brother I know."

Mary leans forward and kisses me on the cheek. "Thank you, Uncle Lummy."

I bring up what I don't want to in this peaceful moment. "Jasper, I best let Rainy know I'm comin'. I guess a message over the wire would be the quickest way."

Jasper leans back in his chair. "It'd be the fastest way, for sure."

Mary offers, "It would get there before a letter could arrive."

I think for a moment. "Yeah, it would, Mary. Would you send him a telegraph for me, please? I don't want to go to Bankston again. What Poole and I did to that place haunts me still."

"I understand. What should I say in the telegram?"

"That I'll be seein' him within the week, and that there's Kimbrell trouble in the air."

"I can do that."

I stand to go back home and finish packing for my trip to where I don't know yet, except to Winn Parish first.

Jasper stretches out his hand. "Isabell, please call the kids. Lummy's about to leave."

Isabell steps out into the dogtrot, wiping her hands on a dishtowel. "When do you leave, Lummy?"

"In the morning, early."

Mary hugs me. "I'm going to miss you, Uncle Lummy."

The kids surround me and hug me all around.

Isabell kisses me. "You take care, brother, you hear?"

I go back to the old Tullos cabin for my last night there and sit for a long time. The silence is so loud you can hear it.

I pack the few things I want to take and fall into my old bed to sleep soundly until a rooster crows.

CHAPTER 5

LEAVING IS THE BETTER PART OF BIDDING FAREWELL

BEFORE DAWN, AUGUST 1, 1886

*The better part of bein' brothers is always
being the same when you see 'em again.*

JASPER RIDES UP on an old mule that looks to have seen its better days. He offers his hand after he dismounts. "Couldn't have had a better brother than you, Lummy. I will see you again, brother."

I pull him close for a good bear hug. "Count on it, Jasper. If not here, then like Granny Thankful used to say, 'In the air on that great gettin' up mornin'.'"

He steps up on the porch and sits in Pa's old rocking chair. "Yeah, that's right. Where will you go?"

"I guess as far as this money will take me."

"Where will you live?"

"I heard a fellow say once, 'I can live anywhere because I belong nowhere.'"

Jasper squints. "Sounds like Rainy Mills."

I grin. "I'm lookin' forward to seeing that old outlaw again before I walk through the thin veil."

"So, Winn Parish first, then God knows where?"

"Yeah, I'll stop for a day or so to say hello to Rainy and Dorcas, and maybe take in that reunion. I'll stop in Vicksburg before I catch the ferry to Looseana."

"Annie Fanny?"

"You know it."

"You better watch that old gal. She'll have you bedded down before you can say 'biscuits and gravy,' and you know that's the truth."

"Biscuits and gravy's 'bout the only thing I'd be good for anyway when it comes to that sort of thing these days. 'Sides, I plan on keepin' my religion when I'm there. Don't you worry, it's been quite a spell since I experienced—how did Pa say it when we were young ruttin' bucks—?"

"A bad case of the red rooster?"

I laugh. "Yeah, that was it. Oh, well, it's the way of the world."

"Ain't it so?" He shakes his head. "And that's just all right, ain't it?"

"Yeah, yeah, it is."

Jasper fidgets. "You thinkin' you might see your boy, Elzey?"

"Not sure. Guess I'll know if that's the right thing to do when I get there." I tie down my saddlebags, shove my Henry rifle into the scabbard, and change the subject. "Let me pay you for the horse. Looks to be a good'n."

"Nothin' doin'. It's my gift to you, brother, to help you on your way." Jasper rocks a bit faster in his chair. He knows I'll be leaving in a bit. "You had a good life here, with Martha and the kids, didn't you?"

"I did, and with all of you, brother. But here I go again, traipsing off to parts unknown, and I really don't know why, except that I cannot stay."

"Like Grandpa Temple always used to say, 'A Celt of the moving kind and a Pict of the settling kind.'"

"Yeah, just wish I could settle in somewhere, paint myself blue, and dance naked around the fire every night up in the hills in the middle of nowhere."

Jasper chuckles. "You ain't never been right in the head, boy. What was it Dan called you? Crazy Deer Dancer?"

In my mind, I can see that buck standing up on its hind legs and dancing in the middle of the road when I left to go find Susannah back in '59. I met Dan Creekwater that day.

I point at Jasper with a grin. "One man's crazy is another man's peace, don't you think?"

"After bein' your brother all these years? I sure as hell can testify to that."

We enjoy a moment of silence. And the memories.

Jasper sits up in his chair. "You gonna be all right, with your war dreams and all?"

"Yeah, I figure I can make it, mostly by stayin' away from people as much as I can, and Dan Creekwater's owl claw here to keep me in the present."

Jasper snickers. "You *do* know you're over fifty now and not what you used to be, right?"

"Like I said, I'll avoid people as much as—"

"Brother, you ain't never had to go lookin' for trouble because it always comes lookin' for you."

I hang my head. "Well, speak to the Good Lord on that one for me. I surely don't need or want any trouble findin' me anymore. I just want to be left alone."

"And that's the ones that irritate the Devil the most and who he comes after in the fury of a tornado."

I look to the sky. "I know."

Jasper changes the subject. "Maybe you'll buy a little farm and settle somewhere quiet-like? You've got the money."

"Probably not. Everywhere I've tried to settle, well, it just ain't worked out too good for me, or those around me."

Jasper stands to stretch. "I beg to differ, but I understand."

I step back up on the porch. I pull his forehead to mine. "See you when I see you, Jasper. I love you, boy."

I mount up, ride past the Tullos Cemetery, take off my hat, and thank Creator for a life lived that only the Master of the Universe could have given. I gently prod my horse on to the next leg of my journey.

"What now, Lord?"

CHAPTER 6

ONE LAST HURRAH BEFORE I GO

JUST BEFORE NOON, SUNDAY, AUGUST 1, 1886

Don't look back if you don't want to leave.
It makes it harder to go.

MY PACE IS slow, and I don't get very far the first few hours. I just needed to walk the hills and hollows of my home one last time. I rub my horse's neck as he waters in Phoenix Creek that runs through our land. I bend down to take a drink for the last time.

"The water's always sweeter at home." I stand to give thought to my first next step. "I need one more look from the highest point, and that'd be Little Mountain. I'll get my last best look at what has been home."

I work my way down Phoenix Creek into Bowie Branch. But there's one place I need to visit before I go to Little Mountain. Bucksnort.

The scraggly little town ain't what it used to be, but neither am I. Known for its whiskey, drunkenness, gambling, fighting, and sporting ladies, Bucksnort has been the subject of many a hellfire and damnation Sodom and Gomorrah sermon delivered by preachers for miles around. Problem is a number of those self-righteous bastards were caught partaking of the devil's doings on occasion in Bucksnort.

Not a good thing.

I step into one of the few remaining saloons just before noon with my hair pulled back and my hat down low. I've never visited Bucksnort, except for passing through. Never needed to, but today I want to sit in the room where Mr. Gilmore won Susannah from her slave master in a card game. I want to toast his profound influence upon my life and how I'm the better man for having known him. It was he who made it possible for me to marry Susannah—even if it was only for a short while.

The old owner of the saloon shouts, "Well, if ain't—" He stops short, realizing he's seeing a different man than he thought. "You're not Elihu, but you sure as hell look a lot like him, only a head taller."

I laugh. "I didn't know that my brother, who regularly sang solos at church, visited here so often he'd be on a first name basis with a saloon owner." Everyone in the place laughs.

"Hymn singer, my ass. Elihu Tullos was one of our best customers and a good friend. Many a day he dropped off a jug of that fine muscadine wine on his way to your church."

I look around the room. "Ain't no churchgoers up in here today, I'm bettin'."

The small crowd shouts, "Here, here!" as they raise their glasses.

"Damn straight. Come on in and have a seat. Any brother of Elihu Tullos is sure as hell a friend of mine."

From the corner of my eye, I catch a man at the bar scowling at me. I have no idea who he is or why he's giving me such a nasty look. I act as if I don't see him.

The saloon owner stops to scratch his head. "Sorry your brother passed on. Heard a copperhead got 'em, right?"

I nod.

He shakes his head and continues wiping drink glasses.

I sit in a corner and nod to the barkeep to bring a bottle and a glass. I throw a silver dollar on the table as he pours my first glass. I scan the room for any other problems than the one sitting at the bar. I guess it became a habit after all these years of experiencing violence when I didn't expect it, but learned how to watch out for it.

The barkeep brings me a half-loaf of fresh baked bread and butter to slather on it. A pot of honey sits on the table. The bread's still steaming. And so is the man at the bar.

Everyone tends to their own business in places like this, but I catch that crusty old man at the bar squirrel-eyeing me ever so slightly with a glower. I know him, but from where? I'm probably mistaken. Hopefully, he is. I don't want any trouble, but I ain't afraid of it either. I sip my whiskey and enjoy my thoughts.

The batwings at the front swing open with a crash and in walk two men I haven't seen in several years. They catch me looking at them and grin.

One asks, "Why, Lummy Tullos, what'n the hell is a God-fearin' preacher man like yourself doin' in this den of iniquity?" The other crows like a rooster. I just hang my head in embarrassment.

"Why, John and Henry, how'n the hell are you boys?" I announce to the meager crowd, "Well, y'all take notice. The Wood boys have arrived, and they ain't scared."

One customer cackles like a crow bird, "That's for damn sure, but they make the finest drinkin' whiskey this side of Tennessee."

The man who's been eyeing me huffs, and then spits into an empty lard can sitting on the floor. I had made the announcement for him.

The saloon owner steps out from the kitchen laughing, hands on his hips. "You bring the whiskey I ordered, or did you boys drink it all before you got here?"

John tips his hat. "We brought you ten hogshead barrels filled with the finest Missip moonshine made from the most heavenly sweet waters of Aaron Wood's Spring. The wagon's pulled up 'round back. We'll unload here in a bit."

The saloon owner waves him off. "Go on and visit with your friend. I'll have my man unload it."

Henry nods. "Thank you, suh, we do 'preciate it."

The barkeep brings over a jug and their payment for the whiskey.

John tosses a slight glance and nod at the grouchy man sitting at the bar.

The barkeep purses his lips and whispers, "He's talkin' under his breath, but he's mentioned somethin' about a black girl in a hotel in Bankston some years back and gettin' the man who shamed him. Don't mind him, he's drunk."

The scowling man throws a coin on the bar and walks out, but not before growling my direction.

I can't resist. I figure I ain't got a whole lot to lose at this point. "You got somethin' to say to me, boy, or are you just good at makin' damn ugly faces? They come pretty easy for you."

He stops at the door. "Your time is comin', and when you least expect, Lummy Tullos."

"Well, I'll tell you, mister. I'm eating this fine fresh baked bread and drinking the finest moonshine in Missip. I don't know which I've had the most of. Either way, I'm in better shape than you if you try to come get some. So, either come with what you got or get the hell away from me."

He stomps through the saloon batwings knowing that with the Wood brothers sitting with me, he doesn't have a chance, even if there were four of him. And he would be correct because the Wood boys, they're always ready for a good scrap.

Henry asks, "Who's that bastard?"

"For the life of me, I can't remember that man. There's somethin' familiar about what the barkeep said, but it escapes my cluttered brain for the moment."

John slaps me on the back. "No worries there, Lummy, let's just enjoy our whiskey."

I turn and smile. "Right."

Then, I tell them I'm leaving Choctaw County. For good.

CHAPTER 7

FAREWELL TO CHOCTAW COUNTY

JUST BEFORE SUNSET, AUGUST 1, 1886

Seein' life from the point of no return sends new possibilities into the soul.

THE SUNSET FLASHES orange and purple as I gaze over the only place I really ever called home.

The view from Little Mountain reminds me of Sky Parlor Hill in Vicksburg. From here you can see just about everywhere, if you have the eyes for it. This will be my last look from this point. This for me has always been a place to leave from, not return to. My soul needs to find new possibilities. They can only be found in the horizon to the west. It's always been that way with Tulloses. But it starts here.

My mount snorts and catches a deep breath after the steep climb.

I feed him a little grain and give him a drink of water. "Take a rest. We ain't got to be nowhere but right here, right now, except I'd like to make it to that old soldier's reunion in Winnfield in a few days. That should be interesting, don't you think?" The horse nuzzles his nose against my chest, and I scratch him between the eyes.

This is a good and most needed moment of peace. This is my church service today. I can't get any closer to Creator than this. I'm not good around people with their religious beliefs that border on sacrilege in my opinion. Just too much talk, judgment, and condemnation without looking to one's own spirituality. I don't have the temperament for that anymore. What's better—a man sitting in the churchouse thinking about being in the woods, or a man in the woods thinking about God? It doesn't have to be one or the other, but rather, it should be both. It's just that ones who can only find God in four walls on Sunday don't seem to appreciate the ones who can't. I'm done with those attitudes.

I stretch my arms to the sky and confess, "I'm ready any time you are, Lord. Take me now, if you want. You know how tired I am." I wait, and nothing happens. "Guess you ain't done with me yet."

I snicker at my own admission.

The late afternoon has become as still as the hills surrounding Vicksburg when the Confederate Army sent up white flags in surrender. The silence buzzes loud in my ears, almost like the booms of the cannon firing on those hills during the siege. Strange, silence being so loud. Nothing moves except the leaves of a small thicket rustle in the slight breeze of a white flowing robe passing by to light by my side like a dove.

"And you would be correct, grandson. Creator still has plans for you, if you are willing."

"Have I ever not been willing, Granny?"

"You've been a bit fussy at times, but yes, for the most part, you've obeyed."

"Will I go alone?"

"You should know by now, boy, that I'm always by your side in whatever Creator has for you to do."

"What am I supposed to do now?"

"Pick up the stone at your feet. It will be your guide and protection." She taps her foot. *"Are you still so dull, Lummy Tullos? Truth is always revealed in the moment most necessary. You will not miss it."*

I pick up the stone. An agate with swirling lines that remind me of the flow of the Universe and how Creator plays everything out in his perfect will.

"Yes, ma'am, but it'd be helpful to know—"

"What you need to know comes for you now, grandson. Prepare yourself to learn what must be done by what happens next."

Granny disappears. My horse snorts and pricks up his ears. A dark shape rushes from the same thicket Granny was in with an outstretched arm wielding a small pistol. I reach for mine, but I'm too late.

"I got you now, you black mammie lovin' Yankee turncoat son of a bitch!

I've been waitin' since that day you made a fool of me in the Bankston Hotel in front of that black girl."

It's the man from the Bucksnort saloon. Now I remember. He'd insulted Ruth, and I took a derringer from him in the same moment I almost took his head with the knife Pa made me. Had Sarge not been there at the time, I'd probably done it.

He aims a small derringer at my head. "Yeah, you recognize the pistol? Same make, same model, same caliber as the one you stole from me that day. I swore the first and last time I would use it would be to kill you, Lummy Tullos."

I remember Rainy Mills telling me this man would come for me one day. I figure with a pistol aimed at my head, I have little to lose. "You must've led a pretty sorry life, holdin' onto a grudge that long. Is that all you got?"

"No, I've got your life in my hands. What'chu say 'bout that, you son of a bitch dawg?"

"You got a name? Surely that unlucky lady who gave birth to you called you somethin'. But I guess as damn ugly as you are, your momma must'a tied a piece of meat around your neck just to get the damn dawgs to play with you." I can't help but snicker at my own words. It just makes him madder.

"I ain't tellin' you my name. You're gonna wander all over hell wondering who shot you between the eyes and spend your eternal days askin' everybody who it was who killed you."

"Well, the way I got it figured? If you make it through this situation, you won't be far behind me, so I'll be holdin' the door open for you when you arrive. I will find you, hell or no hell."

His jaw drops with a twinge of fear, finding no words to respond.

The agate in my hand glows, and I reason if there's something Creator has yet for me to do like Granny said, then this ain't my time to die. So, I trust Creator and figure I might as well enjoy how this plays out.

I chuckle. "If my life bein' in your hands is all you got, I just asked the Lord a few minutes ago to take me now if he's willin'. Maybe he sent you to do me that favor. Kind of comical, don't you think?"

"Ain't nothin' funny 'bout a man gettin' gut shot, boy."

"You'd be truth tellin' on that, but it ain't happened yet, has it?"

"It will now, and I'm gonna make you suffer, Tullos."

"Do your worst, 'cause I will get to you before I die, and then they'll find me sittin' at the base of that old oak over there like I fell asleep, but with your severed head in my lap."

The man lowers his pistol from aiming at my head to my stomach. He gives an evil grin as he squeezes the trigger. I drop down in a flash and sweep his feet out from underneath him with my foot. He's back up like a cat, but so am I. Not as old and decrepit as I think I am. But neither is he. That's the last thing I remember as I start wailing on his head and chest with my fists.

I wake from my rage tripping on a sandstone rock and falling to the ground.

Derringer man laughs and rushes to stand over me, pointing his gun at my head. "You're in luck. No gut shootin' today. I'm puttin' you out of my misery for good, Tullos."

"Make it count, shamed boy."

He backs up as I stand up to face an end that I still don't believe will be mine today. Not yet.

"I'll kill you now."

An arrow with owl fletching swooshes by my head from up in a tree behind me and slams square into derringer man's chest. He screams, then gasps and grabs his chest. He starts to fall backward and points the derringer again to fire. A second arrow finds its way into the man's hand, forcing him to drop the pistol but not before it goes off.

I duck before the bullet passes by my head. It strikes flesh, and a muffled groan comes from someone high in his perch above us.

Derringer man slumps over and falls to the ground, blood bubbling from his mouth. He gets no word out before his eyes close for the last time.

I turn to find an old man sliding down a large oak tree like a bear with a bow in hand. He falls to the ground. The bullet must've struck him good. I rush to him as he hobbles out of the thicket.

Dan Creekwater. Saving my hide one more time.

From the looks of things, maybe for the last time.

Dan chuckles, then coughs. "I knew I wasn't done killin' white men. Well, the evil ones anyway." He collapses.

I drop to my knees as an owl flies into the tall pine above where Dan lays. "Dan, how'd you… oh, hell… we gotta get you to a doctor. Quick!"

He shakes his head and smiles. "No, son, not this time. I'm ready to go to that great hunting ground in the sky." He looks up to the old owl perched above him. "My father said I came into this world with the owls. I guess I'll go out with them, too." Dan takes my hand and squeezes it. "Never forget what you learned in McCurtain Creek Swamp, Lummy. Go find your peace, my son. It's been lookin' for you for a long time." He presses the owl claw into my wrist and smiles. "It's been a pleasure, Crazy Deer Dancer."

I cry as his eyes close. "The pleasure has been all mine, Dan Creekwater."

Three more owls swoop in, each to perch in a different tree. The four sit, staring down from their positions, like they're representing the four corners of the earth. They give a long and loud hooting chorus. I bury Dan Creekwater there, covering him with sandstones. As I place the last stone, an owl feather floats down onto the grave. A fitting tribute to honor a wise man.

On the top of Little Mountain, I sit for a long time. Till dawn. Remembering.

The morning sun breaks over the ridge. I douse my face with water from my canteen.

I tell my horse, "I've got to go somewhere else, where no one knows who I am. Where home is simply where I am, and it doesn't have to be any particular place." I gather myself and my stuff. I mount up and take one long last look at Choctaw County, then ease my horse down the trail to the Old Trace.

"I won't be comin' back here again. Ever." My horse gives a gentle whinny.

I SCRATCH MY mount between the ears as I lean on my saddle. We're standing in the middle of the road on the Old Natchez Trace—a trail that holds many good memories. The best was finding young runaway slave Seth at Brashears Stand and taking him home with me to become part of the family. I'll never know what it's like to be a slave or flee an abusive master, fearing the hounds will rip me to pieces. I don't know what it's like to be taken in by a family who set me free from the chains of bondage and servitude. Susannah tried to explain it after we were married in Winn Parish so long ago, but still, I'll never know.

But because of Mr. Gilmore, I do know what it's like to make freedom happen for a slave. It still makes me sad, and ill, that Captain Tom Ford killed him. There's no telling what Seth and his family would have become given the same opportunity as I have had. That's all right. Captain Tom Ford got his punishment for what he did to Seth. It's really not much consolation.

Memories. Good and bad. Can't have one without the other. But I can choose which ones to give my mind to.

"Which way should we go, horse? Probably won't be comin' back this way again."

I ponder the possibilities. The horse snorts and pricks up his ears.

"What? I guess you don't like bein' called horse?" I scratch my beard. "Okay then, I here and now give you the name Cloud, in honor of the horse that carried me through my time with the First Mississippi Mounted Rifles, and for my great grandfather who came to America from Scotland over two hundred years ago. How about that?"

The horse throws his head up and down like he understands. Maybe he does. Ain't for me to say.

I dismount. Deciding which way to go may take a minute.

"Cloud, we could follow the Trace and go through Clinton. It'd be good to see that professor, oh, what was his name? Oh, yeah, Mister Aquila. He's probably long been in the grave for some time now. His wife sure could cook up the best pies, though." I think for a moment. "Nah, let's go to Carrollton and see if old Dale is still around. But let's make camp for a few hours, get some food in us, and rest. Then, we'll head out."

CHAPTER 8

CARROLLTON AND THE LEGACY OF DALE

NOON, AUGUST 3, 1886

Visiting an old friend on the way is good,
even if he's sleeping in the cemetery.

CARROLLTON, MISSISSIPPI, IS a beautiful town. I thought that the first time I came through back in '59. I pass the old shed I slept in for the night when I first arrived. I made a bit of pocket change working for its owner the next day to help me on my way.

I pass the beautiful courthouse with the stars and stripes flying proudly above. That's always good to see. Even so, there's still a lot of sentiment for the Old South here, and traditions don't die an easy death in these parts. I ease Cloud down the embankment and find the spot where Dale used to tie up his hack when not in use. There's no telling how many trips that man made between here and Greenwood on Big Sand Creek. The one time I traveled with him, I walked away with wisdom that carries me still today. The place has changed, but why wouldn't it have?

A seasoned, sturdy built man wearing a shopkeeper's clothes walks out of a small office building just up the hill from the creek and shakes a customer's hand. He looks my way but starts back to the office. It's not Dale. Another equally built man wearing clothes for working outside walks up the gangplank from one of several hacks tied up to a dock built on the creek bank below the office.

I yell, "Anybody here know of an old coot named Dale?"

Both stop, look at each other, and the man walking up from the boats asks, "Who's asking?"

I smile. "Just an old friend who came by to pay a bit of honor and respect to a man who made a big difference in my life." I hold up the horse head ivory pipe Dale sent me through Rainy years ago.

The one dressed in shopkeeper's clothes squints and turns to his brother. "It can't be."

The other grins. "Has to be." He studies me for a moment. "You're Lummy Tullos, ain't ya?"

"One and the same. Is Dale around?"

The brothers hang their heads and kick at the dirt.

The shopkeeper hangs his head. "Father passed away three years ago, not long after our ma died. He just didn't want to live after she left us."

"Can I ask your names?"

The one in shopkeeper's clothes answers. "Andrew, and my brother's name is Peter, like the two fishermen brothers in the Bible."

"Good men to be named after. Your father was one of the kindest men I've ever met. He must've loved your momma well."

"He was the best thing that ever happened to her, and us, for that matter."

"Y'all still runnin' the business, I see."

"Pa taught us well and left us in good shape."

Peter fidgets a bit. "Is it true, that old cottonmouth that got Pa was the same one that slid over your shoulder when y'all took a hack down to Green-wood years ago?"

"I don't know if it was the same one, but there certainly were plenty enough of 'em to go around. I'm sorry he left this earth that way. I would rather he—"

Andrew speaks up, "Oh, no, that old stump-tail moccasin must've got him good. We found him under a willow tree on a sandbar with a fishin' pole in his hand. A big ole catfish was tuggin' on the line. Pa had the biggest grin on his face." Andrew looks to Peter.

Peter lifts his head. "Yep, that's the way Pa said he wanted to go, and I guess he called it pretty damn close. Don't think he suffered much at all. The doctor who examined him said the poison went straight to his heart. Killed him in less than twenty minutes. Just enough time to get his line in the water and sit down." He sniffles and wipes his nose. "We miss him."

Andrew looks to the sky, then out across the creek. "Yeah, we miss him a lot."

I hold out the ivory carved horse head pipe. "I know you do. Would either of you like to have this pipe? He said his old pap gave it to him before I met him. He sent it to me after the war."

Both shake their heads.

"How 'bout I leave it by his grave then. That be all right?"

Andrew looks to Peter. "It's all right with me."

Peter smiles. "Yeah, that'll work."

I knock what few bits of tobacco are left in the bowl into my hand, and I scatter them like ashes. "Hell, I need to give up tobacco anyway. I've grown too fond of the stuff."

Andrew laughs. "I hear it can become a habit."

I mount up. "Blessin's on you men. I'm the better man for havin' known your father."

I walk Cloud up the hill to the town cemetery. I lay the carved ivory horse head pipe on Dale's gravestone. The inscription reads, A good husband, a good father, a good man, a good life.

I mount up and tell Cloud, "'Nough said." I gaze into the old oaks and cedars surrounding this peaceful place. "Thank you, Dale."

We take the road west out of town, and I tell Cloud, "Let's go to Greenwood and catch a steamer. Then you won't have to carry my heavy ass all the way to Vicksburg."

CHAPTER 9

GREENWOOD ON THE YAZOO

LATE AFTERNOON, AUGUST 3, 1886

Some places you just breeze through like before.

I PAUSE AT the edge of the bluff where the road drops into the flatlands they call the Delta. Some of the richest land this side of Heaven they say. I can see smoke rising from the businesses, homes, and steamboats in Greenwood by the Yazoo River where Jasper and James had a terrible fight against the Yankee Navy at Fort Pemberton.

"Cloud, I'm proud to say that my two brothers and the First Mississippi Light Artillery, Company C, beat the britches off of them Yanks and sent 'em packin'."

I dismount and lead Cloud to a store where I can get something to eat. "Yeah, they must'a gave them hell back in '63. They say it was the first time the United States Navy was whipped soundly by land forces. Huh, I guess that's a fact for the history books, and the Tullos family."

Cloud shakes his head like he's trying to get rid of a horsefly.

"I know, I know. The Yanks won the war, and I'm extremely happy about that, but history is history, and *all* of it should be told." I ponder that thought for a long second. "Otherwise, we'll just keep on makin' the same damned mistakes."

I water Cloud at a trough before I tie him off to a hitching post in the shade. I step up on the boardwalk and realize that I helped build this very stretch with Jake and Eli when I stopped here to make a few dollars before catching a steamer to Vicksburg to find Susannah. I stomp the boards. Still holding up pretty good, I see. As the bell on the mercantile doorbell jingles above my head, a couple of steamboats blow their whistles.

I ask the clerk, "When's the next boat leave for Vicksburg?"

"In an hour, if you're planning on catching it."

"They take on horses?"

"They do, and the price is reasonable on *The Dime*—"

"*The Dime*, you say?"

"Yassuh."

"That old boat's still pluggin' along. Ain't that somethin'?"

"She ain't as pretty as she used to be, but she's the sturdiest on the Yazoo River." He leans up. "And in my opinion, she's got the best captain on the river and makes the quickest run to Vicksburg."

"I think I might catch a ride on her."

"You can make it if you hurry. That whistle was last call for boarding passengers. You should be in Vicksburg by noon tomorrow. The ticket office is—"

"Right next door, I know, in the same place it was when I came through last." I purchase a few items, pay the clerk, and buy a one way ticket to Vicksburg next door.

I walk up the gangplank, leading Cloud. This is all too familiar.

"Tickets please," a deckhand says as he holds out his hand.

I look up at the wheelhouse where the captain stood who gave me a job the first time I rode this boat. A familiar face stares down at me with a grin. The middle-aged man trots down the stairs to where I leave Cloud with the other animals and thrusts out his hand.

"I know you, suh. You're still famous 'round these parts."

I take his hand. "Do I know you?"

"Not really, but my father did." He pulls a silver chain from underneath his shirt and holds out a big gator tooth attached to it. "You ever seen anything like this before?"

I instinctively reach for the gator tooth I once wore on a necklace around my neck for years. It's not there. Then, I remember I gave it to Elzey.

I take his in my hand. "Well, my goodness, where'n the hell did you get this?"

"My father was captain of this very boat when you almost got eaten by that big ole alligator. I was just a boy then, but I saw it all. People still tell that story."

I chuckle. "Yeah, I thought I was a goner when I saw the fire in that dragon's eyes. How'd you know it was me?"

"Ain't many men ever board this boat bein' tall as Goliath. I don't forget faces either, or names, Lummy Tullos."

I'm taken aback for a moment. I never thought of myself as being known for some feat of survival fame or have stories told about me.

"And I've been puttin' words in a journal since I was a kid."

I laugh. "I can still smell the outhouse stank of that gator's breath when it rolled over and died, but not before it gassed me with blood, water, and gut juices when it breathed its last."

"Well, let's get you settled into a room, and join me for dinner, if you will. All on the house, of course, and I won't make you shovel coal down in the boiler room like my father did to earn it. But I will ask you to fill my evening with stories, and—"

"I'll be happy to, and thank you, but first, what's your name, son? I'd like to know."

I guess I'll do as Mary asked, and write down notes about this new adventure I'm on. Anyway, it'll be a good thing to do when I go to the room for the night.

CHAPTER 10

VICKSBURG, FOR THE LAST TIME

NOON, AUGUST 4, 1886

Memories are only as good as they move you forward in
the present and not keep you imprisoned to the past.

I LOOK FORWARD to walking Cloud down the gangway in front of the Prentiss House Hotel. I can still see Martha there on the hotel steps the first time I bumped into her. Life with her saved my heart, and probably my soul. Creator has always put the right people in my life at the right time to keep me from losing myself in all the anger and violence I've endured. Enough of that.

But we don't dock near the riverbank below the Prentiss House Hotel. In fact, we don't pass by the front of Vicksburg at all. On our left, we pass the spot where Desoto used to be. I had forgotten the river cut through Young's Point back in '76. I guess Old Man River did what Grant couldn't do during the Siege of Vicksburg. We all knew that wouldn't work when he tried it. But Creator can carve a path for Big Muddy anytime, anywhere, and anyway he chooses.

I ask a deckhand as I step on the river bank south of Vicksburg, "Where does the ferry go now that Desoto is gone?"

"You look to have been here before but not since the river cut through back in '76, right?"

"I came through a few times before that happened. Lord, what a change Big Muddy made."

"You know it. It's left Vicksburg high and dry. It's kinda hurt business in town, but the city's doin' all right. They started work on cuttin' a canal so the

Yazoo River can go straight through Chickasaw Bayou along Walnut Hills. It should give Vicksburg back her port again."

"Where does the ferry go now?"

He points. "Across over there to Delta, Looseana. It's an easy ferry ride from here."

"What's the schedule?"

"On the hour, every hour, startin' at six in the mornin' in the summer. Goes till dark, and then at night only if there's an emergency."

I toss him a silver dollar.

He grins. "Thank ya, suh."

I turn to throw a wave at the captain's son who treated me so kindly this trip on *The Dime*. He salutes and turns back into the wheelhouse. I paid for nothing but my passage. He wouldn't have it otherwise. I'm grateful. He got a lot of stories for his trouble. It helped me to remember ones I'd forgotten, but I wrote them all down in the first little journal book Mary gave me. I'm kind of enjoying writing them down. And I write the truth, no holds barred, as they say.

I stop off at a nearby stable and pay the livery man to water, feed, and curry Cloud. "I'll pick him up in the morning, say five o'clock?"

"That'll be fine, suh."

"Before you go... would you happen to know when the first train leaves Delta in the morning?"

"You could make the seven o'clock fine with time for a cup of coffee if you get your horse on the ferry by six o'clock."

I pitch him an extra dollar for good measure.

He grins. "I'll be takin' good care of your horse, suh."

I tip my hat and start for Handerson's Café.

Vicksburg has grown south toward the ferry and steamboat landing. That makes sense. Even with the river changing course, Vicksburg seems to be faring all right with new shops, homes, and there's a hustle and bustle that I only witnessed when I first came to town with the Twenty-Seventh Louisiana Volunteer Infantry in May of '62. People seem cheerful enough, and you'd hardly know there was ever a siege here over twenty years ago. There are plenty of shrines and special remembrances of the war, but you'd think it happened a hundred years ago. I don't think I'll go to the Twenty-Seventh Louisiana Lunette this visit. I'm just not up to it. I'll just let those boys rest, and not resurrect any old memories that might send me into one of my war dreams created by that place. I guess I'm moving on. Still, I press the owl claw into my wrist just for good measure.

I walk by an establishment, the sign which reads, *The Lucy Academy, A School for All Children*. "Well, I'll be. She did it."

Children play in the yard behind the building, and there she is, all grown up into a fine woman. Lucy, whose same curly gold locks bounce as she plays ball with children of all backgrounds. She looks up to shade her eyes from the sun. I wave, and she waves back, but I can tell she doesn't recognize me. Just as well.

I walk on and look to the sky. "Thanks, Creator, you're a God makin' dreams come true."

I pass by Saint Paul's Catholic Church as a parishioner steps out, probably having been to confession. I ask, "Sir, could you please tell me if the priest who served this church during the war is still around?"

A sad countenance befalls him. "Sorry to say, brother, he passed on nigh unto five years ago. We miss him terribly."

"He was a good man."

"None better served the Lord and our congregation any better. Sorry, I'm late for an appointment. Nice seeing you."

I tip my hat as he scurries away. I think back on all he meant to me. "I loved that old priest."

A passerby looks at me strangely. Talking out loud again, I reckon.

I take the sidewalk to Handerson's Café and stand in front of it for a moment. Many a good plan was made in this establishment, from marrying Martha to taking down Captain Tom Ford, and to end the West-Kimbrell Gang. Bittersweet. But one thing's for sure, there's never been a sweeter or better pie made than in Handerson's Café. I just hope Annie is still around. I haven't heard from her since Martha died. And that seems like too long ago.

CHAPTER 11

ANNIE FANNY, ONE MORE TIME

1:00 P.M., AUGUST 4, 1886

Some friends live in your heart forever, for what would you be without them?

LITTLE BELLS JINGLE as I close the door behind me. A well-dressed black woman with the refinement of a true lady approaches. "Would you like to have a—" Her eyes grow big as saucers, and she reaches to wrap both arms around my neck and kiss my cheek. "Oh, Mistuh Lummy, I'm so happy to see you."

"Jenny? Ise's Jenny, is that you?"

"In the flesh, as they say, Mister Lummy. Ooh-wee, you just don't know, Ise is gonna cut himself some flips when he finds out you're here. Come take a seat, and I'll go get—"

An old woman, hobbling with a walking cane from the back, cackles, "What's goin' on out here? Who... well, oh, my Lord, if it ain't the purttiest man I did ever see. Blow my skirt up over my head and wearin' no bloomers if it ain't my lover Lummy Tullos."

I believe I just turned five shades of red. That woman can embarrass the hell out of me. I brace myself for what I know comes next.

"Come here, my darling, and give this old bag of bones some sugar."

Jenny turns me loose, and I walk over to Annie, pick her up with my arms under her bottom, lift her up, and give her the best kiss I can muster.

She turns my lips loose with a loud smack and yells, "Shoo-wee, now that man knows how to stir up the fire in a woman's thighs."

I blush when I remember there's a crowd in the room. They break out in laughter and clap all around, the men whistling, and the ladies trying to hide their approving smiles.

I start to set Annie down when she grabs my face with both hands and kisses me again.

"Don't worry. They all know who you are, Lummy Tullos. I've told stories about you over and over so many times they can tell 'em better'n I can. Come over, honey, and let's get you a seat. Jenny, coffee please, and a big slab of your best pie, dear."

Jenny rushes off to the kitchen and has my coffee and pie on the table in minutes.

She starts to leave when Annie says, "No, ma'am, you sit down here with us. You're family with this man as much as I am."

Annie pours Jenny the first cup of coffee. My, the world has changed, and I'm glad to have been a part of helping it change.

I take a bite of chocolate pie and sip my coffee. I catch Annie staring at me with a gleam in her eye.

She minces no words. "You know my Beau's been gone two years now, and I miss him terribly. But that's that." She grins like she did the first time I met her in Desoto when she shook her behind at me after she patched up my injured shoulder. "You know neither one of us is gettin' any younger." The fire in her eyes burns a hole right through me. I can feel her heat. "What would it take for you to stay here with me, Lummy?"

I almost spew out my coffee, and Jenny snickers as she hands me a napkin. I'm thinking fast, but nothing's coming.

"You know I'd just about do anything." Annie cackles again, "I'd even get up on this table and dance nekked if that'd do the trick."

Jenny covers her mouth and pats Annie on the shoulder. "My word, Missus Annie, I ain't never heard of such."

Annie bites her bottom lip as she grins wickedly. "Lummy has, haven't you, dear? Back during the war, on the riverbank that time."

I know my face must look like it's about to catch fire with the heat boiling in my cheeks from embarrassment. "Hell, I don't know what to say, Annie, 'cept, you've always been a beauty in my eyes, clothes on or not."

Annie sits back, patting her colorful Japanese fan lightly to hide her smile, but her eyes still show delight. She starts to speak, but Ise walks in looking like a building contractor.

I whisper, "Thank the Lord."

Annie rubs my leg too close for comfort. "You better. We'll talk later, Lummy honey."

Ise has become an even more powerfully built man who carries himself proudly. I see Susannah in his eyes. I stand to greet him, and he hugs me like there's no tomorrow.

"You look good, Mistuh Lummy." He reaches over and gives Jenny a peck on the cheek. "Hey, darlin', how's business today?"

"Fine, if I can keep Missus Annie's hands off our honored guest."

Annie sniffs. "Nothin' wrong with a woman declaring what she wants." She takes my hand. "You're on your way somewhere, aren't you? You might not even know where right now, but I see it in your eyes. All funnin' aside, you always have a place here, Lummy Tullos."

"Annie, you know I will always love you, and—"

"Yeah, but if we got together, it'd ruin a beautiful and fun relationship, don't you think?"

I smile sadly. "Yeah, I do. But a good roll in the sack with a lovely woman such as you would certainly turn a man inside out." I wink at Jenny and Ise. "Yes, I'm sure of it."

We laugh, and I kiss Annie again, for what I feel will be the last time.

CHAPTER 12

LAST RIVER CROSSING

5:15 A.M., AUGUST 5, 1886

Some crossings leave things behind that are still carried in the heart.

I DON'T LIKE GOODBYES, so I said all those last night as we finished a fine meal in my honor. The well wishes were overwhelming from people who have been nothing short of family. What will I do without people like Dan Creekwater and Annie Fanny in my life? Creator has a sense of humor. I'm sure he'll send new ones. But for now, I just need to be alone with the One who never allows me to be lonely.

I came early to make the first ferry of the morning, so I have a little over half an hour before we board. I tie Cloud to a post. "Stay here. I'll be right back."

I wander down to the river bank in the dim morning light. I think about the letter Mr. Gilmore sent that broke the news of Susannah's death on New Year's Day back in '63. That was the same day Jasper and James came to Vicksburg the first time. I envision the spot where I killed my first man—a Yankee sailor on a gunboat trying to get past the river batteries. The boat didn't survive, and neither did he. I still see his eyes in the darkest nights. A great blue heron glides across the current from behind me without flapping its wings.

"Lord, make my crossin' and gettin' to where I'm going be just as easy as that bird flying across the river. You said you care about even the smallest creatures, even the tiniest of birds. I ask that you take care of me like that. Am I really more valuable than many sparrows, like Jesus said?"

Silence.

I find a log and sit. I pull out the agate Granny gave me on Little Mountain. It sparkles in the sunlight. The wind dies down. Sounds of the riverbank wharf fade away. A beautiful shape with a dark face walks—no floats—my way, enwrapped in silvery robes with beauty and grace.

Susannah.

"You are worth more than many sparrows, my dear husband. But you haven't accepted it."

I stand, shaking with joy and wonderment. "Have you come to take me with you?"

She smiles. *"No, the one who needs you now will not know that until the time of reckoning."*

"When will that be?"

Susannah steps out on the water, turning only to smile. *"You will know."*

"May I come with you, Susannah?"

Susannah gently shakes her head and wafts across the river like a feather drifting in the breeze across the slow moving river toward the Louisiana side. She disappears.

I take a long last look at the city set upon a hill. I'll forever be tied to this place, I reckon.

I ease up to the the ticket collector, who is too young to shave.

"Ticket, please."

I hand him mine, and he punches a hole in it.

"First time in Vicksburg?"

I drop my head and snicker. "Son, I've been through Vicksburg so many times, I do believe if I make it to Heaven, I'll have to go through Vicksburg to get there."

The ticket collector grins. "Well, I hope you make it, sir. You look like you deserve it."

I'm not sure what he means by that, but I ain't asking. I just want to be left alone.

I get Cloud settled and find a seat. I rub the agate in my pocket and scan the wide river. I sigh. "Only one more ferry crossin' to make. The next one will carry me through the thin veil. I hope."

The ferry puts out into the river powered by a chugging steam engine.

The river is low, and the current is easy to manage. A tree floats by as we reach mid-river.

I whisper, "That sure ain't the dragon that jumped up out of the depths to bite me on the shoulder like when I crossed the river trying to find Susannah back in '59." I laugh. "If it hadn't been for that old tree, I never would'a met Annie Fanny. I guess there is always somethin' good that can come out of somethin' bad."

A small but familiar voice dances on the breeze. *"Your healing has begun."*

I turn to the stream filled with eddies and small whirlpools, good reminders of how the Universe works. "Granny?"

"I'm here, grandson."

Another ferry makes its way from the small town of Delta where I'll catch the train. I take in a deep breath. I've always liked the smell of the Mississippi. With the water low, it smells less of murky silt and more of clean freshness. That's what I need right now—to be clean and fresh in my soul as I begin this next part of my life.

I watch the people on the riverbank get smaller and smaller. It's time to leave all of that behind and look to what's coming. As I close my eyes, I can see Martha in her blue dress running down to the landing from Handerson's Café and waving when I left to go fight with the Rifles back in '64. Oh me, I miss that girl.

A small patch of strange fog drifts by the boat. Granny Thankful appears, and I ask, "How many more ferries, Granny?"

She smiles. *"One more after this one before the last one you must take that will carry you through the thin veil."*

As Granny disappears into the fog, the ferry approaching from the Louisiana side passes within shouting distance. Two young men, one white, the other with darker skin, ride at the front. The darker one glances over for just a moment, and I swear I see Susannah in his eyes.

"Can't be. Why would he be coming this way?" I take a last look before they get too far away. The other man with lighter skin surely has the look of a man with whom I spent many years living and working. Ben.

"Naaah, can't be." I pass it off as wishful thinking.

CHAPTER 13

TRAIN RIDE OF NO MEMORIES

6:30 A.M., AUGUST 5, 1886

Is it true that the farther away you get from a place,
its memories will one day fade?

WHEN THE FERRY pulls up to the riverbank on the Louisiana side, I collect Cloud and make my way to the train ticket office. I purchase passage to Monroe, then walk him to the livestock car. I find a cup of coffee and a sweetcake to help me forget some things in the past. The good thing about this part of Louisiana? I have little to no memories here. The "all aboard" whistle blows, and I climb up into the passenger car, find a seat, and settle in for a long nap.

No more memories need resurrecting on this leg of my journey. Only dreams for what will be next is what I want. The clickety-clack of the train ride lulls me to sleep.

It's good to sleep with peaceful dreams. I heard it said that the farther away a person travels from certain places, the less he'll think about some things. It's hell to have good and bad memories about the same place. I guess that's the way of it. Can't have the sweet without the bitter, Ma used to say.

The train stops with a jar, and I snort like a hog waking from my sleep.

A little girl with pigtails, pretty as a kitten, clutches her baby doll and giggles. Her mother gently scolds her for laughing at me, but she can't help but laugh either. Neither can I.

I tip my hat to her mother and say to the little girl, "I'm sorry, little dear. I was raised with the hawgs, and well, I just ain't never really got over it."

She covers her face and laughs.

I wink at her mother, who bursts out laughing.

I stand and stretch. "Y'all have a safe trip, ma'am." I grin at the little girl, "And you, too, little dear."

I miss Delaware and Rosetta already. They grew up way too fast. Memories of my daughters are always sweet.

I deboard and look around. This place has too many memories, not the least of which is watching Susannah disappear as I rode the train to go enlist in the Confederate Army. I put that out of my mind.

I pat Cloud on the neck before I mount up. "Let's go to Winnfield, boy, whatcha say?"

CHAPTER 14

SLEEPING WITH
THE DEAD

LATE AFTERNOON, AUGUST 7, 1886

*You just never know who might show up if
you gaze through the thin veil to the other side.*

I ENJOYED SLEEPING out under the stars last night. As I rein up as the sun starts to go down, I dismount in a place all too familiar.

"Cloud, I guess we could go on into Winnfield today, but why don't we make camp here for the night? I want one more evening by the fire."

Cloud looks around at me like I'm crazy, if a horse can do that. He senses what I already know. This is a place of death. It's the spot on the Dugdemona River where the men of Winn Parish and I took Dawg Smith's gang down, and I removed his head from his body with the knife Pa made me when I was a child.

I pull Cloud's saddle off and lay it on the ground. "And don't ask me why, Cloud, I just felt like I was led here."

Cloud stomps one of his front hooves.

After watering and feeding Cloud, I start a small fire and put coffee on. I walk to the edge of the river to watch the sun dip below the horizon. It's orange and blue in the west. A faint rustling of tiny leaves swirls around across the stream.

It's Granny Thankful. I pull the agate from my pocket, and it catches the last ray of the sun to glow like it's on fire.

Granny smiles. *"Come see me at the tree of the skull tonight, grandson, when today becomes tomorrow."* She fades back into the thicket.

I walk back to the fire and pour a cup of coffee. "This can't be good, Cloud."

I WALK TO the tree, where Dawg Smith's skull once lay, just before midnight. The sign is gone, as is the skull. That's good. I didn't want to see either. Just being here is trouble enough.

I still sense that outlaw's unholy presence, though. An evil aura so overwhelming that chills march up and down my spine like so many little ice soldiers. I shudder like it's cold as hell. It's still warm enough that I'm sweating from the heat of the summer night.

Fiery eyes in the shadowy shapes of wicked men emerge from the river to surround me and the tree where laughter erupts.

Dawg Smith.

I step back, but my feet won't move. I fall to the ground. The demons who once were Dawg Smith's gang surge forward like a pack of coyotes ready to pounce on a wounded animal.

Dawg's fiery skull jaw opens. *"You have fallen, but not completely, preacher."*

I get back up and face the evil. "What do you want, you old heathen?"

Dawg laughs hysterically. *"And the best damn heathen you ever knew."*

"Not quite. Have you seen John West lately? He and the Kimbrells make you boys look like a bunch of church goin' choir boys who corn hole each other after every Sunday church service. But forgive me, you don't have a church where you currently live, now do you?"

"Laugh now, Tullos, but your time's comin'."

"Well, go on, then. Kill me and get it over with, Dawg shit, and make it count, you sorry bastard."

Dawg snickers. *"Oh no, no, no. You don't get off that easy. My claim to fame here in Hell is how I've had the pleasure of tormentin' your sorry-ass soul by reminding you how much I enjoyed raping and killing your wife, heh, heh, heh, and I—"*

Granny Thankful swoops in like a fish eagle over the waters of the Dugdemona and plants her feet to stand beside me. In the sky, Saint Michael with his flaming sword swirls around, keeping an eye on the happenings down here.

I turn to Granny. "I ain't never been a part of anythin' like this."

She squints. *"That is because you have never been in a place where it could happen. Stand strong and in Creator's mighty power."*

"Yes, ma'am, I will—"

Dawg screams, *"You won't do shit except cry like a damn baby when you see what John West has planned for you, Lummy Tullos."*

A voice from the sky erupts, *"Say his name again, demon, and I shall strike you deaf and dumb."* Saint Michael has spoken.

Dawg shrinks back. *"That's all I got to say, except John West said to tell you he won't kill you. He'll do the thing that will torment you until your days are finished. He's comin' for you and yours, boy. You know the one he sends already. West will use him to make you pay."*

Granny shouts, *"Be gone, demon! You and your devilish horde!"*

Saint Michael swoops down and scatters the demon army like a hawk bearing down on a yard full of chickens.

Granny turns to me. *"Show me the stone."*

I hold it up, and it beams like the brightest sunlight on the darkest day. It glows with every color I've ever seen. Dawg Smith and his demons scatter like roaches into the shadows when a coal oil lamp is lit in a cabin.

"This next challenge will be the most difficult because it will be your last."

"But Granny, I don't want to... I can't... I won't...."

In a blast of wind that knocks me to the ground, Granny shouts, *"You must not run from the one thing that will set you free, grandson!"*

I cringe at her power. "What is that, Granny?"

"You must face the red sky storm that comes for you, or your name will be lost."

"I want to be left alone, Granny, but I don't want my name scattered to the winds either."

"Then you must face the one who could end your name. Follow your dearest one now."

"Who is my dearest? Delaware? Rosetta? Who?"

She disappears with only one word spoken. *"Choose."*

I get up, dust myself off, and answer, "Yes, ma'am."

A shooting star races across the sky, changing colors from green to blue to purple to red.

I whisper, "There it is. Red."

THE MORNING SUN bursts through the cypress trees in the shape of a blinding star. I start to saddle Cloud but stop to enjoy the splash of color.

"'Red sky in the morning, sailor's warning,' Pa used to say. I guess that ancient proverb got passed down from great grandpa Claudius who came from Scotland back in the sixteen-sixties." I pat Cloud on the neck. "That's who you're named for, horse. Claudius, what a name. No wonder he took the nickname Cloud. Who'd want to be named for some Roman emperor or general anyway? The Romans were the heathens who thought they had the right to take what wasn't theirs and then call it civilization. No, I figure the people painted blue who danced naked around fires in the deep woods were closer to Creator. But hell, it ain't much different from what the white man has been doing in this country for over two hundred years. Cloud, I've enjoyed listening to Mary's history lessons about our people. I look forward to reading her book."

Cloud nods his head up and down. I put a feed bag on, and he munches grain while I take in the view and jot down what's happened since I left Choctaw County.

"Granny said a red sky storm is brewing. I just didn't know it would start this soon."

A gentle breeze sails through the willows, whispering, *"A warning has been given, my grandson."*

I saddle Cloud, then pack my bedroll and coffee pot.

I get settled into my saddle. "Let's go to Winnfield, Cloud, and see an old friend."

CHAPTER 15

WINNFIELD

MID-MORNING, AUGUST 8, 1886

Some things need to change. Some don't. Old friends need to stay the same, no matter how long it's been since you saw 'em last.

WINNFIELD AIN'T WHAT it used to be, but heck, neither am I since I was here last. The town's gotten bigger, busier, and new businesses have sprouted up and down once nearly empty streets. And me? I've gotten older, grayer, and slower, but I am managing the war dreams a little better these past few days. Enough of all that.

I read the sign that sits over the place where Mr. Wiley used to live. That old man blessed me like no other when I first got here. I miss that old coot. And his fine cooking.

Little bells above the door jingle as I walk into Mills and Son Gun Sales and Repair. Unshaven, hair a bit matted and long, clothes needing to be washed, and the rest of me probably smelling like the south end of a north bound mule, I must look a sight. That's all right. I'm sure it helped me avoid having to talk to people since I left the train at the woodcutter's station. The few I passed by on the road scrunched their noses up at my not-so-human odor.

The train was nice, but I enjoyed sleeping out by the fire on the way here. I feel pretty rested, but I'm certainly ready for a bath, shave, some good food, and a soft bed. Hell, I am getting old.

A voice from the back of the gun shop yells through the batwings, "Be right with you. Make yourself at home."

I have a seat in one of the chairs available to customers. I sniff my underarms. Yep, it's as bad as I thought, maybe worse. Luckily, the smell of gun grease fills the air and blocks out my own stench.

Retracing the steps of my first journey across the Mississippi River to Winn Parish as well as others brings on a flood of memories—being chased by coyotes into Rainy Mill's camp, working with Ben on Mr. Gilmore's farm, marrying Susannah, watching her cry as I left for the war on the train, J.A. and I seeing Annie Fanny by the river after we swam a raft across the river, nearly falling into Dawg Smith's hands after we left Vicksburg and then taking that bastard down, and finally riding the train to take down the West-Kimbrell Gang. Then back home once more.

Home. So hard to find and harder still to hold on to in this world.

Yet the first and last sweetest moments in my life have been finding and marrying Susannah and then returning to Martha after the war for the most peaceful years of my life. Even so, good memories don't always cover over those of death and destruction this path I've walked so freely offered. Funny thing, I sit in what was once the home of the first person I met when I walked into Winnfield that blistering day and whose funeral I did before heading off to fight in the war—Mr. Wiley. God rest his soul, and all the others who have preceded me. Far too many.

So much has happened since then.

I'm not sure I'll ever rest. "Will I, Lord?"

The bat wings that separate the front part of the gun shop from the repair area in the back slap together, jarring me back to where I am.

A man, the spitting image of my best friend in the Vicksburg trenches, clears his throat. "Meaning no harm, but, will you what, sir?"

I'm a little startled. I blink to come back to where I am, but my mind is fuzzy. "Do what?'

The young man puts on his smithy apron and smiles. "How may I help you, sir?'

I wipe my eyes. "J.A.? That you?"

"No, sir, that'd be my daddy. But he's been gone now, oh, nigh unto sixteen years."

"Yeah, I know. Easter Sunday, eighteen-seventy, to be exact."

"You knew my father... wait, you're—"

"Yes, son, I'm Lummy Tullos."

A voice rings out from the back room, "What in the—"

The batwings push open. There stands Rainy Mills, older, a little thicker, and wearing the same smithy apron as Aaron, but not a stitch of black clothing on his person. He bounds out from behind the counter to bear hug me like there's no tomorrow.

"Lummy Tullos, how'n the hell are you, old friend?"

I stand, trying to be cheerful, but I'm tired, body and soul. "Doin' all right, brother, I reckon."

"You look like you've been pulled through a knothole backward."

"And I feel like it, Rainy."

Aaron tries not to snicker. "That doesn't sound so good."

Rainy pops him across the chest playfully. "If anybody in the world knows what that feels like, it's this man right here, son." He points at my chair. "Aaron, get Lummy some cool water, will you, please?"

"Sure thing, Pa, right away."

I follow Aaron out with my eyes. "Damn, Rainy, I thought I was lookin' at J.A. there for a minute. I even saw him with his gray uniform on. I must be goin' crazy."

"War dreams still bothering you?"

"Ain't gettin' no better, but I'm managing 'em all right. I do a lot more talkin' to Creator these days. And my horse for that matter, too."

"That's good. You've always done that." He stares at me, and then grabs my shoulders. "Damn, it's good to see you, boy!"

Aaron brings out a tray with a water pitcher, three glasses, and a bottle of fine whiskey. "Thought we might want something just a bit stronger, Pa."

Rainy pats him on the back. "And you would be correct, my favorite son."

Aaron sets the tray down slowly so as not to spill anything, then laughs like J.A. used to. "Aw, Pa, you know I'm your favorite son because I'm your *only* son."

Rainy squints with a serious look. "Yeah, Aaron, and the best son a father could ever have. You're just like your daddy, God rest his soul."

Aaron's eyes light up like a candle lit in a dark room. "That's what Ma says."

I lean up. "Aaron, I'd be proud as a struttin' rooster if I was you and that man right there said those words to me."

"I am, Uncle Lummy. Proud as a fanned out turkey gobbler in springtime."

"How is Missus Mary Jane?"

Aaron grins. "She's doing very well. She'll be glad to see you. You *are* staying, at least tonight, won't you?"

"Sure, son, maybe a couple three days if that's all right with your folks."

Rainy pours our whiskeys. "You know you're welcome as long as you want to stay, cousin."

Aaron raises his eyebrows. "Do what? You never told that you and—"

"Lummy and I are cousins? Yeah, I should've told you. We have the same great grandfather, I think, right, Lummy?"

"'Tis true. Rainy's great grandpa was Captain James Mills who fought with the North Carolina Continental Army during the Revolution. My Granny Thankful's father was the same Captain Mills, you see."

I notice Rainy shaking his head ever so slightly. I get the message.

"Yeah, Rainy's father, Thomas Mills, was a good man who loved his wife, and well, you see the result of that loving union... a man who has loved you like the son you are, been a husband to a deserving wife, and always a friend who's been like a brother to me."

Rainy smiles a bit red-faced at the compliments. "Aaron, my mother, Epsie, was known to be the sweetest soul in Natchez, Missip. I just wish I'd known her. She passed not long after I was born, and my father died not long before I was born. I was raised in the orphanage there by a good old man who ran the place."

"Thanks for telling all of that, Pa. It must make you a little sad when you think about it."

"Well, when those thoughts come, you know what I do? I think about how happy I am with you and your mother, the life we have, and what you are becoming. That's what I do."

Aaron swells up with pride like a bullfrog about to croak. "Thanks, Pa. That means everything."

Rainy smiles at me for holding secrets that need to stay buried where they lay—in the past.

Some lies are not for the father to tell. It's a weight that a good friend carries for him. No need to bring up what has not been discussed outside our friendship except for a few other trusted men—that Rainy Mills, born as a result of a rape, went dressed in black from head to toe to find his father's murderer and mother's rapist—John Ratliff. After he ended that bastard's life, he finished off the judge who was in on it with Ratliff and didn't bring the raping murderer to justice. Rainy brought justice to them both. I change the subject, but not to a more pleasant one.

I take a sip of whiskey and ask what I don't want to ask. "I see there's a new name above Davis's Mercantile. Did Mister Davis retire?"

Rainy looks to Aaron, and he breaks the news. "I'm sorry to say that Mister Davis passed away three years ago, but peacefully in his sleep, I might add."

I sigh. "If anyone deserved leaving this earth that way, it was that good old soul, and his wife. God rest their souls."

Rainy raises his glass, and we with him. "Here, here. To the best of souls, Mister and Missus Davis."

"Creator ain't ever made any better two from the clay than them." I take another sip of whiskey. I'm feeling a little revived.

Rainy grins sadly. "Damn straight. God don't make them any better."

Aaron chimes in cheerfully, "Mister Davis left everything to Pa, and he distributes what he makes from the property and such to the neediest families around the parish."

I finish my whiskey. "That's good." I eye Rainy, who's staring at me, waiting for what he knows I know. Something will happen, even though I don't know what it is just yet.

After an awkward silence, Rainy ducks his head. "We need to talk about—"

"Tom Kimbrell?"

Rainy appears surprised but not shocked. "Yes, in a minute. But first, let's talk about your son."

I nod. "But not here."

CHAPTER 16

CATCHING UP

BEFORE NOON, AUGUST 8, 1886

Like a man once said about life's troubles,
"There ain't no forgettin'."

MY HEART RACES, and I start to shake. I press the owl claw Dan Creekwater gave me years ago into my wrist like I've done hundreds of times to stay sane when the war dreams come.

Rainy squeezes my shoulder. "That old Choctaw still keeping you out of trouble?"

"Saved my ass on the way out of Choctaw County comin' here."

Aaron starts to leave, but I take his arm. "No, no, son. It's okay. You can stay. You're family."

He smiles and hops on up on the counter. "Thank you."

I nod at Rainy. "You remember the day you showed up in the Bankston hotel to meet Sarge and me before we came here after John West?"

"Yeah, seems like I remember bumping into some big fellow who was threatening you as he walked away from the bar that day."

"Same one. I'd sold my part of the land, said my goodbyes to family and friends, and visited the old cemetery for the last time. I thought I'd stop by a saloon in Bucksnort for one last taste of whiskey before I left Choctaw County for good. I had my drink with the Wood brothers and mounted up to head to Little Mountain, you know the highest place in the county where I met Sarge to join the Rifles back in '64."

"Yeah, I remember."

"It was a pretty day, not a cloud in the sky. I wanted one last look before turning my mount's nose toward Vicksburg, when this long-haired, fiery-eyed, crazy old man came out of the bushes waving a pistol sayin' he's fixin' to kill me and told me to face him like a man. Well, I did.

"He said, 'You don't remember me, do ya, Tullos?' I shook my head, and for the life of me, I didn't know who he was. He pointed his pistol at my head and said, 'I'm the one you shamed in the hotel them years ago, and I aim to collect that debt, right now. Who's shamed now, Tullos?' I told him he still was the shamed one for wastin' his worthless life all this time on a grudge that meant nothin' to me."

Aaron's eyes are big as saucers. "You mean you talked to him like that, and he had a pistol pointed at your head?"

I grin at Rainy. "I'm glad they don't have to go through what we did."

He winks. "Me, too."

"Anyway, I'm standin' there with this pistol stuck in my face. He lowers the pistol, aiming it at my belly, and says, 'I'm gonna gutshoot you. I want you to suffer. Time to die, Tullos.' He was cocking the pistol slowly, enjoying the moment, when from up an old oak thirty feet away, a bow string snaps, and an arrow finds its way into his chest. He just stands there for what seems like an eternity, and when he starts to go down and tries to shoot me before he falls, another arrow slams into his hand. I shift my head to the side just as he pulls the trigger." I pull my hair back to reveal a slight crease on my scalp just above the ear.

"Damn." Aaron covers his mouth. "Sorry, Pa."

Rainy gives him a look and nods to me. "Go ahead, Lummy, show him the other one."

"I got matching marks, one on each side. One for Winn Parish, and one for Choctaw County."

Rainy sees the bit of hurt in my eyes. "What about Dan?"

I shake my head. "When the pistol went off, the shot got Dan and, well, he...." A surge like water loosed from a busted beaver dam rushes through my body. I'm hot. I tremble. My sight goes blank. I talk without thought, like somebody's saying the words for me. "I only got to hear him say a few words before the light went out of his eyes." I'm lightheaded, dizzy, and faint. "Yeah,

I buried him right there on top of Little Mountain where he'll always have the best view and...." It all goes dark.

"Lummy... Lummy!" Rainy is shaking my shoulders with both hands, and Aaron is patting my face with a cold damp rag.

I look down to see the owl claw dug deep into my wrist and blood dripping on the floor. I look up at Rainy and Aaron. "I'm sorry, but losing that old Choctaw really hurt my heart."

Rainy consoles me. "Euripides once said, 'When good men die, their goodness does not perish.' He'll always be with you."

I calm myself. "He was one of the best. Too many good men and women have been lost in my time on this earth. My sister Saleta, Susannah, my brothers Amariah and George, Mister Gilmore and Ben, Granville and Edrow at Vicksburg, Mister Allrice and Momma Sophie, Seth and Elihu, Uncle Rube and my ma, Old Bart and Tom Poole...." I look to Aaron and say, "J.A. and my brother James, my darling wife Martha... oh hell, I can't even name 'em all. Sometimes it's just a bit too much."

Rainy and Aaron remain quiet and just let me have my moment.

"That's why I don't talk about the war. Those old stories send me down a road that I can't hardly come back from. The owl claw has helped a lot."

Rainy smiles sadly. "Yeah, I notice a lot of the fellows from the war don't ever mention anything about what they went through. I just thought they were tired of telling the stories or didn't want to be put up on a hero pedestal by young boys and old women. I guess they have the same problem as you."

"Yeah, and most people nowadays don't understand. They think we should just get over it. There ain't no gettin' over watchin' men die in war that did nothin' but take lives." I tense up. "Damn, what in the hell were they thinkin'? Startin' somethin' like that where thousands of—"

Rainy takes me by the shoulders. "It's all right, Lummy. Just have a seat."

I sit and settle down. "When a war dream comes on me, I can smell the smoke, hear the cannons, shudder at the Yanks screaming as they charge the hill, see the blood splattering everywhere, and watch my friends die." I keep pressing the owl claw into my wrist. Hard.

Rainy winces at the numerous scars left by the owl claw that's kept me sane for all these years. "I understand, old friend." He gently pulls my hand away that's clutching the owl claw. "Let's patch that wrist at the house, get you a hot bath, and a good meal. How's that sound?"

"I'd like that, and maybe a couple 'a day's rest?"

"As long as you want to stay."

"I appreciate it."

"Can I have your guns?"

"What for?"

"Just want to make sure they're in good working condition before you ride out."

"Yeah, right. Thank you." I know he's being courteous, but he's also making sure his family is safe. I appreciate that in him. I've heard about old soldiers who forgot who they were and shot up their family and friends.

"Aaron, take Lummy's pistol to the back and get his Henry repeater from the scabbard on his horse. Look them over for me, please. We'll see you at home for supper later, okay?"

"Sure thing, Pa."

Rainy leans over to whisper, "You've still got that big old knife your Pa made you?"

"Don't go anywhere without it."

"Just hang on to that. You'll feel better."

"Thanks."

CHAPTER 17

TROUBLE JUST WON'T GO AWAY

JUST AFTER NOON, AUGUST 8, 1886

Some of the nicest places just seem to bring on the worst of troubles.

WE STEP OUT into the hot baking sunlight. People mill around, taking care of their daily business, and try to stay in the shade of store awnings.

I take in all the new buildings. "Winnfield sure has grown."

"Yeah, but the courthouse mysteriously burned with all of its records."

"Yeah, I noticed the newly built one when I was here last."

"You and Poole saved the Greensborough courthouse from being burned in Choctaw County during the war, didn't you?"

"Yeah, we did when we served with the Rifles and led the Union cavalry detachment to burn the mills in Bankston. Hell, somebody burned that courthouse down later anyway, records and all. It was a beautiful building."

I notice a man who looks vaguely familiar watching us at a distance.

Rainy points in the direction of his home. "Are you thinking about attending the old soldier's reunion? I know you don't like talking about the war."

"Jasper said it might be good for me to sit with men who could be having the same troubles as me. I guess we'll have to talk about the war some to do that, but it might help."

"Yes, you'll be with men who understand where you're coming from."

We find ourselves in a small crowd crossing a street. Rainy leads the way and gets a bit ahead of me, so I have to speak louder for him to hear me.

"Yeah, I believe you might be right, so I think I'll—"

A hand grips my shoulder like a vise and a knife blade pokes me in the back. The weapon cuts a hole in my jacket, and the blade enters my flesh just deep enough to draw blood. I stop in the middle of the street. People just keep passing by, and Rainy disappears from my sight.

Tom Kimbrell whispers like the snaky demon he is, "I ain't forgot what you did, Lummy Tullos. Your family's gonna pay, and in the worst kind of way."

"Yeah, I got your letter, Kimbrell. Didn't think much about it, to be honest. But it was helpful in the outhouse."

Kimbrell withdraws the knife and spins me around. "I can't kill you right here in front of God and everybody. I'd get hung within the hour, but how 'bout this, Tullos?" He waves his middle finger in front of my face with his knifeblade poking my stomach.

"Yeah, I see it. That's how many friends you had before your dawg died, boy."

A surge of anger empowers my soul like it did in the Vicksburg trenches when the Yankees came up the hill at us. I reach for my knife, but someone grabs my hand from behind.

Rainy whispers, "I knew something was wrong when I turned around and you weren't behind me." He grips my hand tighter. "Not here, Lummy. Keep your head."

Tom laughs. "Yeah, that's right, Tullos. You and that big ole knife ain't gonna do shit. Don't you worry none, preacher. I'm not comin' for you personally. I'm just gonna hurt your family. Real bad. It's gonna make you hurt like I hurt when you and them other bastards killed my family and friends. And then you'll have to live with it the rest of your sorry ass days, you old bastard."

By this time, a small crowd has formed, and Rainy has a hold on my shoulder. Without thinking or having any concern for Kimbrell's knife now poking in my belly, I curl my knuckles up and send a jab to his neck quick as a rattler strike.

Kimbrell drops the blade and doubles over, grabbing his throat, choking, gagging, and coughing.

A man with a familiar face breaks through the crowd. "Whoa, hold on there. What's goin' on?"

He's wearing a badge.

Rainy steps in and says, "Oh, nothing, Deputy. It's just a huge misunderstanding that's getting straightened out right here."

"Straightened out, my ass. That's Tom Kimbrell, and he's drunker'n a jaybird hanging upside down in a crabapple tree."

Rainy snickers. "You called that one correctly, sir." Rainy whispers to me, "Have you ever seen a jaybird hanging upside down drunk?"

"Yeah, every year the jaybirds gathered in the wild plum trees on our farm. Hell, I've seen them three and four at a time, hanging upside down by their feet, swaying and squawkin' like old women singin' at a revival meetin'."

The deputy holds up his hand. "Since you boys have that all figured out, I'd like to get back to my words with this drunk. Rainy, if'n Tom Kimbrell's in it, then there's nothin' but trouble, and I know he started it. He's so damn mean he makes onions cry." The deputy studies me, then grins. "What the hell? Lummy, that you?"

"Why, Jesse Cockerham, you know it is. I see you're still wearin' the silver badge I gave you that the people of Winn Parish gifted me for helping take down Dawg Smith and his gang."

"Yes, sir, I keep it pinned right next to the official one on my vest. I wear it everyday."

Kimbrell coughs and spits. "That old long-haired bastard tried to rip my throat out, and I ain't done shit to deserve it."

Rainy hands Jesse Kimbrell's knife. "He had this in Lummy's back when I conveniently interrupted Mister Kimbrell's plans to hurt our friend here."

I show Jesse the hole in my jacket and the blood on the back of my shirt.

Tom yells, "You and your smart ass words, Mills. You're next on my list!"

Rainy steps up nose to nose with Kimbrell. "I'll watch for you every day, guns cocked and carving knives sharpened, looking forward to our next meeting." His tone deepens. "Deputy Cockerham, you heard him."

Jesse nods. "I did."

"Then you'll know when I kill this son of a bitch, it'll be self-defense."

"I will, and the town'll have a big celebration when you do."

Kimbrell looks at Jesse, back to Rainy, and then me. "You're all in it together, you worthless sons of—"

Deputy Sheriff Jesse Cockerham backhands Kimbrell across the face.

Kimbrell groans, blood trickling from the corner of his mouth.

Jesse smiles. "We have laws against cursing in public, Mister Kimbrell, out of respect for the ladies and children."

Kimbrell giggles like a schoolgirl, almost sounding like he's gone mad. "I can't wait to sample your Mary Jane's fine cookin', Rainy. I'm sure—"

Rainy loses his mind for just a moment and lunges at Kimbrell. I put my arm between them and ease Rainy back.

Rainy calms himself. "I apologize for my outburst, Deputy. The one who talks the loudest is usually the weakest. Be glad the Good Lord and good friends are here to protect you, Kimbrell."

Kimbrell throws his head back, laughing. "You ain't shit, Rainy Mills. Why, I'd—"

I grab his throat, and he stops laughing. "Don't worry, Rainy, he'll get his. Just like his brother, Laws. It's only a matter of time." I pull my knife and thumb it. A bit of blood appears on the blade. I taste it. "And it won't be pretty, that's for damn sure." I lay my blade against his exposed throat.

Tom Kimbrell shudders, but is still defiant. "I'll get you, Tullos. I'm comin', and all of Hell's demons will be ridin' with me."

I snicker as I re-sheath my knife. "Tryin' to be a scripture-quoting, half-assed, Methodist Bible teacher like your old boss, John West?" I grab his shirt collar and pull him close. "Don't bother bringin' Hell with you, son. You'll be there soon enough."

Kimbrell spits in my face. I rear back to punch him again.

Rainy catches my arm before I can hit him again. "I do declare, Lummy Tullos, it takes the both of us to keep each other from killing this sorry piece of street trash."

Kimbrell laughs like a hyena.

"One of my favorite authors once wrote, 'Never argue with stupid people because they will drag you down to their level and then beat you with experience.' I believe that was Mark Twain." Rainy laughs.

Kimbrell lunges at Rainy, trying to break free. "Call me stupid, will you?"

Jesse calls over another deputy. "Would you please take this piece of hawg shit to jail before his head is removed from his body by a man with all the skills and willingness needed to do it?"

Kimbrell growls. "I ain't done nothin' to go to jail for, you sorry ass—"

Deputy Sheriff Jesse Cockerham steps up nose to nose with Kimbrell. "How 'bout I charge you with attempted murder, aggravated assault with a deadly weapon, disturbing the peace, cussin' in public, and just in general for being a horse's ass. You want me to keep goin'?"

Kimbrell changes into the sweetest, kindest young man you'd ever want to meet. "Oh, no, Mister Deputy Sheriff, suh, I'll do what you say, and please, Mister Lummy, I don't know what got into me. Please, suh, I was just—"

Jesse shoves Kimbrell as the other deputy drags him away laughing. "Get his ass outta here."

Tom Kimbrell giggles like a young girl and walks like a monkey, crouched and arms waving. He reminds me of that bastard Dawg Smith.

Jesse squints and snickers. "That boy ain't right in the head."

When Kimbrell is out of sight, my body wilts, and my soul lays faint. I grab a porch post in front of a store and press the owl claw into my wrist.

Rainy scratches his chin as he spits in Kimbrell's direction. "I thought that bastard got hung with his brother Laws over near Austin, Texas, back in '73."

Jesse watches to make sure the other deputy gets Kimbrell to the jailhouse. He turns to Rainy with a scowl. "No, he wormed his way out of gettin' strung up with his older brother. He's pretty good at talkin' his way out of an execution."

I remove my hat and push back my hair. "Yeah, just like he did that Easter Sunday back in '70 when we took John West down." I swat my wrist like a wasp just stung it. It's the owl claw. I pull it out and thank Creator for Ole Dan Creekwater still saving my ass.

CHAPTER 18

OLD FRIENDS MAKE A BAD DAY GO BETTER

12:30 P.M., AUGUST 8, 1886

It ain't easy figurin' out what an outlaw will do when
he doesn't know himself just yet.

RAINY AND DEPUTY Jesse whisper together, but I can overhear their conversation.

Rainy squints. "What do you think he'll do, Jesse? He sent Lummy a letter not long ago but didn't say what he planned to do. And he didn't say in this brief unsavory encounter either."

Jesse asks, "You want to press charges, Lummy?"

"Would they stick?"

"We got his knife and the blood on your shirt as evidence. Be tough, your word against his. Rainy is a witness, though. It could takes several weeks to get a trial goin' and—"

"Oh, hell no, I won't be here that long. Could you just keep him locked up until I leave town?"

"I can't keep him too long if you don't press charges."

I put my hat back on. "Three days?"

"I can do that, for disturbing the peace and cussin' in public."

I shake Jesse's hand. "Thank you."

Rainy takes my arm. "Good, let's get you a bath. You smell like one of those coyotes I shot when you ran into my camp like your head was on fire and your ass was catching."

Jesse laughs. "So, that story is true?"

Rainy snickers. "Right down to Lummy wetting his britches and—"

I chuckle. "You know I ain't never done that, you lyin' sack of turtle shit, and—"

Rainy gets the most serious look in his eye I've seen today. "No, you're right. You're the coolest man under fire I've ever seen." Then, he belly laughs. "Just not that night, Lummy boy!"

Jesse kicks the dirt. "I'll be, and here I thought my pa made that story up, God rest his soul. Said you told him about it when y'all worked together on Mister Gilmore's farm back in the day."

I put my hand on Jesse's shoulder. "I'm sorry to hear that he's gone. You had a good father."

"Yes, sir, I did."

"And he's lookin' down on you, so very proud of how you turned out."

Jesse tugs on the badge I gave him. "Yeah, and the Lord sent the right angel to correct my path at the right time back when we fought John West. I was reckless and raging mad back then."

"Even if it was a death angel he sent?"

"You're still the Lord's angel. One of his best. Thank you, Mister Lummy."

I pat him on the shoulder. "Visit your Pa's grave often. Teach your children to do the same."

Jesse tips his hat. "Yes, sir, I will. Guess I best get my prisoner processed, or the high sheriff will have my hide."

I take Jesse's arm. "One more thing, Jesse. Keep a clear eye. The same people who put that badge on your chest will just as easy put a noose around your neck."

"Bein' with you two when we took down West and Kimbrell taught me that."

He turns, and I watch a good man walk down the street.

Rainy holds his nose. "Let's go. You need a bath. And I mean right now."

"Reckon I do, old friend. Like Elihu used to say to my brothers and me when we took Saturday night baths for Sunday church, 'You gotta wash your cracks, rake your wigs, and brush your snaps before Ma'll let you outta the house tomorrow.'"

Rainy smiles. "I sure am glad I got to know that old ridge runner. He made me laugh."

"Yeah, I wish he was still with us, especially with this Tom Kimbrell trouble brewin'."

Rainy huffs. "Hell, Lummy, if all Tom Kimbrell's got is throwing up his middle finger, then I don't think we have much to worry about."

"Yeah, I'm not so sure 'bout that." I look up the street to the Sheriff's Office. There's trouble on every turn in this world.

Rainy laughs. "What was it you said to Kimbrell when he flashed his middle finger at you? 'That's how many friends you had before your dog died?' Damn, son, I'll have to remember that one."

"What I remember is that if he's anything like his older brother Laws, or John West, there's plenty to worry about."

CHAPTER 19

MISSING AN
OLD FRIEND

LATE AFTERNOON, AUGUST 8, 1886

What makes an old home place home is who ought'a be there, but ain't.

"MARY JANE, AIN'T a better meal ever been prepared, 'cept the ones my ma and Martha cooked, God rest their souls."

"That's a compliment I'll cherish, Lummy. Thank you."

"When did y'all move into town, if you don't mind me askin'?"

Rainy takes a sip of water. "We stayed out on the farm for a couple of years, but, to be honest, it wasn't really working out too well for Mary Jane. I believe it's okay to say"—Rainy takes her hand—"that it wasn't the best place for her to stay."

Mary Jane smiles and squeezes Rainy's hand. "You're right, dear, and thank you for being so understanding all of these years. Lummy, you'll understand this better than me, but the old home place just ain't home anymore if the one who makes it so ain't there."

Aaron wipes his mouth with a napkin. "Pa made the place what it was. I'm glad we moved on into town." He lays a hand on Rainy's shoulder. "And the Good Lord couldn't have brought a better man to take up where my daddy left off. I'll always appreciate you for that, Rainy."

Through a lump in my throat, I say, "Yeah, I do understand that all too well, Mary Jane. But still, bein' with y'all this evening sure makes me feel a bit of home. It's good for my soul."

The room grows quiet, each person lost in his or her own memories.

The silence needs to be broken, so I lighten the mood. "Will somebody pitch me another one of them cathead biscuits before we all go to cryin', please? There's good gravy yet to sop!"

Everyone laughs, but even still, a halo of sadness hangs over the room.

SUPPER'S OVER, AND Rainy and I ease out onto the front porch.

"Your boy Elzey looks just like you, Lummy. Long and lean but just a half foot shorter." Rainy settles into a straight-back chair on the front porch. I sit in J.A.'s old rocker as he leans over and raises his eyebrows. "And I do believe he could be just as fierce."

"He's a Tullos, ain't he? A son is a son, no matter how much you didn't get to be with him." I rock J.A.'s old rocker in a slow rhythm.

"That he is, brother."

I think about Rainy's words as I sip the rich coffee served after a fine meal of ham, corn, potatoes, and gravy, and I swear the best biscuits made this side of Martha's kitchen. "I just hope nothin' comes up that will force him to become as fierce."

"Me, too, brother. Me too."

"I've always hoped that being away from the anger, abuse, and violence I grew up with and had to endure since then, Elzey would become what I was always supposed to be... and everything I never was." I ponder that for a moment. "Not to be me, mind you, but the person Creator always intended me to be. You understand?"

"Yes, I do. After getting to know you and listening to you all these years, I understand better that Creator always had an original creational intent for each person he ever made from the clay. The ancients knew that and spoke of it."

"It wouldn't have worked for Elzey to have grown up in Choctaw County. Look what happened to Seth. I don't think I could've survived Elzey being murdered like that. I only wanted what was best for him, and that's why I left him here. Still, I do feel a bit of guilt and sorrow for not raisin' him myself." I ponder those words. "Hell, that kind of talk just brings a soul down, and ole Satan knows how to turn that against me."

"He surely does, but you're stronger than what he throws against you."

I rub my chin. "Maybe, maybe not."

"You made it this far, old friend."

"Yeah, I'm like an old buck deer wandering off into the deepest cane thickets to die."

Rainy kicks my boot. "Enough of that, Lummy. You have lots of good living left in you. You just need to find the place to do it." He sips his coffee and brings the conversation back to Elzey. "It'd be good if you tell Elzey those things yourself, and more, Lummy."

"Not sure I can do that yet." I scratch my beard. "I reckon it worked out the way it did for a reason, him growin' up here and all."

Rainy nods as he takes a draw from his pipe. "He'll do fine in this world, Lummy. If Ise is any indication of Susannah's people, Elzey comes from fine, hardworking folk on her side."

I wink. "And that'd be the best side of his family."

Rainy elbows me. "I'm sure of it, you ridge runnin', swamp jumpin', moonshine sippin', talkin' out loud son of a bitch who's been about the best friend I've ever had."

I take his forearm and squeeze it. "I feel the same, and to be related, too, even if it is just bein' shirt-tail cousins."

Rainy refills his pipe and offers me a puff.

I shake my head. "Gave it up and left the old pipe you brought me from Dale on his grave when I passed through Carrollton a few days ago."

"Sorry to hear he passed. I would've liked to have known him better."

I nod. "So, tell me about my boy Elzey."

Rainy blows a perfect smoke ring into the night. It hangs in midair as he chooses his words. "He's much of a man, my friend. Strongly built, hair the color of an iron skillet, dark complexion, much like yours, and Susannah's, of course, and he has those same piercing hazel-colored eyes you have. Kind of sets him off from the rest. Good looking kid."

"He got the better part of his momma's looks I hope."

"He's got the both of you in him. Lots of girls around him to prove it, black and white."

"No foolin'? I wouldn't think—"

"Oh, hell, Lummy, you of all people know how lovers slip around. I seem to remember something about a long-haired country boy and his brother James lovin' two sisters of the bronze beauty persuasion."

"Yeah, if it's gonna happen, it's gonna happen." I've thought long and hard about what I plan to say next. "So, where is he? Maybe I can muster up the courage to see him, but don't hold me to—"

"He's not here, Lummy."

"Where'd he go? On a trip?"

"Yes, to find you in Choctaw County."

"What? When?"

"A few days before you arrived. You probably passed him and Tarle on the way going in the opposite direction."

I slap my knee. Hard. "So I did see him."

"Do what?"

"I'd bet the farm that I saw him, and Tarle, on the ferry comin' from the Louisiana side to Vicksburg as I was crossin' the Missip River comin' this way."

"Well, I'll be. I bet you did."

A thousand thoughts race through my head. Why now? Why go look for his father now when he could have all these years? Why didn't I come to him? Why, why, why? Too many questions with so few answers.

"Why? Because you did the best and right thing by leaving him here to grow up, like you said. Choctaw County was too violent a place for, meaning no harm, a mixed race child to grow up. That was easy to see when I was there."

"Yeah, livin' conditions for my Black friends still ain't exactly a whole lot better than when we took down Captain Tom Ford and his Hyenas."

I let it all sink in. My head is swimming, thoughts rushing around like eddies and whirlpools in the Mississippi River, twisting and turning, trying to pull me under. I press the owl claw into my wrist, but it strikes a bandage Rainy placed over the wounds I'd inflicted upon myself.

Rainy clears his throat. "You okay?"

"Yeah. Talkin' out loud again?"

Rainy nods. "You won't ever stop doing that. And you shouldn't. It's the best part of who I know you to be. Talking to God like he's sitting right here with us because he is. You've had a pretty profound effect on me, Lummy Tullos. You helped me exchange dark clothes of death for clothes of light and good living. And I'm the blessed man for it, brother."

"I appreciate you sayin' that."

"And you won't believe this, but Mary Jane's got me going to church with her every Sunday. Has for years now."

"Well, hell, I guess the age of miracles hasn't ceased." I think about that. "I ain't set foot in a church house since Pastor Dobbs passed on to glory some time back."

"Yeah, attending church or not, I've never known another soul as close to Creator as you."

"If it wasn't for my friendship with Creator, I'd done already put a bullet into my brain."

"You aren't thinking—?"

"Oh, hell no. I'd done it a long time ago if I had a mind to. Just ain't in me to do that. And I don't judge anyone who takes that road. Ain't my place, and nobody else's either. You just never know what a person is wrestlin' with that sends them over the edge to make the decision to end their life. I know what troubles my mind has endured, but not everyone can see their way through such troubles of the soul. People want easy answers to tough and confusing questions, then judge a person with their beliefs, not realizing that they're placing greater judgment on themselves for condemnin' another person."

"I say leave it alone and let God handle it."

"That's where I land on the subject. I do wish a person sufferin' in such a way could be asked what it is that's so terrible in this life that takin' your own life becomes the only answer."

"You usually don't get the chance to ask that question." Rainy sips his coffee. "How do you do it, brother? I mean, stay sane with all you've been through?"

I laugh out loud. "First of all, admitting that I'm not sane."

Rainy chuckles. "And then?"

He's serious, and I need to give him a thoughtful answer. And I have one. "Sometimes you just have to sit on the ground with Job of the Bible, throw a bit of dust on top of your head, scrape your sores with a broken piece of pottery, and wait for the Lord to show up."

"That can't be easy."

"It's not."

Rainy fills me in on how Elzey has grown up, his life with Joshua and Sudie Mae, and his education and aims in life. "I've kept a close watch on that young man all these years, helping out any way I could without him knowing it was me. His folks have been extremely grateful."

"I appreciate it, Rainy. You don't know how much."

"Elzey wanted to find you, get to know you, and ask why you never came for him."

"Is he angry?"

"Wouldn't you be?"

"I reckon so. At least he gets that honestly from me."

Rainy smiles. "Oh, he gets a lot more than that from you, my friend. He's a good man."

"He, and Tarle, and Aaron, are best of friends. Tarle went with Elzey to find you. I sent a message ahead to Annie Fanny so they could have a place to land in Vicksburg and see Ise and Jenny. They'll help speed them on. I haven't received a reply yet. Is Annie still with us?"

"Yeah, still creepin' around in her old age but as feisty as always. Her husband, Beau, passed away a few years back. Do you know what that crazy woman suggested?"

Rainy snickers. "I could only imagine."

"That we take up where we left off when she patched up my injured shoulder after I crossed the Missip chasin' Susannah back in '59."

"I don't know, she's pretty nice looking—"

I grin, but I'm serious. "You shut the hell up right now, boy. Ain't nobody in this world can take on Annie Fanny, except Beau Handerson, God rest his blessed soul. She probably wore his poor body to a bag of bones, the fire that lady's got in her thighs for a man." I shake my head like I've got water in my ears. "I can't believe those words just came out of my mouth."

I look at Rainy, and we burst out laughing.

I collect myself. "But I do love Annie Fanny. Always have. Always will. If I took up with her, it'd ruin a wonderful friendship."

Rainy grins. "And she knows that."

"She said as much as she kissed me like a five dollar whore and clutched my backside as I left her café for the last time."

"That's her, all right. Never will change."

"World wouldn't be the same if she did."

Memories flash through my mind.

Annie Fanny. Damn, what a good woman.

CHAPTER 20

A REUNION OF THE RE-UNITED

WAY BEFORE DAWN, AUGUST 10, 1886

My goodness, gray and blue can mix together without things turning red.

THE NIGHT BUGS still sing in the darkness as I walk Cloud to the edge of town.

We ride twenty-five miles from Winnfield to Montgomery to attend the old soldier's reunion. I'm a bit apprehensive, but the best way to handle fear is to meet it head on, Pa used to say.

Things have changed. Montgomery was once in Winn Parish, but Rainy said they took part of Winn Parish and others to create a new one and named it for General Grant in 1869. They did the same to Choctaw County back in '74. Land boundaries change just like the boundaries of our lives. It's just getting tougher to adjust to the changes.

The four hour ride leaves me stiff when I go to dismount. I feel old, not to mention being reminded that this is a reunion for things that happened over twenty years ago.

Montgomery buzzes like a beehive, and the excitement is catching. I leave Cloud at a livery and remove his saddle to give him a rest.

I wish J.A. was here with me.

Then I realize something. He is.

Someone yells across the growing crowd, "Well, if it ain't... can't be. Preacher man?"

I pull my hat down to cover my eyes from the sun's glare. "Sarge? Sergeant Kelly, that you?"

Sarge trots through the crowd, grabs my hand, and nearly shakes my shoulder out of socket. "How are you, Lummy Tullos?"

"Doin' good, Sarge. Wasn't sure if there'd be anybody here who would remember me. Good to see you. It truly is."

"Yeah, I got involved in helping with the event, and now they've asked me to arrange the location of the next reunion. We haven't decided when that'll be, but you come back for that one, too. Unless you're planning on settling in these parts, that is. If you are, I need to get you signed up to become a member of the United Confederate Veterans David Pierson Camp. You could—"

"Right now, I'm just passin' through, Sarge. If I come back this way, I'll certainly give it some thought."

"It'd be like old times." Someone yells from the sign-in booth for Sarge to come attend to some problem. "Sorry, Lummy, duty calls. So good to see you, old friend. Don't leave without us getting a chance to catch up. I'd like to know what you did after Vicksburg. Well, gotta go."

That was more than I wanted, but Sarge means well. Always has. But I'm not interested in talking old war stories, and with me finishing the war with the First Mississippi Mounted Rifles, I kind of doubt they'd want me in their club of veterans—the Rifles being Union and all.

I won't be here long today.

A big man with a mean scowl walks my way like he's headed to a fire. I grip the knife Pa made me, ready to yank it free for a fight. He walks right up to me and stops an arm's length away. He stands there, squinting, like he's trying to decide whether he's going to hit me or hug me.

I break the silence in the middle of the busy street. "John Duncan."

His stern look makes me think we're about to brawl right here in front of everyone. He bites his lip, and then thrusts out his hand. "You saved my life, Lummy Tullos. I was on my way to standin' in front of a firin' squad with the rest of the West-Kimbrell Gang, but y'all hawg-tied me at Shiloh Baptist Church, and well, if you hadn't done that and kept me pris'ner until it was over, I'd be dead right now." He turns loose of my hand. "I have a lovely wife, kids growin' up, a small farm I call my own, and well, just a good life. Thank you, Lummy. If you ever need anything, name it. I mean it."

I let out a sigh of relief. "And here I thought you were gonna shoot me or somethin', John."

He snickers. "I would have back then for damn sure, but the Good Lord has taught me different these past fifteen years or so. I'm glad you came and I got the chance to thank you. I won't forget you, friend." He turns loose of my hand and walks away.

"Wait a minute, John. Tell me what's been goin' on with you since then?"

He smiles. "Thanks for asking. I reformed myself after the West-Kimbrell Gang was taken down, and I've been tryin' to live a good God-fearin' life with my family. I live without all the troubles I had back then and, well, I'm just a simple farmer scratchin' out a livin' on my own land, lovin' my wife, and raising my three kids. It ain't a lot, but it's a good life."

"The best you could hope for, John. I'm real happy for you, brother. I'm glad you came over. Your words have made this trip worthwhile."

"I don't want to bring up all the stuff about Dawg Smith and John West, but I just want to apologize for all the hard things I said about your wife, and for bein' on the wrong side of things with the whole West-Kimbrell thing. Forgive me?"

"Done." I shake his hand.

He grins and disappears into the crowd.

I wade through the growing throng of attendees and stand in the middle of the crowd. Old members of the Third, Twelfth, Twenty-Seventh, and Twenty-Eighth Louisiana Regiments are here. The battle flag of the Twelfth is raised up a pole and several of its members shed tears–not for a lost war, but over lost friends. Those same men turn and salute the Stars and Stripes waving proudly in the breeze above all else. That's good. That was certainly the sight I needed when I switched my loyalties back to the flag I originally gave my allegiance to—the same flag Uncle Silas fought under at the Battle of New Orleans with General Jackson. The Stars and Stripes.

Sarge trots past me, backhanding my shoulder lightly, and saying, "There's over two hundred of us here. Ain't that something?"

I start to say, "Yeah, this is—"

Sarge stops for a moment. "We soldier boys are gathering up to march to the Masonic Square, where there'll be musicians and speakers. It's gonna be great. You get registered yet? They want all the old fellows from the war to sign in so we can keep up with you. Gotta go!"

And so do I. This ain't for me. But I'll stick around for a bit.

The band starts up with patriotic songs. Dignitaries and important people mount a platform to start the proceedings. Old soldiers form up and march in time to the Square. Not me. I did enough marching in the war. Didn't like it then. Ain't doing it now.

I ease on down to the Square with the rest of the crowd and get within hearing distance of the speakers. There's music, a choir, and then to my surprise, Judge David Pierson is introduced and gives an address followed by the song, "Conquered Banner." Those words are certainly true. Pierson was a great help when our little band of men led by Lieutenant McGugarty took down the West-Kimbrell Gang. A kid hands me a program and it looks to be a long day. After David speaks, I go back to the livery stable, saddle Cloud, and head back to Winnfield.

I'm still not ready to celebrate what has given me hell all these years—a war I never wanted to fight in the first place.

On the way out, I did hear Captain Stovall report from the podium, "Company F of the Twenty-Seventh Louisiana Volunteer Infantry, the Winn Rebels, with whom I was privileged to serve, fought proudly and honorably in the former War of Northern Aggression. Of the one hundred men strong who mustered in at New Orleans in March of 1862, only forty men survived the siege of Vicksburg, the bravest of whom went on to finish the war in some form or fashion. The other sixty souls, some of whom gave their lives in the ultimate sacrifice, will always be remembered as patriots who died for a just and righteous cause. And the few who left the fight, well, may God forgive their cowardly...."

His words fade, and so does my concern for what he says next. Some still cling to the hope that the South will rise again. My loyalties changed from the Stars and Bars back to my original oath to the Stars and Stripes when I saw supposedly good Confederate loyalists thrown out of home and shop by Union soldiers because they had hoarded enough food to have fed the entire thirty-thousand man Reb Army at Vicksburg for a whole other month. Selling it to their own people at high prices in the lowest of circumstances sealed my conviction to return to the oath I originally took. The Stars and Stripes waving proudly over the county courthouse in Vicksburg after the surrender brought a good pride back into my soul.

I think about those who died in the trenches of Vicksburg, those who Captain Stovall praised for giving their lives. A bit of anger rears its head like a fiery dragon.

"Horseshit! They died for a cause that became no cause at all, I'm sorry to say." Tears fill my eyes. Granville, Hog Fart. My two brothers, Amariah and George Washington. All gone. "And for what? Politics? State's rights? To keep slavery? To do away with slavery? Who gives an ever-lovin—" I catch myself. "And Cloud, you know what the worst part of it all was? I can still see Susannah cryin' her eyes out as the train pulled away from the woodcutter's station to take me off to the war." I press the owl claw into my wrist.

It's a long, slow ride to Winnfield. Cloud and I camp halfway to give me time to think.

CHAPTER 21

PUTTING WINNFIELD BEHIND ME

9:00 A.M., AUGUST 11, 1886

Just because your body leaves a place doesn't mean all of your soul goes with it.

I EASE INTO Rainy's gun shop just after Aaron turns the *"Open"* sign over. I sit on a stool in front of the counter, and Rainy pours us cups of steaming hot coffee. Without turning his head, he calls, "Aaron, son, Lummy's back." He adds a bit of cream to his coffee and stirs slowly. "How was the reunion?"

"'Bout what I expected. Lots of back slappin' and tale tellin', you know, old soldiers reliving war stories that have grown way beyond what really happened by those who saw little to no action. Those who saw a lot don't say a lot. I guess for the loud talkers, it's all they've got left. Memories, even if they ain't true to the facts." I sip my coffee. "Umm, that's good." I set my cup down. "I guess it's all right that some men stretch the truth if it means the boys who died in the war get remembered."

Rainy lifts his coffee mug. "Here, here."

I drop my head. "'I'm sure there'll come a time when they'll be forgotten."

"I guess it's the way of it, you think?"

"Yeah, nobody remembers the names of people scratched on gravestones a couple of hundred years back, do they?"

"Only those who care enough to honor their ancestors and keep their memories alive. The rest, well, and meaning no harm, are just trying to scratch out a living and live decent lives. Not everyone even gets that remembering ancestors is a healthy part of living. I've always enjoyed bein' around old folks, talkin' ancestors, and hearin' the old stories."

I sip my coffee again. "I guess I'm becomin' just an old story myself, with my niece Mary writing down our family history."

"You sure you want all of that told, you old heathen?"

"Don't worry, cousin, I made sure you're in there, too."

"Did you do okay with the war dreams at the reunion?"

I nod. "Yeah, no troubles. I actually had a good time and spoke to a couple of old comrades. I left before anybody roped me into talkin' about the battles, though."

The bat wings behind the counter swing open, and Aaron brings my guns from the back room. "They're all checked and cleaned, ready to go, Pa. Oh, hello, Mister Lummy. Have a good trip?"

I reach for my weapons. "I did, and thank you for doin' this for me, son."

Rainy inspects my guns to make sure they're in best working order. He smiles at Aaron. "Good job, son." He looks up at me. "You know, you should let me retool this old .44 caliber cap and ball Colt Dragoon so it can shoot centerfire cartridges."

I shake my head. "Naw, that old piece of iron got me through many a scrape, and I reckon it'll keep on. I'll leave her like Mister Gilmore gave her to me. Some things don't need to change."

Rainy packs cap, ball, and powder for the pistol and rifle ammunition in my saddlebags. "Where will you go"

"First, to Susannah's grave one last time. Then, visit Dorcas and the family. After that, hell, only the wind knows."

"Sure wish you'd wait around and see Elzey. He and Tarle'll be back in four or five days. I could send a telegram to Bankston to let them know you're here."

"No."

"I just know he'd—"

I snap at him faster than I want. "I can't. Not just yet." I collect myself. "Sorry, brother, I didn't—"

He waves off my apology and doesn't ask why. We both know it's best to let it lie.

Aaron lays his hand on my shoulder. "Sir, it has been a pleasure seeing you again, the man who saved my daddy's life."

"And the son of the man who saved mine. Just one time too late to…." I choke up and can't talk for a moment.

He pats my back. "Come back and see us, Mister Lummy. You're always welcome here."

I nod. "Y'all tell Mary Jane thanks again for such fine hospitality."

Rainy smiles. "Will do, brother."

I take his hand and hold it firmly. "See you when I see you, Rainy Mills."

The little bells above the door jingle as I walk out. I don't look back. I can't. If I did, I'd want to stay. And I can't do that.

BLACKBERRY VINES COVER the once small cemetery, except one spot.

Susannah's grave.

Elzey, being the good son, has kept his mother's grave in good shape. A cypress wood bench sits a couple of feet away to the side. I sit on the well-worn spot where I'm sure Elzey has had many a conversation with his mother, and Granny Thankful, too, I would imagine.

The cedar branches wave as if a small breeze passes through, but there is no wind.

"I knew you'd come, Granny."

"Don't I always?"

"You have been a faithful guiding light all these years."

"It is mine to do until you join me where I am."

"I'm kinda lookin' forward to that time, Granny."

"But not before your time, though, grandson."

"That I'm comin' to understand." I sit still. "When will all that's about to happen come?"

"You mean, when you must give as Dan Creekwater gave for you?"

"I won't know when the moment of my death comes, but when will the troubles start again?"

"Have they ever stopped?"

"Not really, except for a few years with Martha and the kids."

"A time will come when all troubles will be over."

"Pray tell, when will that be?"

"When Susannah comes for you, one last time."

"Will Susannah visit me today?"

"Not today or again until she leads you through the thin veil. Creator has a special work for her now."

I study the grave where lies the love that Creator set in my heart as a child. "Not much to show for the dreams I had with Susannah."

"A grave marker never marks the life of a good person. Memories do."

"Seems like all I have are memories, Granny."

"You have Elzey." Granny fades into the blackberry thicket that surrounds Susannah's grave.

I sit and recount good memories. For a long time.

CHAPTER 22

DORCAS

AFTERNOON, AUGUST 11, 1886

Sitting with family soothes a weary soul.

SWEAT HAS SOAKED my clothes. It's so hot today. Cloud's coat is dark and lathered. I push aside hanging moss dripping from the old oaks that lead up to Freddy and Dorcas's home.

"Hello, up at the house," I holler.

A flock of strange, gray birds with white heads the size of a chicken sound the alarm like a pack of hound dogs. They screech like rusty door hinges swinging back and forth.

Freddy steps out onto the porch and waves. "Ma, you best get out here. It's your favorite brother-in-law!"

Dorcas hobbles to the door, walking with a cane. "Well, my goodness, Lummy Tullos. Get yourself up on this porch and kiss your sister-in-law."

I tie off Cloud to a porch post and take the steps in two bounds. I hug her close and kiss her neck as I shake Freddy's hand.

"I'm glad to see y'all are doin' so good." I stand there, marveling that I get to see my dear family again. Then, the strange birds gather around, chirping like baby birds, feeding on insects and any scrap of corn they can find. I can't help but ask, "What'n the hell are those things?"

Freddy laughs. "First, you know how your sister-in-law is about cussin', and second, thems what you call Guineas. They're from Africa. They make good watch dawgs and keep the snakes away. They're not too bad on the supper table, and their eggs fry up good as a chicken's."

"I might have to give 'em a try sometime."

Dorcas sits in her rocker. "Have a seat, Lummy. We're doin' well, 'cept child-bearin' has 'bout done me wore out."

Freddy laughs. "It's been a whole lot of fun makin' children, though."

Dorcas swats her handkerchief at Freddy. "Oh, Freddy, stop that, you old coot."

Freddy squeezes Dorcas's arm. "I kinda think child-raisin' was tougher than the child-bearin', you think, dear?"

"You know it, with that dang ole Tullos blood runnin' through some of them children's veins. Yeah, it's good they've gone on to live their own lives and give me a bit of rest."

Freddy kisses her on the cheek. "You certainly deserve it, dear."

Dorcas smiles at Freddy, and then stares at me. "You're goin' somewhere, ain't you?"

I squint. "Yeah, I left Choctaw County for the last time."

Freddy asks, "Where you headed?"

"Not sure yet, but west for sure. Our people always go west when they need to leave a place."

Dorcas studies me. "It's not home for you there anymore, is it, brother?"

"Not since everyone passed except Jasper and Isabell. Just ain't the same." I don't want to talk about that anymore, so I change the subject. "I need a change of scenery, as they say. You know, venture out far enough out to where some of the past can't find me."

Dorcas smiles. "You know that don't ever happen."

I chuckle. "Guess not. But it may keep my mind from goin' places that ain't good for me."

Freddy chimes in, "With that, I do agree. Sometimes a man needs just a little new to keep the old bayed up in a tree like hounds on a coon."

"I reckon so. Where's the children—"

A loud crack like a stone pitcher being dropped crashes, and two boys come running around the side of the house like twin tornadoes sweeping across a cotton field.

Dorcas shakes her head and grins. "That'll be John and James, and they ain't no apostles like in the Bible." She fluffs her skirt and pats it down. "Yeah, they're good boys, though."

"They look just like you, Freddy. I guess they came along after I was here last?"

Freddy scratches his beard. "Yeah, John in '72, and James two years later."

Dorcas lifts her chin. "And that's the last two, mind you. I believe I've done my part for God and country for the number of children I brought into this world." She reaches over and grabs Freddy's hand and smiles. "That is, with two good husbands walkin' with me."

I laugh. "Well, wasn't it the Good Lord who said, 'Be fruitful and multiply?'"

Dorcas chuckles. "Yeah, but time for multiplying is over for this old bird."

Freddy cozies up to her shoulder. "But you're still the prettiest hen in the chicken house."

Dorcas smiles, then eyes me. "Can you stay the night?"

"Are you cookin'?"

"You know I am."

"Well, mine'll be the first feet under the table when the supper bell rings."

"Good 'nough, brother." Dorcas gets up, kisses me on the cheek, and goes inside.

It's good to feel a little bit of home.

SUPPER'S OVER. ALL catching up and talking old times is done. I lie down on the same bed I slept on after we took down Dawg Smith, and before we took down the West-Kimbrell Gang. A haven at the very least. Peace at its best in this place. A soft rain falls and lulls me to sleep.

CHAPTER 23

I CAN'T.
NOT THIS TIME

DAWN, AUGUST 12, 1886

Staying too long deepens the desire to stay. I need to move on.

I STEP OFF the porch with a bag of food Dorcas prepared to help me on my way. Freddy shakes my hand, and Dorcas pulls me close to give me a peck on the lips. Leaving has always been tough for me. So, it's best to mount up, say goodbye, and get going before the sun comes up to reveal the tears. I do just that and trot Cloud down the lane.

I stop by the cemetery for a moment to say my farewell to my brother Ben. "See you in a bit, brother. And don't catch all the fish, you hear?" I chuckle and move on.

THE LIGHTS IN the lone mercantile in the small village of Sikes are flickering through the windows. Pans rattling around tell me someone is getting breakfast started.

I step inside and remove my hat. "Well, now, if it ain't the purtiest cook in all of Looseana."

Madison turns and squints. She smiles and eases over to hug my neck. She gives me a quick kiss and sits down. I sit with her.

"What am I thinking? Let me get you a cup of—"

"How 'bout you sit, and I get us some coffee?"

She grins. "Ain't you the gentleman?"

"You deserve it."

"Where were you when I was of the marryin' age, Lummy Tullos?"

"Oh, heck, Miss Madison, I wasn't fit to be married in those days."

"Just as well, and you can call me Missus Madison now, if you don't mind. I've been a married woman for nigh unto ten years now. No children, though. I figure them old soldiers and crusty worn out farm hands who used to come in here every morning for coffee and talk were my kids." Sadness creeps into her eyes. "Sad to say, they're all gone now."

"Who'd you get hitched up with, Madison? He must be a good'n."

"Oh, you wouldn't know him. He moved here from Alabama after y'all took down the West-Kimbrell Gang. He's a good man, and I love him to pieces, but this is my home. Always has been. I miss the old men comin' in, with their hats cocked to one side, slurpin' their coffee way too loud, and hearin' that cussin' that just sounds good." She wipes a tear. "I helped bury most of those boys. Many had fought in some war and had been wounded or couldn't live with their families because of the war dreams. People don't know how a war can affect a man."

I nod. "Don't I know it?"

"Yes, you do. Let me get you some breakfast, Lummy. I know you're headed somewhere, and I want to send you off right."

"I 'ppreciate it, dear."

After a fine meal of ham and eggs, biscuits and gravy, with the best coffee I've had in a while to wash it down, I lean back in my chair and rub my belly. "You're too good to me."

"I'm just glad to have someone to cook for this morning. Customers have become scarce after the old boys passed on. Now, only a visitor or two comes during the day, and maybe a few locals who try to help keep me open."

"What do I owe you?"

"Nothin', Lummy. It's on the house."

I take out two twenty-dollar bills and slide them under my plate. I stand to straighten my clothes. "Best breakfast this side of my mother's kitchen."

"You're too kind." She stares for a moment. "You won't be back this way, will you?"

I shake my head. "Probably not."

She walks over slowly and pulls me down to kiss me on the lips. "That's for bein' a good man." She kisses me again. "And most 'specially for what you did to help save Winn Parish. Twice, if anybody's countin'."

"Well, if it means a few more kisses, just keep on countin'. It has been my pleasure, more so, makin' good friends who I'll love for eternity." I hug her again. "Take care, Madison."

"I'll see you, Lummy Tullos."

I WALK WITH Cloud for a mile or so to let my food settle before I mount. I'm not in the saddle but a few hours when a rider comes barreling down the road, kicking up fresh earth in all directions. I pull my Henry rifle and throw it across the saddle, ready to fire.

The rider races around a bend in the road yelling, "Rider, hold up there!"

I work the lever of my Henry and take aim.

Rainy's son, Aaron, races up, and his horse's hooves slide in the muddy ground. "Uncle Lummy, you gotta come with me right now! They've got Tarle's wife, Caroline."

As I step out from behind Cloud, my heart drops. "Who?"

But I already know.

"That damned Tom Kimbrell, that's who!" He waits expectantly.

"Tell your pa to send a telegram to Bankston and have Matt Poole run it out to Jasper Tullos's farm. It'll probably get there about the time Elzey and Tarle arrive."

Aaron furrows his brow. "You need to come on, Uncle Lummy. Now!"

I hang my head.

"You're not coming back with me?"

"I'm sorry, son, I can't. Not this time."

"I don't understand. You're the one who—"

"Talk to your pa. He understands."

Aaron races off back to Winnfield.

I take Cloud's reins. I trudge my way down the wagon road leading west. Walking.

Feet as heavy as anvils.

Heart even heavier.

Soul aching.

I pull the owl claw from my wrist. Blood drips. Maybe I should just let it bleed out.

A voice from a switch cane break calls, "Not yet, grandson. One more thing you must do."

I wrap my wound with a bit of salve and a bandage. I need to stop doing that. And try not to think of the wounds that have plagued me throughout life. Especially now.

PART II:
ELZEY

CHAPTER 24

A FERRY TO VICKSBURG, AND THE TRUTH

6:00 A.M., AUGUST 5, 1886

Truth seems to always be found on the other side of a river.

TARLE BACKHANDS ELZEY across the chest as they lead their mounts onto the ferry. "Whoa, what a big ole river. It's somethin', ain't it, Elzey?"

The cool morning breeze wisps against Elzey's hair. He's never been on a ferry, much less crossed a river this size. The ferry from the Mississippi side puffs smoke and heads toward them, but at a safe distance.

Elzey takes in a deep breath and blows it out. "Yeah, it is. Smells a bit like fresh broke ground in the springtime."

Tarle shakes his head. "It's been a long time since my pa took us across thirty something years ago. But that was closer to the city. We crossed over to some place called… what was it? Yeah, Desoto. That was it. That town's probably gone since the river changed course."

"So, you've done this before?"

"Yeah, when I was just a boy. I don't remember much except that I was a bit scared, being so small on such a big rolling river."

Elzey grabs the rail as the boat shudders, breaking away from the river bank. "I'm not sure I like this very much. You sure these things are safe?"

Tarle points to the Vicksburg side. "Hey, look, a ferry's coming this way." He strains to look at the faces of the passengers and their wagons. "They seem so far away, but soon they'll be no more than a good shouting distance."

Elzey snickers. "Let one of them fall out and see how far away they'd get in those whirlpools. That ole river looks mean. A man could get washed downriver in a hurry."

The opposing ferry comes no closer than fifty yards as it passes by. Both toot their whistles at each other out of courtesy. A lone man standing by his horse, hair whipping in the breeze, his foot set up on the rail, stares at the ferry Elzey and Tarle ride.

Elzey elbows Tarle. "You see that old codger staring at us on the ferry that just passed us?"

"Yeah, he had a familiar look."

"He did. He almost looked—"

"Like you, Elzey." Tarle squints at the fading face of the man on the other ferry. "You've come a long way since you told your pap you were going to find your father."

"Yep." Elzey shades his eyes from the morning sun. "One thing's for sure. If that was my father, he's tall as a pine tree."

CHAPTER 25

I WANT TO KNOW
MY FATHER

MR. GILMORE'S OLD FARM, JULY 31, 1886

When your heart says go, no one else can tell you, "No."

"WHEN WERE YOU going to tell me he was my father and not my uncle, Pap?"

Joshua grimaces at the question. "Your ma and me wanted to waits till you wuz big 'nough to understands what we be sayin'."

Elzey fumes. "What do you mean, big enough? I'm a grown man, Pap. Why didn't you tell me before now?"

"'Cause of the red fire I sees in your eyes. You ain't always able to keep dem flames at bay."

"What a dumb thing to do, fooling me all these years, Pap!"

Elzey's mother, Sadie, cuts in. "Elzey Burk Tullos, you will not speak to your pap that way."

"I'm a man, Ma. He should've known that I need to know such things. Things about me."

Sadie bristles. "You know all you needs to know, Elzey. Your father loved you and felt it best you stay here wid us."

"You don't understand, Pap. I need to know who—"

Joshua throws up his hands. "Who yo real pappy is, not just his name, right?"

"That's it." Elzey folds his arms. "Old Nate told me some things, but I can't know who he is by what somebody else tells me."

Joshua takes Sadie's hand. "We've loved you as our onliest son, Elzey. Ain't that 'nough?"

"Pap, Ma, please don't take this the wrong way. You know I love you with all my heart, and you'll always be my pap and ma, but I never did know my real mother. And never will." Elzey purses his lips. "But I can—"

Joshua finishes for him. "Meets and knows yo true pappy."

Elzey lays a hand on each of their shoulders. "I need to see him face to face. I know what you two have told me all these years about Lummy Tullos, but I've got to ask him why he didn't want me, why he didn't take me with him. I have to know."

Joshua nods. "I understands. Guess I'd want to know dat bidness, too."

Elzey growls, "Why didn't Tarle tell me? He's my best friend. I could—"

Joshua doesn't blink. "'Cause I ast him not to, Elzey. Wadn't fer him to say."

Elzey sighs. "Well, no matter how this talk ends, I'm going. I have to go find my father."

Sadie cries into Joshua's chest. "But that's sech a turr'ble and dang'rous road. You knows hows folks feel 'bout a half white, half black child, Elzey. That ain't gonna treat ya right."

"I don't plan to tell them, and I look white enough. Besides, I can handle myself, Ma."

Joshua shakes his head. "You goin' no matter what I be sayin', ain't ya?"

Elzey says nothing more, standing firm and strong in his plan and conviction.

Joshua asks, "How you goin' ta gets there? You ain't got no money to speak of."

Elzey puffs out his chest. "I squirreled away a little money. The rest I can earn by picking up an odd job or two on the way."

Joshua shakes his head. "All right then. You can't be goin' by yo'self."

Elzey straightens up. "What do you have in mind?"

"You goes and gets yo cuzzin, Tarle Tullos, an' see if'n he'll go wich ya. Then, there's a man you has ta go jaw wid, or I'll hawg tie your backside to a barn post, ya heer?"

"Okay, Pap, who would that be?"

"He be knowin' who yo real pappy is as good as any human bein' around. Dat man knows alls 'bout him. Knows him real good. They runn'd together in some purty tough doin's back in the day, takin' down outlaws and sech."

"What's his name?"

"Mistuh Rainy Mills, the gun dealer in Winnfield."

"Then I'll go get my cousin, Tarle, and visit Mister Rainy Mills."

The little bells above the door jingle as Elzey and Tarle ease into Mills and Son Gun Sales and Repair.

A voice from the back yells, "Be out in a minute."

Elzey whispers to Tarle, "I've never been in here before. Never needed to, I guess."

"Really? I thought you would've at least dropped in to see Aaron. I've only been in here a couple of times myself. I got to know Mister Rainy Mills when we took down the West-Kimbrell Gang. He's a tough one. He'll get us on the straight and narrow for this trip."

Elzey covers his mouth when he speaks to lower his volume. "I've never met him, but I've heard stories about him killing his real father for murdering the man who was supposed to be his father and for raping his mother. Then made some judge over in Bossier cut his own wrists with the knife the murderer used to kill his real father for letting him get away with it."

Tarle side-glances Elzey. "No one ever proved any of that, and besides, if it is true, Rainy brought justice where none was till he showed up."

Aaron walks through the batwings, wiping a bit of gun grease from his hands on a towel. "Now just what are you two outlaws up to? Hadn't seen you boys in a bit." He shakes Tarle's and Elzey's hands. "We need to get our cane poles and go get a mess of catfish and have a fry this coming weekend. What do you say?"

Tarle winks at Aaron. "Tha-a-at might have to wait a couple of weeks, but hell yeah! We're always up for eatin' some whisker fish."

Rainy steps out from the back and laughs. "Thought I heard two ruffians out here roughing up my shop. Good to see you boys. How's Missus Caroline, Tarle?

"Fine, Mister Rainy, doin' fine."

"And the kids?"

"Got so many now, I can't count 'em all, much less keep 'em fed and clothed. Then, tryin' to remember their names, well, that's a whole 'nuther story."

Aaron laughs. "Tarle took seriously the Lord's command to 'Be fruitful, and multiply, and replenish the earth.' He didn't say you had to do it all by yourself, though."

Rainy leans back from the counter. "Just how many children do you have now, Tarle?"

"Nine kids walkin' and Erastus who's a year old. Takin' his first steps, though, mind you."

Aaron snickers. "Yeah, Pa, Tarle here don't go to church no more. He's got so many children, he just went ahead and started his own."

Everyone laughs, and Elzey tries to grin, but Rainy notices something's got his mind occupied. Rainy waits for Elzey to speak.

He doesn't.

Rainy stretches his back. "I haven't seen you in a long time, Elzey Burk Tullos. What's it been, ten, fifteen years?"

Aaron elbows Rainy and smiles. "Closer to fifteen, Pa, but I get to see him from time to time, going fishing with Tarle."

Rainy offers his hand. "I know you really don't know me, but it's really good to see you. How have you been, son?"

Elzey grins. "Good, sir. I remember you. You used to wear all black. But no more?"

Rainy smiles. "Yes, I did, son, but thanks to Aaron's father J.A., God rest his soul, your father, Lummy, and my Mary Jane, I changed that color, though black is as beautiful as Creator's canvas behind his sparkling painted stars. It does not represent who I am anymore. It never was about black anyway. It was about the darkness of the soul, you see."

Elzey's face reddens with surprise. "That's what I want. That's why I'm here, Mister Rainy."

"Yeah, your pap came in a couple of weeks ago and said you were asking a lot of questions about your blood father, Columbus Nathan Tullos." Rainy puts his arm around Aaron. "And I'm forever grateful for those who helped me see a better way, especially this one's father, J.A."

"I want to feel that way about mine as Aaron does about his father, too, but I don't. I barely remember seeing him back in '70. Pap told me that my real father left me here because he thought I was better off in Winn Parish and not with him. Didn't he want me as his son?" Elzey shakes his head. "I have little more than contempt and anger toward him for the most part. I just—"

Rainy stares into Elzey's eyes. "I see you still have that gator tooth necklace your pap said Lummy gave you."

Elzey pulls the tooth on a chain out from inside his shirt. "I never take it off."

"As well you should not. That alone says you'll make it."

Elzey tears up. "I can't seem to find my way in all of this."

Rainy lays his hand on Elzey's shoulder. "You'll get there, son. Trust me, if you're willing, you'll get there one day."

Tarle says, "And that starts today, Uncle Rainy."

Rainy changes the subject to give Elzey time to sort through his feelings. "Good. You still got that old double barrel ten gauge goose gun a good friend of mine had cut down to size?"

"I sure do. It might not reach up and take down a duck or goose, but it sure is hell on a deer with buckshot at short range."

Rainy shakes his head. "Yeah, I hated to see those cannon barrels get lopped off. Your pa Ben took down quite a few ducks and geese with that shoulder howitzer. He made pretty good money selling them to riverboats and restaurants, too. But hell, shortening the barrel length was for a good reason. That's another story for another time."

Elzey barks, "I'd sure like to hear it some time."

Rainy loads his pipe with tobacco from a pouch, looks up at Elzey, and snickers. "Maybe you do, maybe you don't." He lights it with a match, takes a deep draw and blows a smoke ring into the middle of the room. "Funny thing, you two being here this morning. I was just thinking about that shotgun yesterday. You know, how it can take down an entire covey of quail with one blast."

Tarle laughs. "Me and my brothers have done just that."

Rainy notices Elzey is still not smiling or taking part in the conversation. He lays his palms flat on the counter. "Glad you came in. What can I do for you boys today?"

Tarle ducks his head and rubs his chin. " Elzey wants to—"

Elzey stiffens. "I want to know my father. I want to go meet him, face to face." His face turns red, and a scowl takes over his demeanor. "I've got a few questions I need him to answer, and—"

Rainy holds up his hands in surrender. "I can see that you're angry."

Elzey barks, "Wouldn't you be?"

"I might be, that is, until I came to understand the truth."

"Well, that's what I'm after. The truth. I've heard all the great and wonderful stories from Pap and people around town about how my father, the hero of Winn Parish, Lummy Tullos, took down evil Dawg Smith and his band of ruffians, and then the murderous thieving West-Kimbrell Gang, but I've never been told much at all about why he left me here that's satisfied me yet."

Rainy takes a draw on his pipe and slowly breathes it out. "Marcus Aurelius wrote, 'It's the truth I'm after, and the truth never harmed anyone. What harms us is to persist in self-deceit and ignorance.' No better way to get at the truth than to get it straight from him. All else is hearsay."

Elzey nods at Tarle, then looks back at Rainy and sighs. "Sorry, Mister Rainy. I got a bit heated there for a minute, but it ain't always been easy growing up a child whose mother was raped and murdered and being left with a father who was never around to help you live with it. I want to know who he is and ask him why he never had me come be with him."

Rainy pats the air. "I understand that better than you're willing to accept right now, son."

Elzey blinks, and his jaw drops. "Oh… um… I'm sorry, Mister Rainy. I know some about what happened to you, and I—"

"You don't know a damned thing, son. It's not easy for anybody growing up in this world. Granted some have it better than others, but you can't let what happened to you define who you are. It matters not what people say you are. It only matters who you believe you are and what you prove yourself to be."

Elzey glares like a new recruit joining the ranks of experienced men of battle. "I know you—"

Rainy barks, "You know nothing, boy. You need to replace 'I know' with 'I don't know,' then maybe you'll learn something. Epictetus once said, 'It is impossible for a man to learn what he thinks he already knows.' You're not the only one who had a mother raped and father disappear. My mother was raped, and I'm the result. My father was—"

Aaron takes Rainy by the shoulders from behind. "Now Pa, Elzey's just—"

Rainy snatches his shoulder away. "Just nothing, dammit." The look Rainy gives Elzey could burn a hole right through him. It does, right through his heart into his soul. "I ain't downplaying what happened to you, son, but what if your father had been murdered before your mother's eyes, and then you had to carry your mother's rapist's blood in your veins forever. How would you feel then?"

Elzey ducks his head and says nothing.

"Answer me, dammit! If you don't, I'll tell Joshua to tie your ass to a barn post, and you'll never meet your father." Rainy spits and looks at Tarle, then Aaron. "He's not ready for—"

Elzey raises his voice. "To answer your question, I'd probably feel just like you do and do what you did to make it right for me."

"Now we're getting somewhere. At least you have your real father around to make that happen. You have no idea what Lummy Tullos sacrificed so you could be right here, right now, so you can have enough sense, enough gumption, and wherewithal to care enough to go ask him. Damn, son, go tell him you love him before he's gone because let me tell you one thing, there ain't much of him left for having given most of himself away so others could have better lives." Rainy wipes the sweat from his brow. "Shit, why am I wasting my time on this?"

Everyone stands in silence.

Elzey says in a small voice, "Because I needed to see how much you love my father, so I can get over myself and love him, too."

Rainy drinks water Aaron brings him. "Well, you've got a helluva way of showing it. Truth is, Lummy already lost one dark skinned son to that devilish coward Captain Tom Ford. He wouldn't have survived losing you, too."

"Seth?" Elzey looks at Tarle, who shrugs.

Rainy takes a deep breath. "Yes, a runaway slave your father found on the way back to Choctaw County after he helped end Dawg Smith's life. He thought he was doing for that young man what Mister Gilmore did for your mother. Sadly, it didn't work out and ended badly, so he decided to leave you here." He drops his head. "Lummy already lost one son to a devilish coward. He wouldn't have survived if he lost you."

Ezley shivers with anger. "Sorry, I just got a bit worked up. I don't want to, but this means a lot to me. And please don't take this as me being unhappy about growing up with my parents. I couldn't have had two better people than Joshua and Sadie to love a child not their own like they did me. It's just, well...."

Rainy reaches to hug Elzey, who melts into his arms. "It's all right, son. Sorry about my outburst. You just don't know how much your father's friendship has meant to me. I—"

"I'm starting to, Uncle Rainy."

"Thank you for that, besides the fact that you know we're kin, sort of, right?"

"Yes, sir, but blood's never been the only thing that makes people family."

Rainy studies Elzey for a moment, then turns to Tarle. "He's a lot like him. Looks, the way he thinks and talks, and especially that hellacious temperament, isn't he?"

"Yep, and that's one reason Elzey wants to get to know him."

Elzey smiles big for the first time since walking into the gun shop.

Rainy sighs. "So, I guess you men are going to Choctaw County, Missip?"

Tarle and Elzey both nod their heads.

"Do you know how to get there and the best way?"

Elzey relaxes his stance. "Not really, but my pap told me I had to come see you before I did anything else, or he'd tie me up and not let me go."

"Good thinking. He's just looking out for you. Are Joshua and Sadie doing all right?"

Elzey nods. "Yes, sir, they're doing fine."

Tarle leans on the counter. "We need to know how to get to Uncle Lummy's place, and maybe a place we can stay in Vicksburg."

"That can be arranged, and no problem at all, if ole Annie Fanny, I mean, Handerson, is still running her café there."

Elzey looks at Tarle. "Annie Fanny? Who is that?"

"A dear friend of your father's that you'll want to meet. She'll put you up for the night and feed you the best meal and pie you'll put in your mouth going there and back. I guarantee it."

Elzey elbows Tarle. "I don't know. That sound pretty good to you?"

Tarle grins. "Well, hell yeah." He scratches his arm. "Do you think Ise will be there?"

Rainy nods. "Last I heard, he and Jenny were married, and she went to work for Annie. Ise had friends in town help get him a job after the war. I'm sure you'll find them both doing well. Good folk, those two."

Elzey asks, "That Ise name sounds familiar, but who is Jenny?"

"Oh, that's right, you don't know her. You were just a small boy when Ise, your father, and a small band of men came here to take down the West-Kimbrell Gang, me and Tarle included."

"So, who is he? Ise, I mean?"

"Your mother's... Susannah's brother."

Elzey wrings his hands, not knowing what to do with them.

Rainy speaks softly, "Jenny is his wife. We rescued her from some pretty evil men on our way here during that same trip." He walks around the counter. "It's all right. I know this is a lot to take in, but you're going to meet people who will love you and care for you even though they've never seen you before."

Elzey kicks at the floor. "I won't know how to act, meeting people I've never known."

"You don't know them, but they know about you. Your father made sure of that."

Tarle squeezes Elzey's shoulder. "They're family, cousin. You're all right with them because they already know about you."

Rainy assures Elzey, "You'll be treated as family the moment they lay eyes on you."

Elzey turns to Tarle and squints. "No fooling?"

Tarle smiles. "He's right. It's the Tullos way, and that name has had a profound effect on many a soul. We'll want to keep that tradition going. Like my pa used to say, 'Remember whose name you wear.'"

Rainy draws in a deep breath. "When you boys leaving?"

Tarle looks at Elzey. "We want to go soon as we can. We don't have much money, but enough to get us there and back. We can always pick up an odd job to make a little extra cash."

Rainy reaches around the counter corner and pulls out a cash box.

Elzey waves his hand. "You don't have to—"

Rainy stomps his foot. "Have to has no part in what I'm doing, son. If you only knew how much your father helped me, and how good his reputation has helped my business thrive here in Winnfield, you wouldn't even think what you're thinking. So here, take this." He hands Elzey a hundred dollars in gold and silver. "Give Tarle half of that so if one of you gets robbed, the other still has money to get you down the road. Use the silver for your day to day needs and the gold only if necessary."

Tarle nods. "Like getting ourselves out of a jam?"

Rainy stares into Elzey's eyes. "Exactly. The road there and back isn't the easiest, I might add. There'll be ruffians on every turn. Stay sharp and keep eyes in the back of your head."

Rainy throws Elzey two small leather pouches. "Y'all put your money in those. Keep it close on your person and never take it out in public. Eyes are always watching. There's a snake under every bush and a bandit behind every tree, you understand?"

Tarle and Elzey both nod.

He turns to Tarle. "How well are you heeled?"

Elzey looks at Tarle. "What does that mean?"

"He's asking how many weapons we have between us."

Elzey turns back to Rainy. "I don't have anything."

Rainy grins. "I figured as much. Tarle?"

"I have the old sawed-off ten gauge Uncle Lummy left with us, but I have no pistol."

Rainy scratches his ear. "Aaron, son, bring the best used pistols we have on hand and another shotgun. Make it a twelve gauge quail gun, you know, a short double barreled one. I want them all to be cartridge shooters. That old ten gauge Tarle has will need powder, primers, and buck and ball loads. Grab a box of the same load in shells for the twelve."

"Yes, sir, I'll start getting it together."

"Fine, son, thank you."

Elzey asks, "What's buck and ball?"

Tarle leans on the counter. "The worst kind of shotgun load. It has both a large round ball and three or more buckshot pellets with a pretty powerful powder load. Close up, it's death."

Aaron gathers up the weapons and ammunition. "I think this'll do it, Pa."

"Good, thank you." Rainy inspects each weapon and, once satisfied, asks Elzey, "How much do you know about guns?"

Elzey rubs the sole of his shoe on the wooden floor. "Not a lot. I fired my pap's old shotgun huntin' rabbits and squirrels, but that's about it."

Rainy scratches his chin. "I see. Let's go out behind the shop. We can practice there."

CHAPTER 26

SHOOTIN' WHEN YOU DON'T KNOW HOW

11:00 A.M., AUGUST 1, 1886

The best way to learn how to handle a gun is for it to knock you down the first time you fire it. After that, you know what to do.

RAINY HANDS ELZEY the twelve gauge shotgun. "Fire both barrels at the same time."

"Both triggers at the same time? Won't that—"

"It will, if you don't hang on tight. Squeeze the triggers. Don't jerk them."

Tarle snickers. "Do what he says, Elzey."

"Okay, here goes nothing." Elzey puts the aiming bead of the double barrel twelve gauge shotgun on an old fruit crate and squeezes both triggers.

The gun goes off like a cannon blast, and a cloud of smoke engulfs the small shooting range.

Rainy looks around, as does Tarle, but Elzey is nowhere in sight.

Aaron laughs. "He's down there.

Elzey struggles to get up. "Damn gun knocked me off my feet and put me flat on my ass."

Rainy snickers. "That's not all it did."

Tarle grabs Elzey's head and looks him in the eyes. "Ooowee, boy. You got the prettiest shiner I believe I've ever seen.

Aaron laughs. "At least it matches that lovely mane of black hair on your head that all the girls swoon over."

Elzey dusts himself off and hands Rainy the shotgun. "Hope I never have to use that thing again." He turns to go inside.

Rainy stomps his foot. "Come back here, son. You ain't done yet."

Tarle suspects what's coming. "Uh-oh."

Aaron grins. "Yeah, you guessed it."

Rainy hands the shotgun back to Elzey. "Load it like I showed you."

Elzey pours powder into the two muzzles, rams a paper patch buck and ball load down each barrel, replaces the two percussion caps on the nipples, and raises the gun to fire. This time, he spreads his feet apart and buries the stock deep into his shoulder. He takes quick aim, fires, and is still standing tall when the smoke clears. Tarle and Aaron clap as he takes a bow.

Rainy barks, "Load it again, and quicker this time."

Elzey has the two barrels loaded in less than a minute, up and ready to fire. He starts to take aim, but Rainy stops him.

"Stop. Do it holding it one-handed, out from your body."

"What? You mean—"

Tarle cuts him off. "He does. If you're going to shoot that thing from a moving horse, you have to be able to handle it with one arm shooting and the other holding your reins."

"All right, but I'll be mad as hell if my arm gets broken."

Rainy snaps, "You'll be dead as hell if you can't manage this gun, boy."

Elzey stiffens his resolve. "Okay, okay. I can do this."

Rainy takes the shotgun. "That's the spirit, son. Hold it like this. Grip it with your hand with two fingers on the triggers and brace the stock against your forearm stiffened out like this." He gets Elzey set. "And don't close your eyes this time. Keep your eyes open and on the target. Raise the gun from your side and fire at the target in one swift motion."

Elzey's muscles flex as he grips the gun. He stretches down his arm by his side, the shotgun now merely an extension of his body. He raises the weapon in quick motion and fires. The shotgun flares up, but Elzey's elbow barely bends with the recoil. Smoke fills the shooting range, and Elzey stands proud that he's done what Rainy asked.

Rainy pats him on the back. "There you go, that's the ticket." He takes the shotgun and hands it to Aaron. "Now, for the hard part."

"What do you mean? The hard part?"

Tarle laughs. "Pistols, Elzey. You have to learn how to shoot a handgun."

CHAPTER 27

DON'T GO

SUNSET AT TARLE'S HOME, AUGUST 1, 1886

When a person close to the Lord says, "Don't go,"
you should probably listen.

ELZEY WASHES UP at the well and takes the steps to the porch in two strides. He's long and tall, but not quite as tall as his father. He stands at the door of his cousin Tarle's house he's visited many times before. This time is different, though. It won't be as pleasant an evening as times before.

Tarle's wife, Caroline, waves him through the children. "Everybody say hey, Elzey."

The children roar, "Hey, Elzey!"

Elzey has come to love their family tradition of making guests feel welcome with a greeting chorus. It also signals the fact that the family is loud and boisterous. Though different from his own quiet home, he enjoys the family's carnival atmosphere.

Elzey stops at the head of the table to stand by Tarle and calls out every child's name in order of age. "James, Sarah, Dorcas, Montacue, Allen Albert, John Bunion, George Luther, Martha Jane, Cleveland, and last, but certainly not least, baby Erastus Tullos. Good to see ya." He works hard to fake the happy feelings to cover up a tornado of troublesome feelings swirling inside.

Tarle nods. "Come and sit here, cousin. Caroline has a place set for you by me."

"Thanks, I appreciate it."

As he sits down on the bench, Elzey eyes Tarle, knowing that Caroline may be smiling now, but that'll change—right after supper. Tarle lightens his cousin's mood.

"How in the h—"

Caroline gives Tarle a look that says, *You better not.*

"How in the world can you rattle the names of my children off with such ease? I can't hardly remember half of their names."

The whole family laughs.

James, the oldest, announces, "Yeah, it takes Pa three or four tries to get to the child he wants. He starts calling, 'James, Sarah, Monty... Allen Albert!' By the time he's called out the one he wants, the whole family is standing in front of him."

All the children laugh and elbow one another at James making fun of his father.

Tarle grins at Elzey. "What can I say? They're right."

Elzey has been used to being with large families where he lives near Mr. Gilmore's old home place. Still, his parents, Joshua and Sadie, had him as their only child in their home. For reasons unknown, Sadie was barren. He always wanted brothers and sisters, but since he didn't have any, he is more than grateful to have his cousin's to be family with.

Whether out of the stress of going to find his father or just being happy to be with his cousins, Elzey stands up and yells, "I want a family just like this one someday!"

Everyone stops what they're doing. Caroline looks to Tarle, who nods for her to handle the outburst.

"Why, dear, you *will* someday, and we will all be there with you, eating a big supper with you, your wife, and your children just like this in your home. The Lord knows what you want, and what you need, and he's a good God."

Elzey sits down, a bit embarrassed. "Thank you for being my family. I trust the Good Lord will give me mine one day. In his time."

Tarle slaps Elzey on the back. "That's the spirit, cousin. Now pass the taters," he says as he sticks his tongue out at the children.

They giggle, and Caroline gives Tarle a furrowed brow look, then bursts out laughing.

Elzey whispers to himself, "This is what I want. More than anything else in this world."

All sound around him fades—laughter of children, plates being filled with food, the rattling of wooden eating utensils.

A voice from the forest whispers through the open window behind Elzey, *"You will have it, great grandson. Learn patience and do what is set before you. All in good time."*

Elzey stands and walks to the window to see flowing robes of a fading rainbow wisp through the brush like smoke. "Granny Thankful."

No one at the table says anything to Elzey. They've come to know him as being a little different, which is all right with them. He returns to his seat and a plateful of food—roast venison, sweet potatoes, cob corn, black-eyed peas, and cornbread.

Elzey stares at the small mountain of food. "It don't get no better'n this."

Tarle elbows him. "Ain't that the truth?"

Caroline finishes laying a spread of food on the table fit for a king. She eyes Elzey and says, "Heard you were stayin' the night with us. Good to have you. Always." There's a twinge of strain in her voice. She sets a basket of corn muffins in front of her husband. "Tarle said we need to have a talk after the dishes are done. That right?"

Tarles looks up to Caroline and shakes his head. "Not now, dear, please."

Caroline speaks her piece. "I woke up with a knot in my stomach this morning that won't go away. I know why now. Whatever this is, the Lord's been tryin' to prepare me for it all day." She wipes a tear. "It can't be good."

James rubs his mother's arm. "You all right, Momma?"

"I am, son. Whatever it is, it'll be okay, God's providence not preventin'."

Elzey sits with his hands folded. "Yes 'um. We *do* need to talk." He senses already this might not be the most pleasant of experiences. But he knows Caroline, and that she loves him like a younger brother. That's not his concern. Hurting her in any way is.

Everything is on the table and set.

Caroline sniffs and asks, "We always give our guest the honor of saying the blessing over the meal, so would you like to do that, Elzey?"

Everything stops. A mouse couldn't run across the floor that wouldn't be heard.

Little four-year-old Martha Jane says, "Cousin Elzey, please pray, 'cause you always pray like God is sitting right here with us. And I like that."

Tarle leans over as Elzey considers the request and says, "My little sister, also named Martha, said those very same words to your father at my childhood supper table after he dealt with Dawg Smith. You know what he said?"

"Just talk to the Lord like you're talking to me because he is right here with us."

"How'd you know that?"

"Granny Thankful taught me that a long time ago once when I sat by my mother's grave."

"You are your father's son."

Elzey glares at Tarle with eyes that look to be shooting knives. "Not yet, I ain't."

Tarle squeezes his forearm. "You will come to see that as a compliment one day, trust me."

Elzey relaxes. "One day. Maybe."

Tarle smiles. "Still want to pray?"

The whole family sits waiting.

Little Martha Jane smiles. "Come on, cousin Elzey, talk to Jesus like he's sitting at the table with us. You do it every time you come see us." She bats her eyes, and Elzey's heart melts.

"Just for you, my little dear."

Martha Jane shivers with excitement. Caroline nods and offers her hands, signaling all to take the hands of the persons on each side, and they close their eyes.

And Elzey prays like the Lord is sitting right there with them. Because he is.

CHAPTER 28

TOUGH TALK ABOUT A TOUGH JOURNEY AHEAD

AFTER SUPPER, AUGUST 1, 1886

The most unpleasant of talks is usually followed
by a desire to do the best and right thing.

CAROLINE STANDS AND places her hands on her hips. "I know that Elzey has to go, but I'm sayin' that I don't want *you* to go, Tarleton Wesley Tullos. Something bad is gonna happen after you leave. The Lord has already laid it on my heart. I feel it in my bones, husband."

Tarle pulls Caroline back down into her chair with grace. "Dear, we won't be gone much more than a couple of weeks at the most."

"It's not that I think you'll get hurt or can't handle yourselves on the way. Lord knows, and I do, too, what you did to help Lummy take down the West-Kimbrell Gang. You were almost—"

"That's why I need to go with Elzey, Caroline. I know Lummy, and I can get us there and back, safe and sound. Besides, Elzey hasn't been any farther than Winnfield his entire life. He needs me to go with him."

"So, you're going no matter what?"

Tarle is becoming a bit agitated. "Just what would you do, Caroline, if you had the need to find a father you never knew? You had a good father who was always there for you."

"So did Elzey."

Elzey sits in silence, wringing his hands.

"He did, but this is different, Caroline, and you know it." Tarle huffs and shakes his head.

Caroline whimpers softly. She sits in silence, contemplating the worst, and thinking through the feelings she's had about what she believes will happen after Elzey and Tarle leave.

Tarle wraps his arms around her.

Caroline straightens up and presses out her wrinkled skirt. "All right. I confess. I would do exactly what you're doing, Elzey. But you gotta be a man about this. You must stay sharp and help bring my husband back home, do you understand?"

Elzey looks at Caroline sheepishly. "Yes 'um, I will do my best."

"And Tarle, you don't do anything foolish, take no chances, and stay away from anythin' that hints of trouble. No saloons, no drinkin', no—"

Tarle squeezes her tighter. "I get it, Caroline. We will do the right thing and avoid anything that even smells of trouble. We're goin' straight to Choctaw County by way of Vicksburg, find Uncle Lummy, get the jawing done, and come home, simple as that."

Caroline whispers as she shakes her head. "That still doesn't ease my mind. Somethin's coming, Tarle. I know it in my soul." She looks to the sky and begs, "Please, dear Lord, keep us in your gracious and mighty powerful hand. We need you."

DAWN BREAKS CHILLY over the ridge. Tarle kisses Caroline and hugs her close. She runs her fingers through his hair. She clutches his full mane and pulls it tight away from his head. "You get on back here quick as you can."

Tarle grins at being bossed and loved by a woman he'd give his life for in a heartbeat. "Yes, ma'am, I will."

She hands him a sack. "Here, this ought'a keep you two fed till you reach Vicksburg."

Tarle pitches the sack to Elzey, who says, "Thank you, Caroline, truly. It's much appreciated."

"It'll be much appreciated you bringing my husband home in one piece, Elzey Tullos."

Elzey squints. Any more words would be inappropriate. He smiles and nods.

Caroline pulls her hair back. "I didn't wake the children 'cept James. Thought it'd go better that way."

Tarle grins sadly. "I looked in on them before I came out."

Caroline turns to go back into the house. "Hold on, I forgot something."

James leads their horses from the barn up to the house. He plants his feet. "Pa, you know if I was a little older, I'd be comin' with you."

"I know that, son, and you would be a great help. That's why I need you here. You're in charge. Listen to your mother, but you do what a man needs to do if trouble comes."

"I will, Pa. Ma's worried about something."

"She is, and she's usually right. You stay close to the house and keep your shotgun handy."

"I will, Pa. I'll take care of things."

"I believe you."

James offers his hand. "Uncle Elzey, I hope you find what you're lookin' for. Everybody needs to know his real pa."

Elzey nods. "Thanks, James. Do what your pa says, now. We'll be back in two weeks."

"Yes, sir."

Elzey mounts his horse and says, "You got a good boy there."

Tarle shakes his head. "Nope, I've got a good man there."

Elzey holds the reins tight. "Damn straight, just like his pa."

Caroline walks out onto the porch and hands Tarle a necklace. He knows what it is.

"Your grandmother's cross?"

"You promise me you'll keep it around your neck till you get back?"

Tarle takes off his hat and slips the silver chain over his head. "How's that?"

Caroline nods and hands Elzey two small books. "One is a pocket New Testament. Promise you'll read from it every night when you say your prayers, the both of you."

Elzey and Tarle both nod.

Caroline stomps her foot. "Promise me!"

Tarle and Elzey say at the same time, "We will."

"And Elzey," says Caroline as she straightens her skirt, "I'm askin' as a favor that you write down in the other book what happens every day, so we'll have the story when you get back. You won't have time to write letters. Don't leave anything out, please. I can wade through what the children don't need to hear. Will you do that for me, cousin?"

Elzey tips his hat. "Yes, ma'am, I will."

"Then shoo, the both of ya, before I…." And she goes back into the house.

Tarle prods his horse. "Let's go. The sooner we leave, the sooner we'll get back home."

Elzey whispers, "So, Vicksburg, here we come."

PART III:
MARION

CHAPTER 29

MARION ARRIVES IN WINNFIELD

JUST AFTER NOON, AUGUST 12, 1886

When a beautiful woman can be as dangerous as she is pretty,
you just listen.

RAINY SITS ON the front porch of his gun shop, feet propped up against a post, smoking his pipe. The sun has ducked behind the buildings across the street to cast a shadow long enough to cool Rainy's spot.

A lone rider walks her horse to the hitching post in front of Mills and Son Gun Sales and Repair. She's dressed like a man but with long, silky blonde hair tied in a ponytail. There's no mistaking she's a fine specimen of a woman. The way she dismounts says seasoned rider. The way she speaks says well-educated lady.

She ties the reins to a post, removes her hat, and pushes back her thick, sweaty mane. "I was told you could help me with a gun repair. Is that correct?"

Rainy drops his feet and stands. "You've come to the right place."

"I need some bullets and gun cleaning supplies, too."

"I have everything you need with the best service and prices in town."

"Good. I also need a room, if you can recommend a place."

"Where are you from? Don't believe I've seen you around these parts."

She gives Rainy a look that could scald him. "Kinda nosey, ain't ya?"

Rainy snickers. "Only with people who want my gun services. I make it my business to know who I'm doing business with, you understand."

She walks back around to mount up. "I didn't come here for polite conversation, or be forced to tell my life story just to get a pistol looked at."

Rainy holds up his hands. "No questions, except what I need to know about the guns. Okay?"

She stares long and hard at him. "Good enough."

Rainy opens the door to his shop. "Come on in and rest yourself. You look to have been on the road a few days. I've got some good cool water, and something stronger if you need it."

She walks in, twin pistols swaying on her naturally swinging hips, rifle and short double barrel shotgun in hand, and saddlebags draped across her shoulder. She's long and lean, and except for the scowl on her face, she's pretty as a peach. She could make any man anywhere turn all the way around just to get a better look at her and then back the way he's going when she gives him the evil eye. She lays her weapons on the counter.

Rainy calls Aaron to the front to take down the order, and he goes to the back to get some water and whiskey for his customer.

Aaron grabs a pencil and pad and looks up. "How can I help you, ma'am?"

"First, by not calling me ma'am. That's for old ladies, wives, and whores when you're paying for their services. I ain't none of them."

Aaron doesn't blink, unafraid of her demeanor. He's dealt with too many "rough as a cob" characters to let her disturb him. "Yes, I can see that. May I have your name then? For the ticket, you understand?"

She stares like she's deciding if she's going to hit him but softens a bit and answers, "Marion."

Aaron doesn't look up but asks as he writes, "Just Marion?"

Marion purses her lips and squints. "Marion Tullos is my name."

CHAPTER 30

KIN AIN'T ALWAYS BLOOD

EARLY AFTERNOON, AUGUST 12, 1886

Blood ain't the only thing that makes a family.

RAINY WALKS FROM the back carrying a tray with water glasses, a stone pitcher, and a decanter of whiskey. Marion is looking through the blinds out at the street like she thinks someone might have followed her. Aaron can't help but notice her shapely backside and feminine curves.

Aaron whispers to Rainy, "That's the prettiest woman I ever did see dressed like a man and wearing a gun."

Rainy laughs. "Better put your teeth back together before your tongue rolls out onto the floor, son. That could be quite embarrassing."

Marion turns around with a scowl on her face. "When y'all get through gawkin' at my ass, maybe we can talk about my weapons?"

Rainy snickers at her testiness. "What can I pour you, Marion?"

"Yes, that's my name. Cool water with just a taste of that whiskey will do. It should simmer me down a bit."

"Everything all right outside?"

"Yeah, I thought I saw someone I recognized, but not so. I don't mean to be cranky, but I haven't had the best of lives, and I'm tired. I need to bathe. I got parts that smell worse than that hawg farm I passed coming into town."

Rainy pours and hands her a glass. "Well, hopefully the worst's behind you, and we'll get you to a room and a hot bath soon as we know what your gun needs are."

Marion drops her head. "Well, we'll see about the worst being past me."
She softens. "I think my troubles are just getting started."

As Aaron inspects Marion's guns, Rainy lays his palms flat on the counter
and says, "Did I hear you say your name is Marion Tullos?"

"You did, but I'd rather not have that spread around."

Rainy grins. "I understand. Let's get what your gun needs taken care of,
and if you're up to it, maybe we can talk. I'm pretty sure I know some people
you might be interested in meeting."

Marion drinks half of the contents of her glass. "Really, now who might
that be?"

"Tullos folk... and me."

She turns up the glass and finishes the drink. "You, huh? Interesting."

Rainy relaxes in his chair. "Yes, me, and at least a couple others."

She grins slightly and slides her glass toward Rainy. "And maybe pour a
full round of that fine whiskey this time, if you don't mind?"

"Happy to oblige. Aaron, you mind taking care of Marion's guns?"

"Not at all, Pa, but I need to go to the mercantile next door for a few
things first."

"You go ahead while Marion and I talk."

Aaron takes off his shop apron and puts on his hat. "I won't be long." The
little bells above the door jingle on his way out.

Marion snickers. "You two sure are the polite ones with all your fancy talk."

Rainy grins. "I guess it's that fine classical education I received at the Natchez Children's Home where I grew up. I left there when I was—"

"You grew up where?"

"In the Natchez Children's—"

Marion leans back in her chair. "Well, I'll be a suck-egg mule if I didn't
grow up in Natchez myself, and in that same damned ole orphanage. My sister,
too, God rest her soul. Fever got her."

Rainy asks, "So, you're a Tullos?"

"I am, but not by blood. My pa saved Silas Tullos's life during the Mexi-
can War, but he was killed in the saving. When our ma died soon after, the
good people of Marion County sent us to the orphanage in Natchez because

no one would take us. I was just a young girl and my sister a baby when Ma passed. It was all I could do to keep the hands of that damn preacher who ran the place off of my ass. I feared more for my sister. I kept him away from her, but me, well...."

Rainy whispers, "No need. I get the picture. I'm sure sorry that happened to you, Marion."

Marion shrugs and wipes a tear. She's not as hardened as she seems. There's a heart in there—a good one. It's just covered over with the scars and calluses of hard years. "Long story short, Mister Rainy, I was turned out of the orphanage at sixteen because I was too much trouble and did the only thing I could do for living in Natchez so I could keep a watch on my sister. No way to say this gracefully, but I worked in a local den of iniquity as a whore." She swishes the whiskey around in her glass and won't look up. "I was so very young." She downs the last of her drink and sets her glass down. "But I'm not that anymore."

"That's easy to see. You're a lady if I ever met one." Rainy decides the rest of that story is for another time. "So, you became a Tullos by way of Silas?"

With that, Marion sits up and takes a deep breath. "I took the name of the man who saved me, as did my sister. He treated us like his own children."

"Sounds like the Tulloses I know," he says as he pours Marion another shot of whiskey.

"Uncle Silas, as we called him, came and got us when he found out who and where we were. He felt he owed our pa a debt for saving his life. I'm glad he did. He was no stranger to danger. He even knifed a man to get me out of that whorehouse. He snatched my sister out of the orphanage and took us to Marion County, Mississippi. Long story short, that same damned ole preacher and a voodoo witch he took up with when I was working in Natchez, and the leader of the trio, a carpet-bagging son of a bitch, hatched a plan to burn the Marion County Courthouse to destroy the land deed records. Once that was done, they figured to beat good, unsuspecting people out of their land by buying up deedless property. They made one mistake greater than destroying the records. They burned up my uncle Silas. He was the night watchman. Everyone else in town thought I burned up with him because I took supper to him and sat with him every night. I loved hearing his stories about his running around the countryside with Sam Dale and fighting with General Andrew Jackson at the Battle of New Orleans. He was just eighteen when he was called up to fight the British. And oh how he bragged on my father."

Marion sighs. "He was more like an old grandpa than an uncle, but damn if he didn't take good care of us." She wipes her eyes with a bandana and stiffens up. She takes a small sip of her whiskey and says, "Damn good man, and I gave those who killed him their just rewards." She holds her glass to her lips and suddenly realizes she just confessed a crime to a man she barely knows. Startled, she searches Rainy's eyes.

He grins. "Hmm, it seems like I remember hearing about two women from Mississippi burning down a gambling house in Waterproof, Louisiana, just up the river from Natchez."

Marion swishes her whiskey around in her glass. "Did you now?"

"You happen to know anything about that?"

"Should I now?"

Rainy smiles slightly. "They left that establishment in ashes but not before three persons of the same low character as you described—a carpetbagger, preacher, and a voodoo witch—were all slain, and in the most horrible of ways, I might add."

Marion's eyes sparkle as she betrays a slight grin. "I don't believe I recollect hearing anything about that, Mister Rainy. But I did hear those two women, who just happened to be sisters, eventually went back to Marion County after the oldest one got redemption in the waters of the Mississippi River on the way home."

"That's what I heard. Seems this particular Marion, whom everyone thought also died in the fire, traded one preacher for another in her life decision process."

"Not sure what you mean."

"She took the life of one preacher who deserved to face his maker with one hand and then was led by the hand by another preacher to get redemption when she stepped off into the Mississippi River to get herself dunked into Jesus. How am I doing so far?"

"You're pert near accurate on the story so far. The other two demons got their due as well."

Rainy cleans a smudge from his whiskey glass with his handkerchief. "Baptism. It's a wonderful cure for sin and salve for the soul, don't you think?"

Marion smiles. "You'd be right on both counts. She was made alive by the hand of the Good Lord and has never looked back. Mister Rainy, she wanted to be counted not among the dead any longer, you understand? People said they saw a whole lot of sin, anger, and guilt floatin' down the Mississippi River that day after she came up out of the water."

"I appreciate your cloaked honesty. It is refreshing to speak with someone who can hide meanings in words that clearly reveal them, if you've shared similar experiences."

"I'd just as soon leave what's been said here 'tween us, if you don't mind."

"Good enough. There are parts of a person's past that need to stay buried in the past."

"Yeah. 'Tween those memories and my sister dying a few years later, I just couldn't stay in Marion County any longer. I made a decision."

Rainy tilts his head to one side. "Yeah, what's that?"

"I decided to become a hunter of outlaws."

Rainy leans back. "Really? That's a—"

"Very dangerous job? Yes, I know. But I seem to have a knack for tracking down the wicked and bringing them to justice. I've brought in seven lawbreakers since Waterproof, and all legal, mind you, but I didn't get any bounty on the preacher, voodoo witch, and carpetbagger. Seeing them dead was enough bounty on those three. And I chalk that one up to gettin' experience. And it did border on, well, you know, maybe murder? Hell, there wasn't enough left of them to take back for any reward anyway."

"So, you think you can become a hunter of men? Rather, I guess I should say, a hunt*ress?*"

"I like that. Huntress." Marion gives that a thought for a moment. "There are humans of the female persuasion who need to be brought to justice just like the men, too, you know."

Rainy tilts his head. "You'd be right about that. One of the worst outlaws was a woman from around these parts named Aunt Polly. I'll tell you that story later."

Marion's brow furrows. "Good, and yes, I know I can be a huntress and do well at it." She lays her palms flat on the table to keep from getting riled. She knows Rainy is a good man and one she'll want as a friend. "I'm not sure you're listening, Mister Rainy." She squints and growls just a little. "I came up the Natchez Trace from the Vidalia side and plan to hit the El Camino road to Texas. I can track a human over a Mississippi River gravel bar after a hard rain, hunt a ruffian down in the dead of night, walk straight into hell fire barefoot, and I can take the life of a man, or a woman, without blinking an eye or shedding one damn tear, all the while smiling and standing still and upright on the Devil's smoldering brimstone." Marion straightens her belt and tucks in a loose part of her shirt into the side of her pants. "Yeah, I think I can be a huntress."

Rainy asks, "Got any friends?"

"I don't really spend time with many people. It's better that way for me."

Rainy snickers. "And for them, too, I would imagine." Marion is not amused, but Rainy follows this line of conversation, mostly because it was the same trail he was on for so many years of his life. "How do you manage to do that in this world?"

Marion smiles, revealing her pearly white teeth. "I do just enough wrong to keep the wrong people away."

Rainy nods. "I know another fellow who used to say the same thing."

"Oh, yeah, and who would that be?"

Rainy winks. "Lummy Tullos. Your uncle Silas's blood nephew. You just missed him."

Marion drops her glass. "Do tell? Uncle Silas talked about him all the time, and about how he and his first cousin, Archibald, came to the Mississippi Territory, and how they used to hunt, trap, and make moonshine together. He told me Archibald and his two brothers, Roland and Burrell, all moved up to Choctaw County, and—"

"One in the same. Archibald was Lummy's pa."

Marion stares into her whiskey. "Uncle Silas said he and Archibald went to Natchez years ago when they were young men, and Uncle Silas fought some famous river rat named Mike Fink. Fink was the toughest of all the riverboatmen. They fought until Fink declared the contest a draw, and he gave Uncle Silas his black hat with a red feather in it. Then, he pronounced Uncle Silas the 'Cock of the Walk,' in honor of their fight. He wore that hat proudly until, well…."

"That'd be the same Silas Tullos. Lummy told me those stories. All of them. You'd like Lummy. You're both cut from the same bolt of cloth, seems to me."

"I hope that's a good thing."

Rainy laughs. "It's for damn sure a good thing."

Marion toys with her glass. "I think one more of these will suit me, if you don't mind."

"And your connection to me? Lummy Tullos and I had the same grandmother. We call her Granny Thankful." Rainy pours the last of the whiskey into Marion's glass. "She shows up from time to time when we don't even know that we need her wisdom." He lets that sink in for a moment.

Marion touches the collar on her shirt. "Some old lady once gave me an agate stone when I was walking down by the Mississippi River. She said it would protect me." She pulls a silver necklace from inside her shirt that has a small rainbow colored stone with wavy lines attached with a gold setting. "I guess it's worked so far." She slips it back into her shirt between her breasts and rebuttons the next to the top button, embarrassed. She quickly looks to see if Rainy is peeking at her breasts.

He's not. He's looking straight into her eyes.

Marion tilts her head. "Most men would've tried to sneak a—"

"I'm not most men, Marion."

She stares into his eyes for what seems like an eternity.

Rainy never blinks.

Marion relaxes the strain in her face and smiles like the innocent little girl she once was so many years ago. "That I can see. Then you're a man I can trust."

Rainy nods. "Yes, Marion, I am."

Marion fidgets in her seat.

He swishes his drink around in his glass. "Something you'd like to tell me?"

"I do, and I don't." She stares off into space, traveling into her past. She tells Rainy the story of her hard and unsavory life.

And then Rainy does the same.

CHAPTER 31

BECOMING
KIN

MID-AFTERNOON, AUGUST 12, 1886

Only the best of kin can you trust with your name, and your life.

RAINY STROKES HIS beard. "All right, then. Since we've established that we're kinfolk, let's just say this is your home for now, and you can come and go as you please. You need a safe place to rest from time to time. In fact, just plan to stay with us here in town. We have an extra room, and Mary Jane loves to have house guests. What do you say? We can talk more about your kinfolks tonight after supper."

Marion studies Rainy with a deadpan face. Then, she throws a grin at him with teeth sparkling like the stars. "All right, I'll do it, and it's much appreciated, Un-n-ncle Rainy," she says sweetly with the brightest smile and batting her eyelashes like a schoolgirl who's just been told she's the prettiest girl in class.

"Damn, girl, you're a heartbreaker if there ever was one. You must have a pack of hound dogs trailing behind you all the time."

She snickers. "I don't need a man in my life now or any time in the un-foreseeable future."

"But you do need a bath, Missus Marion, and soon, I might add."

Marion slaps the table. "I ain't had a bath since I left Natchez three weeks ago. Like I told your son, I smell like a wet dog rolling around on a dead possum that's been lying out in the sun for three days. I've got parts and places that even the most desperate and needy men would turn their noses up at if they caught my scent." She laughs herself into tears.

"Mary Jane'll be happy to help you remedy that problem shortly, if you like."

"Yeah, that'd be good. But I do say, smelling like a shithouse sure keeps the jackasses away."

The two laugh, and then enjoy the silence for a moment.

Marion returns to her somber demeanor. "No one's ever offered me the kind of true and holy friendship that you have today, Uncle Rainy. You don't know how much this means to me."

"You are welcome, Marion."

"The Apostle Paul wrote in Corinthians that 'for though you have ten thousand instructors in Christ, yet have ye not many fathers... for in Christ Jesus I have begotten you through the gospel. Wherefore I beseech you, be ye followers of me.'" She ponders her words. "I know you didn't teach me the gospel, and you aren't my father, but your words of wisdom lead me to ask you to become an instructor for me to follow, Uncle Rainy. I need temperament. I need guidance. I need a home to come back to on occasion. I will take you up on your offer."

"That was my hope when I laid it out there for you to consider."

"I've done some bad things, things that needed doing but were pretty bad just the same. After I got my sins washed away by Jesus' saving red blood in the dirty, brown waters of the Mississippi River, I vowed I would do things the right way, even if they are bad things for the right reasons." She scratches her ear. "I do believe I've come a long ways since that day with that preacher on the riverbank."

Rainy places his palms on the table, looking Marion in the eyes. "Put these words of a man I admire greatly deep in your heart, Marion. 'You are not judged by the height you have risen but from the depth you have climbed.' The great Frederick Douglass said that, and you will do well to accept it in your heart like you did Jesus."

Marion smiles. "I will, Uncle Rainy."

Rainy goes to the back and retrieves a jug with a corncob stopper. "This is the real stuff."

Marion automatically lifts her glass to meet Rainy's. He nods for her to offer the toast.

"To Silas Tullos, who fought at the Battle of New Orleans with, by God,

Gen'l Andy Jackson, and at the Battle of San Jacinto with none other than that man for all occasions, Sam Houston."

Rainy touches Marion's glass with a clink. "Here, here!"

"I'm glad I came here."

Rainy smiles. "Me, too, Marion. You may not be a Tullos by blood no more than I'm a Mills, but we certainly are by heart and soul." The Mills comment goes right by her. Rainy grins. That's talk for a more sober time.

Marion downs her shot of moonshine but drops the glass and laughs. "Guess that needs to be all for me." She shakes her head and blinks her eyes. "Whew, I do believe you're trying to get me drunk, Uncle Rainy."

"No, just helping you relax with your new family." Rainy rethinks his Mills comment. "You'll be interested to know that your uncle Silas's grandfather, Captain James Mills, was my great grandfather."

Marion's eyes light up. "So, that's how we're kin, sort of?"

Rainy grins. "Yes, and you'll be pleased to know that Lummy Tullos, who I mentioned earlier and who used to live here in Winn Parish, is my cousin. He just left for parts unknown out west. He needed to get away from his past, you know, war nightmares."

"Uh huh, I think I'd like to meet him." Marion rubs her eyes and blinks. "I think I've had a bit too much to drink. Shouldn't have had all of that alcohol on an empty stomach. Went straight to my head." She wobbles around in her chair.

"You could catch him if you hurry, but I do believe you're in no condition to do that right now. He left a couple of days ago but was stopping off to visit his sister-in-law, Dorcas Hawthorne, who lives up Sikes way."

Marion sits still, blinking her eyes and humming an old church tune.

Rainy starts gathering gun supplies and ammunition and stuffs them into Marion's saddlebags. He scratches his head. "Where is that Aaron?" He starts looking over Marion's guns. "These look to be in pretty good shape. There are a couple of minor adjustments I need to make and a screw or two missing. I should have you fixed up here in a minute."

Marion stares out the front window, lost in her thoughts. Her head is clearing a little.

Rainy breaks the silence. "Oh, yeah, I almost forgot. Lummy's son, Elzey Tullos, and his cousin Tarle left out a few days ago to go find Lummy. They more'n likely passed each other on the ferry crossing at Vicksburg going in opposite directions. Elzey is Lummy's son, you see, but Lummy felt it best that he stay here and be raised by a good family. It was the right decision, even though Elzey questions it and is a bit angry about it."

Marion stands to stretch and has to catch herself, holding onto the back of her chair. "Why do you suppose Lummy left Elzey here instead of taking him back to Missip with him?"

Rainy squints. "Elzey is Lummy's son by his first sweetheart who was a former slave. He married her right and proper. Her name was Susannah. She passed while he was away fighting the war. Lummy didn't think raising Elzey in Choctaw County was the safest and best thing for his son, a half-black, half-white child. He felt it was too dangerous, and with that I fully agree. I saw what it was like in Choctaw County back in those days. It was the right decision."

Marion peers out at the street through the window. "I may stay around for a bit to meet my newfound family and—"

Aaron bursts open the door, gasping for air, wiping the sweat from his forehead with his sleeve. "They took her, Pa."

Marion quickly draws her knife but slips it back into its sheath. "What'n the hell?"

Rainy rushes around the counter. "What, what? Who took who? Who told you–?"

"Tarle's wife Caroline. Madison from the store came riding into town shouting that they stole her right out of her own home, Pa. They threw her on a horse and took her out of town, somebody said to Texas."

"Who took her? Who?"

"Tom Kimbrell."

"Son of a bitch. I should've known."

PART IV:
ELZEY & TARLE

CHAPTER 32

VICKSBURG

6:30 A.M., AUGUST 5, 1886

Feeling like you've been to a place doesn't mean you've ever been there.

THE FERRY PULLS up to the river dock with a jolt. Animals and people let out a gasp.

The captain yells, "Nothing to worry about, folks. Ole Man River sometimes likes to be cantankerous. We'll unload in just a few moments."

The current swings the boat around to face upriver, and the ferry captain gently maneuvers the craft for a side disembarking. Deckhands secure the boat with ropes as the captain keeps it steady.

Elzey wipes the sweat from his brow. "That about took my heart away."

Tarle elbows him as they take the reins of their mounts. "We gotta toughen you up, boy."

"I ain't as easy as I look. I just don't like being out on the water, especially on this big river."

"Put your mind at ease. We only have to cross the Missip one more time on our way back."

Elzey sighs. "Good." They lead their horses onto the dock and toward a livery stable.

ELZEY AND TARLE TAKE Washington Street into Vicksburg, dropping down by where the river used to flow past the Prentiss House Hotel.

Tarle checks the directions Rainy gave him before leaving. "Says here we're supposed to go up Crawford Street."

Elzey slows to gawk at all of the buildings stretching up the hill. "Would you look at that? Now that's a city for sure."

Tarle looks to his right, and then left. "Like a city set upon a hill that can't be hidden." He glances up from his map and spies a sign. He elbows Elzey, who is taking in all the sights of a bustling town. "There it is. Handerson's Café." He speeds up his pace and says, "C'mon, that's the place Rainy told us about, where the lady Annie Fanny he mentioned will be. She owns the place."

Elzey trots up to keep up with Tarle's long strides. "Is that where my mother's brother is? And his wife Jenny?"

"One and the same. And the best food and pie you can put your mouth on in Vicksburg, Missip, guaranteed."

THE LITTLE BELLS jingle above the door of the eatery as Elzey and Tarle remove their hats. Patrons stop eating breakfast to eye the two men who look like two hayseeds straight from the farm. Tarle and Elzey don't notice them as they marvel at the fancy décor inside the café.

Elzey notices several customers glancing and whispering. He whispers to Tarle, "We must look like a couple of sure 'nough Louisiana dirt scratchers. You see the clothes they're wearin' and the way they handle their forks and knives?" He shudders a little and turns to leave. "Maybe we shouldn't have—"

Tarle grabs his arm and burns a stare through Elzey. "That'd be respectable dirt scratchers to them, cousin. And don't you forget it. Remember whose name you wear, boy."

Elzey stiffens up and says proudly, and a little too loudly, "I'm Elzey Tullos, and proud of it."

The patrons snicker but stop to clap their hands when an older lady hobbles up to them.

"You two boys are Tullos men. I can see that in your eyes and the way you stand. Proud. My name's Annie Handerson, owner and proprietor, though that will change soon." She pats her foot and straightens Elzey's coat. "You have the look of a very dear friend of mine who just left here early this morning. We'll talk about that—"

Elzey blurts, "So, *you're* Annie Fanny? The one Rainy Mills told us about?"

Annie looks around at the customers who overheard the comment. "Just a name from another time in history, friends. Ancient history, that is. A round of buttered biscuits for all, on the house."

The patrons nod and smile and return to their eating and conversations.

Annie takes Elzey's hand and leads him to a corner table. "Son, you've not been off the farm very much, have you?"

Tarle sits and leans over to whisper, "Truth is, neither one of us has been anywhere bigger'n Winnfield, Looesana, except when my pa and ma brought our family through here on our way to Winn Parish back in the mid-fifties."

Elzey gently pulls his hand back, but so as not to offend Annie. He tries to smile as she studies him like a menu.

Jenny walks over with coffee and the fixings. "Missus Annie, would you like me to bring these men something to eat?" Jenny eyes Elzey. "Is that him?"

"Can't you tell?"

"I can. He has the build of his father but the looks of his mother, I'm thinkin'."

Annie takes Elzey's hand again. "Elzey, this is your Aunt Jenny. She married your mother's brother, Isaiah, whom we all call Ise."

Elzey is speechless for a moment, but he stands and offers his hand. "So, we're kin?"

She pulls him close for a hug. "Sure are, Elzey, and proud to call you such. Your uncle can't wait to meet you. He's at work and will get home sometime after dark. Missus Annie, the arrangements we discussed earlier, we still good for doin' that?"

Annie nods and says to Elzey and Tarle, "We'll talk about that in a bit." She taps her chin with her index finger. "When did you boys last have a good meal?"

Tarle grins. "Not since we left Winn Parish. We've been eatin' cold ham biscuits since we left, but we've done all right, and—"

Annie looks up at Jenny. "We still cookin' breakfast?"

She smiles. "Yes, ma'am. I can fix them some sausage, grits and eggs, biscuits and gravy, and we have plenty of pies to choose from if they've a mind to have a piece."

Annie turns to Elzey and Tarle. "How's that sound to you boys?"

Elzey licks his lips and elbows Tarle. "Like heaven, Missus Annie." He digs into his coat pocket and produces a small money sack. "We've got money to—"

Annie pushes his hand back. "No, sir, not in this café you don't. Don't want to hear anythin' else about it, you understand?"

Tarle nods. "Mister Rainy—who incident'ly said to tell you hello—told us it would be like this with you. We sure appreciate you having us."

Elzey grins. "Yes, thank you, Missus Annie. You're every good thing Mister Rainy said about you, and so much more."

Annie sits back and smiles. "Why, boy, you are your father's son." She leans forward and chuckles. "Why, Lummy Tullos could charm the bloomers off the tightest butt of any church goin' beauty with just a wink. Thing is, he never tried. He was too much of a damned gentleman for that kind of doin's. No, it was nothin' but the straight and narrow for Lummy Tullos when it came to women." She stares into Elzey's eyes. "And he loved your momma to no end. No end, you hear me? Still pines for her, even after marrying my sweet sister Martha, God rest her soul."

Elzey's eyes soften. "He married your sister?"

"I've known your father for a long time," Annie replies. "We'll talk about my sister later."

Elzey doesn't know what to say, so he asks, "How long have you known my father?"

"Since back in '59 when I patched up his shoulder that got injured when he rode the ferry across over to where Desoto used to be. I lived there with my man Obe back then and was the worst for wear." She adds a bit of honey to her tea that Jenny just brought in. "I loved your father the first time I laid eyes on his good lookin' ass just like Juliet loved Romeo, if you know your Shakespeare."

Tarle sits up. "We do, but—"

Annie sips her tea, and says, "No buts about it except that I was always tryin' to show him mine. And he did see it across the river when he and J.A., whom y'all knew I believe, crossed the river on a raft after Vicksburg surrendered. I was just skin and bones then, starvin' to death, but your father gave the little bit of money he scavenged from dead Union soldiers and some cans of food he and J.A. found along the way." She sips her tea and gently sets her cup down. "Wasn't long after that he found out about your sweet momma's murder." A tear forms in her eye. "It nearly killed him when he found out. If it wasn't for Old Bart helpin' to patch up his heart, I don't know what he'd...." She wipes the tear with a napkin so as not to mess up her eye paint. "And then he took care of business. Lifted that damn Dawg Smith's head right off his murdering body, dammit. I wish I could've been there to—" She stretches out her hands to calm herself.

Elzey drops his head. "That's when he found out about me?"

"Yes, not long after. He told us all about you later on. He was just too beat up and down and out to care for you like he wanted, son." Annie squeezes Elzey's arm. "But he didn't leave without putting you with a wonderful and loving family who raised you, right?"

Elzey nods. His face is red, and though he maintains his anger, Annie sees it.

"Your father didn't leave you on his own accord. I have it on good authority that he was instructed by the Lord himself to leave you with the people who raised you."

Elzey snaps around to Tarle, who says, "You wanted answers, didn't you?"

Elzey turns back to Annie. "I did, but—"

Tarle laughs. "Well, like Missus Annie said, ain't no buts in this conversation. So, get yours out of the way and listen."

Elzey nods. "Who, Missus Annie? Who told you about this?"

"You're too young to remember Old Bart, who I mentioned a minute ago, Elzey, but Tarle, I'm sure you have memories of that sweet old grandpa."

"I do. He worked with us on the farm when I was a kid. But he was killed when—"

Annie reaches over and puts her finger on his lips. "We'll talk about that in a minute."

"Yes 'um."

"Old Bart had a brother who I believe y'all called Old Nate, right, Elzey?"

"Old Nate was my grandpa all the years I was growin' up."

Annie wipes the corner of her mouth with a napkin. "When Old Bart came through to help your father defeat a wicked outlaw in Choctaw County, where you're headed now, he told me that an old seer named Miss Esther received a word from the Lord that your father, Lummy Tullos, was to leave you in Winn Parish with the good people who are now your parents. When a prophetess of the Lord speaks, you listen and obey."

"Why, Missus Annie? Why would the Good Lord do that?"

"Two reasons. First, your father was in no shape, form, or fashion able to care for a young son. Besides, he felt called to finish the war with the Union Army trying to get the twentieth star for Mississippi back on the flag he gave his first allegiance to, the Stars and Stripes."

"Who'd he serve with?"

"The First Mississippi Mounted Rifles in Company C. It was the only white regiment from Mississippi to fight for the Union. Your uncle Ise was in what they called a Colored Regiment. He and your father were actually on the same battlefield one time and saw each other, though they didn't know each other." Annie sips her tea and sets the cup down. "All your father wanted to do was help end the war and make this world a better place. To do that, he was willing to lead the Union cavalry to his own hometown so they could burn the mills that were making military supplies for the Confederacy." She looks around and whispers, "And he took a helluva lot of shit for doin' that."

Elzey hangs on Annie's every word. He asks, "And the second reason?"

"According to Rainy Mill's report, after he fought alongside your father and others to defeat the outlaws terrorizing Choctaw County, it was simply not the place to raise a mixed-blood child. Rainy affirmed what the prophetess Missus Esther had already revealed from the Lord."

Elzey's mouth is open from the shock of receiving so much information in such a short time. He collects himself and says, "I just never knew... no one ever told me...."

Tarle puts his arm around Elzey. "It's all right, cousin. We got time for all of this to soak in."

Annie stands up. "That's all for now. I'm worn to a frazzle. You boys plan to stay upstairs with Ise and Jenny tonight. Jenny'll make a pallet on the floor and make you comfortable. Enjoy your food, rest well, and let's talk more in the morning over a good breakfast."

Elzey stands. "Did I hear you correctly when you said my father passed through here just yesterday?"

Annie glares at Elzey for a moment, then her face relaxes to a gentle smile. "What I *said* was, we'll talk more in the morning. Let what we've spoken on soak in. See you in the morning."

Annie drifts around the room to speak to her customers, and Jenny leaves the table spread with a fine meal and two pieces of pie each. Annie gathers her things and stops at the front door to give a small wave. The bells above the door jingle as she leaves.

Elzey shakes his head. "I don't understand it. I just don't—"

"Didn't I tell you it'd be like this?"

Elzey scoops up a fork full of grits and eggs. "I just didn't know my father was thought of so highly and so loved by so many."

"And we haven't even made it to Choctaw County yet."

CHAPTER 33

FAMILY STORIES NOT OFTEN TOLD

7:30 P.M., AUGUST 5, 1886

Some stories of shame still need to be told
so that they teach what can be overcome.

ELZEY AND TARLE step into Jenny and Ise's home above the café after having walked the streets and seen the sites in Vicksburg. Full from enjoying a fine supper in the café, both are looking for places to sit and let their food settle. The apartment is neat as a pin and smells of flowers. They remove their hats and jackets, hang them on the pegs beside the door, and stand with their hands in their pockets, wondering what they should do next.

Jenny removes her work apron and chuckles. "Y'all have a seat, please." She calls to the children who play in one of the back bedrooms. "Gabriel, Ruth, Bartholomew, and"—Jenny smiles at Elzey—"Susannah. Come in here, please."

Four stair-step children ages four to seven march out like little soldiers ready to obey their commanding officer. Jenny hugs each one as they walk out.

"Children, this is your uncle Elzey and his cousin, Mister Tarle. Say hello."

As children will, they say together, "Hello Uncle Elzey and Mister Tarle."

Without a thought, little Susannah walks over, takes Elzey's hands in hers, and looks deeply into his eyes. "Am I really named after your momma?"

Elzey fights a tear with a grin. "Yes, little dear, you sure are." He side nods to Tarle. "And this is your cousin, Tarle, who knew my momma."

Little Susannah ponders that for a moment. "Where is your momma now, Uncle Elzey?"

Tears well up in his eyes. "Why, she's in heaven with all the other angels, don't you know?"

Susannah grins from ear to ear. "Then she's very happy."

Elzey wipes his eyes and sniffs. "Yes, she is. But how do you know?"

Little Susannah ducks her chin into her chest and smiles. "Because she told me so." She turns to skip over to the other children who are getting ready to hear their mother read a Bible story.

The door swings open, and in walks Ise. "I'm home! Where's my little darlin's?" The children race to him, and he scoops them all up in one great swoop in his sinewy arms.

Jenny wraps her arms around his neck and kisses his cheek.

Ise starts to ask, "What's for supper, dear, I'm so hungry I could—" He sets the children down when he sees Elzey and Tarle. They stand up as he asks Jenny, "This him?"

Jenny grins and nods. "Your big sister's boy, Elzey, and his cousin Tarle Tullos, Lummy's brother Ben's son. You might remember—"

Ise thrusts out his hand to Tarle. "This good man I know. Tarle, it's been too long, old friend." Ise turns to Elzey and looks him over. "And I do remember Elzey, but as a very young boy, and not the man I see before me." He wraps one arm around Elzey as he shakes Tarle's hand. "Good to see you two men. It's such a blessing to have family visit. Annie told us you'd be comin'."

Elzey asks, "Did she say why we came?"

Ise nods. "She did, and you need to know that we understand what you're doin' and why. We'll help you anyway we can."

Elzey shuffles his feet. "There's really just one thing I'd ask of you two, if you're willing."

Ise stretches his back. "Name it, son, and if we can do it, we will."

"I want to know everything you know about my father, from top to bottom, side to side, good and bad, no holding back."

With the children in bed, the four adults talk into the night. Ise tells the story of how the small band of men traveling from Choctaw County to Winn Parish—Lummy, Lieutenant McGurgarty, Rainy Mills, and he—rescued Jenny from evil men bent on deflowering her with great harm, and about the deaths of those ruffians.

Jenny chimes in when he finishes, "But that ain't the only story that needs to be told about what happened back then."

Ise rolls his eyes and fakes a whine. "Oh, not that again, woman." He grins.

Jenny thrusts up her chin and winks at Ise. "You know you love me tellin' that part about you, husband." She presses out her skirt and folds her hands. "Anyway, this man, before he even knew my name or who I was or anythin', fell head over heels in love with me and wasted no time beggin' me to jump the broom with him as soon as he got back from Winn Parish."

Ise wraps his strong arms around Jenny and squeezes gently. "I loved you at first sight and will until the day my eyes close, my princess."

She melts in his arms. "And Lord, what a sight I was. Barely covered up, mind you, runnin' through the woods like a crazy naked woman tryin' to escape them mean ole men."

Ise elbows Tarle. "And that half-naked part? Yeah, I confess before the Lord, I peeked at her beauty and have been steadily admiring that handsome woman ever since."

Jenny swats Ise's shoulder and tries to hide a grin. "Ise Handerson, you devil you, I'll take a switch to your—"

Ise chuckles. "Ain't nary no devil ever been allowed to view the beauty of an angel so pretty as you, Jenny."

She kisses him lightly on the lips. "You old charmer, you. I do love you with all my heart."

Ise smiles. "You, too, dear."

Jenny gets up and goes into another room and returns with a couple of soft mattresses. She spreads them out on the floor and makes beds of light linens. She stands up with her hands on her hips to observe her work. "I threw on just a bit of cover. The heat won't relax for another hour or so. There's a blanket beside each pallet if you get chilled on over into the morning."

Elzey stands to hug his aunt. "Thank you, Aunt Jenny. Tarle and I surely appreciate you and Ise's kindness."

Tarle nods in agreement.

Jenny swats at the air. "Oh, you hush up, nephew. This is what family does for family."

Elzey smiles. "Yes, ma'am, I'm learning that."

"Good, then." She pulls back a strand of hair that got loose and hangs in front of her eyes. "It's close to midnight, boys. We all best get some rest. We all have long days tomorrow. This has been such a blessin', y'all comin' to see us, stayin' with us. Y'all sleep long as you want, but that rowdy pack of hound dog pups will be up and runnin' early. Best get your sleep now, or you'll wish you had later." She waits for Ise.

"Be there in a couple of minutes, dear. A couple more things I want to tell Elzey."

"Not too long, Ise."

He winks. "Yes, ma'am."

Jenny closes the bedroom door behind her, and Ise rubs his chin, thinking about what he will say next.

CHAPTER 34

STORIES THAT NEVER NEED REPEATING

NEAR MIDNIGHT, AUGUST 5, 1886

There are stories that are not often told. And there are stories
that never should be told but have to be. At least once.

"UNCLE ISE, I'M grown. You can tell me all that needs telling." Elzey stares at his uncle with pleading eyes. "Everything you tell me helps me to know who I am."

Ise smiles. "All right, son. Your father was a fierce man, I mean tougher than a post oak and just as straight. Still is. Now don't get me to lyin', your father had his faults, but no one knew those faults better than him, and I've never known anybody so quick to be honest about 'em."

Elzey sits up to the edge of his seat. "Tell me."

"Your father wanted to do things right, be kind to people, fight for the right things, you understand? And he didn't hold back when it came to fightin' for what was right. He grew up with a hard ass father himself, but that taught him that bullies would not be tolerated... that the right word? Yes, tolerated, that's it. He's a gentle giant who was called on to do things other men could not handle doin' and stay sane."

Elzey's eyes widen. "Is he sane?"

Ise purses his lips and squints, then replies, "Yes and no. He still struggles a bit with all the anger, abuse, and violence he had to go through to have just a few years of a good life with Annie's sister, Martha."

"Yeah, Rainy told me about her."

"Then you should know that he was full of love for his family and people in general." Ise scratches his ear. "But if he had to fight, he was like the devil. In fact, he always said, 'If you're gonna defeat the Devil, you have to become one.'"

Tarle leans over. "I saw that in action when we took down John West and his gang."

Elzey turns back to Ise. "So, what's the not so sane part about him?"

"War dreams. They come on him out of the blue from nowhere and jump on his back like a she-bear protectin' her cubs. He's drawn knives, pulled pistols, raised rifles, and drawn up fists to fight enemies that are nowhere to be found."

Elzey hangs his head. "I bet those times happened a lot with family, and when they least expected it."

"That's right, Elzey. But he did those terrible things so others didn't have to, and the Lord told him to do it."

"How'd he know that it was God who—"

"You ever heard anyone talk about Granny Thankful?"

Elzey jumps up and yells, "You know about Granny Thankful?"

Ise puts his finger to his lips. "Shhh, the children. But yes, your father spoke of her, how she has been his guide, with the agate stones, talks in quiet places, and…."

Elzey sits down. "I've been talking with her since I was a kid. Tarle, too."

Tarle smiles. "It's a Tullos thing, I reckon."

Ise nods. "Good, let her guide you, son. She's never led Lummy astray and kept him from losin' his mind. Most men would've either gone insane or put a bullet in their—"

"So, tell me, Uncle Ise, what was the worst of it?"

Ise rubs his chin. "I'll only tell you these things in this way. Short but truthful. Your father had a severe anger problem he got honest from his father, who got it from his, and so on. He couldn't stand bullies but never looked for a fight. He was long-suffering with the worst of human bein's until there was no more rope to let out. So, here goes, and listen closely. Your father picked a man named Kneehigh up over his head and slammed him down on a hardpan street for makin' fun of your father's love for your mother. Crippled that boy for life. Lummy left home to go find your mother when a good man, Mistuh

Gilmore, won her in a card game so he could free her. Your folks married, but only had a couple of months together before Lummy had to go enlist in the Reb Army. He really didn't have a choice. Your father endured the Siege of Vicksburg in those hills just outside of town where he fought in some of the worst battles, nearly died of fever, almost starved to death, and would've been blown sky high had not the Rebs surrendered. Then, he and his best friend, J.A. Killingsworth, whose son Aaron you know, swam the river to go to Winn Parish. There, your father, J.A., and the men of Winn Parish ended the Dawg Smith Gang, but not before your father lifted Dawg's head from his shoulders with a knife his father, Archibald Tullos, your grandfather, made for him.

"After taking down Dawg Smith, he came back to Choctaw County and fought off Kneehigh's friend and cousin, Lester, who was tryin' to rape and kill your grandmother Mary and your girl cousins. They had been enemies since childhood. I'm told they fought like animals until Lummy knocked the whey out of Lester, who fell on his broken sword. It pierced that man's heart. It always broke your father's heart to have to kill someone. So, to stay true to his new oath, he joined the First Mississippi Mounted Rifles. You understand the seriousness of doin' that?"

Elzey whispers, "I'm sure that I don't."

"He took a helluva lot of trouble for tryin' to help end the war. He even helped lead Union cavalry to his own hometown of Bankston so them soldiers could burn the mills there that was makin' war materials for Gen'l Hood's Reb army. When he joined up here in Vicksburg down the street in December of '64, he took an oath not to kill another man and was able to keep that promise through the rest of the war. So, after the war, he came home, married his sweet bride, Martha, and took her from here with Missus Annie to Choctaw County to live the peaceful life he always wanted." Ise sits on the edge of a chair.

He shakes his head. "It wasn't to be had. A Home Guard outlaw named Captain Tom Ford came after Lummy and his family. They killed a young former slave named Seth, who Lummy had taken in and was starting schools for black children. Captain Tom Ford and his bastard gang killed Seth and other black friends Lummy loved and cared for. My mother Sophie, who I never really knew, died during that time. Your father's brother, James, who fell in love with Ruth, your mother's sister, was beaten nearly to death by those outlaws, but survived. They, at least, had a good life together until James died a few years back. Ruth never remarried as far as I know. She lives there in Bankston where you're headed now.

Elzey looks to Tarle. "That is where we're headed, right?"

Tarle nods.

"But before they passed, your father, Rainy Mills, Lieutenant McGugarty, Matt Poole, the nephew of your father's best friend growin' up, and me went to Winn Parish to wipe out the West-Kimbrell Gang, but you know that story already, I'm sure."

"I do."

"So, can you see that your father has given his life to helpin' other people, doin' things other men couldn't so that they could have the very life he always wanted?"

Tarle lays his hand on Elzey's shoulder. "Lummy did break his promise not to kill another man when he shot John West, just so that I wouldn't have to. He was willing to carry the load so other men didn't have to. So they wouldn't have the troubles he's had, the war dreams, the fits of rage, and hours of melancholy. He gave himself up so others could be saved."

Ise smiles. "Sounds like somebody else I know. You can find him in the Good Book."

"I want to know more about those stories."

Ise stands. "Not tonight, and besides, I'm not the one to tell you. But there is someone you must meet when you get to Choctaw County. She will have all the details of all the stories you'll ever want to hear about your father."

"Who's that?"

"Your cousin, Mary, the school teacher."

"Why so?"

"She's writin' a history of the Tullos family from when they came over from Scotland right up to now."

"And all these stories will be in that book?"

"And more."

"The truth?"

"Every detail, down to the worst of it. Lummy wanted no stone left unturned, no truth hidden, and no story sugarcoated."

Elzey looks at Tarle. "We need to see Mary."

Tarle smiles. "We will in just a few days."

Ise stands. "That's all for now. The rest Missus Annie will tell you in the morning, and Mary later." He stretches his back again. "Boys, I'm goin' to bed. Most likely won't see you in the mornin'. I leave way before daylight."

Elzey hugs Ise. "Thank you, Uncle, for taking the time. Can I come back to visit sometime?"

"You come back often as you like, and stay if you want. I'll give you a job and train you to be a carpenter and businessman."

Elzey turns to Tarle, who shrugs and smiles. "I'll give that some serious thought, Uncle Ise."

Ise shakes Tarle's hand. "Good seein' you." He hugs Elzey.

Ise takes Elzey by the shoulders. "Just want one last look at the closest I'll ever come to seein' my sister until I slip through the thin veil to the other side." He studies Elzey and turns to go to his bedroom. "Night, boys. Don't be strangers."

CHAPTER 35

TAKING A FAMILIAR ROAD YET TRAVELED

DAWN, AUGUST 6, 1886

When the coffee's ready to pour into cups, so are stories ready to be told. But if the teller doesn't come, they may just have to wait. For reasons unknown. As of yet.

ELZEY AND TARLE are up before dawn, not because of the children, but more so because that's how they grew up—starting each day getting up with the chickens, as they say. They ease down the stairs and enter the café dining room and find a table in a corner.

Jenny brings out a hearty breakfast and all the coffee Elzey and Tarle can drink. She sits with them for a moment before the regular morning crowd shuffles in.

"I have to apologize for Missus Annie. I guess she got pretty winded yesterday in all of the excitement of you two visitin'. She said to tell you to stop on your way back through and spend the night again. She'll be feelin' better by then and wants to visit with you some more. Missus Annie has been feelin' a bit poorly lately, I'm sad to say."

Elzey looks up. "But I was really counting on hearing more—" He catches himself. "Yes, ma'am, we will. That'll be fine. Please tell Missus Annie how much we appreciate all of this and what we did learn from her so far. Tell her we count her as kin as anybody we know."

Jenny grins. "She'll like that. I'll pass your words along."

Tarle lays his fork down. "Did I hear Missus Annie say that Uncle Lummy came through here a day or so ago?"

Jenny smiles. "He sure did. Left out early yesterday mornin' before y'all came here. You must've seen him passin' by on the ferry goin' to Looseana."

Elzey looks at Tarle. "That was him. Big and tall, longish graying hair, and fiery eyes that could burn a hole right through you?"

Jenny chuckles. "That'd be him, all right."

Ise steps from the kitchen and sits down next to Jenny. She asks if he'd like anything.

"Just coffee, dear. I'm passin' through on my way from one job to the next."

She gets him a mug from the dish table next to the kitchen door, pours him a cup, and sits back down.

Elzey talks with a bit of food in his mouth, "Glad you did, Uncle."

"Just wanted to check with you boys about which way you plan on travelin' to Choctaw County." He blows on his coffee to cool it.

Tarle says, "We were gonna follow the directions Mister Rainy gave us to go to Clinton, up the Natchez Trace, and then cut across to Bankston. From there, he said it's just a couple of miles as the crow flies to the Tullos farm, where...." He pulls out the paper with the map and directions on it. "Yes, here it is, a Jasper Tullos lives? Shouldn't be too hard to get there."

"Good, good, that's good. Jasper is your father's younger brother, the only one left. They fought right here at Vicksburg in the war together."

Elzey stops eating. "What should we do? Go after my father, or go on to Choctaw County?"

Tarle sets his fork down. "First of all, we don't know where he's headed, and this may be the only chance you'll get to see where your father grew up and his brother."

Elzey puts his elbows up on the table and rubs his eyes. "So, we should go see Uncle Jasper, then try and catch my father when we return?"

"I think so, but that's just me. We could send Rainy a telegram sayin' words to that effect, and if Uncle Lummy comes through, he could hold him up until we get back home."

"Yep." Elzey picks up his fork, ready to take another forkful of food. "That sounds reasonable."

Ise smiles. "You two get along better'n almost anybody I know. That's good."

Elzey elbows Tarle. "The best big brother a boy could've ever had."

Tarle snickers. "Who'll whoop yo ass when you start gettin' out of line."

Elzey grins as he forks another piece of ham into his mouth.

Tarle covers his mouth. "Oh, Missus Jenny, I'm so sorry, I forgot we had a lady sittin'—"

Jenny laughs. "Ain't nothin' I ain't never heard growin' up with wicked white men, no offense, and occasionally a certain black man who used to be in the Union Army." She eyes Ise, who grins and gives her a peck on the cheek. "Don't worry, dear, we have plenty of soap in the washroom if you get to cussin' too much."

Tarle laughs. "You sound just like my ma."

Jenny points her finger at him. "And a good woman she is, I'm willin' to bet, even though I don't gamble."

"Yes, ma'am, of the finest sort she is."

Ise gets a serious look. "Keep a sharp eye while you're on the Trace. It ain't used nearly as much as it once was, and sometimes a ruffian or two are known to hide out there waitin' to rob unsuspecting fools. Don't be one of 'em. Keep your guns at the ready and your eyes all about, you understand?"

Elzey nods. "We will, Uncle Ise."

"Good. When you get to Bankston, Elzey, y'all go to the main hotel and ask for Ruth. She's the head cook there for the restaurant inside. She's been there since the war days. And the best part is she's my sister."

Elzey shivers. "I can't wait to meet her. Thanks, Uncle Ise, for everything."

"Stop back by on your way home and stay another night. We'll talk more then, if you want."

"Yes, sir, that'd be good."

"All right, you men be careful, and see you then."

Jenny follows Ise to the kitchen, where he gives Jenny another good morning kiss and goes out the back.

Tarle sips his coffee. "We, above all men, are blessed."

Elzey sets his cup down. "Ain't it so, cousin, ain't it so?"

CHAPTER 36

THE ROAD TO
MORE TRUTH

DUSK, AUGUST 8, 1886

A well-worn path is easy to follow, but still the end is a mystery.

THE ROAD TO Clinton and the Natchez Trace is well-traveled. But the Trace? It's an old well-worn path, often with steep banks. Plenty of perfect places for thieves and criminals to hide.

Elzey looks around constantly. "This road gives me the shudders."

Tarle looks from side to side and behind him every few minutes. "Yeah, I'm gonna be sore as an old hound havin' to get up off the porch to chase a rabbit doin' all this turnin' and lookin'."

Elzey shivers. "You afraid, Tarle?"

"Oh, hell no. Fear gets you nothin' except killed. It's like cottonmouth moccasins. You got to get over bein' afraid of 'em so you can deal with them with a steady frame of mind. Otherwise, you'll get bit for sure."

"You ain't scared of cottonmouths?"

"Not one bit, but I do have an extremely high respect for 'em. Uncle Rainy marked a spot on the map where we can stay the night. He wrote that there might not be much of a structure left, but there'll be good cover to get out of sight and make camp." Tarle squints. "If I'm reading his writing right, Brashear's Stand. Said he stayed there once years ago."

Elzey snaps his head around. "I heard something."

"Aw, you're just spooked talking about snakes and such. Ain't nobody out there."

"No, Tarle, I—"

"Now that you mention it, I've had a funny feeling, too, like somebody's been watching us."

Elzey shudders. "Me, too. And I ain't been able to shake it."

A voice from the pines whispers, *"Be ready, my great grandsons."*

Tarle stops dead in the middle of the road. "Now *that* I heard, Elzey."

"Granny Thankful, right?"

"Yes. We best get on into camp and maybe not have a fire."

"I don't know, maybe we should do the old Indian trick of having a fire but sittin' a ways out from it, and one of us watches while the other sleeps a bit?"

Tarle grins "Good thinkin', cousin. If there's somebody out there, they'll be tryin' us after we're asleep."

THE FIRE SNAPS and pops, sending embers into the night sky like so many lightning bugs. Elzey and Tarle laugh and talk, whiling away the time like they don't have a clue anyone is around. They lay their bed rolls just out of the light of the fire and stuff their blankets with pine limbs to look like they're curled up asleep. They crawl quietly into a thicket thirty feet away with their jackets on to keep the early morning chill away, and their guns primed and ready. They wait.

A cool breeze wisps through the briar thicket. Owls call to each other in the far away darkness. Elzey snores lightly. Tarle dozes, his head bobbing like a fishing cork when a perch nibbles at the bait. The night seems peaceful enough.

A twig snaps, and Tarle sits up, stretching his neck to see the fire embers glowing bright. His head snaps around at the sound of something brushing against leaves on a bush.

Tarle whispers, "Whew! It's only a rabbit."

The cottontail sits at the edge of the camp, firelight dancing in his small eyes. He suddenly stands up on his hind legs, looking in the direction from whence he came. A small twig cracks on the trail Elzey and Tarle followed into where they made camp next to the ruins of a log building that once was Brashear's Stand.

Tarle covers Elzey's mouth as he wakes him. He mouths, "They're comin'."

They ready their shotguns and level them across two old cedar stumps they'll use for cover. Tarle motions for Elzey to cock the two rabbit ears on his double barrel twelve gauge shotgun. Tarle does the same with his ten gauge.

Tarle leans over and whispers, "Watch the rabbit at the edge of camp."

Elzey nods and pulls his pistol and lays it on the log for an easy grasp.

The rabbit darts away in a flash, and footsteps approach, though ever so quietly. Three shadows skulk through the brush, making little sound except heavy plodding. Muffled voices banter back and forth until one deep voice is plainly heard.

The leader of the ruffians whispers, "There ain't but two of 'em. Y'all slit their throats, and I'll get at their belongin's."

Two shadows ease toward where the bedrolls lie, and the third, larger man, starts to pilfer Tarle's and Elzey's saddlebags with an evil, greedy grin.

Elzey whispers, "What're we gonna do, Tarle?"

Tarle turns with the eyes that would scare the horns off of a demon. "Exactly what your father would do. Keep your head down and do what I say."

When the big man throws down the saddlebags, finding nothing of value, he curses lightly to the wind. The other two kneel down beside the bedrolls, and with knives raised, they rip back the blankets, only to find well-placed pine branches that look like men sleeping. The shock on their faces belie the fear in their hearts.

The big man stands with a pistol in hand, searching the brush. He whispers loud enough for the other two to hear. "We've been tricked."

The other two back their way toward him, drawing pistols. They form a circle that rings the glowing embers of the campfire.

Tarle elbows Elzey. "It's on now. Ready? You aim for the big one. I'll cover the other two."

Elzey shivers and nods. A tear rolls down his cheek as he puts a bead on the chest of the big one. He aims and waits.

Tarle takes a deep breath and lets it out, his hands shaking as he grips his shotgun. "Leave now or die, you bastards. There's too many of us."

The big man is silent for a moment but what seems like an eternity. He drops his head and chuckles. The cylinder clicks as it rotates. The big man has cocked his pistol.

"Two is right, boy, and we know you're carryin' somethin' of value. We aim to get it."

Tarle barks, "I ain't askin' twice."

The big man ducks and yells, "Get 'em!"

They rush the thicket like soldiers assaulting a fortified position. Their pistols spout fire, and bullets whiz through the thicket and slam into the log Tarle and Elzey hide behind. Splinters scatter everywhere at once, one catching Tarle in the eye. He brushes it away, still able to see with his one good eye.

Tarle yells, "Shoot, now!" startling Elzey.

Elzey pulls both triggers at once, but his aim is low. The two loads of buck and ball cut the legs out from underneath the big man. He screams in pain.

Tarle stands like a giant and squeezes off two shots, one each into the ruffians who thought they were going to slash his and Elzey's throats. They both crumple like leaves thrown into a fire and fall into a heap one on top of the other.

Tarle says, "Hold still and stay down until the smoke clears."

A gentle breeze pushes the thick smoke on through the forest where Tarle sees Granny Thankful leading it away. He whispers under his breath, "Thank you, Granny."

Moans from the big man bring Tarle back to the bloody scene. He walks to where the outlaw lays, his legs a bloody mess.

"You done took my legs off, boy."

Tarle shows no mercy. "You intended to take our lives, you bastard."

"We just wanted your money, that's all."

"And our blood to get it. We heard you tell your dead friends to slit our damn throats."

The big man tries to get up. "And I would'a skinned your hides off if I'd got the chance. Go on, get it over with."

Tarle grins and points his cocked pistol at the man's head. "No, I think the Good Lord has you where he wants you. You'll be beggin' scraps the rest of your shitty life."

Elzey asks, trembling, "What're we gonna do with him?"

"That depends on him. Go get the horses saddled."

"Why, what're you gonna do?"

"What he planned to do to us, that's all."

"You can't, Tarle. That's revenge."

Tarle turns to Elzey with a glare. "No, cousin, it's called the reckoning."

Quick as a rattler strike, the big man rolls over, sits up, and aims a pocket pistol at Elzey and fires. But not before Tarle shoves Elzey aside and fires a bullet into the big man's head. The ruffian falls back slowly. His last foul breath takes a long time to exhale.

Tarle pulls Elzey back up and shakes him. He pulls Elzey's forehead to his and says quietly, "That's why, cousin."

Elzey hugs Tarle, and when he releases him, he pulls back a hand with blood splattered on it. "Tarle, your shoulder. You've been—"

Tarle sits down hard on the log by the fire. "It looks worse than it is. Hurts like hell, though."

Elzey helps Tarle remove his shirt and doctors the crease burned along his shoulder muscle with a bit of whiskey, then he ties a rag around it. Tarle just stares into space.

Elzey sniffles. "You saved my life. You jumped in front of that bullet for me, Tarle."

"I did."

"Where'd you learn to do that?"

"Do you really have to ask that with all you've heard lately? Ain't you been listenin', boy?"

Elzey drops his head. "That's what my father would've done."

"It is what Uncle Lummy did for other people all of his life."

"And you're a lot like him."

Tarle wraps his hand around the back of Elzey's head and holds it tight. "And that, cousin, is a good thing. A very good thing. Time's right for you to start believing that, too."

Tarle gets up to see about the dead. He just stands there, rubbing his chin, contemplating.

Elzey feels a bit ashamed. He whispers, "Yeah, it is. Time I started to accept who my father really is, not what I made him out to be."

THE SUN PEEKS through trees red as the blood that was spilled. A sunrise is a pretty sight, but the other, the blood, is a necessary sight. Blood can be washed away with the next rain. But the sun? Thank goodness it always brings hope for something better.

Tarle whispers as he mounts, "We go to something better."

Elzey nods. "Yes, we do."

Their horses walk slowly by one grave that holds three men. Elzey piled brush over it, and Tarle lit a fire whose ashes will hopefully discourage scavengers. And hide the fact that they were ever there.

Elzey looks down on the place of the dead. "Lord, forgive those boys. They only—"

Tarle barks, "They only wanted our lives and what little we got. To hell with them bastards. The reckoning requires no mercy, forgiveness, or compassion. Just settin' things right, makin' them equal again. And trying not to have any feeling about it, like killing a copperhead that's about to strike your child."

"But these weren't snakes. They were men."

Tarle stops his horse. "Oh, really. Guess you forgot already how they slithered in amongst us to strike us when we were asleep."

Elzey rubs his neck. "Don't let this make you hard, Tarle. It ain't you to be this way."

"True, but it is when I have to, and only when it's necessary." He limps along on his horse. "I know how Uncle Lummy feels now." He checks the bandage on his shoulder. "I'll be all right here in a bit. No more talk for now, okay?"

Elzey gently prods his mount. "Yeah, sure."

They ride the Trace together, lost in their own thoughts.

Time is not always the only healer. Silence is, too.

CHAPTER 37

BANKSTON AND RUTH

MID-AFTERNOON, AUGUST 12, 1886

Having a big family just increases your chances of bein' happy.

L ITTLE BELLS ABOVE the door jingle as Elzey and Tarle enter the Bankston Hotel. The barkeep throws down the towel he's wiping glasses with and runs to meet them at the door. Tarle opens his arms and grabs a man he went to war with in Winn Parish against the West-Kimbrell Gang.

"Matt Poole, how in the blue blazes are you, old friend?"

He laughs. "Just that, older and crankier my wife says. Who you got with you there?"

Tarle steps to the side so Matt can see Elzey. "This here is Elzey Tullos. Lummy's son."

Matt's jaw drops. "Never had the pleasure of meetin' you, but you wouldn't have to convince me one bit that you are your father's son."

Tarle turns to Elzey. "This is Matt Poole, who came to help us end the reign of terror brought on by the West-Kimbrell Gang. He's a damn fine cook, too."

Matt turns red in the face. "You're too kind, Tarle. We just did what needed doin', that's all."

Elzey whispers, "Seems like that's the kind of good men my father surrounded himself with."

Matt squeezes Elzey's shoulder. "That's right, and a good lesson for any man to learn.'

Tarle continues. "Matt here is also the nephew of your father's best friend,

Tom. They grew up together here in Choctaw County. Tom and your father rode together with the First Mississippi Mounted Rifles we talked about, and Mister Tom gave his life in defense of his home and your father's family when evil men tried to take this county over for their evil purposes. Elzey, your father told me the whole story. He said no better friend could a man ever have had than Tom Poole, God rest his soul."

Elzey nods. "He said that about Aaron's father, J.A., too, didn't he?"

"Uncle Lummy was blessed with the best of men as friends who became his brothers."

Matt grins sadly. "Thank you for that." They stand silent for a moment. Matt laughs. "What'n hell am I thinkin'? Get over there to that table and rest your weary bones. I'll get us a drink."

Tarle and Elzey find a table in a corner and sit.

Elzey rubs his hands together. "I could use something to eat. You?"

Tarle smooths back his hair. "That, and a good bed tonight. Hope there'll be one waiting for us at Uncle Jasper's."

"If he's like everyone else we've met, we'll sleep good and safe tonight."

Matt brings three whiskeys, mumbling to himself. He smiles, sets the drinks on the table, and says, "Be back in a minute."

Matt steps out and holds open the kitchen door. He takes a beautiful black lady's arm in his and escorts her to where Elzey and Tarle sit. They immediately stand to greet her.

Tarle looks at her, and then at Elzey. "That lady is your kin."

Ruth reaches for Elzey. "I'm your momma's sister. Your father often mistook me for her after she passed. He said we look so much alike."

Elzey is speechless.

Ruth smiles and kisses Elzey on the cheek. "I'm the closest you'll come to seein' what your mother looked like, except for maybe in a photograph." She hands Elzey a small picture frame with Susannah's picture inside. "Your father gave this picture to Momma Sophie years ago. She was our mother... Susannah, Ise, and me. And your grandmother."

Elzey holds the small silver case before him and stares like he's trying to bring Susannah back to life. Then, he cries. Ruth wraps her arms around him and sheds tears herself. All sit down together and enjoy the silent presence of each other.

Ruth stands up. "Oh, where are my manners? You boys will want somethin' to eat."

Matt gently seats her again. "You go ahead and visit, Missus Ruth. I'll get your help to bring out the best of what we have."

Ruth smiles up at him. "Thank you, dear."

The next couple of hours are filled with stories told, good food eaten, love expressed between family members, and memories made to carry with a person for the rest of his life.

Elzey and Tarle rise, having eaten more than they should have. Matt shakes both their hands, and Ruth hugs Tarle, and then Elzey.

Ruth pulls Elzey close. "Your father loves you more than he could express. You must know that, son."

"I'm coming to understand just that." Elzey hands her the small case with his mother's picture. "Here, Aunt Ruth, I know you—"

Ruth pushes it back. "Yours to keep now, nephew. A treasure that will sustain you when the dark days come. And you know they will come from time to time."

Elzey kisses her on the cheek. "Yes, ma'am. Thank you."

Tarle turns to Matt. "What's the best way to get to the Tullos farm?"

CHAPTER 38

THE
TULLOS FARM

LATE-AFTERNOON, AUGUST 12, 1886

When it feels like home, even though it's not, you just sit and soak it in.

JASPER TULLOS STANDS at the well, sipping cool water from a dipper. Two riders ease up the road to the old Tullos dogtrot cabin where he's been making a few repairs before his family moves there. They don't look familiar, but harmless enough. He steps up on the porch where his old scattergun lies within reach. He expects no trouble, but still, he's on his guard.

Elzey and Tarle dismount and walk their horses the last fifty yards up to the house.

Tarle whispers, "Let me start this off, Elzey, all right?"

Elzey nods. "That's probably best. I am a little nervous."

Tarle stops short thirty yards out and cups one hand on the side of his mouth. "If I didn't know better, I'd say I'm lookin' at the better lookin' brother of one Benjamin Franklin Tullos!"

Jasper walks up to the edge of the porch. "Then you'd be correct in what you're sayin', young fella. I ain't heard that name called out in many a year. Nor have I seen anybody look so damn ugly as him!" He laughs. "I don't know which one you are, but I know you have to be one of my big brother's sons."

Tarle trots up to shake hands with his father's brother. "Good to see you, Uncle Jasper. I'm Tarleton Wesley Tullos, Ben's oldest. I wasn't very old when we left Choctaw County for Looseana, but I do remember you. You used to play with us in the yard. I go by Tarle now."

"All growed up, and I bet you have a big ole family like your father did,"

"I do. Can't keep 'em fed, and can't keep 'em in clothes!"

Jasper puts his hands on his hips. "Then you are the blessed man." He steps around Tarle and asks, "And who might this good lookin' young man be? He sure favors... no, it can't be. Elzey Burk Tullos?"

Elzey smiles. "Yes, sir, that's me."

Jasper opens his arms and says, "Well, get over here, boy. Let me hug your neck."

Elzey wraps his arms around his uncle and feels like he's in the presence of his father.

Jasper pushes him back but holds on to Elzey's shoulders. "Boy? Better said, a man. You look so much like your mother but have the strength of your father." He wipes a tear. "If you're lookin' for him, you just missed him by a few days."

Tarle says, "We know, Uncle Jasper, but we wanted to come on anyway. It might be the only time Elzey gets to see the family farm, where his father grew up—"

Elzey interrupts to join in. "My uncle Ise sent Rainy Mills a telegram to ask my father to wait in Winnfield till we get back, if he went that way."

Jasper grins. "Good thinkin' because that's exactly what he did. Y'all stayin' a bit?"

Tarle nudges Elzey. "Yes, sir, overnight at least, and maybe one more, if that's all right."

"All right? Damn, son, you're family. You stay as long as you want and let me tell you, you ain't never ate until you sat at my Isabell's table. Why, you'll think you're in heaven."

Elzey licks his lips and elbows Tarle. "Yes, sir, we believe you."

"You'll be interested to know she learned all she knows from your grand-mother, Mary."

Elzey's eyebrows furrow. "Is she still—?"

"No, son, I'm sorry to say, she passed through the thin veil. She's asleep with the rest of the Tulloses buried up on that hill yonder."

Elzey shakes his head. "I'm sorry, I didn't mean no harm."

Jasper spits. "Son, you're worryin' too much. You're home. This is Tullos land, and you're a Tullos. Just be yourself and that here, you belong as much as any other Tullos family member."

Tarle kicks dirt on Elzey's shoes. "Told you, didn't I?"

Elzey straightens up. "Yes, you did."

Jasper sits back down in his father's old rocking chair and says, "Get them saddles off'n them nags and get up on this porch and sit a spell. We got lots of catchin' up to do."

Elzey and Tarle lead their horses to the barn, give them some water and grain, and brush them down. They amble on up to the house, where Jasper has three tin cups waiting.

Tarle smiles. "Is that what I think it is?"

Jasper holds a cup each over half full. "If you're thinking Wood brothers' moonshine whiskey made from the sweet waters of Aaron Wood's Spring, you'd be right. Pull up a straight back chair and let me do a bit of jawin' first."

Elzey sips the liquid that sets his tongue on fire. He rolls it around in his mouth and finally downs it, smacking his lips like they're trying to stick together. He shakes his head. "Dang, that's liquid fire!"

Jasper laughs as he takes another long sip. "Burn the hair right off of your tongue."

Tarle laughs as he struggles with the stout drink. "Ain't got a hair on my tongue to burn off."

Jasper slaps his knee and laughs. "You for damn sure don't now!"

They laugh until a gray-haired lady, pretty as a peach, strolls around the corner of the cabin.

"I heard that, you old buzzard, and you best quit all that cussin'. You'll get lye soap gravy on your biscuits tonight if you keep on."

Elzey and Tarle stand, cringing.

Isabell gives them a stern look, then covers her mouth as she bursts out laughing.

Tarle steps down off the porch and hugs her. "Aunt Issy, so good to see you and hear that laugh again. Never heard one like it since I left Choctaw County—except from my ma."

Elzey winks at Jasper. "I like her already." He steps to the edge of the porch.

Jasper stands and straightens his jacket. "Missus Isabell Tullos, I'd like to introduce Mistuh Elzey Burk Tullos to you, all the way from Winn Parish, Looseana, no less."

Isabell sits down on the porch steps, almost as if she'll faint. She looks up at Elzey. "Child, I thought I was seein' Lummy when you get out in the sunlight." She stands and opens her arms. "We thought we'd never get to meet you, nephew. Proud you came to see—" She turns to Jasper.

"Elzey already knows Lummy left a few days ago. They hope to catch up with him in Winnfield when they go back."

Elzey slowly steps down to let Isabell wrap him in her arms. The look on his face says that he feels so loved. "Thank you, Aunt Issy. I'm so glad we came to see you. Missus Annie and my uncle Ise said to tell y'all hello."

Isabell releases him. "Y'all stayin' for a while?"

Tarle answers, "We'll stay tonight and tomorrow night, but we'll leave out the next morning. We hope to catch up with Uncle Lummy before he leaves Winn Parish."

"Glad to have the both of you."

Elzey offers, "We can sleep in the barn, if need be. We don't mind—"

Isabell smiles. "Nothin' doin', nephew. Tonight you sleep in the bed your father grew up sleepin' on." She wipes tears with a handkerchief. "I've got so many questions, as I'm sure y'all do. Tarle, how's Dorcas? Oh, you'll have to tell me all about your lives in Looseana and...."

They all talk into the small hours of the night until not long before the rooster crows.

CHAPTER 39

CHASTISEMENT, THE GREAT CORRECTOR

DAWN, AUGUST 13, 1886

A brief chastisement can correct a lifetime of wrong thinking.

FIRST LIGHT BREAKS through the pines to trim off a slight, damp chill. Elzey sips his coffee, feeling at home as much as anywhere he's ever been. He watches little birds peck around in the protection of a patch of briars in front of the dogtrot.

"Uncle Jasper, when I crossed the county line coming here, something just felt right. The hills and hollows, trees and creeks, the smells and sounds. They speak to me, like I'm supposed to be here. Like I've always been here. Am I crazy?"

Jasper squeezes his shoulder and chuckles. "Yes, probably, but you're in good company. You're a Tullos, Elzey, and Tulloses are part of the land from which we all sprung, whether here, back in Scotland where we came from, Virginia and North Carolina where your great grandpas lived before comin' to the Missip Territory, or here in Choctaw County, where I was born. No matter, it's in your blood, son, and there ain't no denying it."

"What's that patch of briars still doing there? Shouldn't they be cut down?"

Jasper stares into the small thicket. "That represents the best of who your father is."

Elzey sits up. "And what is that?"

"That some things need to remain wild and not changed. That people ought to be left who Creator made them to be, not what someone else says they ought'a be. You understand?"

Elzey nods. "I do."

Jasper shakes his head. "Really? Well, it took me quite a while to understand your father. His church is the forest and hills, his chorus the birds and squirrels, and his teacher is Creator. He loves all people, speaks with haints on occasion, and sees the universe in an agate stone. He talks to God like you're talkin' to me. And he picked up a bad habit of talking out loud when he doesn't know he's doin' it." He stares up to the cemetery on the hill. "I miss that boy already. But if the Good Book and Granny Thankful are correct, hell, I'll see him again."

Elzey snickers. "Sounds like they should make my father a saint and paint his picture in a Catholic church somewhere."

Jasper turns and squints. "In some ways, that's exactly what they should do, son. You don't know your father. What he's done to save, protect, and help other people have lives like he always wanted is nothing short of commendable. And the cost has been heavy. That's why he left here. That's why he left you in Winn Parish, son." He scratches at the varnish on the rocking chair arm. His nails are filled with residue.

"It's kinda like the arm on this chair. Lummy put a coat of varnish on this old rocker to bring the wood back to life. Some people do the right opposite. They coat a person with what they put on them to be, rather than scratchin' the surface to see what's really underneath." Jasper stares into Elzey's eyes. "You followin' me, boy?"

"Yes, sir, and I'm feelin' a bit ashamed about how I've been so angry at him all these years. I'm sorry. Now I just want to get to know him, even if I can't always be with him."

"That's the spirit, son. Your father did the same thing with our pa, who, truth be told, was pretty hard on us boys. Your father overcame the hurt and anger he had from the violence and abuse your grandpa Archibald heaped on us. They set things right between 'em before our father died, though. That was a good thing. You will do well to consider doin' the same thing. You only have one father, and despite what you think, he always... *always*, wanted the best for you."

"I'm coming to understand that, Uncle Jasper. What should I do next?"

"You've got an hour or so before Isabell sets breakfast. Go up on that hill there and—"

Elzey stands up. "You mean, up to the cemetery?"

"There are people up there you need to meet and visit with. Your family. I marked every grave with a little sign with each person's name and years lived on this earth."

"What do I do? What do I say?"

"Just be yourself and let it come to you."

Elzey steps out to the porch edge and stares at the hill where his family is buried. "In the dark?"

Jasper snickers. "Ain't no better time. Now go on, git. You got folks waitin' on you."

"Walk me up there, Uncle Jasper?"

"Just to the edge, son."

Jasper leads Elzey up the hill and stands. He breathes deeply of the pungent pine fragrance that graces the hills, hollows, and bottoms that make up the Tullos farm. He turns to scan the place where he grew up.

He smiles at Elzey. "I'll leave you to it, son. Take your time. These are your people as much as they are mine. They know you as well as anybody. No need to be afraid. Though living on the other side of the thin veil, they love you." Jasper scans the small cemetery. "Be waitin' down at the house for you."

CHAPTER 40

WHEN GRAVESTONES SPEAK MORE THAN MEMORIES

NOT LONG AFTER DAYLIGHT, AUGUST 13, 1886

Gravestones never tell the whole story. But if you listen, they may speak a word you've never heard.

ELZEY STEPS INTO the small cemetery like a young deer that's never been in an open field before. An owl swoops down and knocks his hat off. He's shaken but laughs it off.

"I should'a took my hat off before I walked in."

The owl gives a comforting hoot, sitting in a tall pine above his head.

A strong feeling of respect overcomes Elzey's soul. He falls to the ground prostrate like he's in the presence of the Lord. He shakes his head, having never experienced that before. He rolls over to sit up and, without thinking, removes his shoes.

A voice breezes through the cemetery. *"You certainlty are your father's son, great grandson."*

"Granny Thankful?"

"You already know that in your heart, but it's your soul that needs cleansing. Come to know your people, now, in this place."

Elzey stands and, with daylight growing, he stops to examine each grave, calling each person by name, reading the birth and death dates aloud.

He drops to his knees. "Why didn't I get the chance to know all of these people, Granny Thankful? Why didn't I get to grow up here?"

"For now, just savor memories that you never had but are yours. You must find your own peace about such things."

"I don't know how."

"Because you are your father's son, I give you this."

On the ground, an agate stone glows like a bright ember.

Elzey picks it up and marvels at the wavy lines and rainbow of colors. He holds it up to catch more light. "It's beautiful."

Granny smiles. *"As are you, my great grandson, as are you."* She fades into the pine forest, wrapped in a rainbow of flowing robes.

Elzey looks back down at the stone. "The mysteries of the entire universe sit in the palm of my hand."

"No, son, not all, but that you may be in awe of its greatness and humbled by its vastness."

Elzey turns. "Momma?"

Susannah strolls from the woods to stand before her son. *"My son, whom I've never met, but who I have always known. You are the best of your father and me."*

"I'm so thankful, I... I don't know what to say or do."

Susannah's eyes flash blue flames. *"I do. Live the best parts of both your father and me."*

Elzey stands and is stretched upward like he's being pulled into the air.

Susannah speaks in a commanding voice. *"Allow Creator to cleanse your heart, so that your mind thinks correctly and your body does what's right. Then, your soul may have peace."*

Elzey collapses on the ground. He gets up on all fours, agate still in hand, and cries his heart out, confessing all the anger, hate, and evil thoughts he's had about his father since he was a child. When no more tears are to be had, he stands to find a bright ray of sunshine bearing down on him, warming his body.

He looks down at the agate in his hand and says, "All right, then."

ELZEY WALTZES DOWN the path back to the dogtrot with a heart cleansed and lifted. He whistles a tune he's known since he can remember. "Oh, Susanna!" He's never been this happy, or more sure of who he is.

Elzey stops before entering the clearing where his father's childhood home sits. He scans the farm called Tullos land. He looks to the sky and closes his eyes. "Thank you, Creator."

Elzey eats a couple of ham biscuits with Tarle that Jasper brought from home, washes it down with coffee, and wanders around the farm, stopping to savor memories he never had but are his. He rubs the bark of a great old oak down by Phoenix Creek that has a rotting straight back chair leaning against it. A name is carved on a leg. Archibald Tullos. "Grandfather."

He sits down on the ground, hard, for a thousand memories flood his heart, mind, and soul that overcome his body—a place called Scotland and a ship on the ocean, a cobbler's shop and a new road being built into the wilderness of Virginia, a tract of land and a gristmill turning in North Carolina, a black stone instead of a white one in a Georgia land lottery, wagons west to the Mississippi Territory, a fight between his great grandfather Willoughby and a great uncle named Silas who was a stout young man wading the cypress swamps on a battlefield near a place called New Orleans, three brothers driving three wagons rolling north for new land led by Grandfather Archibald, a new cabin raised and a family celebration—

"That's enough for now, great grandson. More will come when you are ready. These are given simply to make you crave more."

"But these are not my memories, Granny, I—"

The force of Granny Thankful's voice knocks him to the ground. *"As long as you have Tullos blood running through your veins, great grandson, they are your memories. Claim them. Let them say who you are. You must know where you've been, to know who you are, to know where you are going."*

"I'm a part of all those memories?"

"You have a thousand ancestors following you, waiting to see where you will go, to witness your deeds, to support you, protect you, and be with you. No one ever walks alone. Not even you, Elzey Burk Tullos. The sooner you learn this, the quicker you accept this, the more you will be at peace, and in turn, bring peace to others. It starts here." Granny Thankful turns, smiling. *"In fact, it comes for you now, great grandson."* She fades into the great old oak, but not before a twinkle of rainbow flashes like a sparkling star.

The sound of a wagon and a carriage coming down the road breaks his trance. The agate in his hand glows, and the feeling of a warm blanket on a frosty night envelopes him.

In this place, at this time, Elzey feels the love of his father.

And he has yet to meet him.

CHAPTER 41

A SURPRISE PARTY THAT LEAVES NO SURPRISES

NEAR NOON, AUGUST 13, 1886

Family is family, whether you've met them or not.
But it's good when you do.

A DUST CLOUD kicks up at the end of the road leading to the cabin. A wagon with one driver and a carriage full of people roll up to the dogtrot. It's the rest of the family come to see their cousin. And a young man unloads three hogshead barrels and sets them on the porch.

Elzey trots up to the old dogtrot cabin, hearing noisy laughter and chattering conversation. Jasper pays the man who drove in the wagon. He starts to leave, but Jasper waves for him to join the festivities.

Elzey rounds a cabin corner to see a small crowd of women and children, young and old. They all stop. One by one, smiles break across faces, eyes squint, and suddenly the silence ends with a blast of greetings, hugs, backslaps, and cheek kisses. Elzey is surrounded by the family he always wanted to know. And they make sure he knows he is welcome and wanted.

Elzey asks, "What is all of this?"

Tarle wraps his arm around Elzey. "It's a surprise party just for you."

"I ain't never been to a surprise party before."

"Well, this one is in your honor, cousin."

Jasper hands Elzey a tin cup with just a splash of Wood brothers' moonshine whiskey and announces to the small crowd, "Y'all all know John Wood's son, Wesley. Wesley, these are my two nephews, Tarle and Elzey Tullos, from Winn Parish, Louisiana. Tarle is my older brother Ben's son, and Elzey is Lummy's son. You know Lummy."

"Yes, sir, I do. My daddy and his brother Henry fought the wicked Captain Tom Ford with Lummy and y'all back in the day."

Jasper smiles. "That's right, and we'd be pleased if you'd stay, but we'll speak no more of that today. Today we celebrate a family member who has come a long way just to be with us."

Everyone stops talking and lifts their cups—adults whiskey and the children milk or water.

Jasper looks to the sky and closes his eyes. "To Susannah, who gave birth to such a fine man we know as Elzey Burk Tullos. To a father who loves him more than can be said. To the Tullos family who opened loving arms to him. To Creator, who walks with each of us from before we're born until we walk with him through the thin veil into heaven. To the hills from whence Tullos folk sprung, from the blue painted Picts who once danced naked around fires in the forests of Scotland to the simple farmers who live meaningful lives right here."

A few in the small crowd snicker.

Jasper grins and winks. "To good friends like the Wood family, who have always been faithful. To Ben and Dorcas for raising up this fine man, Tarle, who we have with us today. And lastly, to Elzey, the best of what the Tullos family has to offer to this world. May he never forget whose name he wears, and that he may wear it proudly. To Elzey!"

Everyone claps, cheers, or whistles.

Tarle raises Elzey's hand. "Here, here! Hurrah for Elzey Burk Tullos!"

Introductions are made all around as the ladies set the table for the celebration feast.

Tarle puts his arm around Elzey and scans the crowd. "This is one of the best days I've had in a long time. I'm happy for you, cousin."

Wesley Wood strides over and offers his hand and firm shake to Tarle and Elzey. "Glad to know you men. My father, John, speaks highly of both of your fathers." He squints as he releases Elzey's hand. "For some reason, I do believe we will have a closer association." He shakes his head like he's trying to get water out of his ears. He stops and cocks his head. "Soon. It will happen soon." He strides off as long-legged as he came over.

Tarle grins. "Interesting man. I'd like to get to know him better."

"According to him, you will directly." Elzey tries to laugh, but tears fill his eyes. "You told me, Tarle. You said it'd be this way. I have to confess, I didn't believe you." He wipes his eyes. "After all this, I have no hard feelings toward my father anymore. He is what Creator made him to be, and did what he had to do to please the Master."

Tarle laughs. "I do believe I can declare this mission accomplished. Agreed?"

Elzey grins from ear to ear. "Damn straight, it is."

Tarle hands him a cup with a little moonshine sparkling like stars at night. "Then let's enjoy the feast and festival."

Elzey sees Susannah waving up on Tullos Cemetery Hill. He waves big with an equally big smile. Granny Thankful joins Susannah and nods. They fade into the pines from whence they came.

Mary the school teacher eases up beside Elzey. "Hello, cousin, mind if we talk? I have stories you will want to know."

"You're the one writing the book, right?"

"Yes. I've collected every story I can that's related to the Tullos family I can find and will have the book, or several books maybe, published for others to read."

"I want to know all the history of my family."

"You will, but now I want to hear yours first."

"Why?"

"So I can include you in my book."

CHAPTER 42

NEWS OF
TERROR

LATE AFTERNOON, AUGUST 13, 1886

When a rider races down the road like the Devil himself,
you can bet Satan is probably in the message somehow.

T HE LADIES HAVE put away the remaining food. The children are getting their last hour of playtime before they're herded into the dogtrot hall for wash tub baths before bedtime. Jasper and Tarle laze back in their chairs on the porch, chewing the fat. Mary, Delaware, and Rosetta surround Elzey, buzzing like honeybees with their talk. Elzey is in heaven with his cousin and half sisters. The sun has set to slowly drift toward the horizon to end a day never to be forgotten. But it's not over. Not yet.

A rider comes barreling down the road to the Tullos farm like Satan himself, kicking up clods high into the air.

Jasper leans up in his rocker to shade his eyes from the sun to gaze down the road. "Who's that ridin' up like his head's on fire and his ass is catchin'?" He shakes his head. "Damn, I've seen this happen before. It ain't never good, whatever it is."

Tarle asks, "What do you mean?"

"The last time a rider came down the road like this, your father was ordered to go to Winn Parish after that bastard John West and his gang." Jasper grabs his scattergun and leans it against a porch post within reach. "Kids, y'all get on in the house with the grandkids. Ladies, you, too, please. Hurry up."

Tarle calls Elzey in a loud whisper so as not to frighten the ladies. "Get your pistol, hide it behind your back ready to fire, and step up to the edge of the porch with Uncle Jasper and me."

Elzey whispers, "Ladies, you will want to step inside, please."

Mary, Delaware, and Rosetta gather their things and walk into the kitchen side of the dogtrot. Mary steadily writes as she takes tiny steps.

Elzey, in a tone like Mary heard come from Lummy's mouth on occasion, gently asks, "Please move a little faster, cousin."

She nods and quickens her step.

The rider stops within fifty yards.

Jasper breathes a sigh. "Relax, boys, it's just Matt Poole." He calls, "Matt, come on in. You might find some leftovers from the party we had for—"

Matt says nothing but turns and slides off his mount and strides right up to Tarle like he's going to hit him. Matt hands him a telegram.

Tarle smiles. "What's this, Matt?"

"I'm sorry, Tarle. So very sorry, brother."

Tarle quickly reads the message written.

> *Come quick. Tom Kimbrell took Caroline to Texas.*
> *Must go after her. Bring Matt and Ise. Make haste.*
> *Rainy Mills.*

Tarle wads up the message into a ball and throws it. He screams at the top of his lungs. He drops to his knees and starts pulling at his hair.

Elzey rushes to him and holds his hands. Everyone comes running.

Tarle stops pulling at his mane and screaming, then calms himself and stands up.

Elzey picks up the message and reads it out loud. He covers his mouth and grabs Tarle.

Tarle has the look of his father's rage but the fierce stance of his uncle Lummy. "I should'a cut that bastard's heart out."

Elzey shakes Tarle. "And we will do just that when we catch up to him."

Jasper tells his sons, "Get their horses saddled and ready. Tie two sacks of grain to each."

They nod and run to the barn.

Jasper takes the telegram from Elzey's hand and rereads it. "I didn't mention this to you boys, but Elzey, your father received a threatening telegram, marked only T.K., just before he left. I should've told you, but I didn't want to ruin the happy time we're having." He looks down at the note and shakes his head. "The sins of the father are often visited upon the soul of the son, though in this case, a nephew. Mister Tom Kimbrell doesn't read his Bible where it says in Ezekiel that a son is no longer responsible for his father's, or his uncle's, sins."

Tarle growls, "I was there with Uncle Lummy when he blew John West's head off. I wish I'd done the same to that pissant sister boy Tom Kimbrell." He breathes rapidly. "I'll get my Caroline back, and I'll kill him."

Jasper squeezes Tarle's shoulder. "This will be made right. You will get your wife back. You will survive this."

Elzey collects their things and grabs their guns.

Isabell walks out with a sack of food. "This ought'a get you to Vicksburg."

Elzey takes the sack. "Thank you, Aunt Isabell."

The boys walk the horses from the barn up to the dogtrot.

Jasper takes Tarle and Elzey by the shoulders. All gather round and lay hands on them or on a person touching them. "Lord, I ain't Lummy, but I'm callin' on the same power you gave him to survive Vicksburg, defeat Dawg Smith, put Lester away, give Captain Tom Ford his due, and destroy the West-Kimbrell Gang. Keep these two men, who we love dearly, safe, and return Tarle's wife back to his lovin' arms. You can do it, God, and...." He opens his eyes and shakes Tarle and Elzey to open theirs. They look into Jasper's eyes as he prays, "And do not let them lose their souls in what they're about to do. Amen." He pulls them close as the others move closer, then pushes them back and says, "Get goin'." He hands Mary the telegram.

Tarle and Elzey mount up and pull down their hats.

Mary hands Elzey a little book and some pencils. "Write down everything you witness, Elzey. Everything."

"But I—"

"Write when you can. Do it for the family. Mail it to me when you're done."

Elzey sucks in a deep breath. "All right, cousin, consider it done."

Jasper warns, "Just go at a steady pace. Not too fast, not too slow, and you can pretty much ride until you get there. Stop for water, but don't give 'em too much, and feed 'em a little grain as you go along, then you won't have to stop. Rest 'em in the shade for at least an hour. Take turns catching a nap. You can make it in two and a half days, if you're careful. Don't run your horses to death. It'll only make the trip longer."

Tarle tips his hat. "Yes, sir."

Matt steps up. "Go straight to Annie's. I'll send a telegram letting her know you're comin'. Take your horses across on the ferry, but catch the train to… wait, what the hell am I saying? I'm comin' with you—"

Tarle softens a little. "No, Matt, you don't have to—"

Though not an imposing man, Matt's temper flares. "I ain't asking, Tarle. It's what Lummy and Poole did for each other, and it's sure as hell gonna be what we do together, too. We know how to do this, you and me. I'm comin'."

Tarle nods. "I feel stronger already with a Poole at my side."

Wesley Wood strides up like a man headed to help put out a fire. "Count me in."

Tarle turns to Wesley. "I've heard about the Wood boys. The sayin' goes that y'all ain't scared. Is that true?"

Wesley trots to his wagon. "You're 'bout to find out. Ask your uncle Jasper. He knows."

Jasper nods. "You will do well to have a Wood boy along with you. They're somethin' fierce. And after bein' with Lummy, I know fierce."

Tarle cups his hands to yell, "All right, Wesley."

Mary walks up to Tarle and Elzey. "I'll go with Matt back to Bankston and send Annie the telegram so you boys can get going." She takes Elzey's hand, and then Tarle's. "It's been a pleasure, cousins. I look forward to our next meeting."

They nod.

Jasper's sons bring another saddled horse for Mary. She and Matt turn to head down the road.

Matt pulls up beside Tarle as Wesley draws up his wagon. "Wesley and I'll meet you in French Camp on the Trace. It's a good place to water and rest your horses for a bit."

Tarle growls, "Matt, you know I can't wait. It'll take you—"

Matt grins. "I think me and Wesley know our own county pretty well, every deer path and rabbit trail shortcut there is. Truth is, Tarle Tullos, we'll be waiting on you." He reaches to shake Tarle's hand. "See you there." He nods at Wesley, who pops the reins on the mule's backs and takes his wagon down the road at a trot. He turns to Mary, "Let's go." They cut across the farm to a trail that will shave off time getting to Bankston.

Mary waves as they disappear down a bank that leads into the woods by Phoenix Creek.

Isabell cries and pats Tarle and Elzey on their knees. "Y'all come back, you hear?"

Elzey tips his hat. "Yes, ma'am, we will." He scans his father's childhood home for the last time and announces, "My only regret is that I didn't have time to get to know you all better."

Jasper walks up and puts his hand on Elzey's arm. "Then you'll just have to come back, won't you?"

"Yes, sir. That I hope to do."

Tarle looks at Elzey with the fiery eyes of a demon and a crooked smile that says he's dead set on what has to happen next. "Let's go, cousin."

Elzey prods his mount. "Lead on, cousin."

CHAPTER 43

VICKSBURG, AGAIN, BUT ONLY FOR A MOMENT

MIDNIGHT, AUGUST 15, 1886

Travelin' fast means you gotta run hard and think quick, all at the same time.

TARLE, ELZEY, MATT, and Wesley rein up their mounts in front of Handerson's Café. Riding night and day as Jasper instructed, they make Vicksburg a bit sooner than they'd planned. Men and horses are exhausted but arriving in the right place to get refreshed before taking off on the next leg of their journey.

Ise sits in a chair on the porch in front of the café, sharpening the short sword he once carried in the war. "You men made good time. Tie off your mounts and come inside. There's food and hot coffee waitin'." He opens the door for them, the little bells above the door jingling.

Tarle notices Ise is dressed differently than when they came through a few days ago. And he has a pistol strapped to his side.

Jenny is dozing in a chair. She's startled by the door closing and jumps up to hug Tarle. "I'm so sorry, cousin, I don't know what to… I'll get you men something to eat." She races to the kitchen and is back with hot coffee and a sweet cake each. She doesn't want to miss a bit of the story. "Ise," she asks, "you want somethin', honey?"

"Just coffee, dear." The four riders fall into their seats.

Jenny smiles weakly. "That'll revive you good men for the moment. I'll get you some real food here in just a bit." She shakes Matt's hand. "Good to see you again, Mister Poole."

Matt slumps. "Just wish it was in happier circumstances, Missus Jenny."

"Me, too." Before she sits, she kisses Elzey gently on the cheek. "You all right, nephew?"

He kisses her back. "Yes, ma'am, I'm good. We're all just worn out." Elzey blows on his coffee before he sips it.

Ise sits and picks up his coffee and pours it into a saucer to cool. "You made good time, and I have to say, your horses don't look too bad." He's giving Tarle time to drink a bit of coffee and take a few bites before he starts asking questions.

Annie hobbles in, wearing a nightgown wrapped in a blanket, not looking well. She sits and nods, then starts a cough she can hardly get stopped, even with several drinks of water. Jenny brings her a steaming concoction of whiskey and lemon. She sips it, and her cough dies down.

Annie smiles faintly. "I ain't doin' very well, boys. But I'm glad to see you."

Tarle says nothing. He just focuses on eating his sweet cake and sipping his coffee.

Elzey says, "Yes, ma'am, you, too. Sorry you're doin' poorly, Missus Annie. We missed you the morning we left for Choctaw County."

Annie takes a long, deep breath that doesn't seem to be getting her the air she needs. She exhales and grasps at her chest. "Oh, that hurts." She coughs a little, and then settles into her chair. She slips into a slight doze, coughing occasionally.

Jenny looks to Ise with sad eyes, and he whispers, "Missus Annie has come down with the pneumonia, the doctor said." Ise says what Jenny can't. "She's dyin'."

Jenny cries. "She's been stayin' with us, but she won't stay in bed. I can't—"

Annie stirs. "What, what's that? Hell no, I ain't stayin' in no bed. Too much good livin' to do in too short a time to waste away under the covers."

Jenny smiles sadly. "Yes, ma'am."

Annie stiffens up and sits straight. "Heard you boys got some trouble."

Tarle looks off into a corner. "Yes, ma'am, we do."

"The kind of trouble a certain man's father used to be engaged in, right?"

Elzey offers a fake grin. "Yes, ma'am, and from what I understand, he'd be the first out the door running right at it."

"You are beginning to understand your father, young man, and...." Annie dozes off again.

Tarle scratches at the table with a fingernail and turns to Ise. "It's one of the bastards we should've killed when we took down the West-Kimbrell Gang. The coward Tom Kimbrell has taken my wife while we've been away."

Ise sets his coffee down. "Rainy sent the details to us, so you don't have to go any further if you don't want to. We know what happened."

Tarle nods and sips his coffee. "Thank you for that."

Jenny straightens up and presses out her skirt with her palms. "Sounds like a story we know all too well repeatin' itself, don't you think, my dear husband?"

Ise nods and turns to Tarle. "Yes, my darling wife, it is, and that's why I'm goin' with 'em."

Jenny wraps her arms around Ise. "And you have my blessin', dear. Make sure you tell them our story again on the way, about how Lummy and you good men rescued me from some wicked men bent on harming me in the most horrible of ways. It will bolster their courage." She stares into Elzey's eyes. "And it'll give this young man an even better understanding of his father."

Ise kisses her on the back of the neck. "I'll do it, dear."

Elzey takes her hand and kisses it. "I'd appreciate it, Auntie."

Annie wakes to cough and spit up. Jenny hops up to care for her. Annie waves her off, though barely able to hold up her hand. She reaches into her gown pocket and hands Tarle a roll of greenbacks. He tries to give it back.

Annie barks, "Take it, dammit. It's the least I can do for a family who rescued me, as well. You go get that wife of yours, and you take care of whatever she needs. There's more'n enough there to do that, get you across the river, and on a train west to your home. It'll cut days off your trip. And you can rest on the way."

Tarle and Elzey say together, "Yes, ma'am."

Annie's voice gets low. "Then, you go get the bastards who took our darling. You spare them no pain, you hear?"

Tarle's hackles rise on the back of his neck, and in the voice of one set on rescue and reckoning, he growls, "You can count on that for damn sure, Missus Annie."

Annie softens a bit. "Now, Jenny will make pallets on the floor for you to sleep on like last time. Get some rest. The first ferry leaves straight up at six o'clock, and the train at seven thirty. You can sleep more then." Tears fill her eyes. "I love you boys and the men who made you and raised you." She coughs into her handkerchief. She tries to hide the blood. "I won't see you again until Gabriel blows his trumpet, but I'll be lookin' for you. We'll all have a grand reunion then."

Annie squints and looks at Elzey with glazed-over eyes. "Lummy, you take care of these boys, you hear, or I'll take a switch to that fine backside you've been totin' around and…." She nearly faints, but her head bobs back up. "Now, Jenny, take me back to bed, please, dear."

CHAPTER 44

WHEN OLD FRIENDS PASS SO THAT OTHERS MAY LIVE

BEFORE DAYLIGHT, AUGUST 15, 1886

The passing of an old friend opens the door for a new friend to live.

ISE SHAKES TARLE and Wesley, then Elzey and Matt, awake. They sit up from their pallets on the floor as Ise sips coffee. His eyes are red and tearful. He sniffs. "Annie Handerson has passed through the thin veil on to her just reward. She just breathed her last not long after you boys went to sleep. It was quick. We chose not to wake you. But rest assured, there was no pain. She just went into a peaceful sleep, praise the Lord."

Jenny steps out of the bedroom where Annie's body lies. "Her last words were to you, Elzey. She said, and these are her exact words, mind you, 'Tell Lummy Tullos that when he gets to heaven, she will find him, and he will be her lover forever.'"

Tarle laughs for the first time since he got the news about Caroline. "Annie Fanny, she just won't quit, will she? I'm glad I got to meet her."

Elzey chuckles. "From what I can tell, if she wants my father in heaven, she's gonna have to wait in line."

Jenny wipes her eyes and smiles. "Yeah, she was a tough old bird, but so easy to love."

Tarle asks, "So, Ise, Jenny, what will you do?"

Ise puts his arm around Jenny's waist. "Don't you know that sweet old songbird gave us this café just a couple of months ago? She made it all legal and everything. She knew her time was about up and swore on the Bible she could hear the angels callin' her name from time to time."

Elzey squints. "I believe it."

Tarle stands to put his shirt on. "Me, too. But meaning no disrespect, I'm sure I know what Missus Annie would want us to do right now."

Ise finishes his coffee. "And you would be right. The horses are saddled and ready, and Jenny has already sacked up food to get us to Winnfield. Get you a couple of ham biscuits and drink a cup of coffee on the way down. We'll get more food on the train across the river."

Jenny whispers to Ise. "I'll let the undertaker know we'll have a memorial service when y'all get back."

Ise kisses Jenny long and hard. "That'll be fine, Missus Jenny. I love you, dear."

"And I'll be lookin' for you every day till you get back, Ise Handerson."

Elzey slips on his boots and buttons his shirt. "Let's go."

TARLE, ELZEY, ISE, Matt, and Wesley ride up to Rainy's shop in Winnfield, quickly tie off their mounts, and burst in, knocking the little bells off the door to the floor.

Deputy Sheriff Jesse Cockersham is waiting inside.

Tarle yells, "Rainy? Where are you? Rainy?" He notices Jesse in the corner sipping coffee. "Oh, sorry for crowin' so loud. Guess you heard about my—"

Jesse stands and takes Tarle by the shoulders. "That's why I'm here. We *will* get that bastard Tom Kimbrell and hang his ass, right after we put your wife back into your arms."

Aaron walks from the back. "Pa will be back in just a bit. He's gathering supplies for the trip you men are about to embark upon."

Tarle smashes his fist into his hand. "I should'a known better than to leave town with that bastard Tom Kimbrell on the loose. Son of a—"

Rainy and Marion walk into the shop.

Marion asks Tarle, "You were saying?

The five men are speechless and gawk at Marion's beauty.

Tarle stutters, "Well… uh, ma'am… I, I… I wasn't expectin' a lady—"

"To be in a gun shop? And if you call me ma'am again, I'll cut your stones off and hand them to you, you understand?"

Aaron shakes his head and whispers, "She does *not* like being called ma'am."

Rainy gently lays his hands on Marion's shoulders. "It's all right, Marion. These are the men I was telling you about. This is Tarle Tullos, whose wife was taken, and his cousin Elzey, Lummy's son." He reaches out both hands to Ise and Matt. "Good to see you two men again." He glances over at Wesley and smiles. "If I'm right, you must be one of the Wood brothers' sons. The makers of the best moonshine you'll ever sip who ain't scared of a damn thing."

Wesley smiles. "John is my father, and he still makes moonshine with my uncle Henry up near Big Sand Rock, where y'all hid out when you took down Captain Tom Ford and his redshirt Hyenas."

Rainy scratches his ear. "Wait a minute. Yes, I remember... what was that... oh yeah, moonshine made from the sweet waters of Aaron Wood's Spring, right?"

Wesley's eyes light up. "Yeah, and you know who stayed at the Big Sand Rock for a spell."

Rainy steps forward with great interest. "Who, might I inquire?"

Wesley puffs out his chest. "The James-Chaney Gang. Yep, Jesse and Frank stayed in the same hole in the ground y'all did under that big ole rock with the the Chaney brothers. Did you know Wood family land stretches from where Chester now sits all the way to Wood Mountain and then some?"

Rainy strokes his beard. "I didn't, but a man could get lost in those small mountains and deep gullies for days if he got turned around. Imagine that, the Jesse James-Chaney Gang, hiding out for a spell at the Big Sand Rock on Wood family land."

"In fact, ole Bill Chaney married my aunt Nancy, and they—"

Tarle has about had all he can stand. "If we're all done with the hand shakin', reminiscing, and honey lovin', can we get about goin' after my wife?" His eyes are filled with tears of anger.

Marion ducks her head and sniffs, then looks him in the eye. "Kinda touchy, ain't you?"

Tarle snaps back. "When it comes to my wife, you're damn right I am, you long-haired, two-bit hussy."

Marion steps up to him and says, "You take that tone of yours and shove it up your—"

Rainy waves a hand. "Hold on a minute, Tarle. Let's save the fight for the right people."

Tarle steps back. Marion doesn't. She glares at Tarle with eyes that could set him on fire.

Rainy takes a deep breath and exhales. "All right, Tarle, this is Marion Tullos. She was raised by your great uncle Silas, who Uncle Lummy often talked about. She's here on business and to take a rest, but now wants to join us to help get Missus Caroline back."

Tarle snickers. "A woman? Ridin' with us? Oh, hell no. I ain't havin' it. No woman—"

Marion's face turns red. "I can outride, outshoot, out drink any of you sissy, squattin' to piss, church goin' choir boys any day and find this Tom Kimbrell in the dark of night while you boys are chokin' your roosters. Y'all *do* have manly parts, I presume?"

Rainy holds up his hands. "All right, that's enough. Really. Marion, would you please—"

Marion stomps her foot. "Please nothing. These silly sacks of shit don't know me, but I'll be happy to show 'em, firsthand, if need be."

Rainy tries to calm her. "Marion, please—"

Tarle grins. "No, Uncle Rainy, let her go and get it all out. I want to know who it is we got here, and if she's fit to ride with us."

Aaron backs up against the wall. "Oh, shit, I wish you hadn't said that."

Marion is incensed. "Fit to ride with you? If you beg just right, you manure shovelin' hawg farmer, I might just let you lick the horseshit off the bottom of my boots."

Tarle blinks. "I ought'a take you to the woodshed and spank your ass right now. But bein' the tough talkin' she-dawg bitch you are, you'd probably enjoy it."

Marion reaches for her knife.

Rainy calmly takes her hand. "It's all right. Nothing wrong with getting the words out now that could hurt us later."

Marion nods and takes a long deep breath.

Tarle asks, "We're fixin' to go up against some pretty bad characters?"

Marion spits. "Do all you Tullos folk talk like you just came out of Sunday school? Damn, man, spit out what you're trying to say and quit sugar-coating it."

Tarle steps up. "What do you do that makes you so sure you could keep up with us? Rainy, Ise, Matt, and I helped take down the West-Kimbrell Gang a few years back, and Elzey and I took down three ruffians a few days on the Natchez Trace before we got to Choctaw County. So don't try and tell me I won't know shit talk when I hear it."

Rainy elbows Marion. "Everybody in this room is either kin to you in one way or another, or at least they should be. Go on, tell them what you do."

Marion looks around the room and calms herself. "I'm whatever the hell you need to call me. A tracker, stalker, trapper, head hunter, a recovery agent—"

Elzey asks, "Recovery agent for what?"

Marion looks again to Rainy, who winks and nods his approval for what she's about to say. "I'm a huntress of men and women who defy the law and need to be brought to justice. I'm a recovery agent of the bad so the good can live peaceable-like."

Tarle snickers. "So, you're a killer-for-hire."

Marion snaps at Tarle, "Don't call me that."

Tarle looks around. "So, you're a predator, then, ain't you?"

"No, I hunt the predators, and you're starting to sound like one yourself. I'm a shadow-dweller with keen skills, but I'm for damn sure ain't no Pinkerton bastard. I hunt men like Tom Kimbrell who took your wife, Tarle Tullos. That's what I do. And get paid for doin' it. You got a problem with it?"

"No, not really." Tarle offers out his hand to Marion and says to Rainy, "I think Uncle Lummy would really like Marion."

Rainy smiles. "I know he would."

CHAPTER 45

WHEN A COUSIN IS BETTER CALLED A FRIEND

AUGUST 16, 1886

Making up with a woman not your wife is always a good thing.

MARION GRINS AND kicks Tarle in the shin. "You dirty rotten sack of snakes. You were playing me all along, weren't you?" Tarle snickers. "I had to know who you really are, cousin. Now we're friends, and I'm glad you're goin' with us."

Marion scans the faces of the men in the room. "All right, the jokes have been on me, but you'll probably best know what I do by the common name, bounty hunter. I don't like it, so don't refer to me by that name. If you just have to call me something other than Marion, make it Huntress. It's my new handle."

Tarle looks to Elzey, Elzey to Ise, Ise to Matt, and Matt to Wesley. They all shrug and nod in agreement.

Rainy hesitates to smile. "All right then. Huntress it is."

She squints at Rainy. "Thanks, Uncle."

Tarle winks at Marion, stands firm for a moment, then collapses into a chair from exhaustion—body and soul.

Aaron brings whiskey for all, and a collective sigh is heard around the room—the kind of sigh good men, and a woman, make when they are resolved to doing what's coming next. In this case, a fight.

Tarle takes a sip from his glass. "All right, Uncle Rainy, now that we're all family here with a singular purpose, what do we do next?"

Rainy pulls a map from under the counter and stretches it out on a small table. "I checked with some of my customers who travel back and forth on the El Camino Road to and from Texas doing business and what not. They keep their ears open and eyes peeled as to what goes on. They've been a big help to keep me informed since this all happened."

"What have you found out, Uncle?" Elzey asks.

"That Tom Kimbrell and his band of miscreants took Missus Caroline down Austin way, where they plan to sell her to the highest bidder in a human stockyard." Rainy looks over at Ise. "And we all thought slavery was over and done with at the close of Mister Lincoln's war."

Ise slams his fist on the map table. "Damn—" He pulls back his hand and looks at the others. "I'm sorry. I had an unpleasant memory about my sweet Jenny and how we found her."

Rainy continues, "That's all right, Ise. I want you to tell that story once we're out on the road, maybe the first night in camp." He scans the eyes of everyone in the room. "We're all a little on edge, but we have to keep our wits about us. They'll know we're coming."

Elzey asks, "How do you know that?"

Rainy smiles and winks. "Because they know that's the kind of people we are."

Tarle chimes in, "And they damn sure know it all too well."

Aaron moves closer to the table and puts his finger on the spot where Austin is located. "Let me take a look at all of this, Pa. I need something to measure with."

Rainy holds out a stick. "Will a ruler do?"

"Perfect." Aaron measures how far it is from Winnfield to Austin by train from two points, Natchitoches and Shreveport. He checks the map legend for scale. "Sit tight. I'll be right back."

Rainy nods. "Where are you—?"

But Aaron is already out the door.

Tarle barks, "Damn, it'll take us a week to get there."

Rainy smiles. "You are your father's son, Tarle, but not so fast. Did you forget how you got here so quickly?"

Tarle settles down. "Dang, I didn't think about taking the train. I thought we'd be riding horses day and night to get there. We'll get to Austin by train."

Jesse sighs in relief. "And them outlaws sure as hell won't take a woman on a train where she could scream for help at the first sign of the law."

Rainy taps his foot. "Y'all get another swallow of whiskey, water, or coffee, and rest for a minute. If Aaron's got an idea, it'll be worth waiting on." He returns to the map. "You're right, Deputy. They've got several days' jump on us, but they can only go so fast driving a wagon."

Aaron returns with a paper in his hand. "I got this train schedule from the telegraph office. They keep them on hand like they do for the steamers." He leans over and traces the railroads from north of Winnfield to Austin with his finger. Aaron motions for everyone to draw in closer. He squints at the map and puts his finger on the town of Shreveport, measures with his index finger and thumb, and traces the route to Austin. He does the same from Natchitoches. He steps back and ponders the possibilities. Then, he reaches to tap his finger on Shreveport.

"Given you make the right connections at the right times, I believe you could get to Austin from Shreveport in less than four days." He counts on his fingers and in his head, whispering to himself. "Damn, you might even get there about the time they do, if you hurry."

Rainy asks, "So, you think going to Shreveport is the best choice, son?"

"I do, Pa."

"Good, then, Shreveport it is. Inform them."

Aaron looks around at the tight circle of rescuers and waves them in closer. "All right, here's what we got so you'll understand. You could ride to Natchitoches, which at best is only thirty-five miles, and catch the train there. But, here's what I'd like to propose."

Tarle asks, "What's that?"

"You ride like bats smoked out of a barn loft to Shreveport and catch the morning run. I know it's a hundred miles, and it'll take longer and be a harder ride, but there are fewer trains running through Natchitoches. You will have to wait longer to catch a train coming through, and the connections might be tight if you start there. But if you take the right train out of Shreveport, you'll get a straight shot to Austin. Otherwise, from Natchitoches, you'll be switching trains, waiting for transfers, and—"

Tarle is becoming impatient. "All right, all right, to Shreveport it is. Can we just go?"

Aaron disregards Tarle's impatience. "...and you could miss a connection if a train is late."

Tarle lays his hand on Aaron's shoulder. "Sorry, brother, I'm tired and will be more so by the time we reach that train. Thank you for this, Aaron."

"Not to worry, cousin. I cannot imagine what you're going through."

Rainy nods. "Good work, son."

Ise agrees. "So, we get to ride in a passenger car, our horses will be well-cared for, and we get to eat and sleep on the train?" He pops Wesley on the shoulder. "Now I like the sound of that."

Wesley smiles. "Me, too. I've never been to Texas before."

Marion clenches her jaw. "If you think this is some sort of holiday, Wesley Wood, then maybe—"

Rainy reins Marion in. "Simmer down, Marion. It's gonna take all of us to do this. Wesley will pull his weight, watch what I tell you."

Marion nods. "Sorry, Wesley."

"That's all right, Miss Marion. I'll try to be more serious from now on."

Marion shakes her head. "No, you stay the way you are, Wesley. We need you, not what anybody else thinks you need to be."

Rainy chuckles. "Sounds like a good man whom I know very well."

Marion grins, capturing everyone's attention with her beautiful smile. "If it's Lummy Tullos you're talking about, then I'll take that as a compliment."

Rainy puts his hands on hips and looks around at the small band of rescuers waiting for their leader to give the orders. "I suggest we gather up and get going within the hour. Aaron and I already have everything ready to go. Fresh mounts, plenty of food, and ammunition for all of your weapons. Tell him what pistol and long gun shells you need. They're on the house."

Tarle purses his lips and nods with approval. "You two have been busy."

Aaron takes a swallow of whiskey. "Pa and I had to do something while we were waiting on you slow ass bastards to get here."

Everybody laughs except Marion.

Rainy asks, "What are you thinking, Marion?"

She looks at Tarle. "What will happen to Missus Caroline if we don't get there in time?"

Tarle straightens up to be the brave one who pronounces a judgment no one wants to hear. "The man with the most money will buy her and take her down to Mexico. Who knows what'll happen to her after that."

Ise grits his teeth. "But we all know what for, dammit."

Rainy squeezes Tarle's shoulder. "The good thing is, they'll do nothing to devalue her on the way to Austin, because—"

Tarle interrupts, "They won't rape her so they can get the best price, right?"

Rainy smiles sadly. "That's right."

Marion slips her hand into the crook of Tarle's arm and pulls him close. "At least she's not being harmed now, cousin." Her eyes betray the heart of one who's experienced the damage that Caroline might suffer. "I'm with you till the day she's freed to go home with you. I'll do whatever is necessary to get her back." She shakes him. "I mean it. Anything." She stares into Tarle's eyes with the vengeance of the Lord. "And I've done this sort of thing before."

Tarle is a bit shocked by her kind but fierce response. "I can see that you have, cousin." He smiles and pats her hand. "We just need to get there before they sell her off."

Ise squints. "And by God's mighty hand, we will do just that."

Marion shakes her head and purposefully looks into each of her new friends' eyes. "Not this time, Ise. God won't be anywhere where we're going, understand? He's sending us into the fires of Hell to kill demons and bring back one of his innocent lambs to the fold. For the Savior said, 'What man of you, having an hundred sheep, if he loses one of them, doth he not leave the ninety and nine in the wilderness, and go after that which is lost, until he finds it?'" She pauses to let her words sink in. "Brothers, we aren't leaving the ninety and nine in the wilderness to go after the one. No, we're leaving the sheepfold and going to where only devils make their homes. The wilderness."

Ise claps his hands and shouts, "Amen, sister!"

Marion holds up her hand, gesturing to the sky. "The prophet Isaiah had this to say when he faced grave danger and uncertainty when the Lord asked, 'Who will go for us?' Isaiah jumped up and said, 'Here am I, send me.'"

Ise, in a singing like voice, says, "Annnnnd off he went to dos the work of the Lord to bring folks to Jesus and—"

Marion recaptures the moment before Ise gets lost in his own sermon. "Yeah, we'll bring 'em to Jesus all right. They'll all be meetin' him face to face after we're done with them."

Silence betrays an appreciation of what Marion is doing to bolster these men's courage. She takes advantage of the moment to bring the group together even closer under one banner. "If you claim to be a believer, then repeat after me. If you're not, then hedge your bet by saying these words anyway. What have you got to lose?"

Everyone straightens up and stands at attention.

She calls out the confession, and they repeat in kind. "I believe... that Jesus Christ... is the Son... of the living God... amen."

A collective "amen" rises.

Marion smiles. "Now we're ready. The Good Book says if we go with that confession on our lips and in our hearts, then the gates of hell cannot prevail against it. And we're goin' against the gates of Hell in Texas."

Ise shouts, "Hallelujah," as the others nod and say their amens.

Rainy whispers under his breath, "And Lord, I thought we lost our preacher when Lummy went west."

Marion snaps her head around. "I'll take that as a compliment, Uncle Rainy." She gathers her guns and saddlebags, then stops to sit and listen.

Elzey asks, "Uncle Rainy, why didn't my father stay to help us? Aaron said he caught up with him leaving Sikes."

Rainy drops his head. "I'd think you'd understand that better by now."

"I do, but the way y'all talk about him, we need him here."

Rainy smiles. "He is here with us in spirit, and that means a lot."

Elzey shakes his head. "Still, it just ain't the same."

"Sure it is, son."

"How do you figure that?"

"You're here. And his blood runs through your veins."

CHAPTER 46

TIME TO GO

AUGUST 16, 1886

Trouble has a way of bringin' family together for a singular cause.

A GREAT SILENCE blankets the room. Somber faces belie ruthless determination. All know what must be done and that the risk will be great. Lives could be lost.

Wesley chimes in. "It's gonna be an ugly sight when we're done."

Ise responds by taking out his short sword and thumbing the blade. He licks the spot of blood that appears. "That's for damn sure."

Rainy looks up from the map. "Matt, Jesse, what do y'all think?"

Jesse signals for Matt to speak first. "I think we need to get our asses out to Austin, Texas, as quick as we can. I'm familiar with the buyin' and sellin' of goods. So, I could pose as a buyer of spices or some damn thing and gather information about these outlaw bastards' location. I can also keep y'all supplied with food and such until the deed is done."

Rainy asks, "Jesse, what's going through your head?"

"We need the best guns we can get and more bullets than we can carry. I fully believe this will be a war like it was with Dawg Smith." He turns his sad eyes to Elzey. "But this time, son, we *will* get our lady back, in honor of your mother."

"Thank you for that, Jesse." Elzey shudders. "Do you think we have what it takes to bring 'em down like y'all did the West-Kimbrell Gang?"

Marion smiles with fiery eyes. "Do you know your scripture, cousin Elzey?"

"Pretty much. I—"

Marion speaks in a tone that could rival any brush arbor stump preacher. "'The Lord is greater than the giants you face,' the Apostle John wrote."

Ise grins. "It's clear you know your Scripture, Marion."

She huffs a chuckle. "Yeah, I do when I need it."

Ise squints. "We need it now, sister."

Rainy tries to soften the mood. "All right then, it's all over but the leaving. Get your stuff and meet me at the livery. We'll light out to catch the train at Shreveport. We have to travel north before we turn west, but Aaron's right, it's the quickest route. From there, we head directly southwest to Austin."

Jesse hooks his thumbs in his belt. "And we won't be worn out from ridin' and sleepin' out for days."

Rainy gathers the map up and makes for the back room to gather up his gear. "Exactly."

Everyone shuffles to the door. Aaron reaches down to retrieve the little bells that were on the door that were knocked off when Tarle burst in earlier. He looks them over, thinking about how to fix them.

Marion takes them from his hand. "I'll take those."

Aaron instinctively lets them go. "They're busted and good for nothing, so—"

"That's how I've felt most of my life. Besides, I have an idea about these little bells," she says as she rolls them around in her hand and then stuffs them into her pocket.

"What's your idea?"

"You'll know when your pa gets back and tells you."

Aaron smiles. "I wish I was going with y'all."

Rainy steps up behind Aaron and pats him on the back. "You being here to give folks a fake story about where we've gone and being close to the telegraph office if we need anything is just as important as you going. Besides, we need to carry on business as usual to keep suspicions down, and somebody's got to keep your mother from worrying too much." He stops. "Enough of all that." He hugs Aaron. "You're the man of our family while I'm away. And with your father's blood coursing through your veins, I have no fear. Keep a clear eye, though. Tom Kimbrell still has friends in the parish, and they can get communiques to and from him at any time by telegram. You understand?"

Aaron pulls his apron up to reveal a pistol in his belt. "And I have a der-ringer in my back pocket as well."

Rainy pulls Aaron's forehead to his. "Take care, my son."

"I will, Pa. You come back all in one piece."

They hug again, and Marion whispers to Rainy as they walk out of the gunshop door, "You are a blessed man, Rainy Mills."

He puts his arm around her shoulders. "And so are we for knowing you."

WHEN RAINY AND the rest arrive at the livery stable, Mary Jane steps down from her carriage seat and starts gathering the food sacks stored on the back seat.

Rainy gives her a kiss. "Thank you for getting all of this ready for us, dear."

She waves her hand across the group standing before her. "No trouble. I fixed a sack for each of you. Come get one. I believe it will carry you to Texas."

Everyone thanks Mary Jane and checks their mounts.

Mary Jane grabs Rainy by his shirt collar and shakes him. "You better come back to me, you old outlaw."

Rainy grins. "You know what they say, niece. 'It takes an outlaw to catch an outlaw.'"

Marion snickers. "Yeah, and that very same man said, 'It takes a devil to kill a demon.'"

Ise whispers, "Yes, and he was right."

Marion leaps into the saddle in one bound. "Oh, yeah, who was that?"

"Your uncle, Lummy Tullos."

Elzey asks Rainy, "Just how much of a devil was my father when it came to this kind of doin's?"

Rainy purses his lips. "You really don't want to know, son, but I'll tell you on the way."

Everyone secures their mounts and gear and pulls together into formation.

Mary Jane wipes sweat from her forehead with the back of her forearm blouse sleeve. "Now that's a picture that ought to be painted. Maybe I'll do that someday." She takes out a piece of paper and quickly sketches the scene and the position of each rider. "There, I have it." She starts to cry.

Rainy dismounts and pulls her close. "Pray hard, dear, that we come back so you can finish your drawing."

"It'll give me something to do while you're away, Rainy."

He hugs Mary Jane like he never wants to let her go, kisses her, and turns to mount up again.

Mary Jane waves and covers her mouth and nose with a handkerchief. Aaron walks up behind her and wraps his arms around his mother.

Elzey eases his mount close to Aaron and his mother. "Missus Mary Jane, if it wouldn't be too much trouble, I would like a copy of that picture when you're finished, please, ma'am."

"No trouble, Elzey. Printers can do amazing things these days."

Elzey nods and gets back in formation.

Rainy calls each person by name. "Tarle, Elzey, Ise, Marion, Matt, Jesse, and Wesley... to the train."

They ride west into a setting sun.

Marion eases up beside Rainy at the front of the column. "See the horizon?"

Rainy grins. "Yeah, pretty, isn't it."

"For now."

"What do you mean?"

"You've heard the old saying, 'Red sky at night, sailor's delight, red sky in the morning, sailor's warning?'"

"Yeah, but that sky is as blue as the dress my wife was wearing."

"It's not about what you can see, but what's going to happen that you can't see."

"And what's that?"

"A red sky storm." Marion catches Granny Thankful standing in a cane thicket holding a demon by the neck that's scratching and clawing to get free.

Granny squints. *"Riding west into a red sky horizon means blood troubles are on the way."*

Rainy looks in the same direction and witnesses Granny's power. "Yes, I see. A storm of blood it will be."

Marion drops to the back of the line of rescuers to be alone. And Rainy gets lost in his thoughts.

Both pray—one at the front of the column, and the other in the back.

CHAPTER 47

TRAIN OF WISHFUL SILENT CONTEMPLATION

AUGUST 17, 1886

*The gentle rocking of a moving train offers great
solitude and silence, if you're left alone.*

AFTER LEADING THEIR mounts to the rear car of the train when they arrive in Shreveport, Rainy and his band of rescuers make for the passenger car they've been assigned.

They settle into their seats, exhausted, Tarle and Elzey the most for not having rested since arriving in Winnfield. They all look forward to a quiet, restful sleep. Hats are pulled down, arms are folded, and feet are propped up to give Marion and the men the most comfortable ride possible. It's not long before light snoring is heard as passengers find their seats.

A nosey acquaintance of Rainy's strolls down the aisle to where the group rests. Rainy sees the man coming, recognizes him as a competitor in the gun business. He pulls his hat down in hopes the man will pass on by. He doesn't.

He lifts Rainy's hat with the end of his cane and offers his hand. "Well, if it's not Rainy Mills and his finely-bred associates, I might add."

Rainy feigns sickness and doesn't shake his hand. "Not feeling well, Oliver Yates, so please excuse my unwillingness to greet you properly."

"No, no, that's quite all right." He studies the group. "And who might this fine collection of backwoodsmen and a lady be?"

Rainy shakes his head slightly. "We haven't slept since leaving Winnfield late yesterday evening, some longer than that." He waves his hand around at the group, trying to give a hint. "My friends here need to rest, if you'd be so kind. Maybe we can talk later, Oliver?"

The man doesn't move, and it's obvious he fully intends to aggravate Rainy.

Marion barely opens one eye, thinking, This is gonna be good.

"But Mister Mills, where would you be going at such a time?"

Rainy slinks down in his seat, trying to give the signal that he doesn't want to talk. His competitor doesn't take the second hint.

Rainy sighs and sits up. "Hunting."

Oliver shifts from one foot to the other. "This time of year? For what, if I may ask?"

"You already asked, but if you have to know, deer, maybe a bear, and such."

"You don't appear to be going hunting. Where are your sporting guns? You look like you're heading to a fight. I just want to know what—"

Rainy adjusts his jacket. "Tell you what, I'll make a deal with you. I'll tell you a story that'll speak to your curiosity. I guarantee you will walk away satisfied when I'm finished. Agreed?"

He nods and says, "This ought'a be good. Let's make a bet of it. What do you say?"

Rainy rubs his hands together. "All right, then. Here's the bet. If you leave after I tell the story, you'll not bother me again. It won't be a long story mind you, but you have to pay for our meals for the entire trip."

He smiles. "And if I win?"

Rainy gives a devilish grin. "I buy your meals and passage, give you the real purpose of our trip, and send three good paying customers your way to boot. How's that sound?"

"That's bait that even the least hungry fish in the river cannot resist." Oliver chuckles.

Rainy grins and offers to shake Oliver's hand. "It's a bet, then?"

Oliver is reluctant to take it but nods and shakes his hand. He wipes his hand on his jacket when Rainy turns loose.

"Okay then, here goes. A young boy was sitting on the porch of the mercantile, busily eating candy. He was stuffing peppermints and lemon drops into his mouth as fast as he could chew them up. A gentleman, much like yourself, was passing by and couldn't help but notice the young boy eating candy so quickly. He asked, 'Son, don't you know that eating that much candy that fast isn't good for you?' The young boy finished chewing the candy in his mouth. 'Well, sir, my grandpa lived to be a hundred.' The gentleman rubbed his chin and asked, 'Eating candy like that?' The young boy smiled and said, 'No, sir, tending to his own damn business.'"

Everyone in the passenger car laughs out loud.

Oliver is visually embarrassed. He gasps at the insult and unmistakable threat. "Well, I never—"

"Yeah, you did, Oliver, just now."

Oliver turns to walk away, but Rainy takes his arm. "Satisfied?"

Oliver jerks away and huffs. "I am," he growls as he turns to walk back to his seat.

"Then go on about your business and don't bother me, or us, again, understand?" Rainy signals the conductor and in a loud voice says, "Mister Oliver Yates will be taking care of our food bill for the entire trip."

The conductor, who had been listening, smiles and says, "Very good, sir. I will adjust his bill accordingly."

All the passengers clap. Rainy stands and takes a bow. "And good people, don't forget the name, Oliver Yates, an unruly gun dealer who associates and does gun business with known men of low to no account. Remember that name when you need firearms or ammunition of any sort. And then come see me, Rainy Mills, in Winnfield at Mills and Son Guns and Repair. Mention this incident when you come in, and either I or my son Aaron will give you a substantial discount." They all clap again.

Tarle laughs and elbows Elzey. "Reminds me of an old friend, Mister James T. Gilmore, who my pa worked for years ago. That man should've been an actor."

Rainy sits. "That he should have been. But what he did freeing slaves had a far greater reach in real life than play-acting on a stage."

Marion sits up. "Damn, Mister Rainy, you do have a way of telling a story with a singular point. You believe that he was truly satisfied?"

Rainy slouches down in his seat and covers his eyes with his hat brim. He lifts it up just enough to see Marion and give a devilish grin. "Yep, satisfied enough to know that he wouldn't live much longer if he kept on pestering me."

Elzey sits quietly, taking it all in and writing it all down, as quickly and accurately as he can.

CHAPTER 48

A BIBLE TRUTH BEFORE THE RED SKY STORM

AUGUST 17, 1886

A river always has to be crossed to enter a foreign land.

THE TRAIN ENGINEER blows the whistle, and the train lurches forward. As it picks up speed, Marion peers out the window. She elbows Rainy. "What river is that we're about to cross?"

"Why, it's the Red River."

Marion snickers sarcastically. "That figures. It always seems like when an army has to go into a foreign land, they have to cross a river. And we're crossing over the same color of blood into a red sky storm ahead."

"Yeah, but we have the blood of the Savior on our side. At least that's what you said."

Marion nods. "Remember the story of when the Philistines took the Ark of the Covenant?"

Ise sits up. "I do."

Marion rubs her hands together. "Well, they got it back, but not before—"

Tarle shuffles his feet, trying to wake up. "So, my wife is like the Ark of the Covenant, and we're goin' to bring her back?"

Marion nods, and Ise says, "Makes good sense to me. It helps to keep the Lord before me for what we're doin', Tarle."

"You're right. And I appreciate every time you bring the Lord into what we're doin'. Helps me stay sane when I want to run off in all directions, like a chicken with its head cut off."

Marion smiles. "Glad to be of service, cousin." She looks around at those listening to her Bible lesson. "Y'all don't forget how you feel about me now when you witness what'll need to happen to get Missus Caroline back. Say you forgive me in advance."

They all nod and agree.

"Good, 'cause what I think I'll have to do will make you think the worst of me, unless you truly are men God claims as his."

Wesley asks, "What do you have in mind, Miss Marion?"

"You'll just have to wait and see."

Ise, starry-eyed at Marion's command of Scripture, laughs. "You sure know the Bible, Miss Marion."

"Backward and forward, upside down and right side up, Ise." The corner of her mouth curls into a slight grin. "And I live it. Most of the time."

A whistle blows long and loud, startling sleepy passengers awakened at an unreasonably early hour. The conductor yells, "We're in Austin, ladies and gentlemen. All passengers deboarding, please gather your things and animals before we move on. This train leaves again in fifteen minutes. Thanks for traveling with us. We hope to see you again."

Rainy rouses everyone, and they make for the livestock cars at the rear of the train. When all the mounts have deboarded, Rainy asks, "Anybody want coffee, and maybe breakfast?"

All hands shoot up quickly, and they walk their mounts to the closest café.

Rainy whispers to Marion, "Crossing the Jordan don't make Texas the Promised Land."

Marion sighs. "Yeah, and even though their God was with them, it still wasn't easy."

Rainy straightens his hat. "No, in fact, it appears their troubles increased a hundredfold, if my memory serves me correctly."

Marion checks her clothes before entering the café. "You're right, but the difference is, we aren't staying. We're just goin' to get back what's rightfully ours. I do believe the Good Lord appreciates this kind of work as long as we Israelites obey to the letter of the law."

Rainy asks, "How do we do that with what we're going to do when we find Tom Kimbrell?"

Marion grins. "Ah, and therein lies the question which truly possesses an easy answer."

Rainy opens the door to the café, and the little bells at the top jingle.

Marion gives them a quick glance but says before entering, "Do what we must and trust in the grace of a good Creator who already knows what's about to happen and searches our hearts." She stops dead still and turns to a small band of men who bunch up running into each other. "Y'all stay pure of heart, calm of mind, and trusting in your soul so that your body will be used to complete the work God has given us, understand?"

The men remain quiet.

"I asked if you understand."

They all nod and speak words of agreement.

Marion turns and smiles, whispering, "Lord, help us."

PART V:
RED SKY STORM

CHAPTER 49

THE PLAN

CAMP, OUTSIDE AUSTIN, TEXAS,
MORNING, AUGUST 22, 1886

If you want the best performance from an actress,
get one who's played the part in real life.

THE SKY IS particularly red this morning. No one mentions that a storm is coming. Everyone knows it. And they're thinking about rain, unless it's hellfire and brimstone.

Jesse removes his hat and scratches his ear. "Somebody's gotta get close to 'em. Somebody they don't know."

Everyone looks around at each other, except Rainy. He's staring at Marion.

Rainy stands to straighten his clothes. "Someone once said, 'A very little key will open a very heavy door.' Charles Dickens, I believe it was." He works his teeth with a blade of straw. "And Marion, you are that key."

She squints and blinks, counting the cost. "All right, dammit, I'll do it."

Rainy doesn't blink. "You're the one who can get close to that son of a bitch, if you still have the skills." He grins slightly, baiting her.

She winks at Rainy. "Oh, no need to poke me, Uncle Rainy. It won't work, and there ain't no need. I know what must be done to get the information we need."

Tarle asks, "And pray tell, what would that be?"

"Listen, cousin, you know about as much about me as I do the rest of you all put together. But that's a story for another time." She ponders her next words carefully. "Let's just say I know the whore game better than they know it themselves. Why, I can make this hiney jiggle like two wildcats fightin' in a gunny sack."

Matt's eyes widen. "Lord, I ain't never heard nobody say anything like that before, but I am convinced Miss Marion has the goods to do it."

Marion smiles with an evil grin. "Damn straight, I do. But you just keep your eyes only looking into mine and not on my ass when I get gussied up, you hear?"

Matt ducks his head, grinning. "Yes, ma'am."

Wesley asks, "But who's gonna go along with her—you know, in case somethin' goes sideways?"

Rainy looks around the group and comes back to Wesley. "You're the only person here besides Marion he doesn't know. So, guess who?"

Wesley rubs his face and nods. "Okay. I can do that."

Rainy taps his foot. "I trust the Wood boys. They ain't scared, as a good friend used to say."

Wesley starts to get up, but sits back down to contemplate what he just agreed to doing.

Rainy studies Marion, who's ringing her hands. "You sure you're up to doing this?"

"Oh, hell yeah. It's just my game."

"Well," Rainy whispers, "sometimes a wicked past can be useful for the right purpose."

Wesley, wide-eyed with jaw dropped, blinks like an owl. "What're you gonna do, Marion?"

Marion smiles with a look that Delilah would have been proud of. "I'll show enough leg to make Tom Kimbrell drool all over himself, rendering him unable to walk because of the red rooster standin' up to crow in his britches."

Rainy laughs with the other men. "I swear, Marion, you *do* have a way of describing things."

She winks, "And gettin' better at it every day."

Rainy brushes off his pants. "Then let's go into town and get you the clothes of a soiled dove." He and Marion start for their horses, and Rainy turns to Wesley. "You, too, you ridge stomping, stump jumping, swamp running son of a moonshine maker."

Jesse walks with them to their mounts. "Be careful. We don't know who owns the law in this town, and Kimbrell will have lookouts everywhere lookin' for anyone new or anything suspicious."

Rainy nods and tips his hat. "Let's go before it rains."

It doesn't rain.

CHAPTER 50

THE

DECEPTION

EARLY EVENING, AUGUST 22, 1886

The only problem with acting is when it becomes too real.

WESLEY STUMBLES IN like he's half-drunk and sits at a table near the batwings. He signals the barkeep for a drink. When the barkeep brings a bottle and glass, he asks with a slur, "Does it rain around here?"

The barkeep wipes the table with one hand while clutching the bottle in the other. "Only when the Devil lets it rain, son. Why, what's it to you?"

"Oh, I thought I might need to get a room if that red sky comin' in the mornin' brings on a flood."

The barkeep laughs. "Get used to that red sky, son. It comes every other day. Ain't been no deluge 'round these parts for some time. You just drink your whiskey and stay dry in here. Leave a dollar on the table when you leave." He chuckles as he walks away. "Dumb ass kid."

Marion slinks into the smokey bar like a snake on the scent of a mouse. Her long blonde hair put up on top of her head, a fancy evening gown that accents her every curve, and a sultry smile that catches the attention of every man in the saloon completes the picture. She knows just how to swing her hips to keep their eyes on her feminine assets and not on her face so much. She spies the man Rainy and Jesse described as Tom Kimbrell sitting in the corner with his men, laughing, drinking, and talking about the money they'll make at the next day's auction. They disguise their words with terms about livestock and such.

Marion smoothly slides her bottom onto a stool at the bar, looking around as if disinterested with everything she sees. She pulls her split-leg long skirt over her lap, but when she nods to the barkeep for a drink, her dress falls open, revealing that she's wearing nothing underneath. From the corner of her eye, she catches Tom Kimbrell following her leg from her red shoes up to her exposed thigh. When he looks up and their eyes meet, she gives him a seductive wink. His smile widens like a kid who's just been given all the candy in the mercantile. That's when she knows he's taken the bait.

Marion waits. She figures the trap is set, and it won't be long before Kimbrell's curiosity gets the best of him. He's still watching her. She wiggles just enough to make the little bells dance and jingle on her breasts. Kimbrell licks his lips like a hound about to be thrown a hambone. Marion gets sick to her stomach reliving a memory from the whore house in Natchez. She steadies herself. Those thoughts could send her into a temper fit, and she can't let that happen. What she's doing is too valuable to getting Missus Caroline back. She draws in a deep breath, takes a sip of her whiskey, and fixes a bit of hair that has fallen. She winks at Kimbrell again. It's the last stick put on the fire to boil the water that makes her completely irresistible to Kimbrell.

He finishes business with his men and saunters over to where Marion sits. She pulls her split skirt together, puts one elbow on the bar, and rests her chin in her palm. She slowly turns and smiles at Kimbrell, batting her eyes.

Kimbrell, trying to be suave, takes the seat beside her and asks, "Now who might you be, you long-haired blonde beauty with the dancing bells?"

Marion looks him up and down like he did her. "Well, you guessed it. They call me Belle. All I have to do is ring these little bells, and whoever I want comes running." She pauses and grins. "Like you, whoever you are."

Kimbrell stares at her breasts. "The sweet sound of those bells certainly calls to me. Tom Kimbrell is my name. Where are you from?"

Marion laughs. "Here, there, everywhere, and maybe nowhere. Who needs to know details when my name is enough for where I believe this is going?"

Kimbrell, the weasel that he is, wastes no time getting to the point without grace or poise. He tells his men, "Exactly. Why waste time talking when life needs to be lived?"

Marion stares into his wicked eyes with the same intensity. "My sentiments exactly, Mister Kimbrell."

A man wearing a minister's collar staggers in drunk. Marion shudders at being reminded of the preacher in Natchez who had his way with her when she was just a girl.

Kimbrell asks, "You all right, preacher? Looks like–"

The preacher acts like he's stumbling but falls into Marion with his hands on her breasts. "Oh, sorry ma'am, I didn't–"

Marion front and back hands the preacher hard enough to make him take two steps back.

Kimbrell points. "Preacher boy, get your ass over to that table with the rest of the men, or I swear, I'll–"

Marion ever so gently caresses Kimbrell's face. "It's all right. No harm done." It's all she can do not to kick the preacher boy in the stones.

Kimbrell nods to his men, the signal that he has captured yet another damsel he plans to distress. "Think I'll get some air and go for a bite to eat. Miss Belle, would you join me?"

Marion swirls the last of her whiskey around in her glass and downs it. "Why, thank you, Tom Kimbrell. I believe I would. I only dine at fine restaurants, you understand?"

"Like you frequent fine saloons, my dear?"

She hadn't counted on that comment. "I like my men rough and salty, but my cuisine, succulent and divine."

"I know just the place. And then, we—"

"We will see what happens." Marion gives Kimbrell a side wink and grin.

He offers his arm. "This way, my dear."

Marion almost pukes playing this scene she's done too many times. But those times were for real. They step through the batwings to the street and start down the boardwalk in the opposite direction of restaurant row.

Wesley waits a moment, then slides out the door unnoticed.

They pass several dark alleys, and Marion realizes the plan is not going the way she'd hoped, but exactly as she planned. Her guard is up, and she knows he'll make his move any moment.

Marion turns her head slightly when a voice from across the street calls, "You there, young man, stop. I want to talk with you."

Wesley bolts down the street, and the deputy starts in after him.

Kimbrell laughs. "Another vagrant who'll pay a hefty fine to get out of jail in the morning. We make pretty good money off of newcomers."

Marion cringes. Wesley's no longer in the picture, and Kimbrell is working the same game of robbing and murdering newcomers as he and the West-Kimbell Gang did back in Winn Parish.

Marion masks her nervousness and asks, "May I ask where we are going?"

"Oh, I thought maybe we'd go out to my ranch just outside of town. I have a fine chef, and she'll prepare anything your heart desires. Better'n anything this town has to offer."

"That sounds interesting. Is it a big house?"

"One of the finest in the county."

"Where is it?"

"Oh, about three miles out on the road that goes by the lunatic asylum. Our place is at the headwaters of Waller Creek and—" Kimbrell stops short and becomes visibly suspicious. "Why do you want to know where it is?"

Marion jokes it off. "A lady needs to know where she'll be laying her head at night to know how to get home when she sneaks out early the next morning." She rubs his chest and pulls him down to kiss him on the cheek. "Understand now?" His rancid breath almost makes her heave.

"I do. We sell horses and cattle, among other things, and do pretty well for ourselves." He can't keep his eyes off of her breasts. "You know, I'm a successful man, and I've been thinking about finding the right woman, you know, to settle down with and have some kids."

"Oh, you're getting a little ahead of yourself, don't you—"

Kimbrell spins Marion around and covers her mouth with his tobacco-fouled hand. He drags her, kicking and fighting, into a dark alley where no one will hear. He's strong. Too strong. He stops and slaps her hard before she can scream. She purposefully goes limp and feigns fainting.

Memories of the preacher at the Natchez orphanage and the whorehouse attack her mind. Her heart races, and her mouth is dry. She wants to fight but knows it's not the right moment. Not yet. Visions of the so-called man of God putting his hands on her body flood her soul. Horrible memories of being raped and treated every way but right as a lady start overtaking her mind. She's losing her will to fight. She's weak, feeling overpowered like she did as a young girl at the orphanage. She wants to give up and die. She's had enough. She can hear the wicked laugh of the preacher who ran the orphanage. It's too much. She goes limp.

Marion prays. "Lord if ever there was a time…."

Kimbrell laughs. "God ain't nowhere to be found out here, don't you know, whore bitch?"

She thinks to herself, *I have to do something, or I'll be found with my throat slit tomorrow morning.*

Marion scratches her wrist. She focuses on that pain to block out the memories that are sending her to the wrong places. She must get back to Rainy with what she's learned.

She whispers like she's moaning, "I can do this. I can make it through."

Kimbrell stops and asks, "What did you say?"

She just moans, "Oh, don't hurt me anymore."

"That's what I thought you said, my sweet Belle." He drags her deeper into the alley abyss, snickering all the way. "All I want to do is get into this lady's bloomers and leave her for the rats to finish."

Kimbrell throws Marion on a cellar door and pulls her skirt apart. His eyes feast on her naked body. He starts unbuckling his pants. An alley cat that jumped up on a stack of crates screeches, and Kimbrell snatches his head around.

Marion sees Wesley sneaking up. She whispers, "Now." She sits up and kicks him in the groin as hard as she can.

Kimbrell doubles over laughing. "You missed, Belle, my foolish dear. But I'll not be fooled again." He grabs the front of her dress and yanks it hard enough to tear it down to her waist. Her breasts spill out.

Kimbrell is mesmerized, not realizing he's holding the little bells in his hand with a piece of her dress. "By God, would you look at those? Maybe I will consider settlin' down." He stares for a long moment.

Marion pulls the derringer Rainy gave her from her garter.

Kimbrell bends down to kiss her.

She puts the derringer to his forehead. "Mister Kimbrell, I do believe it's time for me to leave. You certainly are not the gentleman you pretend to be."

Kimbrell starts to move, and she cocks the small weapon.

"Move again. Please. Do it."

Wesley dashes from his hiding place and slams a gun butt on the back of Kimbrell's head. He and Marion stand over Kimbrell who is on all fours, shaking his bleeding head.

"You know I'll find you, Belle, or whatever your name is, and whoever this piece of rat filth is. I know everybody in town, and the law is all bought and paid for. We'll find you, both of you." He takes his wallet and throws it behind some old crates. "Now I can have a warrant put out on you for robbery. I'm sure the sheriff wouldn't mind sharing a sweet thing like you up in the jailhouse for a few nights and beat the hell out of this runt kid."

Marion tries to tie up her torn dress the best she can. "You should really learn how to treat a lady, you heathen." She finishes and says, "Get your rooster in the dirt, Kimbrell."

She keeps the derringer pressed hard against his head as he lies down. He grabs at her foot, but she's quicker, and Wesley kicks him in the face. He rolls over moaning and rubbing his eye.

Marion and Wesley sprint down the alley through several back streets to their horses and ride like the Devil's mistress and her escort because that's how she's felt all evening.

And Marion cries all the way back to camp.

CHAPTER 51

THE TRAP
IS SET

BEFORE MIDNIGHT, AUGUST 22, 1886

When the rat takes the cheese, all that's left is for the poison to take effect.

MARION BURSTS INTO camp and slides off her horse. Wesley grabs her reins. Everyone jumps up, weapons in hand. Her torn dress flaps in the breeze as she races to sit by the fire. She shudders, not from fright, but for having to restrain herself from killing Tom Kimbrell for trying to rape her. She doesn't realize that her blouse has fallen open. She quickly pulls it back together to cover her breasts. The men look away out of respect. She gets herself together.

She rocks back and forth and says, "Tonight. We gotta go tonight. They plan to have the auction tomorrow at noon."

Rainy brings her water and sits on a log beside her. "Tomorrow?" He slams his fist into his palm. "All right, then. We don't have a choice. We go tonight." He turns back to Marion and puts his arm around her. "I'm so sorry, dear. Are you okay?"

She's trying to tie up her dress, but her hands are shaking too much. Wesley squats in front of her to calm her hands that are working like bees in the hive. She lets go, and he gently fixes her dress in a way that will keep her covered.

Wesley's calm spirit sets Marion at ease. He looks at the group and says, "Bravest woman I ever saw."

Marion takes in a deep breath and leans on Rainy's shoulder. "I'm all right, Uncle Rainy. Just shaken up a little, but thank you." She sits up straight and sips the coffee Matt brings over. A bit revived, she laughs. "You should've seen me play the part. I reckon I'll always have the skills to lure a man into giving me whatever I want from him."

Wesley's boyish charm gets the best of him. "Meaning no harm, ma'am... uh, not ma'am... I'm sorry. Oh, shit, I'll just say it. Judgin' from what I just witnessed, you have the beauty to charm King Midas out of all the gold he ever made with the slightest touch."

Marion glares at Wesley, then snickers. "Like what you saw a minute ago, young feller?"

Wesley says, "Oh, yeah. You look more beautiful than one of them goddess statues in Greece I saw in a picture book." He catches himself. "I mean, damn, I'm sorry, I —"

"Good. Now that you've had your show, if I ever catch you peeking at me while I'm dressing or taking a bath, I'll make marbles out of your eyeballs to go with the stones I'll clip from between your legs, understand?"

Wesley covers his mouth to keep from laughing and nods. "Yes."

"The rest of you men, I thank you for your kind respectfulness whilst I was exposed and unaware." She bursts out laughing and throws a stick at Wesley. "Oh, hell, what am I sayin'? If I saw a man who looked as good to me as I do to you gents, by God I'd gawk at him, too."

Ise brings Marion a blanket, and Matt pours her more coffee.

"Thank you." She takes a sip, and then shares the information she gathered at the saloon.

Rainy says, "All right, men, gather closer." He takes a stick and draws on the ground. "Here's the plan." He looks into the eyes of every man around the campfire, some of whom he knows may be dead this time tomorrow. "All right, everyone clear? We surround the house and position ourselves to cover the windows and doors. Marion and I go through the front door. The rest of you know your places, right?"

All nod, though some fidget out of nervousness.

"Good, then." Rainy elbows Wesley. "Son, I know no good Wood boy would go anywhere without at least one or two jars of fine moonshine whiskey."

Wesley smiles. "I just happen to have two pints."

Rainy nods. "Break them out. Let's make a toast to our upcoming success."

Wesley hands one jar of moonshine to Rainy, who asks, "Didn't you say you had two jars?"

"I do."

"Are we not going to get to savor a full cup each of its fine burn this evening?"

Wesley holds up the jar he's keeping in his hand and looks at the stars through it. "Nope, I'm savin' this one for somethin' special."

"What's that?"

"Like Miss Marion over there said, you'll get to see later."

Elzey stands away from the fire, fiddling with something hanging around his neck.

Rainy takes him a portion of moonshine. "How are you doing, Elzey?'

"I'm all right, but I have to admit, I've never done anything like this before."

"Truth be told, none of us have done anything quite like this before. You will be all right, son."

Elzey turns and pulls what he's been toying with in his shirt out for Rainy to see. "I was told by my father many years ago as a boy, when I thought Lummy was my uncle, that this gator tooth would keep me safe and bring me luck."

Rainy smiles. "I remember that tooth and the story behind it."

"Tarle told me that story. My father told it when he lived and worked with Ben."

Rainy lays his hand on Elzey's shoulder. "So, you know that your father is with you now."

Elzey holds the gator tooth up so that the metal sparkles in the shifting firelight. "I do, Uncle Rainy. I feel like he's real close."

Rainy grins and puts his finger on Elzey's chest. "He always is, right in there."

CHAPTER 52

THERE'S MORE'N ONE REASON TO KILL AN OUTLAW

BEFORE DAWN, AUGUST 23, 1886

Hurtin' animals says more about a man than how he treats humans.

THE BAND OF rescuers surround Kimbrell's ranch house. Thick brush hides within earshot of the house makes it easier to hear what's going on. Rainy and Marion crawl up to the east side of the house, stretching out on the ground to wait. It's still dark, but light is peeking over the hill that leads away from the house in a long upward slope.

Tom Kimbrell walks out onto the porch that faces the east. He stretches, and the little bells that hung around Marion's neck last night now hang around his.

Marion whispers, "That's him with little bells. That's Tom Kimbrell." She fidgets like ants are crawling all over her.

Rainy puts his arm over her shoulders. "It's all right, Marion, everything will be fine." He elbows her and grins. "So, that was your plan for the little bells, even back in Winnfield?"

She looks long and hard into his eyes. "Yes, and what I did last night, too, and what I'll have to do here in a bit to get Missus Caroline back. Granny Thankful has already declared it."

"What is it?"

She grins, shakes her head, and turns to watch the porch. "You don't want to know."

Kimbrell sits, sipping his coffee and wiping sleep from his eyes.

His mother, whom everyone calls Aunt Polly, follows him out with fresh baked biscuits and a cup of steaming coffee in her hand. She sets them down on a small table between them and goes back inside. She brings out a saucer and sets it at the edge of the porch. She pours milk into it from a stone pitcher.

Kimbrell asks, "What's that for?"

Aunt Polly smiles with her front teeth missing. "Watch, you'll see."

Tom Kimbrell looks to the east as light breaks over the hill. "I like this time of day. It's a good time to be in the woods huntin' squirrels, rabbits, deer, and such. I miss home, Mother."

Aunt Polly sighs. "Me, too, son. Ain't no place on God's good green earth like Winn Parish, Looseana." She taps her foot, sounding the call for something to come to the milk. "It's always been my favorite time of day, too, son. By this time, we'd already be done with the killin' of the migrants and cleanin' up the blood. John West and your brother Laws would be on their way to throw the bodies down a well. They'd come back for breakfast, and then were off to work on gettin' rid of the loot we took from them poor, defenseless, ignert ass pilgrims, heh."

Kimbrell laughs. "Poor little babies, bless their hearts."

Aunt Polly takes a noisy slurp of her coffee. "What'cha gonna do with that bitch inside?"

Kimbrell leans up. "I don't know if I want to love on her for a while, sell her outright, or cut her up into little pieces just for the fun of it. I'm still hacked about Lummy Tullos blowin' John West's head off. What do you think?"

"I think that whatever you do, do it this mornin'. Somebody will come lookin' for her, and we don't need anybody snoopin' around here. Sell her and use the money to buy more cattle. We're makin' pretty good on them critters."

Kimbrell breathes in deeply and looks up the long sloping hill. "Look at the sky, Ma. You know what they say about red sky mornin's?"

"Yeah, that a storm's a'comin', hard and fast." She takes a bite of biscuit and talks with her mouth full. She spits biscuit crumbs as she talks. "You best be decidin' what you're gonna do with that she-dawg inside, or—"

"I am, Ma, I am. I just wanted the boys to get a little more rest. Besides, I like sittin' out here with you before the sun comes up."

Aunt Polly pats his arm. "That's my sweet boy."

Tom Kimbrell lays his hand on hers. "Love you, Ma."

Aunt Polly taps her foot, and a small kitten gingerly climbs up the steps and meows.

Kimbrell kicks at the small bundle of white fur. "Where'd that damn thing come from?"

Aunt Polly tries to defend the kitten. "Oh, leave it alone. Ain't hurtin' nuthin'. The little thing wanders over from the farm next door everyday for its breakfast. I guess they ain't feedin' him and, well, I've been givin' him milk every morning."

"I don't want that damn thing around here. That meowing is nerve-rackin'. Get that damn thing out'a here."

Aunt Polly stomps her foot. "It ain't hurtin' nothin'. Leave him alone."

Kimbrell sets his cup down. He grabs the kitten and throws the animal like an apple as far as he can. It lands in the brush next to Marion's face. She starts to reach for the injured kitten.

Rainy grabs her hand and shakes his head. He mouths, "Don't."

Marion growls, "I'd kill him just for doin' that. There's more'n one reason to kill a bastard outlaw."

Rainy pats Marion's arm. "Maybe we'll come back for him."

She snatches her hand away. "Why don't we just kill that bastard now and get it over with?"

"Patience, my dear, he will get his soon enough. I guarantee it."

CHAPTER 53

CREEPING UP ON THE RANCH HOUSE

SUNUP, AUGUST 23, 1886

Ending a bad dream always takes waking up
and putting one step toward reality.

R AINY AND MARION watch the old house from their perch in the rocks just above the cabin.

Marion shudders and whispers, "This is like a bad dream, Uncle Rainy."

He elbows her. "You better get awake, my dear, for it doesn't get any more real than this. And we're about to take the first step toward ending this whole damn business."

Kimbrell and Aunt Polly sit quietly, enjoying the solace of the early Texas morning, unaware of what's lurking in the surrounding rocks and brush. Not a breeze, not a sound stirs. Only a cricket here and there and a wood thrush calling from a bush near where Rainy and Marion hide.

Aunt Polly gets up to stretch, pushing on her back from behind. "It'll be full light soon." Her joints crack and pop like a pine wood fire. She snickers. "Reminds me of the time you broke that old man's leg bones when he wouldn't tell us where he hid the gold. His old bones sounded like kindling getting snapped into smaller pieces for the fire."

"Those were the good old days." He looks around. "I think that old hammer is around her somewhere. I might need it this morning when the fun starts."

Aunt Polly drifts back to another time in Winn Parish when the West-Kimbrell Gang ruled the Natchez Trace and El Camino Roads. She snaps out of her daydream. "Get the boys up and ready. I'll get breakfast goin'. Do ham, grits, eggs, biscuits, and gravy sound all right?"

Tom Kimbrell rubs his belly. "Couldn't be any better if you're doin' the cookin', Ma."

She smiles and kisses his forehead. "Thank you, dear. You've always been the good son."

Marion looks at Rainy and whispers, "These people are completely mad."

Rainy nods. "And that's what makes them so dangerous."

Kimbrell gets up to open the door for his mother. "I like breakfast before I start carvin' up a woman. I'll start right after I eat. I've other things to do this afternoon."

Aunt Polly shakes her finger at her son. "All right. Get the preacher boy up and in the right spirit. Tell him not to go into town for church this mornin'. I want a lively service today. Tell him get up a good sermon. I'm in need of some encouraging words from the Good Book."

Kimbrell nods and snickers. "I'll tell him, Ma. We'll need to ask forgiveness for the things the Lord has for us to do today. Preacher will be the first one I rouse this mornin'."

"Take him a cup of coffee and put his Bible in his hands. Tell him he don't have to do chores this morning. I want him all studied up by ten o'clock."

The door slams behind Kimbrell and his mother. Loud talk and joking erupt inside the farmhouse. Not a sentry can be found watching for the impending doom that waits in the rocks and bushes surrounding the Kimbrell lair.

Rainy asks, "How many of them are there, you think?"

Marion counts in her head. "From watching their comin's and goin's all night to the outhouse and such, I say eight, including the one Kimbrell called Preacher." She turns and grins like the Devil himself. "He's mine."

Granny whispers through the brush, "Sometimes it's the wicked, self-proclaimed man of God who gets his due first."

Rainy squints. "It's not a dream anymore, is it?"

Marion rolls over on her back and checks her pistols. "Not anymore, it ain't."

RAINY SIGNALS THE others to make their way to the farmhouse. Just as they get in position to rush the house, the front door creaks open, and a tall, skinny man tiptoes out wearing only long johns, boots, and a reverend's hat. He trots over to the outhouse like he's got stomach trouble.

He hurries inside and breathes out a long and loud sigh of relief. "Whew, I made it."

Rainy and his band of rescuers stop dead in their tracks and drop to the ground. Wesley and Ise hide behind the outhouse and quietly put their backs against the back wall of the small building.

Rainy whispers to Marion, "Damn, wasn't counting on that. Who is it?"

Marion growls, "The preacher boy who was with Kimbrell in the saloon. He came in drunk as a skunk and grabbed my titties. I slapped him twice before he got the message. Kimbrell's men just laughed. I wanted to kill 'em all right then and there, but we wouldn't have found out where Missus Caroline was. That preacher boy may be the most lustful man I've ever met, next to the one I killed in Waterproof, Louisiana, some years back. I saw the same devil in that preacher boy's eyes. I want him."

Rainy notices Marion scratching her wrist. It's bleeding and scarred like she's been doing it for a while. Just like Lummy. "Marion, it's all right, dear. Everything is going to be all right." He looks into her eyes, and it's like nothing's there. It's as though he can look all the way down deep inside her where a great hollowness resides. Not even a soul.

He shakes her, and she comes back to where she is.

Rainy consoles her. "From what you told me so far, it was bad."

She smiles. "You can not even imagine." She pushes her long blonde hair back and says, "I'm all right. You don't have to worry about me. I know why I'm here and what the most important thing is. Gettin' Missus Caroline out of there alive." She squints at the outhouse. "But that preachin' son of a bitch is gonna get his."

Rainy turns to eye the outhouse. "You're good."

The preacher hums and sings, "We shall come rejoicing, bringing in the sheaves. Yes, we shall come rejoicing—" His singing stops, and he's silent except for a bit of moaning. Then, he passes gas so long and loud that Ise and Wesley almost start laughing out loud.

They hold their noses, and Ise mouths, "Damn, the Devil done crawled up in his ass and died."

Wesley snickers, and the preacher stops singing.

Wesley covers his mouth, and fortunately a bird lands on top of the outhouse whose chirp sounds like Wesley's snicker.

The preacher resumes his melody and in step with the tune, sings, "I certainly am rejoicin', passing all that gas." He laughs at his own joke as he hums all the way back to the farmhouse.

Marion looks at Rainy with eyes that burn like fiery embers. "He won't be laughin' soon."

RAINY SIGNALS THE small band of rescuers to move toward the ranch house. They make no sound as they slip up close to cover every door and window.

Marion smiles. "Me first, Uncle Rainy."

Rainy nods. "Right behind you, my darling niece."

Marion yells, "Blessed be the Lord my strength, which teacheth my hands to war, and my fingers to fight!"

Marion and Rainy rush in the front door, pistol in one hand and a knife in the other. Ise lets loose a shotgun blast through the window that cripples two of Kimbrell's men. He drops the shotgun and dives through the window, his short sword in hand and a knife blade in his teeth. He rolls to land on his feet to finish the two-shot. They moan as his knife slits each of their throats.

Jesse and Wesley gun down two outlaws trying to slip out the back door. Jesse kicks their weapons away and stands in the doorway. Wesley quickly gathers their weapons.

Rainy rushes to knock a shotgun from Aunt Polly's hands before she blasts Marion, who has squared off against the biggest man he's ever seen, even taller than Lummy Tullos.

Marion laughs and screams like a panther as she battles him tooth and nail. She moves around the room like a monkey in a cage, ducking and dodging the giant's every knife thrust and effort to get a shot off with his pistol. Finally, she gets behind him and climbs up his back like a catamount up a tree and buries her knife into the back of the giant's head.

He goes down like an old rotten tree as Marion shouts, "Goliath, you ain't got shit on us!" Marion grins at Tarle as she severs the giant's head like David did in the Bible. "Didn't I tell you that God is greater than the giants we came to kill?"

"You did." He frantically looks around for his wife. He screams, "Caroline!"

Caroline's cry comes behind a door next to Marion. She drops the giant's head and bursts into the bedroom, where the preacher boy is fondling and squeezing Caroline's breasts.

Preacher cries, "The angel of death has arrived." He raises his gun, but Marion is quicker. She blows the pistol out of his hand and three fingers with it. He screams, "Oh, God, help me!"

Marion kicks him in the groin, and as he falls, she growls like a panther. "Ain't no God here to help you, Preacher. The fool says in his heart there is no God."

He cries out like a squealing pig as Marion steps on his bloody hand. "But I believe in God, and if you do, you won't kill me."

Marion's lips tighten. "I know you do, Preacher. You say there is a God but live like the Devil and expect him to be all right with that?" She reloads her pistol as Tarle rushes to Caroline. "What have you got to say for yourself, Preacher?"

"That I've been a damn fool."

"Kinda late for makin' a confession, ain't it?"

"If I make one to you, will you let me go?"

"Make it then."

The preacher whines, "I'm a damn fool for the way I let my daddy beat the hell out of me and beat my momma to death. It's his damn fault that I did what I did, but I was the one who…." His words fade into the background, and Marion hears no more as he babbles on.

Marion weakens, remembering how she was treated in the Natchez orphanage by that preacher and later in the whorehouse. Uncle Silas's face comes to mind, and she thinks about how he was murdered by a preacher. She feels herself scratching the same spot on her arm and regains her composure.

The preacher smiles in hopes that he's said enough to save his life. "There, I've made my confession." He looks into her lifeless eyes. "Please forgive me."

"I'm not the one you need to speak with about that. You need to talk to the one who is above all and forgives all. Creator is his name."

"I've been a damn fool."

Marion cocks her pistol. "Then a damn fool it is." She blows a hole through his temple, and he collapses in a puddle of his own blood. She falls into Tarle and Caroline and breathes a heavy sigh. "I'm not sure that I'm really cut out to do this kind of work," Marion mutters as she watches the preacher's blood spread across the floor, "There ain't no saving blood of Jesus for a wicked, lyin' ass preacher who never walked the path he preached." She spits on him. "Touch my titties, will you?"

Matt, who's been guarding their horses, walks in the front door just as Wesley pushes a man out the back door. Matt follows Wesley. He pulls a small jar and holds it up while he keeps his pistol trained on his enemy.

Matt asks, "It's not really the time for a drink, don't you think?"

"I agree with you whole-heartedly, but it is time for this man's good morning sip of fine Wood brothers' moonshine made from the sweet waters of Aaron Wood's Spring."

Wesley takes a sip and empties the pint jar on the wounded outlaw, covering him from head to toe. While the ruffian swats his hair and claws at his eyes like he's being attacked by a swarm of yellowjackets, Wesley strikes a match just as the outlaw starts to lunge at him.

Wesley cooly says, "This'll prepare you for where you're goin' next, you son of a bitch."

The outlaw screams and rolls around on the ground, trying to quench the flames with dust.

Matt pulls his pistol and says, "Enough," and fires, killing the man.

Wesley stands and wipes his hands on his shirt. "Yes, that's good enough," he says as he pats Matt on the shoulder and walks back into the farmhouse.

Matt whispers, "Damn, you Wood boys ain't scared."

Rainy, who's been guarding Aunt Polly, is hit in the back of the head by an outlaw who was hiding in the pantry. Rainy whirls around just as the man raises a knife to stab him and grabs him by the throat with one hand and squeezes with all his might. The outlaw slashes at his arm, but Rainy's jacket is thick enough to protect it. The man gasps for air and wretches in pain. He drops his weapon and shivers like he's got the malarial shakes.

Rainy yells like he's charging a hill on some battlefield. "No more!" He whips out the throwing knife his blood father used to murder his real father, and with one slash opens the man's neck at the jugular vein. He growls, "That's in honor of my mother who was treated like this good woman we saved today."

Aunt Polly drops to her knees and prays.

Rainy spits. "Ain't no amount of praying going to help you today, sister."

Everyone goes into the bedroom, where Tarle is on his knees crying and hugging his wife.

"Oh, my dear wife, I was so stupid to—"

Caroline calmly says, "Tarle, I'm okay. Would you please get me out of these ropes, dear?"

Marion gets up to help Tarle.

Caroline laughs. "I told you not to go, didn't I, husband?"

Tarle is speechless, then stutters, "Yes, I-I... know Caro—"

"Let's talk about all of this later." She smiles and walks out of her prison room. She looks at the dead men scattered about for a moment. "Time to go, Tarle." She nods, letting him know she'll be fine. He takes her arm and has her sit down to rest for a moment.

Rainy squeezes Tarle's shoulder and whispers, "Son, she's been through a lot. She's still in shock. Be gentle and give her time. Let this tragedy make you a better husband. Forego self-blame and pity and put yourself into loving her, you hear?"

"Yes, sir, I will."

Rainy scans the room. He and Marion look at each other and say at the same time, "Where's Elzey?"

CHAPTER 54

THE

EXCHANGE

9:15 A.M., AUGUST 23, 1886

If you want to beat the Devil, then you have to use his rules.

TOM KIMBRELL SCREAMS, "Rainy Mills, get your ass out here and all the other bastards you brought with you, especially that whore bitch who got me into this."

Marion whispers to Rainy, "You and me?"

He nods. "The rest of you stay here and don't make a move."

Kimbrell yells, "Send out my mother, now."

Rainy nods, and Aunt Polly rushes out the door. "Oh, thank you, son, for savin' your old ma."

Kimbrells barks, "Now, you, Rainy Mills, and you better not have any weapons on you."

Marion shakes her head. "I don't go anywhere without—"

Rainy puts his finger on her lips. "You will today, except for what you carry around your neck in the back."

"My derringer?" Marion grins. "I'll get changed."

Rainy snickers. "Play the part well, whore bitch."

She backhands him on the shoulder and then motions for the other men to turn around and look away. She strips down to only her long button-up shirt with nothing underneath.

Rainy slips a twine necklace with the small, one shot derringer round her neck. He moves the derringer to hang in the back and asks, "You ready?"

Her squint speaks of hesitation while the fire in her eyes says she's determined to see this through. They move to the door, and Rainy takes her by the back of her collar and holds his pistol to her head. She opens the door, and there in the corral with a lone horse, saddled and ready to go, stands Tom Kimbrell holding Elzey with a knife to his throat. Blood is dripping down his neck, and Elzey looks to be on the verge of fainting.

Kimbrell cocks his head. "What's this?"

Rainy smiles and says, "How about we trade?"

"You're not gonna... wait a minute. What kind of trick is this?"

Rainy edges Marion closer, her shirt flopping open just enough to keep Kimbrell's eyes on her and not Rainy. "No tricks. This woman doesn't mean shit to us. That boy does."

Kimbrell rubs his chin. "Interesting."

"Now, I know you and Lummy Tullos have had your differences, but this is a deal to put all that behind you."

"How's that?" Kimbrell asks as he wipes the drool from the corner of his mouth.

"Even trade, the girl for the boy."

"Naaagh, that ain't enough. I'm goin' to get a whole lot of pleasure out'a killin' this one. Just like Lummy Tullos did when he shot off John West's head and severed Dawg Smith's with that big ole huntin' knife. I'm goin' to peel this one's hide off a little at a time."

"And miss the skills this girl has mastered? Why, she was trained in the art of pleasuring a man in the best of sporting houses in none other than Natchez, Mississippi. You could have your way with her, and when you're tired of her, you could still sell her for a huge price. You would have firsthand knowledge of those skills, if you know what I mean."

Tom Kimbrell fidgets like he's got ants in his breeches. It's not ants, but the uncontrollable need for a woman that grows in his pants. "All right, but this is how it's gonna go."

"Then spit it out."

"Bring me three horses, saddled and ready to go. Ma and I take the boy and the girl. You give me an hour head start. I'll know if you start anytime before that because my route takes me up that sloping hill. I'll see what's comin' behind me for a couple miles. I see you, or anyone, following me, I kill the boy and still keep the girl, understand?"

Rainy nods and retrieves three horses from the barn.

It dawns on Kimbrell that only Rainy and Marion are outside the old farm house. "Where's the rest of you?"

"I told them to stay inside. I didn't want one of them to get trigger happy and mess up this good deal. Besides, your men are all done in."

Kimbrell laughs loudly. "Good thinkin', Rainy. Them other fellers? Hell, they're just cannon fodder, like John West used to say. You know he and Lummy Tullos fought in the same shithole rifle pit together during the Siege of Vicksburg."

Rainy hands the reins to Kimbrell. "Yeah, seems like Lummy told me about that one time."

"I hate that Preacher didn't make it. I kinda liked him. Ma did, too." Kimbrell pats his mother's shoulder and yells, "Get your rooster in the dirt, Rainy Mills. I ought'a just kill you, but I ain't. You go back and tell Winn Parish what happened here, and tell that Lummy Tullos, if I ever see him again, I'm just gonna go to shootin' because I know he's come to kill me."

Rainy mumbles. "I got it."

Kimbrell waits. "You hear me?"

Rainy scowls at Kimbrell. "I hear you. Now get on with what you've got to do."

CHAPTER 55

A SHADOW BRINGS OUT THE BEST OF CREATOR'S LIGHT

10:00 A.M., AUGUST 23, 1886

*Out of the deepest and darkest pits of Hell do the strongest
of Creator's angels rise.*

A S SOON AS Kimbrell and Aunt Polly and their two hostages are out of sight, Rainy signals for the rest to take the right and left flanks in the scrub brush. He motions for them to move slowly, placing his finger over his lips. They understand. They heard everything that was said between Rainy and Kimbrell.

With Wesley and Ise in place on the right and Jesse on the left, Rainy whispers, "I'll stay here in plain sight so Kimbrell doesn't get spooked. If I don't, he'll kill Elzey." He grimaces at that thought. "Hopefully, he can't keep his eyes off Marion and y'all can get the drop on him." He scratches his beard. "Matt, you bring up the horses when I signal you."

Matt nods and takes off at a dead run.

Ise and his band of rescuers look at each other, wondering what to do next.

Rainy points to the sky. "Remember who is with us." They nod, and Rainy says, "You can do this." Then, he realizes their dilemma. No one's in charge. "Ise, you lead them."

Ise salutes and motions the little band of rescuers in the direction that Kimbrell went.

KIMBRELL GETS TO the top of the long sloping mountain and turns to see

Rainy standing in front of the old farmhouse. He waves, and Rainy signals back that he sees him. Kimbrell leads his two hostages into the brush off the road. Aunt Polly follows along behind them.

"I've got just the place for what happens next for you two."

Kimbrell turns for one last look and, satisfied he isn't being followed, he stops to partake in a different kind of satisfaction.

"Ma, stand over there where you can watch Rainy Mills. I don't want him or his men sneakin' up on us."

Aunt Polly is getting nervous. "Get on with your cuttin' and carvin'. We need to leave soon."

"Yes, ma'am." He turns to Marion. "You got away last time, Belle—or whatever bitch dawg name you wear. This time I'm gonna work you every which way but Sunday go to meetin'." He snickers hysterically, like a horde of demons crawling alive in his soul. "Strip, bitch!"

As she removes her shirt, Elzey turns to hide his face from the wickedness about to occur. He grabs the gator tooth and prays.

Kimbrell laughs and kicks him in the side. "Oh, no, you ain't doin' that. You turn around and watch how a real man handles a woman."

Marion tries to pull the derringer around to shoot Kimbrell, but the string gets caught in her hair.

Kimbrell turns and slaps Marion hard enough to make her mouth bleed. "What? You think you were gonna shoot me in the back when I wasn't lookin'?"

Marion spits. "You treat women like you do the sheep and goats you hump, shitface."

Kimbrell binds her hands together, throws the rope over a tree limb, and pulls it tight before tying it off. "There. I'll be with you in a moment. I have a bit of unfinished business to attend to with Elzey Burk Tullos."

Marion screams, "What? You can't do that! Rainy made a fair trade. You better honor it, or I'll spend the rest of my days hunting you down, and when I find you, it'll take years to finish you off, one small piece at a time."

"Which is exactly what I'm fixin' to do with this lad—and you're next."

A moan drifts from Marion's soul. "Oh, please don't. Do with me as you will, but not him."

"Don't worry your pretty little head. I'll make it quick for him." He grins. "But not for you, whore bitch."

Elzey lies on the ground, faint from blood loss, waiting to be executed. Kimbrell learned well from his mother the skill of how to bleed a hog slowly so blood wouldn't get everywhere. She didn't train him on hogs, but rather on women traveling west with their husbands who stopped for the night at the Kimbrell house for a meal and a night's rest.

Elzey holds his bandana against the wound on his neck. Fortunately, it looks worse than it really is.

A shadow slips through the brush, making no sound.

Elzey can hardly hold up his head. "Granny Thankful?"

A whisper comes with a slight breeze from the east. *"I am here, child."*

He sees her face glowing like an agate stone of many colors. Elzey squeezes the gator tooth on the necklace that was once his father's and prays, "Creator, whatever happens in the next few minutes, please make a way for Missus Marion to go free."

Kimbrell stomps over to where Elzey is on the ground trying to get up. "Get on your feet, boy. It's your turn to receive the Devil's due."

Elzey drops his head, and then frantically looks into the brush to find Granny Thankful again.

She's there, smiling. As her face fades, another one replaces Granny's. It's the face of the man he saw on the Mississippi River ferry.

Elzey coughs and whispers, "The Devil's due, huh, Tom Kimbrell?"

"Yeah, that's right."

Elzey barely mumbles out something unintelligible.

Kimbrell unsheathes his blade and takes Elzey's hair in hand. "I didn't hear you. What's that?"

Elzey takes a deep breath and speaks in a clear tone. "Look, for the Devil has come for you."

In the speed of a bolt of lightning and just as powerful, a graying long-haired angel rushes forward with a blade that could only be made in the hills of Mississippi by a father who always wanted his son to be protected. The avenging angel slices through the mop of hair Tom Kimbrell has gathered in his hand, and Elzey falls free. He slashes right and left until Tom Kimbrell stands still with no ability to defend himself.

CHAPTER 56

THE DEVIL TO DEFEAT
A DEMON ARRIVES

NOON STRAIGHT UP, AUGUST 23, 1886

When the Devil comes for one of his misbehaving demons,
there's extra hell to pay.

TOM KIMBRELL QUIVERS from intense pain and can barely speak.

"Lummy Tullos, I thought—"

Elzey reaches up a hand. "Father."

Silence.

I come to my senses. "I am Lummy Tullos, and today you die, Tom Kimbrell." I spit on the ground at Kimbrell's feet. "You and your kind, damn you all to hell. I'll go to my grave ridding the earth of your wickedness."

Kimbrell stands paralyzed, mouth gaped open in surprise.

I turn to Elzey and say, "Lie down and do not watch."

Elzey obeys.

I walk to where Kimbrell stands shuddering. I look at the knife that my father made me so many years ago in Choctaw County. The blade that removed Dawg Smith's head from his body and... now is not the time to reminisce.

Aunt Polly runs over and drops to her knees, begging, "Please don't kill him, he's the only son I have left. He didn't mean to—"

"Oh, ma'am, yes he did."

Kimbrell squeals like a stuck pig as I slowly run my blade from his crotch up his body to split his rib cage open, finally stopping at his jaw. Before he collapses, I remind him as he takes his first steps into hell, "You just don't treat people like that." I drop the knife, never to pick it up again. "All is accounted for and made equal again."

Elzey whispers, "So, this is what a reckoning looks like."

Out of the brush burst Ise, Wesley, and Jesse with guns cocked and ready for a fight.

I turn, crouching like a catamount ready to spring.

Ise yells, "Whoa, whoa, whoa, Mister Lummy. It's us, your friends."

For a moment I see Susannah's face, but quickly realize its Ise, who looks so much like her. Then I remember.

Marion mumbles a verse from the Good book, "For I the Lord thy God will hold thy right hand, saying to thee, Fear not, I will help thee."

I yank off my shirt and rush to cover her naked body.

"Thank you, Uncle Lummy. I knew it was you who came for us when you busted out of the thicket like a she-bear defending her cubs."

I smile as I untie the ropes holding her up. "Why am I so blessed to be called your uncle?"

The ropes loosen, and young Marion drops to the ground, but not before I catch her.

She kisses my cheek. "You're everything anybody has ever said about you, Uncle Lummy."

I shake my head. "Uncle? I don 't understand."

"I'm Marion Tullos, raised by your uncle Silas in Marion County."

I blink twice and shake my head. "Well, I'll be. Never knew Uncle Silas to have any children. Last time I saw him I was only ten years old, but—"

Marion puts a finger to my lips. "That's a story for another time. Right now, I'd like to get covered up decent-like."

Matt brings up the horses.

Rainy rushes to bring Marion her clothes. "So sorry you had to go through with this, Marion."

"I'm all right. You don't worry about me. Let's get Elzey patched up." Then, she nods in my direction. "I guess you know that old coot over there."

He steps back when he sees me standing off to the side.

"What the... Lummy?"

I grin and nod. "Betcha didn't expect to see me again so soon."

Rainy snickers. "Hell, I'm wonderin' what took you so long."

"Didn't you tell me one time that Napoleon said, 'Never interrupt your enemy when he is making a mistake?'" I kick the dirt. "Well, I waited till Kimbrell made his last."

Rainy shakes his head, grimacing. "You and that knife become one when it comes to times like these."

I squint. "Not anymore. That was my last fight. Ever."

THE HORSES ARE ready. Everything is packed where it should be. Matt and Caroline ride up in a buggy he took from the farmhouse. Everyone gathers before mounting up as Marion finishes dressing behind a rock.

Rainy waves his hand at a pile of wood and kindling. "Matt, Wesley, bring that wood over here, would you? We need a fire."

Marion walks out and points at Aunt Polly. "What do we do with her?"

Aunt Polly folds her hands like she's praying. "Oh, you sweet dear, I know you have the compassion to let this old woman go free. I know you won't—"

Marions slaps Aunt Polly so hard she lands on her back. "What? Kill you? Why I'll—"

Rainy grabs Marion around the waist and whispers in her ear, "It's all right, niece."

I say with no emotion, "No, we won't kill you, Aunt Polly. We're gonna leave you here, tied up for the coyotes to come for you. But not before you see the last of your world go up in flames."

I throw a match to light the fire. The dry wood ignites to burn fast and hot. And it's not long before Tom Kimbrell becomes ashes. We watch in silence until he is scattered to the wind.

I turn to Aunt Polly, who is shaking so hard her teeth rattle. "Marion, tie her to the same tree her son bound you to. Tarle, scoop up some of Tom Kimbrell's blood from that puddle and spread it on her legs. Elzey, get some paper and write a note, saying, 'The Kimbrells are no more,' and stick it in her pocket."

It's done, and I need to pray.

I look to the sky and beg, "Creator, please forgive the wickedness we had to dish out on wicked men. Let these good men and women who gather with me in prayer now return to their lives, never having to do anything like this again. Carry us home now on the wings of angels."

I look to the brush, and there stands Granny Thankful, that faithful soul who has guided and protected me since I was a child. I nod, and she blows me a grandmotherly kiss.

I turn to Elzey. "I'll stay the night so we can talk, son, but then I leave in the morning."

Elzey grabs me around the waist. "But why, Pop? Why can't we be together now?"

"Let's talk about that tonight."

He nods.

Rainy pats me on the shoulder. "Let's go, old friend. We've got a fine camp and good food to celebrate our successful retrieval of Miss Caroline and you saving your son's life."

I rub my forehead. "Guess I didn't think of it that way."

Rainy squints. "Granny Thankful made it so, didn't she?"

I hold up my agate stone. We ride for a moment, and I ask, "Camp and good food, you say?"

"That's what I'm offering."

"I hope there won't be any coyotes this time."

Rainy chuckles. "No, there won't. They'll all be at supper together at Aunt Polly's tonight."

We turn our mounts to head east toward camp.

Rainy stops for a moment. "Marion, you coming, dear?"

"Yeah, be right with you. There's something I need to grab before we go."

Marion picks up my knife, thumbs the blade, and slides it into her belt, leaving the blood of her attacker on it. She stuffs it into her belt.

As she mounts up, Marion licks the blood from her thumb and whispers to the setting sun, "Thou hast a mighty arm and strong is thy hand, and high is thy right hand. Justice and judgment are the habitation of thy throne, O Lord. Mercy and truth shall go before thy face. Blessed are the people that

know the joyful sound for they shall walk, O Lord, in the light of thy countenance." She gently pats my knife and smiles. "And Creator's blade is sharp.
Very sharp."

CHAPTER 57

THE
LAST NIGHT

EVENING, AUGUST 23, 1886

Telling old stories, good and bad, heal the soul and help it move on.

ELZEY SHIVERS A bit. "Gets kinda cool out here at night."
Ise chews on a piece of dried grass. "Nothing like a good fire to warm the heart, mind, body, and soul."

Jesse looks across the valley from their hilltop campsite. "It's kind of nice out here. Not near as muggy as back home. Them damn swamps make breathin' hard and breedin' skeeters easy."

Matt picks up the remaining empty tin plates, having cooked a fine meal in celebration of having Missus Caroline back safe and sound. Everyone thanks him for the good food and being such a willing hand. He smiles as he completes his work. "I wouldn't want it any other way, either. You folks are my family."

Wesley, still feeling new to the group, says, "I'm just happy to be here with y'all." He fidgets around a bit. "I gotta confession to make." He hesitates.

I throw a small stick at him and laugh. "Well, go on, son, spit it out. I've never known a Wood boy to be scared of anythin'."

He throws it back. "All right, kinfolk, I'm gettin' to it. I-I… well, all right, dammit. I want to start courtin' Mister Jasper's daughter Isabell when we get back home. There it is. I said it."

Rainy asks, "Do we shoot him now or wait and let Jasper do it?"

Everybody laughs.

I laugh. "Heck, Jasper'd marry off his daughter right now if it meant gettin' a free supply of that fine Missip moonshine whiskey made from the sweet waters of Aaron Wood's spring."

Wesley jumps up. "I can surely make that happen."

I wave for Wesley to settle down and sit. "It's all right, son. Jasper's already noticed you eyein' his daughter." I elbow Rainy. "And like my oldest brother Elihu used to say, 'He ain't got nothin' against it.'" I feel for my knife to make a joke, but it's not in the sheath. I'm good with that, but I still want to make my joke. I pull my old pistol. "See this old pistol, Wesley?"

He shivers a bit. "Yes, sir, I see it."

"Then you know it's pretty old, and the mechanism that makes it work is pretty worn out. I have to watch it. It can go off if I don't handle it gentle-like and right, like you should treat a fine woman worth marryin'. Jasper's kind of like this old gun. Old, a bit worn out, and can easily go off if things aren't like they should be, like his daughter bein' mistreated. You get my meaning?"

"Yes, sir, I do."

"Don't forget Jasper fought at Vicksburg and threw grenades at the enemy when the cannon ordnance ran out, and went hand to hand against the Yanks when they got past the grenades and thunder barrels." I feel a war dream coming on. I press the owl claw into my wrist.

Rainy pulls my hand away and smiles. "It's all right, Lummy. We're all here in Texas, and Wesley is a good man. He'll treat Miss Isabell with gentle and graceful behavior."

Marion, who's said nothing since arriving in a camp rest, quotes the Bible, "So ought men to love their wives as their own bodies. He that loveth his wife loveth himself."

Wesley lifts his chin. "Yes, Miss Marion, that'll be my every intention. I'll do my best."

Marion grins. "I believe you will, Wesley Wood."

Wesley thanks Marion and gets up to get more wood for the fire.

Tarle holds Caroline closely, and he says to all around the fire, "I will forever be in your debt. You are family. Better said, you are my good friends. Someone once said, 'There is a friend that sticketh closer than a brother.' That's you. You're better than family, and our home is always open to you, day or night, anytime." He smiles at Caroline, who cuddles in his arms like a kitten. "We will be offended if you come through and don't at least come see us."

Caroline stands, brushes back her hair, and straightens her raggedy skirt. "Well then, I have something I need to say, too. I'll tell a story to do it. I'm told Tarle's father Ben used to tell this tale. Said he was there when it happened. It'll make my point. An old blind man who was hard of hearing was sitting in his house waiting for his children to bring his supper after they finished work. The sound of a great wind came, but the old man had heard stormy winds blow before. He felt the air whipping around, going in and out of the house, and breezing through the windows. He felt a crash, and then the winds disappeared. He thought to himself, 'All right, I'm okay.' Soon he heard voices, yelling, sounds of a door being kicked open. Startled, he asked, 'Who is it, what's goin' on?' His son rushed in and checked him for any wounds. 'Pa, don't you know where you are?' The old man replied, 'I'm right here where I always am till you and your sweet wife bring me my supper. Why do you ask if I know where I am?' His son thanks the Lord and says, 'Your house was picked up by a tornado that just came through. Now it sits two hundred yards from where it used to be.' The old man rubbed his chin. 'Alls I heard was some fierce wind and felt the house shake a bit. I do sense that I'm sitting facin' a different direction than I was, and it did get a bit air-ish up in here.' His son squeezed his shoulders. 'Weren't you afraid?' The old man said, 'No, I wasn't afraid, but I was just a little concerned when I thought the house was spinning like a child's toy. No, I was fine because I knew that no matter what happened, I knew you'd come. You always come.'"

Everyone remains still. Quiet.

Caroline looks to the starry sky and says, "Tarle, boys, Rainy and Ise, Miss Marion, no matter what happened in this difficult time or how strong the winds were or how turned around I got or afraid I might have felt, I knew you would come." She starts to waver from exhaustion but girds herself up. "Thank you, men, and you, too, Missus Marion. You saved my life, and I will never, ever, forget what you have done here. It will be a story my grandchildren will tell theirs until the Lord comes for us all." She cries and hugs Tarle. "My children thank you, too."

Elzey writes everything down as fast as he can. I'm sure he'll be sending this story to Mary for her book.

Caroline sits, and Ise starts humming "Amazing Grace." Then everyone, in low but grateful tones, sings words that bring comfort and peace. And watch the fire into the night.

CHAPTER 58

IT'S FINISHED, AND FOR GOOD

BEFORE DAWN, AUGUST 24, 1886

When a thing is done, let it be. For good.

MATT HAS COFFEE ready before dawn, and the smell of salt pork and biscuits drifts toward the sleeping men and women. One by one they rouse, wash their faces, traipse off to the bushes for a moment of privacy, and get their things packed. Ise, Jesse, and Wesley get the horses saddled and ready.

I sit quietly by the fire, watching Marion gather her things. She pushes the tail of her shirt aside but covers something up with her hand. She moves her hand to reveal the knife my pa made me years ago.

I squint and cock my head, whispering, "I wasn't expecting that."

Marion carefully cleans the blood from the hilt and blade with a damp rag, caring for it like a precious jewel. She pulls a whetstone from her saddlebag and begins sharpening the blade in a slow, circular motion.

I clear my throat. "I thought I left that knife back where we took care of Tom Kimbrell."

Marion doesn't look up. "You did."

"I wanted it to stay there."

"Your knife did, Uncle Lummy."

"But like I said, I wanted it to stay there."

"And like I said, Uncle Lummy, *your* knife did. It's mine now, and it's on me to carry on the family tradition."

"What family tradition?"

Marion grins and whispers, "Ridding the earth of the wicked as God would have it."

I ponder her words, then nod. "All right, then. Just keep the blade clean and the edge like a razor. It will serve you well. As long as you do things as God would have it." I summon up the courage to pass the mantle of authority and responsibility to one who is no blood kin but every bit a Tullos, through and through. "Marion, you will be in my prayers. Every day."

Marion winks. "Thank you, Uncle Lummy. That means everything to me."

"Where will you go next?"

Marion ties down her saddlebags. "Hangin' Judge Parker always has a list of ruffians that need rounding up and brought to court. I like his style of justice, fair and swift. Maybe I'll start there."

I'm still rattled a bit from the battle. I'm thinking it might be good to keep some company on my way to where I'm going next, at least until my head gets sorted out after the battle.

I decide. "I hear Texarkana is a pretty place in the fall. Mind if I ride a ways with you?"

"It's on my way to Fort Smith. And havin' you along for company? Well, hell yes, please."

I look Cloud over. "Maybe tell me more about my uncle Silas? I've always wished I'd had more time with him. The stories he told me when I was just a boy have carried me a long ways."

"I'd like that. Uncle Silas was the best man I ever knew, until now." She winks and pats my old knife stuck in her belt. "You can show me some tricks with this big ole knife."

I pull the sheath I made for it years ago from my belt. "Might as well have this, too."

"Thank you." She looks it over, runs her belt through it, and slips the knife in. She smiles and asks, "Mind if we go north? I want to see Fort Worth."

I make a request. "I'm good with that. No trains, just horses."

"Suits me fine. I need time to unwind a bit."

"Then it's done."

CHAPTER 59

I SAY
GOODBYE

DAWN, AUGUST 24, 1886

*Saying goodbye may be the hardest thing you tell someone you
love, even when it's the right thing to do. And as much as it hurts.*

ELZEY WALKS UP. "Where will you go, Pop?"

I rub my shoulder where the log rose up out of the Mississippi River
and injured it so long ago. "Oh, somewhere quiet, I reckon."

"Why not Winn Parish? You could help me run Mister Gilmore's old
farm. I would—"

"Son, I know this is hard to understand, but I can't be around people for
a time. A long time."

"How will I know where you are, how you're doing?"

"I'll try to send a message to you when I can. You go have a good life, find
a wife, work the farm, have some children. It's all I ever wanted for you, son."

"It's also all you ever wanted, too, Pop."

"Yeah, and something the Good Lord decided I could only have for short
periods of time." I rub the back of my aching neck. "It's all right, Elzey. I get
lots of satisfaction knowing you will have what I always wished for with your
mother, God rest her soul. I reckon I'll have mine when I see her again on the
other side." I look to the north. "I think I'll ride for a while, maybe to Arkansas.
I heard there's some places over there where a man can get lost for as long as
he wants. I need some wilderness time. Time to be still and relax my soul and
hope that healing comes in the quiet moments ahead. I'll let you know, son."

Elzey rushes to me and wraps his arms around me. "I don't want to be
without you."

"Son, for what's goin' on inside of me, you need to be without me." I gently push him back and hold his shoulders with a firm grip. "I'll let you know how I'm doin', I promise."

"And maybe come visit me sometime?"

I don't answer. I just nod. I feel like an old buck deer headed off into the cane breaks to live out the few days he has left.

At least I'll have Marion to ride with for a few days. Then, I'll fade into the shadows for a long time. A very long time.

As I look toward the east, a faint rustling stirs the bushes. It's Granny Thankful. *"It will be in the shadows of your new life that the light will shine brightest, grandson."*

PART VI:
LUMMY: MY LAST HOME

CHAPTER 60

NEVER HAVING A HOME
IS HOME

MID-MAY, 1904

I can live anywhere because I belong nowhere.

MOVING AROUND HAS made life interesting—seeing new places, meeting new people, and leaving when I've needed to. Living pretty much on my own for the years after we rescued Caroline from Tom Kimbrell has been relatively peaceful, except for the scrape Marion got us into when we arrived in Fort Worth. That's a story for another time. That Marion, boy, what a wildcat that girl is. I'm proud to have known her and ridden with her for a bit. It's been too long since I've seen her, or Elzey, for that matter. I received letters there for a while after our little band of rescuers went our separate ways, but no visits, and that's all right. He's got enough on his mind with his family to worry about this old man whose mind is drifting away.

The war dreams are nearly unbearable these days—for me and for my daughter, Rosetta, with whom I've lived for a number of years. Her husband, William Gauden, certainly has been a prince out of a storybook in his love for Rosey and how he's taken care of me. He's had to hold me down, sometimes for an hour at a time, when the demons come. They know just when to strike. I can't ask my sweet Rosey and William to give their lives to what is about to end mine. The doctors say I have acute mania, brought by the shock of the violence I'd experienced growing up and from the horrors of what I went through at Vicksburg.

I feel like I'm lying in those trenches now. Just a bag of bones. Skin hanging off of my arms from starving. Sick all the time because of extreme weakness. But the strength I can muster when my mind tells me that the Yankees are charging up the hill is more than Rosetta and William can manage. I'm still too strong. I'm unhappy with this. I want to go somewhere that I can be cared for and not hurt anyone. I haven't yet, but I feel I'm losing all control. So, I applied for a bed in the Old Soldiers' Home at Fort Leavenworth, Kansas. My pension for having served with the First Mississippi Mounted Rifles came through back in 1890, and provision was made for the care of people like me who have gone crazy because of a war that we never should've had to fight in the first place.

Damn. I'm just ready to get on through the thin veil. There's got to be a better life waiting there for me.

"Lord, come and get me anytime you want. I'm ready."

CHAPTER 61

MY LAST HOME
BEFORE I GO

AFTERNOON, JUNE 18, 1904

It's that last full surrender that takes you fully home.

HERE I AM in Kansas. Columbus Nathan Tullos, lying on a bed in the Old Soldiers' Home, high upon a hill near Fort Leavenworth. Hills run thick in Tullos blood, and the Lord has made it so that I can finish my life on top of one. Creator is kind. I can see the Union flag from my window, now with forty-five stars, flapping at the entrance to the National Cemetery. A steady, warm, westerly wind rises to fully extend the banner as like in a painting. No furling, no flapping, just straight out.

I try to sit up. "I can see it! The twentieth star for Mississippi!" I try to stand up, but the best I can do is roll over on my side and prop myself up on one elbow. I've become too weak. The doctors say the acute mania has taken its toll.

Heck, it's been taking bits and pieces of me for years since Vicksburg.

I gaze into the bright sunshine blanketing the cemetery that for me will soon be eternal light. I reminisce about the war for a moment, and my mind goes to another place.

Soldiers rise from their eternal rest to stand in front of white tombstones, dressed in perfectly arranged blue uniforms. In one motion, they all stand at attention and salute.

Someone shouts, "At ease!"

The men visit, shake hands, and congratulate each other. They laugh and backslap at each other's jokes. They turn and wave for me to enter the cemetery gate guarded by the Union flag. I fall back hard like when the Yankee minie ball struck the button over my heart during the Siege of Vicksburg.

A nurse rushes over. "It's all right, Mister Tullos." She straightens my pillow and gives me a sip of cool water. "Can I get you to eat a little?"

"No, thank you, dear." I'm exhausted. Worn smooth out. Ready to go. I've been in this bed almost three weeks now, but I won't stay long. I rise up on one elbow again and wave at the rows of tombstones of the soldiers gone on to meet their Maker. "Be there soon, boys."

I'VE HAD A good life. I gave it the best I could. I have only a few regrets. Things I wish could have been resolved before I go. But all will be made right after I walk through the thin veil between the seen and unseen. Lately, I've been more there than here.

Rosetta and William brought me here from Ryan town in the Indian Territory. The train ride was difficult at first—too many nightmares and too many visits from old enemies. The sleep medicine the doctor prescribed before we left helped little. Funny thing, my first train ride was in a cramped cattle car filled with a bunch of scared and stinking volunteers going to get trained for war at Camp Moore. My last was to Fort Leavenworth trying to leave it all behind. I'm glad the Old Soldiers' Home will be my last station before I cross the Jordan River. I won't need a train to take me to the other side.

Oh, how I wish Martha was here. Loving her and helping raise the children brought happiness I never got to have with Susannah. Now our children are scattered across this growing nation that somehow managed to survive the worst of family disputes. Susannah and Martha. Two loves, and the brightest stars in my soul. They have been kind to come each evening in the night sky to sweep aside the eyes of the men I've killed. They comfort my soul.

I strain to see the flag again. It rests untouched by the wind now. So many new stars since the war. Forty-five, if I remember correctly. These past few years, though, Delaware and Rosetta became the new stars in my flag soon to be lowered. My condition has worsened these past few months. This acute mania thing I have, I still don't understand it. I don't eat and can't sleep. They say I'm dehydrated and starving to death, and the delusions, well, they are getting to where I can't tell what's real and what ain't. It won't be long now. I'm ready. William and Rosetta did the right thing bringing me here.

The war took a terrible toll on me, and it's worsened through the years. And though Susannah and Martha try to block the eyes of the men I killed at Vicksburg, they still come to visit in the darkest part of night. I'm just thankful I didn't kill anyone after that. Except those ghost riders of the West-Kimbrell Gang who terrorized innocent souls. I don't count them. They weren't men. They were worse than animals. The stuff of bad dreams. I relive killing John West and Tom Kimbrell over and over. They just keep coming back, and I keep fighting them. I feel myself losing control. I feel for the owl claw Dan Creekwater gave me so many years ago, but the nurse took it away because the wounds from using it bled constantly.

I need it now.

I slap my wrist. "Stop it! I've had enough killing for anyone's lifetime! Just like the men who rest in the beds next to mine! Why do I have to keep reliving this?"

The nurse sits and takes my hand. "Mister Tullos, your family is here."

William and Rosetta have come to say their goodbyes. They don't stay long, thinking I'm out of my mind and don't know what's happening. I do. But it's okay.

Rosey cries out, "I can't bear to watch him die. I want to remember him for the good father he was. This ain't him. It's the Devil stealing his last moments. I can't do this anymore." She leaves, but the door creaks back open. Rosetta falls on me, hugging me like she'll never turn me loose.

I pat her on the back gently. "It's okay, Rosey, dear. I'll be with your mother soon. You and William have been too good to me, but it's time for me to go."

I fade into a vision of Grandpas Cloud, Captain James Mills, and Temple, and Uncle Silas, and all Tullos folk from centuries back until now, who ask, *"When will our stories be told?"*

I reach for them, but they stand, waiting for my response. "Mary, my niece, will make our lives forever known."

They disappear into the sunlight.

I point to the small table drawer.

Rosetta opens it to find a small box. "What's this, Pop?"

"Notes about my life since the last time I sent Mary a batch. There's a few thoughts and some letters from old war friends in there. They tell my story, our story, and your story. Please write down what's going on here and where they'll lay me to rest… I need rest."

Rosetta wipes my forehead with a cool cloth and offers me water.

I take a little sip. "Promise you'll pass them on to Mary so we won't be forgotten? She said she'd begin seeking a publisher on the day I pass. It might be a pretty interesting book."

"I will, Pop. More importantly, I'll never forget your love for me." Rosetta leaves, wiping her tears and clutching the box.

William pats my shoulder. "I'm sorry, Pop. It's just that she loves you so very much."

I wave my hand. "It's all right, son. I'm not alone. Never have been. I've always had friends with me that no one else could see. I've always had Creator surrounding me, don't you know?"

William kisses my forehead, tears dripping. "We'll be here when they lay you to rest." He straightens up. "You've been the only father I've ever known. The Lord couldn't have given me a better one. I love you, Lummy. We *will* see you again on the other side."

I smile weakly. He closes the door. I lie in this bed, alone but not. I sense the presence of the Great Alone and all those on the other side waiting for me. I just have to walk through the thin veil. This journey no one can make for me, or go with me. I must go, alone but not.

I WAKE FROM dozing and scan my surroundings. I can feel it. I'm not long for this earth. I'm glad to be here. When I first arrived, I enjoyed talking with fellow soldiers. Sharing old war stories has been good, like a final purge to free my soul. When I leave, it'll be like going on the final leg of a trip without having to carry any bags. I'll leave everything behind when I cross the river soon. What a relief.

This is a good place. The orderlies are kind but firm, talking me down when my emotions go high-low in an instant or if I get agitated. They hold me down when I go to fighting the Yankees in the Twenty-Seventh Louisiana Lunette again or think I see Lester, Dawg Smith, Captain Tom Ford, John West, or Tom Kimbrell lurking outside my window. The orderlies comfort me when I sing "O Susanna!" and cry for my darling to come be with me. The nurses put cool damp cloths on my face when I see my dear Martha or laugh with Annie Fanny and when I call out for Susannah.

I wish Susannah was here. Martha, too. They would've liked each other. What am I saying? They like each other now. I can feel it. I wish Ma could give me words to calm my spirit. I wish I could horse around with my brothers and go squirrel hunting one more time with Pa and Elihu. I wish I could tell Ben again that he's all right with me. I wish I could talk with Josiah and Rainy Mills, Mr. Gilmore and Sarge, Old Bart and Old Nate, Mr. and Mrs. Davis and Mr. Wiley, Poole and J.A., Hog Fart, Seth and Granville, Momma Sophie and Mr. Allrice, Pastor Dobbs, the Catholic priest at St. Paul's, and Dan Creekwater. It hits me hard. Creator has always put good people in my life. What am I saying? I'll see them soon. I'm looking forward to it.

It won't be long. I sense it in my spirit.

This is my last home living in this world. Choctaw County was always my first best home, although Winn Parish with Susannah could've taken its place. I remember Ben saying that he never felt like he had a home because our pa did all within his power to make the house where we grew up a place he wanted us to leave. Maybe Ben and I could've had *home* together in Winn Parish. I don't know. It doesn't matter now. Ben and Pa have a home together now in heaven.

Returning to Choctaw County after mustering out of the First Mississippi Mounted Rifles, I remember worrying what my brothers would say about me changing horses in the middle of the stream. Like I should've expected, Jasper and James welcomed me home, saying that I did what I thought best, and that was good enough for them. Love between brothers is far greater than love for some damned cause. They surely came through when we had to take down Captain Tom Ford and his redshirt Hyena gang. I shudder, thinking about how we ended the Night Rider's storm of terror. That's all behind me now. And my son Elzey is living a full and good life in Winn Parish. My greatest dream was that he could have the life I always wanted. It cost me, but I'd not do a thing different. It was worth it. All of it.

"Now I can rest, dammit!" I snicker. "Never did defeat that cussing demon completely. Oh, well, gotta have somethin' for the Lord to get on to me about when I see him."

Truth be told, Creator's got plenty of dirt on me. I'm asking for mercy.

CHAPTER 62

WHEN AN OLD ENEMY
SETS ME FREE

EARLY EVENING, JUNE 18, 1904

The last person I thought I'd see was the person I hurt the most in this life.

I'M GRATEFUL CREATOR has seen fit to allow time so I can sort through everything before his angels come for me. Creator is kind. Always has been.

Marrying Martha Brock and helping her children get started in this world makes for good memories. She made life truly home for us. The best was having our beautiful girls, Delaware and Rosetta. But my Martha died way too young, and I've had to live too long without her. My heart is beginning to ache. I'm getting upset, so I turn my thoughts to times spent on the sandbar by the Mississippi River through the years. Those moments of sitting with God kept my soul and feet going in the right direction. I calm myself.

But in my short years, I've realized that a good life lived is always pointed homeward. So, home is where I happen to be in the moment, and who I'm with. Even here, I find peace and....

I awaken to the western sun spraying rays of sunshine through my window to form a small rainbow on the wall.

The door creaks open, and I sense someone peering at me.

The nurse lays her palm on my forehead. "Mister Tullos, you have an unexpected visitor today. Are you all right with that?"

I nod and try to sit up. "Sure."

The nurse helps me up.

A graying man with a cane hobbles into my room and shuts the door behind him. I strain to see him through his thick long hair. I don't recognize him. Maybe he's a chaplain come to say last rights or pray over me or something.

He speaks with a gravelly voice that I'm starting to recognize. "I'm here today to say thank you, Lummy Tullos. You probably don't remember me, but you saved my life. And my soul, for that matter."

"Kneehigh? What? How'd you ever find me?"

He holds his hands up, and I stop talking. Nehemiah explains that not long after I left Choctaw County in '59, he parted ways with his cousin, mostly because Lester had no use for a limping half-cripple.

"That certainly told me how he felt about me. If I was of no use to him, he didn't want me around. I never did like that bastard, but bein' the runt of the family, I stayed close to who I thought would protect me. Lester only did me harm. When the war started, I left my ma and went north to where our people came from. I joined the Union Army. They wouldn't let me fight but said I could be a clerk, since I could read and write. My mother never forgave me for that, so I never went back home. I married a fine woman and had a sack full of kids. I stayed in the Army, finally taking a post here at Fort Leavenworth as a prison guard for years, until I got a job in records at the Old Soldiers' Home. My kids moved away, and my sweet wife is with the Lord now. But I've had a good life, Lummy, all because you made me see that my life was goin' nowhere fast with that bully Lester, so full of hate and violence. I should be retired by now, but I don't have anything but my work to keep me going."

"So, my name came across your desk when I arrived here?"

"It did, and I hoped it was you. It took me a few days to get the courage up enough to come visit you. I don't know if you want to see me or not, but I'm here offering my hand of apology and thanks. I said and did some pretty bad things to you back in Choctaw County." He sits down in the chair beside my bed and hangs his head.

I lay still for a moment, a thousand thoughts racing through my head. I thrust out my hand, and he takes it. "Kneehigh. Nehemiah, I am so very glad you came. The one thing I felt I left undone was not apologizing for cripplin' you."

Tears form in my eyes. He wipes his own with a handkerchief.

Nehemiah blows his nose. "No, no, I was in the wrong. You helped me get back on the right road. I may have walked with a limp all these years, but I've walked straight and tall in my soul."

We talk of old times and about our adventures with family, in the war, and of old friends. He prays for me to recover.

"I appreciate the prayer, Nehemiah, but I'm ready. And you helped set me free, brother."

With a few more stories and words of gratitude, Kneehigh leaves. I stare out the window into a starry sky of the eyes of those who'll help me make my next move. I have only one step left.

CHAPTER 63

LIFE IS ALWAYS LIVED HOMEWARD

SUNRISE, JUNE 19, 1904

*Last breaths are best taken with the man who has become
what I was supposed to be.*

I LIE IN this bed, pouring over my life this early morning of June 19, wishing some things had been different, but thanking God for all the good I've enjoyed. The doctor says I have only moments left and asks if I want a priest or preacher. I shake my head and tell him I have a priest who will soon send friends to walk me through the thin veil.

A nurse whispers, "He's reaching for something on his bed stand."

"This old rock is all that's here." The doctor places it in my hand. The multi-colored agate Granny Thankful gave me back in Vicksburg glows. I am now complete. Almost.

The doctor's lips are moving, but all sound disappears. The light fades, and only faint shadows move slowly around the room. Suddenly, my eyes are filled with the light of the sun rising brightly across the Mississippi River.

Hands reach for me. Familiar hands. Soft but firm hands gently pull me toward the warm sunrise. I stand on the water in the middle of a great swirling stream beneath my feet.

Shadows become forms. Faces take shape.

Pa and Ben reach to hug me. *"All is made right in this place of light."*

Ma cries, *"My son is truly home, never more to roam."*

Granny Thankful kisses me on the back of the neck and takes the multi-colored agate from my hand. *"This goes back to the river of life so that another may find their way here."*

Mr. Gilmore laughs. *"Finally, you can meet the true Master."*

Granville runs by, yelling, *"I can play chess now, Lummy, and I'll beat your socks off."*

Edrow chases after him, laughing, *"Hey, you can't call me Hog Fart here, Lummy dummy."*

Mr. Wiley snickers. *"No more battles, my son."*

Old Bart and Old Nate, now young men, laugh with their heads back, say together, *"We're all free here."*

Annie Fanny, wearing a beautiful gown of sparkling gems, grins. *"I still got an eye for you, Lummy honey."*

Martha squeezes me tight, whispering, *"You were the husband and father I needed, my beloved."*

Mr. Allrice whispers, *"Heaven truly is a place where all praise God with one voice in many languages. Didn't I tell you?"*

Sophie smiles. *"Home is where all get to sit at the same table together."*

Lester, Dawg Smith, Captain Tom Ford, John West, and Tom Kimbrell walk stiffly into the growing crowd, presenting themselves before me with lowered heads. *"You were right, Lummy,"* they say together. I shake their hands. They move aside, smiling.

And there before me is a thin veil, like the curtains in Mr. Gilmore's house back in Winn Parish. A shadowy form eases forward, and I recognize her shape, her beauty.

Susannah steps from behind the veil, and her voice sounds like a cool trickling spring in summertime. *"Now we can live the life we always wanted, my dearest."* I rush to wrap her in my arms, but she raises her hand. *"Not yet, my love. Not until you are fully here."*

I look about the place. It's the most beautiful land I could ever imagine— mountains tall with snow and rolling hills green with forests of perfect trees and swaying grasslands. We stand on the surface of a great river as fish of all kinds swim underneath our feet and myriads of birds fly above our heads. Great crowds of every race imaginable walk a street paved with gold through a gate of pearl to a throne where the brightest of all rainbow lights shines forth in every direction.

Susannah takes my right hand, and Martha the other, who's arm in arm with her first husband, William.

William pats me on the back. *"Thank you for raising my children, Lummy."*

We join the crowd, gliding across the waters to the great light of the throne. All fear and anger, anxiety and depression, hate and violence, and guilt for killing vanishes into the light. Peace passing all understanding is mine. Peace I could only imagine on the sandbar alone with God. What once was only a dream then is reality now. I'm here. I'm really here. We stop and raise our hands to the source of the great light.

As Susannah and I walk hand in hand, the light becomes brighter. I turn loose of Martha's hand to shade my eyes. I peer at two men standing by the gate of pearl. It's Grandpa Cloud standing arm in arm with Grandpa Temple.

Granny Thankful smiles. *"The Tullos family is no longer Celt pushed by enemies, and no longer Pict painted blue, or any color, dear Lummy. Here, we are no longer of the moving kind. Now, we're people of the settled kind. Forever."*

The small welcoming crowd turns to the bright light shimmering in every imaginable color, and all say together to Creator, *"Lummy, your son, is now home."*

Susannah drifts away. *"Soon, my love. We will be together forever soon."*

A loud chorus erupts. It's not the sound of men charging a hill in battle. No, it's all men and women praising the One who sits upon the throne. I go to see him. I've never felt anything like this before, I....

A hand touches my cheek, and I open my eyes to a blurry figure standing over my hospital bed. A voice I haven't heard a great while whispers something about me seeing his mother soon. My eyes clear. It's Elzey. He's come to be with me in my final moments. My heart swells with joy.

Elzey sits on the bed by my side. "I just had to come see you once more, Pop. I know you have to leave, but I'm here, like you were for me all those years." He leans over and kisses my forehead. "How are you doin'?"

I have little strength left to speak. "Oh, I'm so tired. There ain't much of me left, son."

Elzey smiles. "Thought you'd like to know what day it is, Pop. It's a holiday we celebrate, at least our black family does. You ever heard of it?"

I struggle to speak. "Not sure I have. I'm all out of sorts, son. Why?"

"They call it Juneteenth, when the last slaves were freed in Texas after the war. It's today."

I shake my head and struggle to say, "Well, ain't that somethin'?"

Elzey lightly pats me on the chest just above my heart. "It is, Pop."

I look out the window and find the twentieth star on the Union flag and grin. "My, my, what a day to leave this earth on, Elzey."

"Yes it is, and you did your part to help black and white people have better lives. You sacrificed yourself so others could live the life you always wanted." He wipes tears with a handkerchief. "I'm so proud to be your son, Pop." He puts his palms on my cheeks. "You are my father, Columbus Nathan Tullos, and I am the better man for it. I love you, Pop."

"I'm so worn out, Elzey." My mind goes back to the last letter I wrote but never sent to Susannah. "Well, son, the world did change, and I'm okay with dying today."

Elzey's face fades into the light as he whispers, "That's all right. No more a Celt of the moving kind or a Pict of the settling kind. You can rest. Your home, now and forever, is...."

Susannah touches my soul. *"It's time, dear."*

I whisper as I breathe my last, "Praise Creator, I'm makin' my last move."

My eyes close to see a starless sky glowing with all the colors of the rainbow.

I awaken with just one thought. "I'm home."

COLUMBUS NATHAN TULLOS—Lummy—trots off to meet his Creator....

A TALE OF TWO COLORS

FREE
TO GO

A SHORT STORY

THE STORY OF SILAS TULLOS

EFFINGHAM COUNTY, GEORGIA, 1809

If one should get to go free, then should all.

"ANNA, GET EVERYTHIN' you want to take with us out on the porch. We leave come first light."

"You best watch your bossing, Willoughby. I ain't one of your slave women."

"Woman, would you just hush up and do what I tell you? I want to get to the so-called 'Promised Land' before Christmas."

"Christmas is six months away, Willoughby, dear."

"We'll be spending it here if you don't stop your jawin' and get to work. It's July, and I want to get land cleared and ready to plant by spring."

Anna smiles. "They say Mississippi Territory is the land of milk and honey."

"Promised Land, my foot. They ought to get rid of the Indians between here and Mobile like the Israelites did the Philistines. We've plenty of work to do when we get where we're goin' to be worryin' about savages."

"Stop complaining, Willoughby. Your slaves do all your land clearin', like we really need them. We got sons and your brothers for that. Why don't you set them free?"

"If I told you once, I told you a thousand times, they ain't slaves. They're servants. Speakin' of servants, where's that son of yours? He's probably flutterin' away the day doin' nothin'."

Anna snatches her skirt around to go into the house. "God never made a meaner man than you, Willoughby Tullos. Only man I know God made from clay but treats others like dirt." She huffs. "Lord, I do wish he'd free those slaves."

Archibald tries to sneak past his father.

Willoughby barks, "Archy, where do you think you're goin'? Go get the mule at the blacksmith's like I told you."

"But I promised to help Mary's folks get ready to leave."

"Wearin' your church clothes? You ain't goin' to load a wagon. You were gonna let Henry get the mule, weren't you? I know you're sweet on Mary and y'all been courtin', but blood family comes first. Besides, y'all ain't hitched yet."

Archy turns, unbuttoning his shirt. "She'll be blood soon as we're old enough to marry. I love her, Pa."

"That ain't all there is to it, boy. You got to make a livin' and support her. Love don't put bread on the table. You gotta make somethin' of yourself. Money only grows out of the ground if you work it. You got a long ways to go yet, sapling."

Archy strips off his good shirt and puts on an old one. "Work hard, build somethin' with your own two hands, huh, like you do, Pa, working your slaves to death? President Jefferson said you can't buy slaves off the ships in Savannah no more."

Willoughby heckles. "Yeah, but I can breed as many as I want."

"It's wrong puttin' women in breeding cages. God isn't happy with that."

"You're gonna tell me what makes God happy?"

"What if my sister Sarah was in one of those cages? How would you feel?"

Willoughby pinches his arm. "See that? It's white. Guess I don't have to worry about that."

"God doesn't see color, Pa. He wants them married, like us."

"You don't pay a preacher to marry a bull and a heifer so she can have a calf, do you?"

"I guess if you make a human an animal, you can treat her like an animal."

"You got that right."

"But that don't make it right."

"Well, my slaves will be your slaves one day."

Archy steps forward with a furrowed brow. "I'll never own a slave, ever!"

"Boy, I'll take a hickory handle to your back if you keep on."

"I'll speak my mind, even if you beat me. Slaves are human beings, just like you and me. They deserve lives, homes, families, land, and even romance."

"The preacher says slavery is perfectly legal. Go read your Apostle Paul about that."

"I won't be standing anywhere near your hating ways when Gabriel blows his trumpet."

"Go get that mule before I backhand you!"

Archy buttons his shirt and steps off the porch. He calls to the barn, "Let's go, Henry."

"Yassuh."

Archy whispers, "You ready to leave?"

Henry grins. "Got everythin' packed and ready."

"Still running to the British?"

"If I can make it to Florida like you said."

"Follow the coast south until you cross Saint Mary's River. Tell the first redcoat you see that you want to join the British Army."

"Then I'll be free?"

"Yes, but you have to stay in the army as long as they say. Run off, and they'll shoot you."

"They'll give me food, a musket, and a uniform?"

Archy nods. "War's comin' soon with the British. I guess they didn't get enough the first time around. Don't come back here."

"I understand, Massuh Archy."

"Master no more, Henry. Just Archy to you, brother. I'll do my best to take care of Lucille."

"Just keep my girl out of them cages, please, Massuh, uh, I mean, Archy."

"You know Pa's all business."

"I'll fetch her when I can. What about your father?"

"Cousin Silas and I've got that figured out. You best go." Archy hands Henry a small purse. "This'll help you on your way."

Henry cries as he trots to a small boat on the riverbank. "I never know'd a good'a man as you. Please tell my best friend I'll see him again one day."

"I'll tell Silas you said that." Archy turns for home and to face his father.

———————

WILLOUGHBY MARCHES OFF to the passport office, mumbling, "Dang that Archy, anyway. That girl's messin' up Archy's thinkin'. Besides that, I've got to go almost to the Mississippi River to get good land. Why don't the damn Creeks just give up theirs? I'd be happy to settle in Alabama. I could haul crops and goods to Mobile easy as the sun comin' up in the mornin'."

"Mobile? I hear they got some pretty girls."

Willoughby turns with his fists balled up. "How long you been listenin'?"

Silas throws up his hands. "Whoa, Uncle Willoughby. I trotted up just now as Archy left."

Willoughby takes long strides to leave him behind, but Silas has longer legs.

Silas chuckles. "You know why the Creeks won't leave? They've got the best ground for growing corn and sorghum in the South. Would you give that up?"

"Don't sass me, Silas. I'll beat you with a plow line like you was my own."

Silas chuckles. "You'll have to catch me first."

"Where's your father? He's supposed to help me load the wagon today."

Silas grins. "Probably sippin' a little moonshine. It's Saturday, you know."

"Temple better not be drunk, or I'll—"

"Oh, no, Pa's a fine, upstanding Baptist, just like you. He doesn't guzzle. He sips his shine a little at a time. He's always first on the road when the church bell rings for Sunday preaching."

Willoughby cuts his eyes toward Silas. "Upstanding? Yeah, right. What do you want?"

"Pa told me to get passport papers so we can move to the Mississippi Territory next year."

"Lazy hound dawg. I told him to get his papers turned in. I knew neither of us would do any good in the Georgia land lottery. Black rock, white rock, what'n the hell is that anyway?"

"It's how God made decisions in the Old Testament. Preacher called it urim and thummim."

"I don't know about all that, but I know they cheated us. They pulled two black stones from the sack on purpose, one for me, and one for your Pa."

Silas scratches his ear. "I guess the Good Lord let the rocks do the choosing."

"Folks don't want us around here anymore."

"Well, you do raise a stink regularly, and you're pretty hard on people."

Willoughby stops in mid-stride. "Only about important things, like how war's comin' to where we're headed. Every settlement on the Federal Road we'll be travelin' is in danger if the British keep arming the Creek Indians. Your pa better come on, or he'll lose everything if them red heathens get agitated."

"They're no more heathen than the heathens trying to steal their land."

"Americans don't talk like that."

"Don't you say that to me!"

"Boy, I'll slap you sideways lookin' both ways for Sunday."

Silas bristles. "You will try, suh."

Willoughby walks in silence the rest of the way. After all, Silas stands six foot six.

The passport clerk hands Willoughby his application. "Read this over to make sure the information and spelling is in order."

"Heck, it ain't changed since I filled out my papers." Willoughby snarls and reads it out loud.

Executive Department
Monday, 18th December 1809

ORDERED

That passports be prepared for the following persons to travel through The Creek Nation of Indians,
to wit – One for Mr. William Tullos, one for Mr. Thomas
Tullos, one for Mr. John Tullos, one for Mr. Willoughby
Tullos, with a family of nine whites and seven blacks
and one for Mr. Walter Davis and family which were
presented and signed.

The clerk peers over his spectacles. "Well?"

Willoughby snaps, "Like I said, nothin's changed."

The clerk blows on the ink and holds out the completed passports. "Are you taking them all?"

"Yes!" Willoughby throws money on the clerk's table, snatches the passports, and stomps off.

"And thank you, kind sir," the clerk says sarcastically. He waves Silas up. "What can I do for you, son?"

"I need passport applications. We'll follow my uncle there to the Mississippi Territory soon."

"He's your uncle?"

Silas leans up. "Yassuh, but I usually don't tell anybody."

The clerk hands Silas the papers and snickers. "He's mean enough to pioneer new land."

"Meaner than a black panther treed by a pack of hounds."

"I'm surprised he got people to vouch for his character."

"Heck, folks stood in line to help get Uncle Willoughby on down the road." They both laugh. "I'll have these back soon as I can."

"Don't forget the filing fee."

Silas tips his hat and heads to the blacksmith's shop to get Willoughby's mule.

ARCHY SPIT SLICKS his hair down and straightens his shirt. He fidgets as he knocks. Mary comes to the door. Archy nearly faints as his heart flutters. He holds out the bouquet of wildflowers he picked on the way. She smiles and holds them to her dainty nose, breathing in the sweet fragrance.

"Mary, if you ain't the prettiest girl in Georgia."

Mary blushes. "Archibald Tullos, what a sweet thing to say."

"And one day you will be the most beautiful married lady in the Mississippi Territory!"

"Why, Archy? Are you sweet talking me?"

"Every chance I get."

A lady calls out from inside the house. "Mary, who is it dear?"

A man's voice barks, "Hope it ain't that Tullos boy, unless he's willin' to load the wagon."

Mary hides her face behind the bouquet, embarrassed by her father's insult. "It is, and he's here to help, Pa."

"Good, my old war wound is actin' up again."

Mary stares deeply into Archy's eyes.

"Don't just stand there, girl, let him in."

"Yes, Pa."

Mary's mother brings in sweet bread and hot tea.

Her father sits up with the help of a cedar cane that has a man's head carved on the handle. He sticks it out at Archy. "Have a seat, son."

Archy sits slowly, keeping an eye on the end of the walking cane.

The old man asks, "See that?"

"Yassuh, Mister Davis."

"Know why I carved a British soldier's head as a handle for my walkin' cane?"

"No, suh."

"So every time I take a step, I'm pressin' down hard on the British Army me and the Swamp Fox Francis Marion whooped back in the war."

Mrs. Davis hands Archy a cup of tea on a saucer.

"Thank you, ma'am. My pa says war is coming soon."

"Yep, but Americans ain't scared of no redcoats, and we're meaner'n any redskins."

"Like my pa?"

"Yep, I'm glad we're travelin' with y'all tomorrow. Willoughby's mean as a swamp cat and fast as a rattler. Bring on them dang Creeks. We'll take 'em in a good fight."

Mrs. Davis trembles. "Keep talking about Indians, and you'll be going to the Mississippi Territory alone."

"Calm yourself, woman. Just bolstering up my courage, that's all."

Archy winks at Mary. "Well, sir, we have enough guns, ball, and powder to fend off any attack. The Tulloses ain't fearful men."

Mary clears her throat. "Talk is there's been no incident for some time."

Mr. Davis barks, "Yeah, but you don't know Indians like I do. They're unpredictable. Dang Creek will shake your hand and have a knife hid behind his back."

Archy chances, "Guess he's thinking the same about us. White folks haven't been the most trustworthy either."

Mr. Davis shakes his cane at Archy. "That ain't American! I'll not—"

Archy stands up. "Suh, I believe you have a wagon to load? I'm here to help, if needed."

Mr. Davis calms down. "Shouldn't have said that to you, son. That's one thing I love about this country. You can speak your mind and disagree."

Mrs. Davis hands Archy a piece of sweet cake and smiles. "And that is American, son."

Archy loads the wagon, sneaks a kiss from Mary, and trots home.

SILAS WAVES AS he leads Willoughby's mule. "C'mon, Archy, or Willoughby will think we all ran off."

Archy catches his breath. "You pay the blacksmith?"

"Yeah, you get Henry on his way?"

Archy nods. "I did. I sent him to the British down in Florida."

"Good, that's good. I've never had a better friend than Henry."

"I know, Silas. He's gonna miss you, too." Archy points to the back of his head. "Put a small gash here so my hair will cover it up when it heals. Make it bleed, or Pa won't believe Henry knocked me in the head."

Silas taps Archy's head with his hatchet.

Archy winces. "Dang, you didn't have to split my skull open."

"You said make it bleed."

"Guess we best go tell 'Pharaoh Willoughby' that I let an Israelite go."

Silas chuckles. "This I got to see."

WILLOUGHBY BELLOWS, "WHERE'S Henry? He and Lucille need to try and make another young'un."

Archy leads the mule into the barn, glancing at the breeding cage where Lucille lies trembling. Tears roll down his mother's cheeks. Her whimper sounds strangely like Lucille's.

Archy marches toward his father and screams, "Enough!"

Silas whispers, "What about Henry's escape story?"

"Don't need it."

Willoughby wheels around to slap Archy.

Silas steps between them. "Not today, Uncle."

Willoughby squints. "You takin' his side?"

"I'm takin' the right side."

Willoughby laughs. "Archy says we can't buy slaves off the ship no more. What else can I do?"

Archy steps up. "I want her out of the cage."

Willoughby peers through narrowing slits. "You want her out? Take her. She ain't dropped a calf in two years anyhow. She's yours."

Archy glances at his mother as Silas elbows him. Anna nods.

"Sign her over to me. I'll take her."

"Done! Now get out of my sight."

Archy and Silas gently help Lucille from the iron cage.

Anna takes her to the well to wash up.

Archy turns to his father. "I'll never be like you."

"You're free to go anytime you please, boy."

Archy whispers, "Soon enough."

Willoughby jerks his head this way and that. "Where's Henry?"

Archy grins as he rubs the back of his head. "Like you just told me, I told Henry he was free to go."

Standing: Edna Tullos—Elzey's and Francis's daughter. L-R 2nd row: Elzey Burke Tullos, wife Francis, and Martha Curry and William Curry—Francis's parents. 1st row: Elzey's and Francis's younger children.

AUTHOR'S NOTE

R EADERS OFTEN ASSUME that the people of A Tale of Two Colors are, like many fictional characters, simply figments of my imagination. Some, like Rainy Mills, "Annie Fanny" Handerson, and Marion Tullos, are just that. Others, however, are much more. Columbus "Lummy" Nathan Tullos was a real person, who made many of the travels and fought many of the battles I have conveyed throughout this series. He was my ancestor, and when I heard the story of a man who switched sides in the midst of the Civil War, I had to know more, and my research led me to write this story.

While I will admit that there is more than just a little bit of me in the Lummy you have come to know and love, his experiences are my best guess at how he lived and what he felt through it all.

Lummy is not the only true to life inspiration for the characters of this story, though. Jasper Newton and James, their parents, Archibald and Mary, and siblings, for instance, were all real persons.

Since I have yet to find a picture of Lummy, I thought it fitting to leave you with a picture of Lummy's son, Elzey Burke Tullos.

ANTHONY WOOD grew up in historic Natchez, Mississippi, fueling a life-long love of history. Not long after high school, he lived and worked in Alaska for several years. He returned to the South and ministered for nearly three decades among the poor, homeless, and incarcerated. Leading an effort that planted five urban churches inspired him to co-author *Up Close and Personal: Embracing the Poor* about his work in Memphis, Tennessee. He also authored a number of articles and stories about inner city ministry.

Anthony is a member of Turner's Battery, a Civil War re-enactment group, the Civil War Roundtable of Arkansas, and serves as President of the White County Creative Writers group. His short stories and poetry have won multiple awards and have been published in *Saddlebag Dispatches, The Vault of Terror,* and *The Avocet: A Journal of Nature Poetry.* One of those stories, "Not So Long in the Tooth," won a Will Rogers Medallion in the Best Western Short Fiction category for 2021. Anthony was also the Arkansas Writers' Hall of Fame inductee for 2024.

When not writing, Anthony enjoys roaming and researching historical sites, camping and kayaking on the Mississippi River, and being with family. Anthony, and his wife, Lisa, live in Arkansas.

www.ingramcontent.com/pod-product-compliance
Lightning Source LLC
Chambersburg PA
CBHW030936260626
47169CB00002B/503